Athelstan Riley

Athos

The mountain of the monks

Athelstan Riley

Athos
The mountain of the monks

ISBN/EAN: 9783337287214

Printed in Europe, USA, Canada, Australia, Japan

Cover: Foto ©Andreas Hilbeck / pixelio.de

More available books at **www.hansebooks.com**

ATHOS

OR

THE MOUNTAIN OF THE MONKS

BY

ATHELSTAN RILEY

M.A., F.R.G S.

𝔚ith numerous 𝔍llustrations

LONDON

LONGMANS, GREEN, AND CO.

1887

TO

MY DEAR AND VALUED FRIEND

THE REV. ARTHUR EDWIN BRISCO OWEN, M.A.

December 1886

CONTENTS.

CHAPTER I.

INTRODUCTION .   .   PAGE   1

CHAPTER II.

DEPARTURE FROM LONDON—A STIFF WINDOW—BUCHAREST—A
FUNERAL—RUSTCHUK—VARNA—A WEDDING—ARRIVAL AT
CONSTANTINOPLE.   8

CHAPTER III.

. CONSTANTINOPLE—ST. SOPHIA—DEDICATION AND DESECRATION
OF ST. SOPHIA—TRIPLE WALLS—SEVEN TOWERS—VISIT TO
THE ŒCUMENICAL PATRIARCH—PROSELYTISM—IGNORANCE
AS TO THE ENGLISH CHURCH   19

CHAPTER IV.

WE LEAVE CONSTANTINOPLE — CAVALLA — ARCHBISHOP OF
CAVALLA — TURKISH BARGAINING — DESCRIPTION OF OUR
PARTY—ARRIVAL AT ATHOS—A TERRIBLE SUPPER   .   .   34

CHAPTER V.

VATOPEDI—ATHOS ARCHITECTURE—CEMETERY—COURTYARD—
PHIALE—DESCRIPTION OF AN EASTERN CHURCH—CATHOLI-
CON—RELICS—MIRACULOUS STORIES—ORIENTAL MONASTI-
CISM—CŒNOBITE AND IDIORRHYTHMIC—LIBRARY—A THEO-
LOGICAL DISCUSSION   46

CHAPTER VI.

PAGE

'LITURGY OF ST. GREGORY DIALOGOS'—ROAD TO CARYES—
CARYES—GOVERNMENT OF ATHOS—THE HOLY SYNOD—AN
IMPOSING RECEPTION—CIRCULAR LETTER—'GOD GRANT US
UNITY' 73

CHAPTER VII.

VATOPEDI—SEMANTRA—A MONASTIC BATHER—PREACHING—
MUSIC—HISTORY OF THE MONASTERY—PRIORIES AND HER-
MITAGES—CHURCHES 90

CHAPTER VIII.

DEPARTURE FROM VATOPEDI—PANTOCRATOROS—FOUNDATION—
CHURCHES—CATHOLICON—LIBRARY—ANCIENT BOOK-COVER
—WE DISCUSS 'FILIOQUE' AND BAPTISM—CLERICAL MAR-
RIAGES—ABRUPT TERMINATION OF THE DISCUSSION . . 101

CHAPTER IX.

SKETE OF THE PROPHET ELIAS—RUSSIAN HOSPITALITY—STAV-
RONIKETA—HISTORY—CHURCHES—THE NOISY EPITROPOS—
AN APPALLING SUPPER—LEVINGES—'FAIR AS THE MOON' . 114

CHAPTER X.

STAVRONIKETA—CATHOLICON—ST. NICHOLAS—MYRON—LI-
BRARY—AN UNEATABLE COCK—'ALL ROMAN PRIESTS ARE
IMMORAL'—IVERON—DISH OF SNAILS—HISTORY OF THE CON-
VENT—CHURCHES AND CATHOLICON—THE PORTAÏTISSA—
LIBRARY—ST. EWTHYM'S MS.—CLOCK 125

CHAPTER XI.

PHILOTHEOU—THE GLYKOPHILOUSA—CATHOLICON AND LIBRARY
—FOUNDATION—PORT OF LAVRA—THE LAVRA—MONASTIC
CURIOSITY—A KELLI—FOUNDATION OF LAVRA—ST. ATHA-
NASIUS OF ATHOS—SKETES, HERMITAGES, AND CHURCHES—
CATHOLICON—RELIQUARIES—JOHN COUCOUZELE—DOUBTFUL
LEGENDS 145

CHAPTER XII.

LAVRA—LIBRARY—THE EX-PRIMATE OF SERVIA—AN ANGLICAN
EUCHARIST — OBSTINATE LOVERS — QUIETISM — THE UN-
CREATED LIGHT—SKETE OF THE PRODROMOS—CAVE OF ST.
ATHANASIUS—MIRACULOUS ICON 182

CHAPTER XIII.

THE PRODROMOS—SELF-CONVICTED SLUMBERERS—DOG-FACED
ST. CHRISTOPHER—MONASTIC TIME-TABLE—ASCENT OF ATHOS
—KERASIA—CHURCH OF THE PANAGHIA—WE REACH THE
SUMMIT—CHAPEL OF THE TRANSFIGURATION—MAGNIFICENT
VIEW—DESCENT TO KERASIA 204

CHAPTER XIV.

ROAD TO AGIOS PAVLOS—MONASTERY OF ST. PAUL—THE HER-
MIT'S GARDEN—FOUNDATION OF ST. PAUL'S—CATHOLICON,
RELICS AND TREASURES—SKETE OF ST. ANNE—WE LEAVE
THE ARCHBISHOP—MONASTERY OF ST. DIONYSIUS—CATHOLI-
CON—ST. NIPHON—LIBRARY—FOUNDATION 216

CHAPTER XV.

MONASTERY OF ST. GREGORY—LIBRARY AND CHURCHES—ROW
TO RUSSICO—A DEVOTED LOVER—THE RUSSIAN QUESTION—
RUSSIAN COLONIZATION OF ATHOS—HISTORY OF RUSSICO—
FOUNDATION OF ST. ELIAS AND OF THE SERAÏ—RUSSIA AND
ENGLAND 235

CHAPTER XVI.

RUSSICO—MY LORD ABBOT—BONE-HOUSE—GREAT SERVICE—
LIBRARY — CHURCHES — XEROPOTAMOU — FOUNDATION —
CATHOLICON—RELICS AND TREASURES—CHURCHES—RIDE TO
CARYES—THE SERAÏ—COUTLOUMOUSSI—RAT-OIL—GREGORY
THE SON OF DEMETRIUS 251

CHAPTER XVII.

PAGE

THE POSTMASTER OF CARYES—THE PROTATON—PANSELENUS—
SCHOOL OF PAINTING—THE SERAÏ—HEAD OF ST. ANDREW—
CEMETERY AND BONE-HOUSE—PHOTOGRAPHING IN CARYES—
FAITH AND MIRACLES 271

CHAPTER XVIII.

THE CAIMACAN — DEPARTURE FROM THE SERAÏ — RIDE TO
CARACALLA—BENIGHTED—THE MONKS SUSPECT TREACHERY
—FOUNDATION OF CARACALLA—CATHOLICON AND LIBRARY
—BACK TO RUSSICO—CURIOUS SERVICE—VENERATION OF
ST. MARY 287

CHAPTER XIX.

SIMOPETRA—ROMANTIC SITUATION—CHURCHES AND FOUNDA-
TION—RETURN TO XEROPOTAMOU—THE ARCHBISHOP PER-
FORMS THE OFFICE OF A DRAGOMAN—RETURN TO RUSSICO—
BISHOP NILOS—STATE VISIT TO THE ABBOT 308

CHAPTER XX.

THE ARCHBISHOP'S MASS—XENOPHOU—CHURCHES—CATHOLI-
CON AND RELICS—THE MISSING VOLUME—CAUGHT IN A
STORM—DOCHEIARIOU—CATHOLICON—THE GORGOŸPECOOS
—FOUNDATION — THE ARCHBISHOP FAVOURS US WITH A
SONG 325

CHAPTER XXI.

RIDE TO CONSTAMONITOU—'WHERE'S MY CLOAK'—FOUNDA-
TION OF CONSTAMONITOU—CATHOLICON—CHURCHES—GIVE,
AND IT SHALL BE GIVEN UNTO YOU 343

CHAPTER XXII.

ZOGRAPHOU—FOUNDATION—PICTURE OF THE PAINTER—MIRA-
CULOUS ICONS—SIX-AND-TWENTY MARTYRS—RETURN TO
VATOPEDI GREAT SERVICE—SKETE OF ST. DEMETRIUS—
THE ARCHBISHOP'S REVENGE—ESPHIGMENOU—FOUNDATION 352

CHAPTER XXIII.

PAGE

CATHOLICON AND RELICS—ST. AGATHANGELOS—LIBRARY—TREA-
SURY—CHURCHES—CHILIANDARI—HISTORY AND CHURCHES
—CATHOLICON—THE THREE-HANDED PANAGHIA—LIBRARY—
FAREWELL TO THE ARCHBISHOP—BACK TO VATOPEDI . . 371

CHAPTER XXIV.

FINAL DEPARTURE FROM VATOPEDI—XEROPOTAMOU—THE ATHE-
NIAN PROFESSORS—RUSSICO—WE LEAVE ATHOS—SAIL UP
THE GULF—XERXES' CANAL—ST. NICHOLAS—MONASTIC
FARM-HOUSE—SALONICA—CALAIS—CONCLUSION . . . 385

APPENDIX.

I. THE DISPERSION OF THE WOOD OF THE CROSS . 405
II. GREEK ECCLESIASTICAL MUSIC . . . 406

LIST OF ILLUSTRATIONS.

(Mostly engraved from the Author's photographs.)

FULL-PAGE PLATES.

PHIALE AT THE LAVRA . . . . *Frontispiece*

ALL THE MONASTERIES (FROM A MONASTIC ENGRAVING) *To face p.* 34

THE LAVRA (FROM A MONASTIC ENGRAVING) . . . „ 188

MONASTERY OF ST. PAUL . . . . „ 217

MONASTERY OF ST. PAUL (FROM A MONASTIC EN-
GRAVING) . . . . „ 220

MONASTERY OF ST. GREGORY (FROM A MONASTIC
ENGRAVING). . . . . „ 238

MONASTERY OF SIMOPETRA . . . . . . „ 309

INTERIOR OF CATHOLICON AT DOCHEIARIOU . . „ 336

WOODCUTS IN TEXT.

THE HOLY MOUNTAIN (FROM A RUSSIAN PRINT) . *Title-page*

PAGE

COURTYARD OF VATOPEDI 49

GROUP OF MONKS AND PHIALE AT VATOPEDI 94

MONASTERY OF PANTOCRATOROS 102

ANCIENT BOOK AT PANTOCRATOROS 106

PAGE

PORTION OF THE EASTERN SHORE OF THE PROMONTORY,
  WITH STAVRONIKETA IN THE FOREGROUND, AND MOUNT
  ATHOS IN THE DISTANCE   . . 118

IVERON   . 131

MONASTERY OF PHILOTHEOU .   . . 148

PORT OF THE LAVRA   .   . . 153

THE LAVRA   .   . . 159

COURTYARD OF THE LAVRA 161

CAVE OF ST. ATHANASIUS, WITH THE HERMIT   . . 200

MONASTERY OF ST. GREGORY   .   . . 235

HIGH STREET, CARYES   . . 283

CARACALLA   . 292

MONASTERY OF SIMOPETRA   313

MONASTERY OF ST. XENOPHON 326

CONSTAMONITOU 344

OUR CAVALCADE   . . 359

MONASTERY OF CHILIANDARI 379

PLAN OF AN EASTERN CHURCH .   . . 52

MAP OF ATHOS .   *At the end*

KEY TO THE DESCRIPTION OF THE MONASTERIES.

	PAGES		PAGES
Vatopedi	43–100, 359–365	Xeropotamiou	258–262
Pantocratoros	101–113	Seraï	277–287
Prophet Elias	114–117	Coutloumoussi	264–269
Stavroniketa	118–130	Protaton	272–276
Iveron	130–144	Caracalla	289–299
Philotheou	145–151	Simopetra	309–314
Lavra	153 197	Xenophou	327–333
Prodromos	197–208	Docheiariou	335–342
St. Paul	217 224	Constamonitou	347–351
St. Anne	224–227	Zographou	352–358
St. Dionysius	228–234	St. Demetrius	366
St. Gregory	235–238	Esphigmenou	368–375
Russico	241 258, 300–307, 317 325	Chiliandari	376–382

MOUNT ATHOS.

CHAPTER I.

The sanctuary of the Greek race, which is in a great degree the sanctuary and refuge of the whole Eastern Church, is Athos—'the Holy Mountain.'—STANLEY'S *Eastern Church*.

THREE years ago an improvement in railway connection placed Constantinople within five days of Paris. The Oriental express running direct from the capital of France to the ferry across the Danube at Rustchuk, in communication with a train to Varna and a steam packet sailing thence to Constantinople, enables the traveller to undertake with but little difficulty a journey to the great metropolis of the East, and, if he be of the more adventurous sort, to prolong his voyage to the maritime cities of Asia Minor, or wander along from island to island in the Greek Archipelago. Few more delightful journeys than these can he undertake, and few will so repay him in refreshment of both mind and body; for in Oriental Europe there are still to be found secluded paths, fresh scenes, and many an untouched mine of rich and varied interest, whilst over all there hangs that soft and dreamy Eastern charm, quite indescribable and only to be appreciated by those who have at some time revelled under its delicious influence.

If ever, reader, you should be fortunate enough to

B

undertake such a journey, as you pass through the blue waters of the Ægean on your way from ' The City' to Athens, you may chance to see, if the weather be clear and your eyes open, as it were a high and rocky island lifting itself out of the waters far away on the northern horizon. You ask one of the ship's officers to tell you what it is. He replies, ' The Monte Santo,' the Holy Mountain. If you can draw into conversation that Greek sailor who, with shaded eyes, is gazing so earnestly over the sea, and ask him to supplement this meagre information, he will call upon you to bless God that He should have permitted you but to cast your eyes from a distance upon so holy a spot, the Agion Oros, the Mountain of the Hermits and the Saints.

Yes, the island to the north is but the peak, rising above the horizon, of lofty Athos, the very centre of the Eastern Church, the proud Christian fortress that has never yet yielded to the infidel, but has preserved its independence through three long centuries of Moslem rule, the one spot to which every Orthodox Eastern, from sultry Egypt to the icy shores of the White Sea, turns his eyes, as the nursery of all holiness and the impregnable fortress of the Christian faith.[1]

[1] There are about a hundred millions of Christians belonging to the Holy Orthodox Eastern Church. Those who divide Christendom into Protestants and Roman Catholics will do well to remember this vast body of Christians who stand aloof from both, protest against the Papal pretensions as much as any Protestants, and yet reject the novelties of the sixteenth century, appealing, as the Church of England does, to antiquity and the inspired decisions of Christ's Undivided Church. Amidst our endless religious controversies in the West it is something more than a relief to turn to this great Church, which has been all the time far removed from the questions which trouble us, whatever difficulties she may have had of her own.

You cannot see more of Athos if you would, for the swift steamer hurries you along without a stoppage until you reach the capital of modern Greece, where you will find that the excursion would mean a voyage to Salonica and a forced stay in that town, probably extending rather over weeks than days, before an opportunity occurred of transporting yourself to the monastic shores. An out-of-the-way place, indeed, and it is well that it should be so, for the very difficulty of access affords the chief protection to the monastic life; and when the long-projected railway connects Salonica with Europe, and brings the eager tourists to the threshold of the Holy Mountain, the guardians of the sacred shrines will do well to add to the severity of their laws and increase the jealousy which guards their borders.

From the south of Macedonia there stretches into the Ægean Sea an irregular tract of land about the size of Norfolk, bounded on the west by the Gulf of Salonica and on the east by that of Contessa, these being known anciently by the respective names of the Thermaic and Strymonic gulfs, and the projecting tract of land itself as Chalcidice. From the southern, or, to speak more accurately, the south-eastern side of Chalcidice three promontories of almost equal length run side by side into the sea, the easternmost being that of Athos, the others known as Longos and Cassandra, but the three anciently as Acte, Sithonia, and Pallene. The promontory, or rather the peninsula, of Athos (for not far from its base, at the spot where Xerxes cut his canal, it measures but a mile and a half across) is long and narrow, having an average breadth of about four miles, whilst its length is forty.

A ridge of hills runs down the centre of the peninsula, beginning from the narrowest part near its base and reaching some height where the monastic establishments commence, at a distance of fifteen to twenty miles from its extremity. From this point the ridge rises gradually from 1,000 to between 3,000 and 4,000 feet, when it suddenly shoots up into a mountain nearly 7,000 feet high [1] and falls into the sea. There is but little level land on Athos; the sides of the central ridge slope as a rule down to the very shore, whilst round the end of the peninsula, especially on the western side, the mountain drops by rapid descent or breaks away in steep and rocky cliffs. Every part of the promontory is covered with vegetation, the east side being the more conspicuous for luxuriance of growth; and its position in the waters keeps the forests of Mount Athos fresh and green when all the neighbouring country on the mainland is burnt up by the summer and autumnal heats. The mountain is one vast mass of white or whitish-grey marble, clothed with trees to within a thousand feet of its summit and then rising in a bare and conical peak. From the top can be seen the islands of Thasos, distant thirty miles; of Lemnos, forty (upon which the shadow of Athos is said to fall as the sun sets [2]); of Samothraki, sixty; and on a clear day the Thessalian Olympus, distant ninety miles; whilst, on the other hand, it can itself be seen from the shores of Asia Minor on the plain of Troy.

Round the shores of Athos stand the twenty ancient monasteries to which the whole peninsula belongs, and

---

[1] Various heights have been given, from 6,349 feet to 6,900.
[2] Ἄθως σκιάζει νῶτα Λημνίας βοός.—Sophocles.

which form the monastic republic of the Holy Mountain. The origin of this ecclesiastical state is lost in the obscurity of centuries. When the hermits first chose this romantic spot, and when they first were gathered into monasteries, is uncertain ; but though the establishment of religious houses by the great Constantine may be a myth, we have evidence of the existence of hermits on Athos for the last thousand years ; [1] we know that the founder of one monastery lived in the tenth century, and another convent was *restored* nine hundred years ago. Comparatively few vicissitudes have befallen this strange community since its foundation ; the Latin conquerors of Constantinople, it is true, pillaged the monasteries in the thirteenth century, but by the lavish support of succeeding Greek emperors it not only recovered but soon surpassed its former estate. Passing from the jurisdiction of the Christian emperors to that of the Ottoman, it alone preserved its self-government and its ancient privileges when all the rest of the Byzantine Empire was crushed beneath the feet of the victorious infidels. At the beginning of the present century the War of Independence brought heavy burdens on many of the convents, and the confiscation of their lands first in free Greece, then in the Roumanian provinces in 1865, inflicted a heavy blow upon their fortunes. But now the community seems to have again recovered, to have made good its losses, to be increasing in numbers, and to be extending its establishments, and, with the exception of the universal want of learning, which seems to date from an epoch not much posterior to the Turkish Con-

---

[1] By a document of the Emperor Basil in the year 885.

quest,[1] when arts and humanities fled from the East
to find a home in Western Europe, the Holy Mountain appears to be in much the same condition as it
was in the Middle Ages.

Such is Athos, a land of great and varied beauty, a
mountain and a garden in the sea. If it please you
we will together wander up and down this eastern
fairyland, peep into its venerable religious houses, talk
to their grave inhabitants, and examine the treasures
which centuries have heaped together within their
walls ; we will refresh ourselves with a visit not only
to another clime but to another century, and we will
seize upon this one changeless spot as a solitary mark
by which to take our bearings when all the world and
we within it have drifted to and fro upon the ever-
varying tide of human restlessness. There is something of fascination in this thought, is there not ?

But stay ! Do not promise too rashly. My companion must be of chameleon temperament, and able
to change at will from grave to gay and gay to grave ;
for there is in all connected with Athos a strange mixture of grotesqueness and religion, so much that forces
merriment from Western travellers, whilst as we laugh
the mysterious power of the Christian faith on the spot
devoted to its cultivation checks the motion of our
thoughts and leads them into other channels. And so,
though we jog on like any other travellers, and crack
our jokes and curse our bed and board, yet we shall be

---

[1] ' Les Grecs des sus-dicts monasteres estoyent le temps passé beaucoup
plus doctes qu'ils ne sont pour l'heure presente. Maintenant il n'y en a
plus nuls qui sçachent rien ; et seroit impossible qu'en tout le mont Athos
lon trouvast en chaque monastere plus d'un seul Caloiere sçavant.'—*Les
Observations de plusieurs singularitez et choses memorables trouvées en
Grece, Asie, Indée, Egypte, Arabie et autres pays estranges.* Par Pierre
Belon du Mans. Anvers, 1555.

pardoned if sometimes a touch ignite a train of thought, out of place in any other journey save that across a land saturated through and through with the energy of faith, for we will quench the flame as speedily as we may and trudge again along the proper and accepted track of statistics and description. My companion too must be one able to leave all prejudices behind, and be content to reflect on what he sees, and, may be, sometimes learn a thing or two from those poor folk whom the world despises and contemns, the humble and illiterate peasant monks, possessed of nothing save a dauntless hold upon the ancient faith of Christendom. Such companions are hard to find; there are but few to whom a journey to the Holy Mountain will bring any profit or even pleasure. Perhaps, dear reader, you are one of these few; if so, will you come ?

CHAPTER II.

The love of Greece, and it tickled him so
That he devisèd a way to go.
Old Song in 'Monsieur Thomas.'

On Friday, July 20, 1883, at twenty minutes to eight
A.M. I left London for Bucharest. I was to travel
alone, for it had been arranged that my companion
should follow in the course of the next thirty-six hours
and join me in the capital of Roumania. That night
I slept at Cologne, putting up at that most comfortable
house, the Hôtel du Nord.

Starting the next day at noon, I passed the night
in the train, was turned out at the early hour of four
o'clock on Sunday morning to pass the custom house
at Passau, and reached Vienna at half-past ten.

The remainder of this day I passed pleasantly in
the Austrian capital; went in the evening to Schön-
brunn, and lay that night at the Hôtel Métropole.
On Monday, July 23, I left Vienna at 3.30 P.M. to
travel direct to Bucharest. All went well until after
passing Pesth; only two other men were in my com-
partment, and I was looking forward to a comfortable
night, when at ten o'clock we were invaded by an old
gentleman, his wife, and his daughter. Our compart-
ment was now *complet*; paterfamilias occupied the
seat in front of me, and the mother, who was of such
proportions that she had had considerable difficulty in

squeezing through the doorway, filled, or rather over-flowed, the seat on my right. Presently the daughter complained of the draught, and the old gentleman shut the window. At the end of a quarter of an hour the atmosphere of the carriage became perfectly unendurable to me, although none of my fellow-travellers appeared to be uneasy.

What was to be done? I could not insist upon fresh air in the face of the majority, so I determined to try what politeness would effect. Seeing that the mother was endeavouring to compose herself to sleep, I offered her my air cushion to support her head, and under cover of this small courtesy, which was accepted with bows and thanks, in Hungarian, I pointed to one of the ventilators and proposed by signs to open it.

'Ist good?' said I.

'Good!' replied the old gentleman; and opened it was.

Still the heat and stuffiness were intolerable—it was a sultry July evening, remember—and I began to cast about for a new relief. Just then we happened to stop at a station.

'Szegedin,' said the old gentleman to his family.

'What!' said I, a brilliant idea occurring to me, 'Szegedin?'

'Szegedin,' repeated he.

Down went the window in an instant, and out went my head. It was pitch dark, and of course under any circumstances there was nothing to see. As the train moved off I proceeded to shut the window, as in duty bound. It was a very unfortunate thing, but the window would not quite shut. Whereupon the old gentleman hastened to assist me, and we both pulled and

pushed with apparently equal earnestness.   Finally
we both desisted, with mutual smiles and shruggings
of shoulders.   Triumph number two, ventilation se-
cured, and I soon fell into an innocent slumber.   Late
in the evening of the next day I reached Bucharest,
and put up at the Hôtel Otteletchano, a comfortable
house, with fairly reasonable prices for a town where
everything is dear.

Bucharest is a city of gardens in a flat plain, in
character half Russian, half Oriental.   The Dimbovitza
runs through the midst of it, a river highly praised by
the native poets.

> Dimbovitza, apa dulce.

But when I had the pleasure of gazing upon this
renowned stream it bore a strong resemblance to a
very large ditch filled with singularly dirty water.
On the farther side of the Dimbovitza stands the
metropolitan church of Bucharest, on the top of a
considerable eminence.   There is nothing in the
church itself to repay one for the toil of climbing the
steep ascent, but from the platform outside one gains
a really fine and comprehensive view of the town,
which looks its best from this point.   The meanness of
its buildings is not discernible, whilst one's eye rests
with pleasure upon the expanse of white houses, green
gardens, and the many domes of the churches and
monasteries ; some painted in the brightest colours,
others plated with sheets of tin, which light up brilliantly
under the cloudless Eastern sky.   One of the things
that most strikes the English traveller in Bucharest is
the degraded condition of the women of the lower
classes, who are employed literally as beasts of burden.

When I was in the town building and rebuilding were
taking place on a very large scale, and in every street
women and girls of all ages, and burnt by the sun to
every shade of brown and black, might be seen mixing
mortar, or painfully carrying loads up inclined planes
to the top of scaffolding, where their lords and masters
were engaged in slowly and deliberately putting the
bricks into their places. It is exceedingly unfair to
judge of a people from a hasty visit to their country,
more especially if that visit be to their capital, where
a nation usually exhibits its worst side ; and, indeed,
the Roumanians do not appear to be very proud of
their chief city, if the following proverb rightly ex-
presses their sentiments towards it : ' Here flowers
have no smell, men no honour, women no virtue.'
Still, without pretending to estimate their national
virtues or their national vices, one cannot help noticing
that miserable desire to imitate French manners and
customs which seems to have taken root throughout
the East, especially in the little Balkan States which
have just begun to toddle by themselves. Unable to
distinguish between the good and bad of *mores Gallici*,
eager to hide their rude native characteristics beneath
the veneer of Western civilisation, the men of the
upper classes copy the vices, the women the fashions
of the West. French architecture is transplanted into
countries where it looks ridiculous ; French republi-
canism tinges the politics of nationalities but just
emancipated from tyrannous despotism, whilst the
common people keep more or less to the customs of
their fathers, unable to appreciate exotic manners and
caring little or nothing for political freedom.
     Thus one class losing touch with the other, division

arises, and patriotism is either sorely injured or altogether extinguished.

Whilst walking about the town the day after my
arrival I suddenly came upon a large funeral procession, evidently that of some person of consideration,
as two mounted soldiers rode in front to clear the way.
They were followed by an undertaker dressed in a
black suit trimmed with gold lace and a cocked hat,
carrying a basketful of unlighted candles. Then
came a second undertaker, bearing a disc of painted
cardboard, and two more behind him carrying another
disc between them, all three being attired similarly to
the first. After the undertakers came four carriages,
each containing two priests ; then a fifth, in which were
seated two deacons, one of whom bore an episcopal
staff in pieces ; a closed carriage followed, in which was
the prelate. All these ecclesiastics were in full vestments. Then came two horse undertakers, dressed
like their brethren on foot. A mounted undertaker is
an odd idea, I admit, but very gallant these gentlemen
looked nevertheless on their prancing steeds, supporting by hand and stirrup long poles with swinging
lanterns at the ends, like a pair of sepulchral lancers.
A quire of men and boys followed, chanting dolefully :
these were in ordinary dress. Immediately behind
them came the hearse. It was much more like a
circus car, for the canopy over the coffin was supported by four wooden knights, nearly life size, clad
in complete armour and richly gilt. A red pall covered
the coffin, and on it, surrounded by wreaths of flowers
and evergreens, was the deceased's best tall silk hat.
Wreaths and ribbons of the Roumanian colours hung
round the car and its canopy. Four horses, each led

by a footman carrying a candle, drew the hearse, and
on the box there sat a gentleman in a cocked hat with
a large white plume nodding over his eyes. In the rear
of the procession were fifteen male mourners on foot, one
carriage in which rode the chief female mourners, and
eight other vehicles containing the friends and relatives
of the deceased. I noticed that all in the streets un-
covered when the hearse passed, and some saluted the
bishop in a similar fashion. I must confess that I had
considerable difficulty in preserving the gravity of
countenance proper to the occasion.

No, I do not find the water of the Dimbovitza
palatable!

Undeterred by the sight of the river to-day or by
its ominous colour in the carafe this evening, I have
tried it, but I do *not* appreciate the flavour. On an
appeal to the head waiter he tells me, with a fine and
undisguised contempt for my taste, that everybody, including the King, is only too glad to have the chance
of drinking the water of the Dimbovitza, that all the
aërated beverages· are made of it, and that no other
water is obtainable unless I like to pay a franc and a
half for a bottle of imported Apollinaris! I end by
drinking my wine undiluted.

The next day, Thursday, July 26, O— arrived,
bringing the good news that he had succeeded, though
with great difficulty, in persuading the customs
officials at the various frontiers that the five her-
metically sealed tins of photographic dry plates (to
open which would have been, of course, destruction)
did not contain tobacco, dynamite, or other contraband
articles. The following morning we rose at half-
past three o'clock, in order to catch the 5.15 A.M.

train for Varna. There was some doubt as to the station from which the train started, but on the authority of ' Bradshaw ' and our landlord we were persuaded that the right station for Varna was the one known as ' Philarète.' To ' Philarète ' we accordingly went, and reached it at four o'clock, congratulating ourselves on being in such excellent time. There were only two men about, one of whom was washing what we supposed was our train, but neither of them could speak any but their native language. Time passed on, and, as at five o'clock no other officials had appeared and the ticket office had not yet opened, we began to suspect that something was wrong, and our worst fears were confirmed a few minutes afterwards by our seeing the express crossing a distant junction on its way to Varna. It had left the other station.

We roused the slumbering station master, who soon appeared, half-dressed, and through the medium of some execrable French we drew from him the explanation that there had been a recent alteration, owing to the establishment of the Oriental express, so that now travellers bound for the East started from the arrival station instead of having to drive across Bucharest. Of course the landlord of the Otteletchano must have known that he was sending us to the wrong station, and he no doubt expected to see us back again to spend three more days under his roof ; so we vowed that he should not profit by his iniquities, and determined to devote the three days to visiting other places on our route.

There was a train leaving for Giurgevo at half-past seven, and this we resolved to take, as it would give us an opportunity of seeing Rustchuk, the second town of Bulgaria and celebrated in the late Russo-Turkish war. In four hours we arrived at this place, situated on the Danube, across which there is a steam ferry to Rustchuk. On board the steamer we made a frugal meal, which we had hardly finished before we arrived at the Bulgarian shore. The instant we had disembarked we found ourselves surrounded by a crowd of men and boys, all eager to carry our luggage. One grabbed one thing and one another, which we hastily snatched back and piled up on the quay. Finally we seized upon the best looking of the party, who spoke a little Italian, and put ourselves under his guidance; the crowd was then cuffed and kicked in various directions, and three Turks were selected to carry our baggage into the custom house. The dry plates proved the only obstacle to our speedy release; finally these had to be bought with backsheesh, and we then drove in a carriage over a bad road to a miserable place that called itself an hotel.

Rustchuk is not a prepossessing place. Whatever it was before the war, it is now most dilapidated and poverty-stricken. The streets are mere sandy tracks except in places where they appear to have been paved at some remote period and still preserve a few odd stones. Wooden houses of one storey totter on either side, and here and there a half-ruined mosque reminds one of the late rulers of the town. A palace had just been built for the Prince by a Bulgarian merchant. It stands on the high bank overlooking the Danube, and bears a striking resemblance to an English suburban villa. We walked in at the open door and inspected it; for it was not quite finished, although a soldier was keeping guard and the Bulgarian standard floated proudly over the roof.

We visited the chief church, which, however, hardly repaid our trouble, and, as we were assailed by myriads of fleas, we soon made our escape. As we passed through the doorway the guardian of the church advanced and sprinkled our hands with lavender water from a silver bottle. Our guide (the youth we had picked up on landing) then conducted us to the principal mosque, into which he contemptuously strode with some other Bulgarians, trampling over the matting without removing his boots. A few Turks were saying their prayers, and it was curious to see how the conquered race did not even deign to notice the insult they were powerless to avenge. Truly the tables are turned in Bulgaria, and all the Turks that can afford to do so have left the country.

Our dinner was abominable this evening; the steak which our landlord had provided for us was like leather, and so gritty that we wondered if it had been accidentally dropped in the sandy street outside. Our bedroom also was full of vermin, and we were not sorry when the time came to bid farewell to Rustchuk, which we did early the next morning, taking the 7.30 A.M. train for Varna. The landlord had very foolishly brought the bill to the station, thinking, no doubt, that, in the hurry of departure, the amount, equal to what one might have paid with grumbling at a first-rate hotel in Paris for a night's board and lodging, would have been handed over to him without much difficulty. But we were his match, for, O— having duly registered the baggage, I called for the bill, and on observing the total simply turned the paper over, made up my own account on the back, item by item, at fair prices, added it up, and presented the sum to our host. He recognised that he was beaten, for he quietly pocketed the money without a murmur.

It is a golden rule worth remembering when travelling in these countries : *If you intend to dispute your bill, see that your luggage is safely out of the landlord's clutches*; he has then but little hold on you.

The railway to Varna lies through a flat, uninteresting country. Before reaching the coast the line passes through a large marsh; tall reeds shut out the view on either side and even brush against the carriages. Varna itself is situated at the mouth of a long arm of the sea, and is a clean and flourishing town with a population of about 20,000 souls. We reached the terminus at 4.30 P.M. and drove at once to the Hôtel de Russie. The room allotted to us was comfortable enough, but on asking the price we found it so enormous that we instantly demanded a cheaper apartment. This was declared impossible, but we argued the point and reminded the landlord that we were not in an European capital.

'No,' said he, 'but, you see, this hotel must be supported, and no one would ever stay here unless he had missed the steamer, as you have done.'

This, I dare say, was true enough. However, we came to terms at length, and I am bound to say we were very well treated during our stay. We had a delicious bathe that afternoon, although we unfortunately managed to choose a spot where the rocks were most painfully sharp. The next day being Sunday we went to the Church of St. Athanasius, and found a wedding taking place. In the centre of the nave were the bride and bridegroom before a desk upon which was placed the Book of the Holy Gospels. They had

C

wreaths or crowns of orange blossoms on their heads,
and stood clasping each other's hands.   In front of
them was the bishop, who officiated ; behind them an
old clerk held two lighted candles adorned with twisted
bands of muslin.   Two priests and several readers,
standing in stalls, chanted at intervals. The day was terribly hot and the church pretty well filled with people.
One kind lady friend occupied herself with fanning the
bride, and at intervals an old man went up behind the
happy couple, and removing first the bride's crown and
then the bridegroom's, mopped their streaming faces with
a handkerchief, replacing the orange blossoms after the
performance of this kind office.   Towards the conclusion of the ceremony the relatives and friends kissed
first the Gospels, then the bishop's hand, and finally
the newly married couple on both cheeks.

When the service was over the people rushed out
of church and formed a procession to conduct them to
their home.   This was headed by two fiddlers, a man
with a clarionet, and two other men playing instru-
ments resembling guitars, but struck with a quill instead of the fingers; and a curious noise this Bulgarian
band made.   On the Monday we left Varna by the
Austrian Lloyd steamer 'Ceres' at 3 P.M., and early
next morning, after a calm night's voyage, passed the
ancient Cyanean rocks and entered the Bosphorus.
We were not long in steaming down that enchanting
stream ; we were soon abreast of the Castles of Europe
and Asia, and a few minutes later, off the village of
Candelli, the distant view of Constantinople burst upon
us, the dome and minarets of St. Sophia rising above
the green cypresses of the Seraglio gardens.   At 8 A.M.
we cast anchor in the Golden Horn.

CHAPTER III.

WITH a description of Constantinople a volume could be filled, and if one were to spend a twelvemonth in the imperial city, and, having visited the ordinary sights, were to search amongst courtyards and gardens and dive into cellars and modern Turkish houses in quest of the antique and the historic, not one but many volumes would have to be written to treat of those relics of departed Byzantine glory which are to be found beneath the dust of Stamboul.

As for ourselves, we are bound for another place ; we cannot afford to waste time on our journey thither, so I shall be accorded grace, I am sure, if I touch but briefly upon a city which demands something more than a passing notice.

We have visited the Hippodrome, have seen the Delphic column and the obelisk of Heliopolis ; we have descended into the great hall called the Thousand and One Pillars, formerly the cistern of Constantine ; we have strolled through the bazaars, jostling with every kind of Asiatic and delighted with the sight of wares brought from every part of the world. There are no bazaars like those of Constantinople, none one

quarter the size, none so rich in the products of both
East and West, for here alone do both civilizations
meet.

Constantinople was no new ground to me, so I had
the pleasure of being a cicerone to my friend. Acting
upon the experience of my first visit, I arranged that
we should see the other great mosques before that of
St. Sophia ; as the latter furnished the inspiration for
the architecture of those built after the conquest, and
far surpasses them in almost every particular, one's
interest is better kept up by reversing the usual pro-
cedure of travellers.

The exterior of St. Sophia is disappointing ; the
church presents but the aspect of a confused mass of
buildings, irregular and somewhat mean in character and detail, above which rise a flat central dome,
several half-domes abutting thereon, and four inelegant
minarets. But having passed the outer porch, or
exonarthex, and gained the inner porch, or esonarthex,
with its sixteen bronze gates, nine of which lead
directly into the nave, the glory of the great church
begins to dawn upon us ; for we find, on looking
round, that we are in a hall, 200 feet long by 30 feet
broad, the walls of which are panelled with variegated
marble, though dull with age and neglect, it is true, and
above the marble we gain our first view of mosaic work.

We pass impatiently into the nave, and pausing in
the centre of the church cast our eyes around. No
disappointment awaits us here. Like the heavenly
Jerusalem, this Christian temple 'lieth four-square,
and the length is as large as the breadth ;' and if we
were to measure the height from dome to pavement
we might still further the comparison, for we should

find that, speaking roughly, 'the length and the breadth
and the height of it are equal.' Above us, supported
on four arches resting on four massive piers, is the
aërial dome, so called because, by reason of its extreme
shallowness in proportion to its diameter—fifteen feet
more than that of the dome of St. Paul's Cathedral,
in London—it is supposed to resemble the vault of
heaven; it is constructed of pumice stone and bricks
of an especial lightness. On the north and south
sides, between the dome piers, stand eight great
columns of green marble, four on either hand, said to
have formed part of the Temple of Diana at Ephesus,
brought, it is certain, from that town by the Prætor
Constantine. Eight more columns of porphyry came
from the Temple of the Sun at Baalbek, and ninety-
one other pillars of every variety of marble, brought
from many ancient buildings, support the galleries and
vaulted roofs, making up the total number of one
hundred and seven. There is but one apse; here
stood formerly the high altar, and before it the screen
or iconostasis, partly of carved and gilded wood, partly
of gold itself. This apse is lighted by two rows of
three windows each, in honour of the Holy Trinity,
according to the direction of an angel who appeared
to Justinian during the erection of the building. The
walls are veneered with jasper and variegated marbles,
or adorned, like the vaulted ceilings, with mosaic; but
here and there plates of marble have fallen off, and the
present possessors of the church have supplied their
places with plaster painted in imitation of the more
precious substance; the mosaics too are for the most
part hidden behind a layer of plaster, as representing
human figures inadmissible in a mosque.

There are two chapters in the history of St. Sophia upon which I like to dwell when treading the pavement of that great church. The first carries one back thirteen centuries, to December 27, 537, when the Emperor Justinian solemnly dedicated the completed building to the worship of the Eternal Wisdom. The Patriarch, we are told, rode in the imperial chariot, accompanied by all the ecclesiastics of the city; Justinian himself followed on foot at the head of his people, giving thanks as he went for the mercy vouchsafed to him in having been permitted to finish the holy work; and thus the vast procession wended its way from the Church of St. Anastasia to the new basilica. The Emperor enters: he gazes around upon the gorgeous marbles, the glittering mosaics, all fresh from the hands of the craftsmen; he sees the great iconostasis of wood overlaid with gold, the splendid sanctuary, the walls of which are encrusted with forty thousand pounds in weight of silver, the doors of cedar, of amber, and of ivory, the holy table one mass of jewels held together by gold, for that precious metal was thought too poor to be used alone. Thousands of lamps and candles are suspended from the arches and the dome, or burn in silver standards upon the marble pavement. The sunlight streams through the windows and lights up the curling incense-wreaths. Justinian is surrounded by a dazzling crowd of bishops and senators, priests and courtiers; all that is noble in the empire is gathered within those splendid walls. He stands in front of the altar screen; he gazes upward at the great vault suspended, as it were, over his head, and as he does so the cry bursts from his lips, 'Solomon, I have surpassed thee!'

The curtain drops. We raise it again when nearly a thousand years have elapsed, on May 29, 1453. The vast city of Constantine, which the first Christian emperor had founded to be the capital of the Christian world, is in her death throes. For fifty-two days the fifteen miles of wall had been successfully defended by 8,000 soldiers against nearly 300,000 infidels ; the siege had almost been raised in despair, when Mahomet executed his famous stratagem and sailed his fleet over the dry land into the Golden Horn, and on the evening of the 28th all knew that the end had come. The brave Emperor Constantine Palæologus, having made his last speech to the valiant defenders, and received for the last time the Lord's Body at the altar of St. Sophia somewhere about midnight, bade farewell to the trembling inhabitants of the palace, forgave and asked forgiveness of those around him, and mounting his horse rode to the great breach by the Gate of St. Romanus in the land wall on the farther side of the city. At eight o'clock that morning, the Feast of Pentecost, Constantinople was taken.

Twenty thousand people of every age and rank rushed in the vain hope of sanctuary to St. Sophia. ' In the space of an hour the sanctuary, the choir, the nave, the upper and lower galleries were filled with the multitudes of fathers and husbands, of women and children, of priests, monks, and religious virgins.' [1] A mighty cry goes up, ' Kyrie eleison ! Kyrie eleison ! ' ' Have mercy upon us, O Lord ! have mercy ! ' A thousand hands are outstretched in agonized supplication to where the calm, majestic face of the Virgin Mother looks down from the mosaic vaulting upon the

[1] Gibbon's *Decline and Fall of the Roman Empire.*

frantic crowd; a thousand voices implore the aid of the
great archangel, who, a prophecy asserted, would appear to deliver Constantinople at the eleventh hour.
Ah, poor souls! It is too late now to cry for mercy,
for the hour of judgment has come. In vain do
you seek the intervention of the Blessed Ones, for
their will is the will of God ; Mary has veiled her face
and Michael is sorrowfully leaning upon his sword.
Ten centuries have filled to overflowing the cup of
wickedness ; the sins of the great Christian city have
reached unto heaven, and God hath remembered her
iniquities. Alas! alas! that mighty city! for in one hour
is her judgment come! A roar of voices is heard outside ; shouts of 'Allah!' drown the Kyries ; the doors
resound with heavy blows ; the axes crash through the
brazen gates : the Turks rush in.

They meet with no resistance ; the crowd is like a
frightened flock of sheep. Some few, indeed, are cut
down by the flashing swords ; battle axe and mace
beat down the upturned faces of those who block
the entrance of the conquerors, but these are already
satiated with blood and tired of slaughter, eager now
for the captives and the spoil.

The miserable wretches are dragged out into the
courtyard and bound together in rows, amidst tears
and wailing ; daughters are torn from their mothers,
wives from their husbands, the men to cruel bond-
age, the women and girls to grace the harems of
their masters.[1] Some are forced down by the press
and trodden underfoot ; shrieks and groans resound
through the church and mingle with the battle cry of
the infidels, 'Allah! Allah!' Tradition asserts that at

---

[1] Phranza, 3, 8.

one of the altars in the southern gallery a priest was
celebrating the last mass in St. Sophia; for the last
time the blessed words of institution had been pronounced within these venerable walls, for the last time
the spotless sacrifice had been offered up, when the
Turks streamed up the inclined planes which serve
instead of staircases and threw themselves amongst the
terrified throng above.   One quick glance behind him
upon the advancing infidels, one imploring cry to God,
not for himself but for the holy mysteries, that they
might be preserved from profanation, and then the
priest, bearing the Sacred Gifts before him, passed
through the solid wall, leaving behind no trace either
of the manner or of the place of entrance.[1]   Will he
ever return and complete that unfinished Eucharist?
Some think he will, on the day when St. Sophia
is solemnly restored to the worship of the Christian
faith; others, and they are the more part, doubt the
possibility.   For myself I have no opinion on the
matter; but one thing I know, that if that tradition be
true and the priest again appears after his long sleep
to assist in the re-dedication of the profaned sanctuary, the nineteenth or twentieth century will persuade itself that he is but an optical delusion; it
will need something more than the reappearance of
an old priest to shake the world out of its material
conceits.

Below the work of destruction has commenced:

[1] During the restoration of the church in 1847–49 by Monsieur Fos-
sati, an Italian, called in by the Sultan Abdul-Medjid to save St. Sophia
from the ruin which threatened it through long neglect, this architect had
the curiosity to open the wall at the spot where Turkish and Greek
traditions alike declare the priest to have entered.   He found a little
chapel in the thickness of the wall, with a descending staircase encumbered with rubbish.

the great screen is hewn into fragments; the jewelled
sheathing of the icons and the countless silver lamps
that burn before them become the prey of the maddened
soldiery. The costly hangings and veils, the curtains
of scarlet and of purple are torn down and parted
amongst the spoilers; the holy table is hacked to pieces;
the crosses are defaced. The crowd pours into the
sacristies; the vestments and the sacred vessels of
priceless worth become the property of the furious
infidels; the bodies of the saints are turned out of their
precious shrines; the temples sanctified by the Holy
Ghost are thrown to the swine and to the dogs. In a
few short hours the heaped-up treasures have been
swept away for ever, and nothing but the empty shell
of St. Sophia remains. Then a cry goes up for the
utter destruction of the Christian church; the Turks
have already commenced to cut away the mosaics,
when the Conqueror himself appears and sternly
claims the building as his own. He rides proudly
into the church;[1] his charger's hoofs clatter on
Justinian's pavement; he stops before the eastern apse
and there proclaims the Church of the Eternal Wisdom
to be henceforth sacred to the religion of the Prophet.
That evening the muezzin ascended the principal tower
and called the faithful to prayer:

La Ilah il Allah we Mohammed resoul Allah.

St. Sophia was lost to Christendom. But—so say
Turks as well as Christians—not for ever. And in the
eastern apse, above the muttering Moslems, may still
be traced the image of the Divine Redeemer with all-

---

[1] Ducas seems to contradict this tradition; but the historian was not
present on the occasion.

embracing Arms stretched out in benediction, appearing through layers of paint and plaster; and over the western doorway may yet be read the words, written on a brazen tablet, 'Come unto Me, all ye that labour and are heavy laden, and I will give you rest.' *Viventne ossa ista? Domine Deus, tu nosti.*

It is a long ride or drive from Pera to the triple wall which defends the land side of Constantinople, but it is worth undertaking, for it offers the most perfect specimen extant of mediæval fortification, never having been touched since the Turkish conquest and presenting the same shattered aspect as when the city was stormed in 1453. At the corner where the triple wall joins the wall on the south side of Constantinople, which runs along the shore of the Sea of Marmora, is the citadel or fortress known as the Seven Towers, formerly used by the Ottomans as a State prison, but now entirely dismantled. From the circuit of the castle walls a fine view is obtainable; the inclosure is bare and empty, but in the vaults under one of the towers visitors are shown the place where the unfortunate prisoners were confined. Until comparatively recent times, on war breaking out between the Porte and another Power, the ambassador representing the hostile government was hurried to the prison of the Seven Towers, instead of being politely handed his passport, as in these days. Of those confined within the castle few ever regained their freedom; the sword, the bowstring, and the torture did their work, and many a gloomy story those walls could tell. On the walls of what was formerly a dark vault, but which is now opened to the light, many names are scratched in European characters. One imperfect inscription I copied out.

Prisoñie
urs qui dans
les miseres,
gemissez dans
ce triste lieu
Offrez les de
bon Cœur à
Dieu et vous
les trouverez
légér.

But a few broken words, and yet a touching tale is hidden here. Poor prisoner! without a name, without a history.

One night we went to dine with some English friends at their house at Candelli, on the Asiatic shore of the Bosphorus. After dinner we sat on a terrace overhanging the water and enjoyed the coolness of the evening, listening to the heavy sighs of the porpoises as they frolicked in the rushing stream. As it grew late, we embarked in our host's caïque to return to Constantinople. The old Greek boatman took us into the middle of the stream, and then, equidistant from Europe and Asia, we were partly rowed, partly carried by the swift current towards the city. We were reclining lazily on the cushion at the bottom of our little craft when Constantinople rose before us in the darkness like an enchanted city of the 'Arabian Nights.' It was the festival of Bairam, and every minaret in Stamboul was illuminated with rows of lamps—a scene most weird and wonderful, but, like most good things, too transient, for the stream was swift, our old boatman strong of arm, and soon our sharp prow grated against the dark quay of Galata.

Before our departure for Mount Athos it was

necessary to obtain a letter of introduction to the
·monks, and for that purpose we arranged for a visit
to Phanar, where lives the Patriarch of Constantinople—
the Œcumenical Patriarch, as he is called in the East—
to present the formal letter of introduction with which
we had been furnished by our ecclesiastical authorities
and to pay our respects to his Holiness.

Having received intimation from the Patriarchate
that an audience would be granted us on a certain
afternoon, we left our hotel at Pera at two o'clock that
day and drove, attended by our dragoman and a
cavass from the consulate, to Phanar. We were received at the gate of the Patriarchate by several
servants, who conducted us up a long flight of steep
marble steps to the room of the Grand Vicar, a rather
young man with black hair and beard. About ten or
twelve other ecclesiastics were present, and we soon
got into conversation, as they were very inquisitive
and asked innumerable questions over the sweets;
coffee, and cigarettes which are the invariable prelude
to all business in the East. So we told them that we
belonged to the great Anglican Church of which the
Archbishop of Canterbury was the patriarch : that we
were not like the Lutherans or the Calvinists ; that
we had nothing to do with the Presbyterian missionaries, but had the greatest respect for the Eastern
Church and much wished for unity. Then we exhibited certain photographs, with which we had provided
ourselves before leaving home, of the Archbishop,
St. Paul's Cathedral, and other English churches.
These called forth endless questions, which we had not
time to answer before word came that the Patriarch
had finished his siesta and was ready to receive us.

Accordingly we got up, bowed to our friends, and were taken into the presence of Joachim III. His Holiness was sitting in a good-sized, airy room, furnished in the French style with a row of high-backed chairs and a sofa covered with crimson velvet. A few sacred pictures hung round the walls, amongst them an engraving of Murillo's Madonna in the Louvre. A small writing table covered with books, at which the Patriarch sat, completed the furniture.

As we entered his Holiness rose and gave us his hand. We all sat down, and he remarked that he was very glad to see me again (I had had a short interview with him in 1882), and pleased to make the acquaintance of my friend, who, he hoped, was satisfied with Constantinople. Then O— drew from the pocket of his cassock our commendatory letter, saying to the interpreter, 'Tell his Holiness that I have the pleasure of bringing him a letter from the Most Holy and the Most Learned the Bishop of Lichfield.'

The Patriarch took the document and read it through carefully from beginning to end, and then began it again and read the whole of it for the second time. Apparently he was much pleased with it, for he said ' Polycala' (Very good) several times, and then handed it to the Grand Logothete, or principal layman, who was the only other person in the room.

The episcopal seal of wafer and tissue paper hardly excited less interest than the contents of the letter, and both Patriarch and Grand Logothete twisted it every possible way to see how it was done.

We conversed about the English Church, and his Holiness said that he was very sorry to hear of the death of the late Archbishop of Canterbury, and asked after the present one, whereupon I told him that our Lord Edward was much interested in Eastern Christendom, and that on my return to England I should relate to his Grace all I had seen.

Then we exhibited our photographs and began the subject of unity by saying that there were many people in England who wished for the union of the two communions. The Patriarch said that the wish was a good one, and he hoped it might be fulfilled. ' But,' added he, referring to what was evidently on his mind, ' unity should be procured without individual proselytism.'

' Of course,' said we, ' that is very wrong.'

' But the Protestants and the Americans proselytize,' said his Holiness, ' and the American college here does its best to draw away our people from the faith of their fathers.'

Here it was necessary to insist very strongly on the fact that our Church had nothing whatever to do with the Protestant missionaries in Constantinople. These missionaries themselves are at great pains to inform the Greeks that they belong to our holy religion, for however much they may attack the Church at home they like to wrap themselves in the mantle of her prestige abroad. So we put the matter quite clearly before his Holiness, and asked him if he had ever found our people proselytizing amongst his flock.

' No,' said he, ' with Anglicans we have no fault to find.'

We next spoke about a Greek deacon whom the Patriarch had sent to Oxford to study English theology, and said that we were all much gratified at his sending him to us, taking it as a great compliment to our Church. At this the Patriarch's face quite

brightened up ; he was evidently pleased at hearing
that his action had been appreciated, and he twice
repeated that he would send some more. The Patriarch
then discussed our journey, and commended our purpose of visiting the Holy Mountain. Soon afterwards
we rose to take leave.

His Holiness bade us adieu in a very kindly manner,
asked us to visit him in the event of our returning to
Constantinople after leaving Athos, and finally said,
'I am always delighted to see any member of the
English Church, and you must be sure to convey my
salutations to the Archbishop of Canterbury.'

So we bowed and withdrew.

After visiting the Patriarchal Church of St. George
and leaving a card upon the Metropolitan Bryennius,
the learned editor of the Διδαχὴ Ἀποστόλων, whose
acquaintance I had made the previous year, we left
the Patriarchate and returned to Pera.

Two days after our interview an archimandrite and
a secretary waited on us at the Hôtel d'Angleterre
with a letter from the Patriarch, recommending us to
the synod of Mount Athos. The following is a literal
translation of it :

Joachim, by the mercy of God Archbishop of Constantinople,
New Rome, and Œcumenical Patriarch.

Most Holy Presidents and Overseers of the Synod of the Holy
Mountain of Athos, Our beloved sons in the Lord, Grace be with
you and peace from God.

The bearers of our present letter to your Holinesses, English
travellers, the Most Reverend Priest of the English Church Arthur
E. Brisco Owen and Athelstan Riley, eminent professors of the
renowned University in Oxford, visiting Eastern parts, journeyed
also to Constantinople to see what is most worthy of inspection
therein, and came to Us provided with a commendatory letter from
the Most Beloved of God William, Bishop of Lichfield, in England,

who requires that they, who are about to visit the sacred abodes of the Holy Mountain, shall be properly recommended.

We, therefore, assigning to these persons who have been introduced to Us befitting dignity, as being illustrious persons and strangers worthy of all honour, writing by this present Patriarchal epistle of Ours, exhort your Holinesses, that, having received with hospitality these distinguished guests, ye furnish them, besides necessary protection, with every other facility, that making the circuit of the Holy Mountain they may see also whatever is worthy of inspection therein and may carry away with them the most pleasing impressions of your friendly and kindly customs.

The Grace and Endless Mercy of God be with you.

July 21, 1883.

+ Of CONSTANTINOPLE *your bedesman in Christ.*

Before leaving the capital we visited the chaplain of the Crimean Memorial Church, Canon Curtis, who gave us three copies of Palmer's ' History of the Church,' a work which he had translated into modern Greek, asking us to give them away at Athos as presents from him.

He spoke much on the utter ignorance respecting our Church which exists in the East, and told us an amusing story in illustration of this.

During the late troubles in the Bulgarian Church, which have culminated in a sort of partial schism and separation from the Patriarchal see, Canon Curtis received a letter, signed by high ecclesiastical and lay members of the Bulgarian Church, asking him to use his influence with the Archbishop of Canterbury to get them admitted into the Anglican communion ; 'for,' said they, 'you have so many sects in your Church—Presbyterians, and Lutherans, and Calvinists, and many others—that it cannot do you any harm to have one more ; so please take the Bulgarians as well.'

D

CHAPTER IV.

In cities should we English lie,
  Where cries are rising ever new
And men's incessant stream goes by—
  We who pursue

Our business with unslackening stride,
  Traverse in troops, with care-fill'd breast,
The soft Mediterranean side,
  The Nile, the East,

And see all sights from pole to pole,
  And glance, and nod, and bustle by ;
And never once possess our soul
    Before we die.   MATTHEW ARNOLD.

ON Saturday, August 4, N.S., we left Constantinople
at 3.30 P.M. in the 'Calypso,' one of the Austrian
Lloyd Company's steamers. The Sea of Marmora
was as smooth as glass, and we had a glorious view of
Stamboul and Scutari as they gradually disappeared
from sight. There were hardly any saloon passengers
—only a Greek tobacco merchant, a Turkish officer on
his way to Salonica, and one other man. As we were
drinking tea in the cabin after dinner the Greek merchant, who spoke a little English, imparted to us the
unwelcome news that the ship in which we were had
just returned from Alexandria, with only ten days'
quarantine at Beyrout and two in the Dardanelles ;
that she had been engaged in Turkish transport service
in the Red Sea, when two privates and one officer had

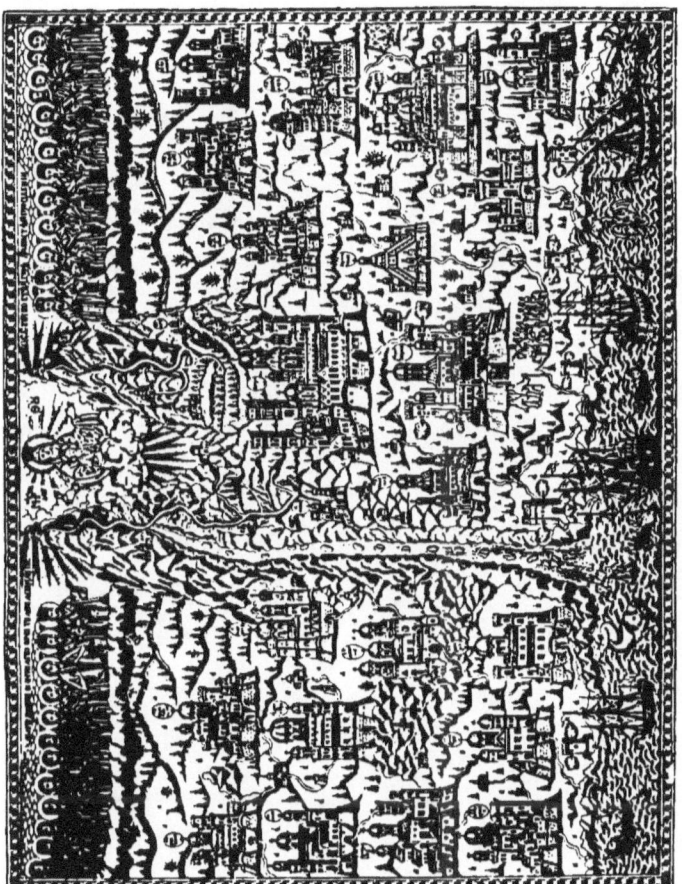

ALL THE MONASTERIES, FROM A MONASTIC ENGRAVING.

(It will be observed that the artist, wishing to represent both sides of the promontory, has given a double top to the mountain.)

died on board of cholera; that one of the numerous deck passengers had only just recovered from cholera, and that he himself had seen his papers, which testified to that effect. Here was a cheerful prospect—to be cooped up for forty-eight hours in a choleraic vessel, with the uncomfortable feeling to boot that the Turkish officer *might* have died in one's berth! However, there was nothing to be done; we put as cheerful a face upon our circumstances as possible, and after all were none the worse for our voyage.

On Sunday morning, at 4.30 A.M., we anchored off Gallipoli, and at eight o'clock passed through the Dardanelles, which are perhaps a trifle narrower than the Bosphorus, but not nearly so pretty.

At four in the afternoon we reached Dedeaghach, and, as the steamer was to remain there until midnight, took the opportunity of landing. The town consists of between fifty and a hundred houses scattered over a sandy plain; in fact, a more miserable place it would be difficult to imagine. The next morning, quite early, we touched at Lagos, and soon after leaving it saw the mountainous island of Thasos in the distance. Passing this we cast anchor in the bay of Cavalla a little after noon.

The town of Cavalla is extremely picturesque. Occupying a rocky promontory, it is surrounded by the sea on three sides; the houses rise one above another until they are crowned by an ancient fortress at the top of the rock, and the whole is encircled by walls in perfect preservation, I think of Genoese construction. The promontory upon which the town stands is connected with the mainland by an isthmus; here a fine Roman aqueduct conveys water from the neighbouring

hills to the inhabitants, of whom there are at present
11,000, 6,000 being Turks and the rest Greek Christians, with the exception of a small colony of 150
Italians.   Almost the whole population is concerned
in one way or another with the tobacco trade ; for the
tobacco plantations of Cavalla are only second to those
of Yenidjeh, which lie a little inland.

On landing we found the city quite as pleasing in
its interior as in its exterior ; the streets are narrow,
steep, and tortuous, the dresses of the natives thoroughly Oriental.   Here turbans are still in fashion,
and the women are clad in the brightest-coloured silks
and wear the *yashmak* more closely than their sisters
of Constantinople, tying it in a different way, with the
end of the veil hanging down their backs.

There being no British consul, Signor Pecchioli,
who represents Italy and Germany as vice-consul, has
been appointed our acting consul.   This gentleman
insisted upon our accepting his hospitality during the
term of our enforced stay at Cavalla—although we
were perfect strangers and had no letters of introduction to him—and took upon himself the conduct of all
our affairs.

The consul went with us for a walk on the afternoon of our arrival and showed us a plane tree of great
size and between 400 and 500 years old, growing in
the court of a mosque.   Near it, under a pump, is a
stone trough which tradition asserts St. Paul used for
baptisms.   But half a mile from the town, on the other
side of the bay, is a relic which is more certainly connected with the great Apostle, the old Via Ignatia,
which here leaves the sea and stretches across the
mountains to Philippi.   This part of the old Roman

road is still in perfect preservation and is paved with blocks of stone. The scene from it, looking back over the bay, is a beautiful one, and can be but little changed since the Apostle's days ; probably the town itself presents much the same aspect that it did 1,800 years ago. We returned to the town towards evening, stopping first, however, at a little wayside café to refresh ourselves. We sat down in the garden facing the bay and had some Turkish sweetmeats and water. In front of us we could just make out the outline of Mount Athos through the mist, rising up out of the distant sea.

Whilst we were thus enjoying ourselves an ecclesiastic appeared, preceded by a cavass gorgeously apparelled in blue and gold. He was walking with a long silver-headed staff in his hand, and was introduced to us by the consul as the Lord Archbishop of Cavalla. He took a seat at our table, and we entered into conversation, the prelate speaking a little French.

We told him that we were waiting for a boat to take us to Mount Athos.

' Why, then,' said the Archbishop, ' you must be the two Englishmen of whom the Œcumenical Patriarch wrote in his letter to me. I too am going on a pilgrimage to the Holy Mountain for the first time, and when the Patriarch sent me my letter of introduction he told me that I should probably fall in with two distinguished English travellers, in which case I was to show them every civility. So we will go together.'

Of course nothing could have been more advantageous for us, and we arranged the matter over a cup of coffee. The Archbishop would go as soon as we wished, and as we wished. And thus it was that our friendship began with the genial fellow-traveller who was to contribute so much to the pleasure and the profit of our ' memorable and fortunate journey to Athos.' [1]

But it was no easy matter to get to the land of the monks. Though under its very shadow, it seemed as far away as ever. The consul refused to aid us in going round by land, as recent intelligence had reached him of brigand bands in the vicinity, and he would not take the responsibility of abetting the journey. We tried a sailing boat belonging to two Italian sailors, but they said that we might take three days to reach Athos if the wind was unfavourable, and this intelligence was quite enough to make me refuse the experiment. One course was still open to us, to charter a little Turkish steamer, that was to touch at Cavalla on its way from Salonica to Smyrna, to take us to our destination. This vessel arrived at 10 A.M. on the second day of our stay, Wednesday, $\frac{\text{August 8}}{\text{July 27}}$, and we instantly sent to make arrangements with the captain and the agent. The answer was that they would take us for the modest sum of 25*l*.!

Then the usual bargaining began. Two or three messages passed between the steamboat office and the consulate, with the result that two hours later the captain paid us a visit to inform us that after due consideration, to oblige Englishmen, &c. &c., they had agreed to take 12*l*. or 300 francs ; this was the *very* lowest price. So we thanked him for the trouble he had taken in coming to see us, and told him that upon second thoughts we had come to the conclusion that a sailing boat would be a far more pleasant means of transit.

[1] So the Archbishop described it in a letter to me after my return.

The captain pointed out that the wind was contrary. 'So much the better,' we replied; 'we shall have the more for our money;' whereat he departed.

'Ah,' said the consul, 'give him another hour, and he will be here again.' And sure enough the little steamer in the bay showed no signs of weighing anchor, and at one o'clock the captain returned with the agent of the company.

He said that they thought it right to warn us that a storm was brewing, and that it would be extremely dangerous to attempt the passage in an open boat.

We thanked them for their kind thoughtfulness, but said that, having quite decided to go by the sailing boat, we must trust to our *kismet*. If we were fated to be drowned we should be; but if otherwise, *Inshallah*, we should arrive at Athos. The agent then observed that having spent the last hour in minute calculations he had found that the amount of extra coals needed for the trip would not come to more than 11*l.*

'Well,' said I, 'as you are so very anxious for us to take your steamer (though for my part I *much* prefer a nice little boat in which one can take one's ease for a day or two), perhaps we might give you ten Turkish pounds.'

'Certainly,' said the agent, 'but as Englishmen you will pay in English pounds.'

'Oh, no!' said I; 'we could not think of that; it would be an insult to the country we are in. In Turkey we always pay in Turkish pounds.'

And so the bargain was struck—ten liras (about 9*l.* sterling), and we might start at once.

We took leave of our kind host and his wife, and were soon on board; the Archbishop and his servants joined us a few minutes later ; we weighed anchor and made for the Holy Mountain.

The deck was encumbered by Turks and Greeks with their goods and possessions round them, placidly smoking their tchibouques and cigarettes. All were bound for Smyrna, and were consequently being taken some way back in the direction of their starting-place, Salonica ; altogether the digression for our benefit would entail about ten hours' extra voyage. But what matter ? Time is of no value to an Oriental ; he never makes an appointment, or if he makes one he never keeps it. Now that our party is finally made up, and before we reach the scene of our toils, the pilgrims will do themselves the honour of making their introductory bows to the reader.

First comes the Altogether Most Holy One Philotheos, by the Mercy of God the Most Reverend and Divinely Appointed Archbishop and Metropolitan of the Most Holy Metropolis of Xanthe and Christo-polis (Cavalla) ; Highly Esteemed and Right Honour-able.

The possessor of these superlative titles is about five-and-thirty years of age, in person short, not more than five feet three inches, but looks much taller on account of his lofty hat and the extreme dignity of his demeanour before strangers on all official occasions. Over his purple cassock he wears a grey cloth cloak lined with white fur, and over this again, at stated times, a voluminous cloak of black stuff. Genial, kind, and full of good-nature towards his equals, whilst haughty and unbending towards his inferiors, indolent beyond belief, absolute idleness being his chief delight, in character he is a pattern Oriental.

He is attended by two servants, Pantele and Peter. The former is his cavass, or soldier servant, whose duty it is to ride or walk before him, carrying his long silver-headed staff. His dress consists of a pair of loose blue trousers fitting tightly below the knee, a short jacket of the same colour, both jacket and trousers being covered with gold embroidery, a forage cap, a sword by his side, and a sash round his waist containing knives and pistols. He is a Montenegrin, and does justice to his nationality—quick, handy, obedient, possessed of a fine upright figure (he has a curious way of bringing his feet together in the 'first position' when halting, which gives him a particularly smart air), and in addition to these good qualities extremely devout and well-behaved in church, where he is accustomed to strike his forehead with such resounding blows on the pavement that the exercise seems to partake more of the excess than defect of devotion. Peter : The bosom friend of Pantele and his inseparable companion through evil report and good report, through archiepiscopal storm and sunshine ; in nearly everything except religion his friend's antithesis ; short, thick-set, with a light brown beard, dressed in untidy European dress surmounted by a fez. In character humble, submissive, he is kept in constant attendance on his master—not an easy one to please—whom he serves as valet and general slave for the magnificent wage of a mejidieh and a half a month (about six shillings) and what he can pick up when resident at 'the metropolis.' Peter will tell you that his one great ambition is to become a deacon, and that his master has promised him that if he is *very* good, and serves him well and faithfully, *perhaps* he will make him one. Peter has, therefore, already commenced to grow long hair, which escaping from beneath his fez adds to his general unkempt appearance. Probably he hopes by this means to keep the promise constantly before his lord's notice; for he has misgivings that the Archbishop prefers his present services as servant to his doubtful diaconal assistance, and Peter being remarkably quick with his needle and an expert mender of the archiepiscopal wardrobe, I have no doubt that there is good cause for his fears. Now, Peter, off you go with a salaam and make room for your betters.

The Reverend Arthur E. Brisco Owen next appears before you—an old Oxford friend of mine, a tried fellow-traveller, whose sunny presence and mirthful humour have relieved many a dreary hour; in every respect an ideal companion for the journey upon which we are engaged. In height—well, he has the advantage of Philotheos; in dignity, a good second. Now you know as much about O— as you will learn from me, for to describe a friend is not only an improper but an impossible task.

Angelos Melissinou, our dragoman: In person tall, broad-shouldered, and—to use a polite word —stout; his weight I should be sorry to mention. O— always speaks of him to me as 'your ox'! Dresses as much like an Englishman as possible, and prides himself on being taken for one. He speaks our language like a native, having been engaged in his business from his youth, chiefly on board English yachts in the Levant. He knows his profession well, and is usually employed by travellers in Greece, with whom he is a general favourite. Being a native of Athens, he thinks it grand to exhibit a mild form of

scepticism, has given up fasting, and in church makes
a little sign of the cross an inch long, as if he were
ashamed of it. His chief delight is to torment the
Archbishop by telling him, with an air of great superiority, how they have given up this or that piece of
religion at Athens. The Archbishop rejoins by per-
tinent allusions to hell fire ; Angelos appeals to us ; we
back up the Archbishop, and so the controversy sub-
sides for the next forty-eight hours.

. Lastly there is your humble servant. Well, perhaps
the less said about him the better. By the time we
have completed our journey you will know as much
of him as is necessary.

So here we all are, three Greeks, two Englishmen,
and a Montenegrin ; and having introduced ourselves
we will think about landing, for we have nearly reached
the great promontory with its white monasteries dotted
along the shore, and we are just entering the Bay of
Vatopedi.

The British ensign was run up to the mainmast,
the Turkish flag (to denote the presence of the Archbishop, who was a Turkish subject) to the foremast ;
the steamer gave several loud whistles and cast anchor
in the bay.

It was now eight o'clock and dusk, but through the
gathering darkness we could see two or three small
boats coming towards the steamer, propelled by monks
in tall hats.

Into one the Archbishop, O—, Pántele, Peter, and
myself entered, but not without the greatest difficulty,
as the boat all but upset. Angelos followed in another
with all the luggage.

We soon reached the pier, were assisted to land by

a crowd of monks, walked a little way towards the monastery, and then sat down on a stone bench to await the luggage. When it arrived a Turkish custom-house officer was greatly desirous of opening it, but by strenuous exertions Angelos prevented this, and we all proceeded to the monastery. On our arrival the great gate was thrown open, and a monk carrying a taper in his fingers went before us. It was now quite dark and we could see nothing of our surroundings, but followed the monk through what seemed a laby-rinth, through courts, up flights of stairs, along passages, across the tops of ancient walls, now under cover, now, as we could tell from the stars overhead, in the open air. Finally we reached the set of rooms provided for us—a large sitting-room, into which two bedrooms opened, one for the Archbishop and one for us, con-taining clean iron bedsteads, and three or four other bedrooms on the other side of a passage in which our retainers settled themselves.

Supper was announced almost immediately, and the Archbishop, ourselves, and Angelos were conducted to the room where it was prepared.

We seated ourselves round a table with four of the chief monks, and the meal was immediately served.

But what a repast! Our hearts sank within us as we thought of the gastronomic trials in store for us during the next few weeks. The first dish consisted of raw tomatoes and chillies steeped in strong-smelling oil. This was placed in the centre of the table, each person helping himself with his own fork. The second course was soup, delicately compounded of fish and oil, the first spoonful of which positively took my breath away, it was so inexpressibly nasty. The soup was followed by hot fish cooked in oil ; this was just eatable. Then cold cooked tomatoes stuffed with herbs and garlic. The fifth dish consisted of a white paste looking like cornflour, which we were told was made of ground beans ; this was a sort of sweet, but being flavoured with garlic it did not suit our palates. At the sixth course we returned to the fish again, and ended with water melons, which all ate with their fishy and garlic-scented knives. The redeeming point in the supper was the wine, which was both plentiful and good. After the meal we left the table and reclined on the divans to take our 'after-dinner' glass. Whether we afterwards got accustomed to the fare or not I cannot say, but this supper seemed to us to be un-questionably the worst meal we ever had at Vatopedi ; we never had anything to complain of in the food set before us on subsequent occasions in this hospitable monastery.

We returned to our rooms, had coffee whilst re-ceiving several monastic visitors, and retired at half-past eleven for our first night's rest on the Holy Mountain.

CHAPTER V.

In spite of the novelty of our situation we slept well, and did not awake until the sun had been up many hours and the heat of the day had begun. Before dressing we hastened to the windows of our little bed-room to see where we were, for our rambling walk through the monastery the previous night had left us in utter ignorance of the points of the compass. We found that our room was at an angle of the walls, where there had been originally a great tower, which, having been evidently considered useless and out of date by the monks, had been levelled to the height of the walls and then been built upon. This is the usual modern development of Athos architecture, and if my reader will take the trouble to look at the illustrations of the monastic exteriors he will find examples of it in nearly every convent. Thus at Vatopedi the rooms are continued along the top of the wall the whole way round, with two exceptions, where the ancient battlemented towers have been allowed to remain. A second architectural peculiarity is that these rooms, which are built on the top of the wall, overhang it considerably on the exterior, and are, therefore, supported by brackets of stout timbers. Sometimes, indeed, these hanging rooms are built in several rows one over the other, as at the Monastery of St. Dionysius. This gives a curious pic-

turesqueness to the walls of the convents, although there
is a drawback in the feeling of insecurity which forces
itself disagreeably upon the visitor as he leans out of
the window at the back of his divan and discovers that
he and the divan upon which he is reclining are not
upon *terra firma*, as he fancied, but overhang a precipice.

But I must return to our chamber at Vatopedi.
Our first peep gave us a slight foretaste of the glorious
scenery that was in store for us during our six weeks'
sojourn on the Holy Mountain. Immediately beneath
us was a sort of moat supplied with water from one of
the numerous rills which flow down from the hills;
beyond the moat an open space of ground led up to
the gate of the monastery, before which was a domed
porch supported on four marble pillars. Close to the
gate there is a little kiosk, or summer house, where the
monks sit in the cool of the evening and enjoy the
balmy breezes from the sea, which is only a few hundred yards distant and here takes the form of a beautiful bay. A few small craft were lying at anchor,
discharging cargoes of bricks and iron rails for the repair of some buildings recently burnt. Just outside the
monastery and opposite to our window are the stables,
where a hundred fat and well-groomed mules belonging to this convent have their head-quarters, wandering
about the neighbouring pastures when they are not required, each with his little tinkling bell round his neck.
Then comes the cemetery, a marvellously small piece
of ground for the number of inhabitants that live and
die in and around Vatopedi, if it were not for the invariable custom which prevails here, and generally
amongst the Greeks, of digging up the bodies three

years after burial ; the skulls are then neatly labelled with
the names of the owners and the dates of their deaths,
and placed in the crypt of the cemetery church, whilst
the other bones are thrown confusedly into a large chest.
The crypt at Vatopedi contains 3,000 skulls. In the
hole out of which the skeleton has been dug (corpses
are buried without coffins) another body is buried, and
so on *ad infinitum*. How the soil manages to absorb
so much animal matter I cannot tell, but it is a very
rare occurrence for a body to be found entire at the end
of the three years, and a popular superstition hands
over the owner of the said body to the Fiend in the
case of non-decomposition. Passing the cemetery and
the various little cottages all covered with vines and
creepers which lie between the convent and the sea,
where dwell the muleteers, artisans, and labourers
belonging to the monastery, you arrive at the garden
in which the good monks grow their herbs and vegetables. It stretches for some distance along the sea-
shore, from which it is separated by a stone wall.
Every evening this garden is carefully irrigated from a
large reservoir, and in consequence is very productive.

After we had gazed for some time at the scene I
have just described we called for Angelos, who was
sitting talking with the Archbishop in the next room,
and made him fetch water for our bath. And here let
me recommend to all travellers that great luxury, a port-
able india-rubber bath. Mine goes into the compass
of a large sponge bag, and does not take up more room
in the portmanteau than an ordinary night shirt. It
has been many thousand miles with me, and is in as
good condition as when I first bought it at the cost of
seventeen shillings and sixpence. We dressed rapidly,

and having startled an old monk beneath by emptying
the water from the bath into the moat, joined the Archbishop in the parlour. It was now time to go to breakfast ; but O— had to take his departure without me,
as the dainties I had consumed the previous evening
had proved too much for me, and I breakfasted in my

COURTYARD OF VATOPEDI.

bedroom on plain boiled rice. Towards noon, however, I recovered and joined O— in an examination
of the interior of the monastery.

It is built on a hill rising from the sea, so that the
courtyard, which is very extensive, is on a considerable incline. Within this is the catholicon, or principal
church, the ancient refectory, another church dedicated
to the Holy Girdle, and various offices, such as kitchens,

E

oil stores, bell and clock towers, &c. The courtyard is
surrounded by the monastic buildings, of vast extent,
partly within the great walls, partly built on them in
the manner described above. There were originally
twelve towers ; now only two remain as such, the rest
having been levelled nearly to the walls. Curzon in
his delightful book [1] describes the monastery accurately
when he says, ' This convent well illustrates what some
of the great monastic establishments in England must
have been before the Reformation. It covers at least
four acres of ground, and contains so many separate
buildings within its massive walls that it resembles a
fortified town.' Some idea of its extent may be realised
when one considers that it contains no less than sixteen
churches within the walls. Of course many of these
are mere chapels, but still each is a perfect church with
its interior divisions and its dome over the roof. The
entrance, which, as before said, has a porch,[2] is defended
by three gates placed at intervals along a narrow and
tortuous passage, so constructed as to be easily defended in case of need. In this passage Clarke, in 1801,
noticed two guns on carriages ; there were then, he
says, many cannon in the embrasures of the walls. In
fact, until 1820 all the monasteries were provided with
cannon ; in that year the Turks removed them. On
the second gate (the old outer gate, the present one

---

[1] *Monasteries of the Levant.*   London, 1850.
[2] Nearly all the convents have similar porches. They generally contain frescoes of the Blessed Virgin and the Holy Child, the two archangels Michael and Gabriel, the two soldier saints George and Demetrius,
and the patron saint of the house. Lamps are suspended before these
representations of the guardians of the monastic gate, and it is customary
to bow towards the principal picture over the doorway and to cross
oneself on entering or leaving the convent.

having been added 150 years back) is a small handle fashioned into the rough likeness of a dog, and the story goes that it was presented by a Turkish officer who contemptuously brought his bitch within the sacred precincts (probably during the occupation at the time of the Greek Revolution), when the animal was instantly stricken dead. The door is thickly plated with iron and is of great weight.

Between the west end of the catholicon and the refectory is a charming little court planted with orange trees, containing the *phiale*, or fountain, which is always to be found close to the catholicon, generally at the west end, throughout the Athos convents.[1] It is used for the blessing of water at the Epiphany and on the first day of each month, though anciently it was probably intended for the performance of ablutions before entering the church,[2] as is the custom of the Mussulmans at the present day; indeed, this reason has been given for its discontinuance amongst Eastern Christians. In the West the phiale has been replaced by the holy water stoup; in the East holy water at the church doors is unknown, although I have heard it stated that there are exceptions where the Easterns have been brought into contact with the Latins. At Vatopedi the phiale, dedicated to St. John Baptist, has a dome supported by a double row of white marble columns, connected by a carved parapet of the same material. Under the dome is a large marble basin.

---

[1] On the phiale of St. Sophia at Constantinople was the following inscription, which, it will be observed, reads both ways :

ΝΙΨΟΝ ΑΝΟΜΗΜΑΤΑ ΜΗ ΜΟΝΑΝ ΟΨΙΝ.

[2] Eusebius, *Hist. Eccl.* x. 4. See also Texier, *Byzantine Arch.* p. 71.

The catholicon is one of the most ancient buildings on the Holy Mountain, and is particularly well proportioned. From internal evidence it would seem to have been built about the ninth century, possibly as late as the end of the tenth, as there exists a tradition that the monastery was restored at that time after it had been destroyed by the Arabs. The monks assert that the

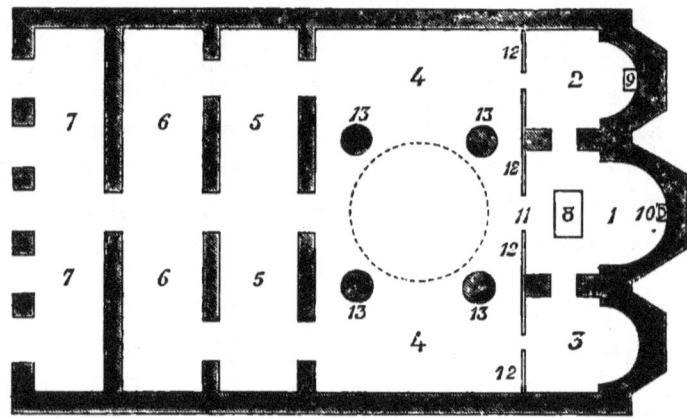

PLAN OF AN EASTERN CHURCH.

1. Bema.
2. Chapel of the prothesis.
3. Diaconicon.
4. Nave.
5. Esonarthex.
6. Exonarthex.
7. Pronaos.

8. Holy table.
9. Table of the prothesis.
10. Bishop's seat.
11. Holy doors.
12. Iconostasis.
13. Pillars supporting the central dome.

four massive columns of porphyry which support the central dome were gifts of the Empress Pulcheria,[1] being brought hither from Ravenna. Pulcheria died in A.D. 453, and the church is certainly not as old as the fifth century, but it is quite possible that these

[1] Another tradition alters *Pulcheria* to *Placidia* : see history of the monastery, below.

pillars may have belonged to a more ancient church which was only partially destroyed and was afterwards rebuilt much on the old plan.

Before giving a description of the interior of this catholicon it will be necessary for me to explain to some of my readers how a Greek church is built, for it differs so widely from a Western interior that if I omitted to do so my remarks would be for the most part unintelligible.

It will be seen, looking at the accompanying plan, that the church is divided into three principal portions, the *exonarthex*, or exterior vestibule, with the *esonarthex*, or interior vestibule, the *nave*, and the *bema*, or sanctuary. The exonarthex and esonarthex are frequently merged into one division, called simply *the narthex*. Generally in addition to the nartheces there is a *pronaos*, or porch, sometimes called the *proaulion*. Besides these divisions there is theoretically always a quire, situated in front of the bema in the centre of the church, but at Athos there is no proper quire, as stalls are fixed against the whole of the walls of the nave and narthex.

On each side of the bema is a chapel, that on the north being the *chapel of the prothesis*, that on the south the *diaconicon*, or sacristy. These chapels are sometimes completely separated from the bema, being entered from it by doorways in the dividing walls, but more often, especially in modern Byzantine churches, they are only architecturally separated.

The bema, the chapel of the prothesis, and the diaconicon are separated from the nave by a high and solid screen called the *iconostasis*, which reaches at least halfway up to the roof of the church and is covered with *icons*, or sacred pictures, in which, as a

general rule, only the faces and hands of the figures
are painted, the rest of the subject being rendered in
repoussé metal work, usually of silver gilt, and set with
precious stones.   This screen is pierced by three doorways, the centre one called the ἅγιαι θύραι, or *holy doors*,
opening directly on to the holy table, which is situated in
the bema about three feet behind the iconostasis.   The
icon next to the holy doors on the south side is that of
our Saviour, that on the north of the Blessed Virgin.
This order is invariably followed in every Eastern
church ; the other icons on the iconostasis may be of
any saints.   Besides the holy doors a curtain or veil
(βηλόθυρον), drawn across their interior face, completely
shuts off the bema from the nave if, as is frequently
the case, the doors are of open carved wood work.
The door on the north of the holy doors leads into the
chapel of the prothesis, that on the south gives access
to the diaconicon.

The bema contains the *holy table* (ἁγία τράπεζα),
which is usually rather low and square in shape, having
four pillars at the corners supporting a canopy or
baldakin like that over the high altar in St. Ambrose
at Milan.   On the holy table is kept the Book of the
Gospels, always magnificently bound, a cross used for
blessing the people and for them to kiss, and a cor-
poral of linen or silk called the *antimins*, which has a
small portion of relics sewn into a little bag in the
corner.   The antimins is always kept carefully wrapped
up in a piece of silk, and is not allowed to be touched
by the laity.   On the eastern side of the holy table
are a cross and candlesticks, as with us.   The Eucharist
is frequently reserved in a little box suspended by
chains between the two eastern pillars of the baldakin.

Behind the altar a seat generally runs round the wall of the apse, having in the centre the seat of the bishop of the diocese, called the *synthronos* (σύνθρονος), so that when seated in it he faces the holy table. The walls of the bema are often hung with small icons, valuable chiefly on account of their antiquity—for the older an icon is the more it is worth in the eyes of its owner—and therefore given a place of honour in the sanctuary; there are also generally a few cupboards containing the relics and the more precious of the monastic treasures.

In the chapel of the prothesis is a small table. This is used for the office of the prothesis, or the preparation for the liturgy, in which the priest and the deacon prepare the bread and wine in a very complicated and symbolical manner. On this table are usually kept the chalice and paten and certain other articles connected with the liturgy.

In the diaconicon are chests for vestments, charcoal for incense, censers, &c.

In the nave (this term includes the transepts) stalls (στασίδια) run completely round the walls. These are furnished with *miserers*, as in the West. They are principally used for standing places, as the monks rarely sit during Divine service. The esonarthex is also provided with stalls. In the chord of each transept is placed a high octagonal stool panelled all round to the ground and usually inlaid with tortoise-shell and mother o' pearl; this is called the analogion (ἀναλόγιον). On these stools or desks the canonarches (κανονάρχης), or ruler of the quire, rests his book as he goes from side to side prompting the cantors—generally three or four monks who sing the psalms without books. The last

stall on either hand, nearest the centre of the church,
is a place of honour; these are usually fashioned
like thrones; that on the south side is the bishop's
throne and may be used by *any* bishop, and so differs
from the seat in the bema, which may only be used
by the bishop of the diocese; that on the north side
is the throne of the abbot or superior of the monastery. Against the pillars which support the central
dome icons are frequently placed, and before every
icon are lamps and standard candlesticks. Beneath
the dome hangs a corona ($\pi o \lambda v \epsilon \lambda a \iota o s$), generally of
open brass work and suspended from the roof by long
chains. This corona, usually of the same circumfer-
ence as the dome itself, is filled with candles of every
size, and from it are suspended ostrich eggs and
occasionally lamps as well.

Besides this large corona the smaller domes are
frequently provided with others; and candelabra of
brass and silver of various sizes are suspended from
other parts of the roof.

At Athos the whole of the interior of the church,
without exception, is covered with frescoes of Scriptural and historical subjects and of saints. In the
narthex is represented the martyrdom of the saints;
in the pronaos the favourite subjects are the Last
Judgment and scenes from the Apocalypse.

The floors of the various parts of the building are
paved with coloured marbles and mosaics, and, as there
are no carpets or seats other than the stalls round the
walls, these variegated marbles add to the general
richness of the decorations. Along the east side of the
pronaos is a seat of stone or marble. The gates
between the pronaos and the narthex are called *the*

Beautiful Gates ; the gates between the narthex and the nave are also sometimes called by this name, for Byzantine ecclesiology is very confused in its terms. This Scripture name reminds one of the symbolical character of a Byzantine church, which reproduces to a certain extent the divisions of the Temple.   Much of the worship and the ceremonies of the Eastern Church are borrowed from the Jewish ritual, and are probably very similar to those of the early Christian converts from Judaism, who would naturally adapt their worship from that of the Temple.   This is a very interesting subject, which it would be here out of place to follow up.

Briefly, then, the symbolism is the following :

> The Bema represents the Holy of Holies.
> The Quire represents the Holy Place.
> The Náve represents the Court of the Jews.
> The Narthex represents the Court of the Gentiles.

This will be the better appreciated, and the different degrees of sacredness appertaining to the various parts of the church will be more easily understood, if I quote a passage from Texier's work on Byzantine architecture.[1]

The Christian community was then divided into three classes : the first consisted of those who ministered in holy things, and had the power of conferring the ministry on others ; the second, of those who had been baptised and admitted to communion ; the third and last, of those who had been excluded from Christian communion and had returned to the right path with tears of repentance, imploring forgiveness from God.   Included in the last class were also those who, though devoted in spirit to Christ, had not yet received baptism, but were being taught the principles of the Christian faith.   They bore the name of Catechumens.

[1] Texier and Pullan's *Byzantine Architecture*, chapter on the ' Ceremonies of the Primitive Christian Church,' p. 70.

To the first order the most secret part of the temple (the sacrarium, bema, or sanctuary) was open. This part was separated from the rest of the temple by veils and barriers, in order that it might appear still more sacred, and that the sight of the service should be hidden from those who were not worthy to see it.

The second had access to the middle part of the temple, the nave, where the faithful assisted at the service.

The third and last were admitted to the exterior portico, called the *narthex*, only, and did not enter into the church except when they were summoned, and went out the moment when the deacon, mounted on a raised place, proclaimed with a loud voice that it was time for their expulsion.

The Auditors [he has explained before that these were Gentiles who were anxious to learn something of the Christian faith] remained in the lower part of the *narthex*, or in the *exonarthex* (exterior porch) ; the *esonarthex* (interior porch), where there were two porches, being reserved for the Catechumens.

In modern times (and in speaking of the Eastern Church 'modern' goes a long way back) these distinctions have been, to a very great extent, abolished, through altered circumstances; for there are but few catechumens in these days compared with those in the first ages of Christianity, and penitential discipline has been relaxed, so that deadly sins no longer necessarily bring the ecclesiastical punishment of excommunication ; thus the nave and nartheces are now used indiscriminately by all worshippers, and their varying dignity is only acknowledged by certain portions of the services being performed in different parts of the church. But the sanctuary still belongs to the clergy alone. No layman may remain behind the iconostasis during Divine service ; none but the clergy may at any time pass through the holy doors or walk between the altar and the iconostasis. No woman may enter the sanctuary even out of service time. One more point in connection with the interior of the churches needs a brief notice. In the East it is forbidden for more than one mass to be celebrated at the same altar on the same day. To avoid this where there are many priests it is usual to find side chapels, or *paracclesia*, connected with large churches. A paracclesi differs from a Western side chapel in being invariably distinct from the principal church, only communicating with the latter by a door. It always 'orientates' and is a complete little church, with iconostasis, bema, narthex, &c. The favourite position for these chapels is on each side of the nave, so that they are entered from the exonarthex of the principal church, which is continued along beyond the north and south boundary of the nave so as to form the nartheces of the paracclesia. They are frescoed and decorated like the principal church.

The catholicon at Vatopedi (dedicated to the Four Evangelists) has an esonarthex, an exonarthex, and a pronaos. The nave is $37\frac{1}{2}$ feet from the west door to the iconostasis; the extreme width across the transepts is 50 feet; and the bema is 17 feet from east to west and 15 feet across, not including the side chapels of the prothesis and diaconicon. The apse of the bema is polygonal.

Attached to the catholicon are four paracclesia, two on the ground floor and two on an upper floor. Of those on the level of the church that on the north side of the nave is dedicated to St. Demetrius of Salonica, that on the south to St. Nicholas. The other two are dedicated the one to the Archangels, the other to the Assumption of the Blessed Virgin. We were very much struck with the interior of this church; it was the first we had visited on the Holy Mountain, and it is one of the finest, if not the finest, of all the Athos churches. The frescoes, which completely cover the walls, the richness of the marble pavement, all of *opus Alexandrinum*, the glitter of the metal work, the icons, the lamps, the candelabra, partly of brass, partly of silver gilt, and lastly the enormous corona of open brass work, hanging under the central dome, all this wealth of colour and brightness is softened by the subdued light which the few and narrow windows admit, so as to form a picture not easily to be forgotten.

The frescoes, unfortunately, have been repainted; probably extensive restoration was necessary after the troubles of the war of independence, when Turkish troops were quartered on the monasteries for several years. Over the doorway in the exonarthex is a mosaic representing Christ with St. Mary and St. John; two other mosaics, one on each side of this doorway, represent St. Mary and St. Gabriel. These mosaics furnish additional evidence of the antiquity of the building, this form of decoration being very rare at Athos. We were conducted behind the iconostasis to see the relics and some of the principal treasures, which are kept in a cupboard in the bema. The relics are a piece of the reed used at our Saviour's Passion, a large piece of the True Cross (nearly every convent on Athos claims the honour of possessing a portion of this great relic, and, considering their intimate connection with the early Emperors of Constantinople, if not with Constantine himself, their claims are not unreasonable [1]),

---

[1] St. Paulinus, writing seventy-seven years after the Invention of the Cross, boldly asserts that the Holy Wood multiplied itself to provide for the pious wants of the faithful. ' Quæ quidem crux in materia insensata vim vivam tenens, ita ex illo tempore innumeris pene quotidie hominum

a piece of the girdle of the Blessed Virgin, the skulls of St. Gregory the Theologue, St. Andrew of Crete,[1] and St. Modestus.[2] From the last proceeds a sweet odour (εὐωδία), which one constantly perceives on closely approaching these Eastern relics.

The Greeks maintain that this is a supernatural perfume, a sort of 'odour of sanctity.' Whether this is the case, or whether it merely proceeds from the spices with which the body was originally embalmed, and so has given rise to the superstition, I cannot say.

St. Mary's girdle is a narrow strip of some red material, as far as one can judge, sewn with gold thread and ornamented with pearls.[3] It is sent to Constantinople or great cities of the Levant when the plague appears in them. Mr. Jerningham says of it,[4] 'It is a curious fact, but one which I can vouch for as correct, that cholera cases actually diminished from the very time of the appearance of the girdle in Constantinople;'

votis lignum suum commodat, ut detrimenta non sentiat, et quasi intacta permaneat quotidie dividua sumentibus, et semper tota venerantibus' (*Ep.* 31, written to Severus, A.D. 403).

St. Cyril of Jerusalem, writing before this, only twenty years after the Invention, instances the distribution of the Wood of the Cross as one of the testimonies to Christ. Τὸ ξύλον τὸ ἅγιον τοῦ σταυροῦ μαρτυρεῖ, μέχρι σήμερον παρ' ἡμῖν φαινόμενον, καὶ διὰ τῶν κατὰ πίστιν ἐξ αὐτοῦ λαμβανόντων, ἐντεῦθεν τὴν οἰκουμένην πᾶσαν σχεδὸν ἤδη πληρῶσαν (*Cat.* 10, 19).

[1] Archbishop of Crete in 712. He was a great hymnologist, and composed the hymn beginning, 'Christian! dost thou see them?' and another of 300 stanzas, called the *Great Canon*, which is sung through on the Thursday in Mid-Lent.

[2] Consecrated as Patriarchal Vicar of Jerusalem on the capture of the Patriarch Zacharias by Chosroes II. in A.D. 614. After the death of Zacharias, Modestus succeeded to the See.

[3] Discovered in the time of Leo the Great and originally preserved in the church at Chalcoprate. See Du Cange, *Constant. Christ.* 4. 2. 6.

[4] *To and from Constantinople*, by Herbert Jerningham. London, 1873.

he adds, 'so powerful is prejudice in the popular
mind.'

The cases which contain these relics are very fine,
especially the *inner* cases of the relics of the Cross and
of the girdle ; the *outer* are comparatively modern.
The skulls are all set in wrought silver.   Besides the
relics there are several other most interesting objects.
One is a cross called the Cross of Constantine, and is
said to have been made out of one of the five pieces
into which the Labarum of Constantine the Great was
afterwards divided.   Most of my readers will remember
the story of the apparition to Constantine of the fiery
cross in the heavens before the battle of Saxa Rubra,
A.D. 312, with the words, Ἐν τούτῳ νίκα ; how the
Emperor caused a cross to be made as his standard, and
having defeated his enemies, ordained that the Labarum
should be the sacred standard of the empire.[1]   The cross
appears to be of oak ; it is covered with plates of
silver gilt of ancient Byzantine workmanship.   There
is also a jasper *patera*, said to have belonged to Constantine ; it is set on a foot of silver gilt, and two
dragons of the same metal form the handles.   Behind
the altar (for convenience' sake I shall frequently use
the Western synonym for the holy table, though in the
language of the Eastern Church the whole bema is
called *the altar*) is an ancient icon of the Blessed
Virgin, before which is a large candlestick.   The story
goes that in the ninth century, during the irruption of
the Saracens, the icon and the lamp which burnt before
it were put down a well for safety.   Many years afterwards, when the hidden treasure was hauled up again,
the lamp which accompanied it was found to be still

---

[1] Eusebius, *Vita Const.* I. cc. 28-30.

burning. This light is now inclosed in the large candlestick, and a lump of wax placed near the wick keeps it continually alight. Before leaving the sanctuary I ought to mention that the silver incense boats and thuribles which are kept there are of fine workmanship, and are for the most part ancient. Two sorts of censers are used in the East, one with chains, as with us, the other somewhat like a hand candlestick ; this is held in the hand and waved by a motion of the wrist. Both invariably have bells attached to them, which tinkle as they are moved. The iconostasis is of eighteenth-century carved wood work, heavily gilt. At the south end of the narthex are the tombs of certain benefactors, and their effigies are painted on the wall above the place where they lie.

In a little passage which runs between the narthex and the paracclesi of St. Demetrius is an icon of the Virgin which is said to have one day called to the Empress Pulcheria [1] as she was going to her devotions in the great church, saying, 'What do you, a woman, here ? A queen you are, it is true, but there is another Queen here. Depart from this church, for women's feet no more shall tread this floor.' It seems rather hard that poor Pulcheria should have been banished from the monastery she loved so well and from the church she had adorned ; but the monks say that the holy empress obeyed the heavenly direction and never again saw her beautiful columns nor prayed on that sacred floor, and that from that day no woman or female animal has been allowed to set foot on the shores of the Holy Mountain. This, then, is the

---

[1] Other historians, e.g. Comnenus, again substitute *Placidia* for *Pulcheria*, and put the date of the occurrence as A.D. 382.

monastic tradition concerning the origin of this extraordinary prohibition.[1]

In the narthex of the chapel of St. Demetrius[2] is another miraculous icon, about which we were told the following story : A deacon being late for supper was refused his usual commons ; wandering sulkily about the courtyard, he entered the church, and in a fit of anger struck his knife into the painting of Our Lady on the wall, when, to his horror, blood issued from the wound and slowly trickled down the picture. Instantly moved to repentance, he spent three years in a little open cupboard (which still exists) opposite the picture. When he died he was buried in peace, but, at his own request, the offending hand was cut off before his body was consigned to the earth, since he wisely preferred to enter into life maimed rather than having two hands to be cast into everlasting fire ; for the Holy Virgin had appeared to him in a dream, and had told him that she forgave *him*, but would never forgive *his hand*. This hand is still preserved in a box and was shown to us.

One more icon, and my stories are at an end. Near the south end of the pronaos is another fresco of the Virgin on the wall, and here on a peg are hung the keys of the church, under the guardianship of the Panaghia. One day the hegoumenos, or abbot, was about to take them down to open the church, when a voice proceeded from the icon warning him not to do so, as there were robbers about.

After we had thoroughly examined the catholicon we crossed the court of orange trees to the refectory,

[1] I infer from a note in Muralt's *Essai de Chronographie Byzantine* that there was a nun at Athos who died about the year 1098.

[2] Of Alexandria, A.D. 189–231.

which is a cruciform building of brick and stone of considerable antiquity. It is now only used on feast days, when monks and pilgrims dine together after the liturgy is over ; for Vatopedi is no longer a *cœnobite* monastery, but has changed its government to the *idiorrhythmic* rule, and in a convent of this kind the monks do not eat at a common table save on great occasions. The refectory contains a number of marble tables, of all shapes and sizes, provided with rude stone seats. Twelve tables are placed on each side of this hall, with one at the west end for the presidents or other great persons ; two more are situated in one transept and three in the other.

As I have already had to use the words *cœnobite* and *idiorrhythmic*, it may be proper to explain in this place the difference between the two forms of government, as well as the system of Oriental monasticism.

We are in the habit of calling the rule by which Eastern monks live the Rule of St. Basil, just as we speak of the Rule of St. Benedict or the Rule of St. Dominic in the West. As a matter of fact Oriental monks are not governed by any code of laws laid down by any particular saint or founder, but are bound by the *canons*, i.e. the monastic disciplinary enactments of the Œcumenical Councils of the Catholic Church, especially of that part of the Sixth Council known as the *Concilium in Trullo*. Added to these fundamental laws are various traditional customs which have descended for the most part from antiquity, customs of universal acceptance and customs of particular religious houses. Many holy monks and hermits, it is true, have inculcated in their writings precepts of monastic virtue, as St. Basil, or have left bright examples in

F

their lives, as St. Anthony ; but none ever compiled a formal code of rules, as the founders of the great Western orders did. Another point of difference between Eastern and Western monasticism is, that whilst the latter became, to the undoubted advantage of the world, the guardian and the teacher of universal learning, so that the cultivation of the arts and sciences has now come to be looked upon in the West as an attribute of monasticism, in the East the old idea of the religious life has existed to the present day—that the monk is one who has left the world simply for the sake of a closer union with the Unseen, and that the study and the propagation of worldly learning, though not forbidden, form no essential part of the system, but are rather the accidents of time or place. Thus to an Oriental the highest ideal of a religious would not be a Duns Scotus or a Mabillon, but rather a simple and uninstructed ascetic, living in a cave, far removed from men and human interests, possessed of no books save perchance the Holy Scriptures, a few service books, and the writings of the saints, if so be that he can read, spending his time when not in prayer in the cultivation of the vegetables that form his daily food. But, although all Eastern religious follow but one rule, there are the two classes of monasteries of which I have already spoken, the coenobite and the idiorrhythmic. The former is on the lines of a Western monastery, with inmates governed by an abbot to whom they owe implicit obedience, and having all goods in common. In an idiorrhythmic monastery each monk lives as he pleases ; if rich he has a suite of apartments, if poor he shares a cell with a brother. Discipline is kept up by public opinion rather than by authority ; a monk is not *bound* to attend vespers, but if he omitted to do so two days running without valid excuse his brethren would begin to talk about his laxity and to show signs of disapproval. Instead of an abbot an idiorrhythmic convent is governed by a deliberative assembly and two or three annually elected presidents. Several minor points in connection with this form of rule [1] will be found in the subsequent chapters of this book.

As to the history of these two kinds of convents, but little that is definite can be said. Monasteries arose from the custom of hermits living together for mutual benefit, and were at the first nothing but collections of hermitages. The establishment of a distinct cœnobium, with a common life and a single ruler, was a later development. One would like to discover in the modern idiorrhythmic convent a survival of the old *laura*, or hermit village, but it seems probable that it is a comparatively modern return to the ancient custom, the product of laxity of discipline rather than that of anachronistic conservatism.[2]

Gass is of opinion that this rule took its rise from the fact of rich men entering the monastic order and becoming troublesome to the abbot, and he states that the first trace of it is to be found in the fourteenth century.[3] It is extremely curious that no travellers on Mount Athos before 1840 notice the distinction between the cœnobite and idiorrhythmic monasteries,

---

[1] I shall use the expressions cœnobite *rule* and idiorrhythmic *rule* for the sake of convenience.

[2] But Vatopedi *became a cœnobium* in 1557 (see 'Ο Ἄθως, by Manuel Gedeon, Constantinople, 1885); so it seems that it was before that date idiorrhythmic, as now.

[3] *Zur Geschichte der Athos-Klöster*, 1865.

although it is certain that they must have existed side by side for at least a considerable period.

The monks are divided into two classes, the *dokimos* (δοκιμός), or novice, and the *caloyer* (καλόγερος, literally *a good old man*), or professed monk.

The caloyers, again, are divided into three grades—*rhasophoria* (ρασοφορία), *the little habit* (τὸ μικρὸν σχῆμα) and *the great habit* (τὸ μέγα σχῆμα).[1] The great habit is a sort of black scapular, in shape not unlike the *epitrachelion*, or Eastern priest's stole, worked with the cross, lance, sponge, skull and cross bones, and other pious designs in faint outline. This scapular is, I think, only assumed for the Holy Communion, and is retained in wear during the rest of the day after the reception of that Sacrament ; ordinarily there is nothing in their dress to distinguish the monks of the great habit from the others. The monastic habit consists of a double-breasted cassock, generally of black, but sometimes of a dark and sober tint of brown, confined at the waist by a belt. Over this the monks wear a gown with loose sleeves in church and on other public occasions, as well as a veil or hood of light material, which is thrown over the high hat and falls behind below the shoulders. Like the Nazarites of old they never cut their hair on head or face.

To return to our exploration of Vatopedi : After visiting the refectory we were taken to see the oil stores. They are vaulted with brick, and contain enormous jars and marble receptacles like sarcophagi.

---

[1] But very few enter this, the highest monastic grade, which entails almost complete withdrawal from earthly things and a life entirely devoted to religious exercises. The great majority of the Athos monks belong to the second grade, of the little habit, though many assume the great habit on their death beds.

Opposite the entrance is a marble tank in which the oil
was miraculously replenished, as in the widow's cruse,
but not at the prayers of Elijah or of Elisha, but at
those of the Mother of God, whose icon is placed close
to it. Not far from the oil stores is a building containing the great winepress. It is constructed of heavy
beams and timber, and is said to be capable of holding
200,000 okes of grapes, or *rather over* 253 *tons*. This
is clearly an exaggeration, although it is certainly of a
very great size.

Each of the 220 monks of Vatopedi draws his
commons of wine every day ; so do their 130 servants ;
and, as at the Monastery of Iveron I was told that a
hundred hermits and poor people are fed there with
bread and wine every day, besides the pilgrims that
come on great occasions, we may reasonably suppose
that an equal number of mendicants are supplied
with wine at Vatopedi, for Vatopedi is about the same
size as Iveron. Thus the consumption of wine in the
course of the year must be enormous. Probably the
monks meant that the total weight of grapes used in
the year amounted to 200,000 okes.

The library is a pleasant, well-arranged room, situated in one of the towers on the sea front of the monastery. There are 627 manuscripts, besides a number
of printed books. A monk of Vatopedi, called Neophytus of Brousa, took the trouble to make a catalogue,
which he began in 1867 and finished in 1874. Among
the manuscripts we noticed a fine illuminated evangelistarium, the whole of the works of St. Chrysostom
(eleventh century), a small quarto psalter of the same
age, a late illuminated manuscript of the liturgies, and
a very curious old geography of Ptolemy with maps.

We were next taken over the hospital, which is on the
east side of the monastery, built in the form of a square,
three sides of which contain rooms for the sick, supported over cloisters ; the whole is clean and airy.   A
Greek doctor—from Athens, I fancy—is maintained by
the monks at Vatopedi and has rooms in the hospital.
We sat on a divan at the end of the passage under a
window which looks towards the sea, and there amongst
a crowd of eager monks we held forth on the subject
of the English Church and the unity of Christendom.
The principal speakers were ourselves, our friend the
Archbishop, and the ephoros of the hospital, a very intelligent old man, by name Eugenius, the other monks
merely listening attentively and every now and then
giving vent to exclamations of surprise or pleasure.
Round went the photographs of English churches and
the Archbishop of Canterbury, and I took the opportunity of distributing several of the leaflets of the
Association for the Promotion of the Union of Christendom, in Greek.   Eugenius had read the Thirty-nine
Articles, and said he only objected to No. 19.   I was
anxious to keep the discussion to points of agreement
between our two Churches and to avoid differences ;
so, resolving not to defend my position but to beat a
dignified retreat, ‘ Ah,’ said I, ‘ perhaps we are wrong ;
only one Church is infallible.’   This of course produced
a general laugh and a chorus of ‘ *Polycala.*’

‘ When in doubt play a trump ’ is an old whist rule :
Rome is the trump card here.

In the cool of the evening we walked towards a
little kiosk behind the cemetery, which overlooks the
gardens by the sea.   On the way we met the Archbishop and two of the epitropoi, or presidents of the

monastery. One of the latter, an old man with a long grey beard, presented us with a little bunch of sweet basil, which they had just gathered from the garden.[1] The trifling courtesy of this venerable monk quite touched us ; it was bestowed with such quiet dignity. At sunset we had supper, and a very fair one too. Afterwards we had a discussion with a theological professor of Chalki, the archimandrite Baphides, like us a visitor to Athos, on Transubstantiation and Anglican orders. With regard to the former he said :

'We believe the same as the Latins, for we admit the word *transubstantiation* into our formularies.'

The latter statement is true ; the Greeks have adopted the word as a synonym of *transmutation*, but as a matter of fact they do not attach the same meaning to it as the Romans do, never having accepted or even considered the scholastic philosophy on which the Roman theory of *substance* and *accident* is based.

We pointed this out to the archimandrite, and after some discussion he admitted the truth of our criticism. 'For,' said he, 'we hold the doctrines of the holy fathers without any addition whatever, and by the term *transubstantiation* we do not intend to define the doctrine of the Eucharist after the philosophy of the schoolmen ; we merely use the term for the sake of convenience.'

The Greeks derive their information respecting Anglican orders chiefly through Roman channels—that is to say, when they obtain any information about them at all—so the archimandrite was very anxious to

[1] According to the popular belief amongst the Greeks it was in a bed of this tender herb that Our Lord's Cross was invented. On this account they love to have the plant about them, in their gardens and in their houses.

discuss the subject with us, especially as he was writing a Church history for the use of the students at Chalki (the principal ecclesiastical seminary of the Constantinopolitan patriarchate), and intended to devote a chapter to the Anglican Church.   Our conversation lasted till past midnight, when we went to bed somewhat tired by our day's exertions.

CHAPTER VI.

August 10 / July 29. This morning O— celebrated the Anglican liturgy, the Archbishop, the archimandrite Baphides, and several monks of the highest dignity being present at their own request.   Afterwards, during breakfast, the Archbishop turned round to us and said, 'Your liturgy is the liturgy of St. Gregory Dialogos.'[1]   We ventured to doubt this exalted origin, and replied that we had every reason to believe it was compiled by certain excellent gentlemen who lived in the sixteenth century; but the Archbishop was not to be contradicted.

' No,' said he; ' I have studied it carefully, and it is the liturgy of St. Gregory Dialogos, and a very good liturgy too.'

The monks had told us that we ought to take the earliest opportunity of going to Caryes, where the Holy Synod of Mount Athos sits, to present our credentials and to receive at its hands a circular letter of commendation to all the monasteries; so word had been sent early this morning that we intended to do ourselves the honour of visiting the Holy Synod that day.

When breakfast was over we were conducted to the gate of the monastery, where our mules were waiting for us.   Rich carpets being thrown over the heavy

---

[1] Pope Gregory the Great.

framework of the saddles, we mounted and rode off in
the following order : On the first mule was Pantele,
the Archbishop's cavass, carrying his master's long
silver-headed stick ; he was preceded by one of the
Christian soldiers in the service of the monks (two or
three of whom are stationed at each of the principal
monasteries) in his picturesque Albanian dress of a
fustinella, or voluminous white calico kilt, and a jacket
embroidered with gold, carrying an old-fashioned flint-
lock musket with an immensely long barrel.   Pantele
was followed by the Archbishop, with his cassock
tucked up and gaiters over his full Oriental trousers ;
then came O—; then myself ; the Archbishop's valet,
Peter, and lastly our dragoman, Angelos, with some
muleteers on foot.

The road to Caryes is paved with large rough
stones.[1]   As we were not accustomed to mule-riding on
Athos roads, we thought the path very steep in places.
Afterwards, when we had completed the circuit of the
monasteries, we travelled over this road again, and
wondered how we could ever have called it bad.   As
a matter of fact it is about the best on the peninsula.
After leaving the monastery we mounted to a considerable height, from which we had a splendid view of
Vatopedi, its beautiful bay, and the Strymonic gulf,
with the island of Thasos in the distance.   On our
left were the ruins of the college founded in 1750 by
Eugenius Bulgaris—a doubtful experiment, which failed
five years later.   They occupy a commanding position
on the top of the hill overlooking the bay of Vatopedi
and the sea.   We did not visit them, but from the

---

[1] The Athos roads were first paved by an ex-Patriarch of Constantinople, Dionysius by name, about the middle of the last century.

distance they appeared to be but little injured, though roofless. They consisted of a master's lodge and 170 small rooms for students. Eugenius Bulgaris was advanced to the see of Chersonesus by the Empress Catharine of Russia.

The ride to Caryes is certainly one of the most delightful on Athos; the whole road is shaded by beautiful trees—sweet chestnuts, oaks, and beeches—with thick shrubberies on either side of box and laurel, whilst vines, and honeysuckle, and creepers of every kind twine themselves round the tree trunks or hang in festoons over the path. After we had reached the highest point of our road we continued along the east side of the central ridge. At one spot we rested to enjoy the distant view of the Monastery of Pantocratoros; at another we watered our mules at a pretty fountain fed by water from the hills, and refreshed ourselves by sitting for a quarter of an hour under the shade of the trees. The Archbishop was anxious we should taste this water, which he said was 'light' and far superior to that at Vatopedi, which was 'heavy.' Just before entering Caryes we passed the Seraï, or Russian skete of St. Andrew, on our left, and had a view of it through the trees. We now encountered a troop of hermits and beggars, most of whom rushed up to kiss the Archbishop's hand and to receive his blessing. Many of them were Russians.

Caryes is situated high up [1] on the side of the hill, which is covered with luxuriant vegetation and the hazel groves from which the town is generally said to derive its name ($\kappa\alpha\rho\acute{\upsilon}\alpha\iota$, *hazels*). It seems to me, however, that a more likely derivation is from $\kappa\acute{\alpha}\rho\alpha$, *a*

---

[1] 2,195 feet above the sea.

head, as being the chief centre of the promontory and the seat of government. I do not remember to have seen this derivation suggested by any writers except Didron, and he gives another and a curious reason for it.

La capitale du mont Athos s'appelle Karès ; suivant la plupart et les plus instruits des moines, elle prendrait son nom de κάρα, tête, parce qu'un pape, revenant de Constantinople, où on n'aurait pas voulu reconnaître son autorité, aborda au mont Athos et fit trancher les têtes de tous les moines de Karès qui refusèrent de lui prêter serment.[1]

The town consists of a collection of houses amongst orchards, gardens, and vineyards—through which countless little streams run down from the mountain side—and one long irregular street with two or three lesser ones opening into it. In this street is the bazaar, and awnings are stretched across it to shelter the wares and their owners, for the most part monks, who sit outside their shops and gossip the whole day through. Nearly all the goods are exposed for sale on stands outside the shops themselves, which are sometimes of one story, but often consist of only a ground floor. This bazaar with its awnings and cords across the street, the trellised vines which hang over the houses, and the picturesque crowd of sombre caloyers and gay *cosmicoi*,[2] with here and there a turbaned Turk, form a charming picture. The chief wares are shoes, coarse cloth, ready-made garments of various descriptions, monastic hats and lay brothers' hats ; the former high and stiff for the professed monks, lower and soft for the dokimoi, or novices ; the latter small and grey in

[1] *Manuel d'Iconographie Chrétienne*, 1845.
[2] Laymen ; literally ' men of the world.'

colour, usually with some religious mark impressed
upon the crown. Besides these articles of dress there
are groceries, barrels full of rice, sugar, and coffee,
American tinned lobster, tinned sardines (both of these
being in great request), and dried octopus hanging up
on nails.

Three or four shops are devoted to the sale of pious
pictures, rosaries, wooden crosses carved by hermits,
and other religious objects of Athos manufacture;
also incense, of which there are two sorts, the com-
moner, that comes in lumps from Palestine, and a
more precious and expensive kind made on the Holy
Mountain. Coarse tobacco may be purchased here;
one or two persons undertake the repair of clocks and
watches, and there are several brass candlestick and
bell founders.

One does not immediately perceive the chief
peculiarity of Caryes, for the strangeness of the entire
life of Athos deadens one's senses to all impressions of
the unusual, and it is not until the traveller has walked
up through the bazaar and down again that it suddenly
strikes him that all the people who throng the little
street are men! And so it is. Here is a tinker
mending pots and pans, but no wife stands in the
doorway or prepares her husband's supper. Next door
there is a cobbler, hard at work at his last; the tall
hat proclaims him to be a monk, so in his case a
spouse would not be expected. There are, it is true,
a few boys, who have accompanied their fathers from
the mainland; but you may listen in vain for infant
cries or the treble voice of the fair sex. No pretty
face peeps out from the vine-clad windows; no lover
waits in the street below. Caryes is still what it has

been for centuries, the only town in all the world without a single woman.

We arrived at the house belonging to Vatopedi at about two o'clock, having occupied between two hours and a half and three hours on the journey. A young monk, whose name was Dimopoulos—to whom I had brought a letter of recommendation from a Greek friend in England—received us; he was the secretary of the Holy Synod. Two other monks from Vatopedi looked after our wants, first bringing us the inevitable glyko (preserves or sweetmeats), mastica (a coarse spirit flavoured with mastic), and coffee, and then preparing an excellent luncheon of fish, which, as we were very hungry after our long ride, we thoroughly enjoyed. Afterwards we sat on a divan and smoked and drank more coffee whilst we conversed with the monk Dimopoulos on all sorts of topics until the time came to visit the Holy Synod.

It may be as well to insert in this place an account of the government of Athos, the particulars of which the secretary of the Synod himself gave me.

When Murad II. was overrunning the Empire of the East and, though repulsed from before the walls of Constantinople in 1422, had taken Thessalonica in 1430, the monks of Mount Athos, deprived of the imperial support and determined to accept the inevitable, submitted to the Turkish Sultan whilst they could make terms; thus they put themselves under his rule on the condition that their ancient privileges should be respected and that they should be allowed to govern themselves. To these terms the conqueror acceded, and the Holy Mountain became incorporated into the Ottoman Empire about the year 1448, five years before

the fall of Constantinople. Since then the monks
have enjoyed the practical independence which still
belongs to them.

The present Turkish staff at Caryes consists of the
caimacan, or governor, his secretary, a chief constable,
an assistant constable, a sergeant and ten zaptiehs, an
officer of customs with eight assistants, and an officer
of health. As all these officials, including the caimacan, are of course obliged to leave their harems
behind them, I fancy the posts are not much sought
after. The Holy Mountain being in the vilayet of
Salonica, the caimacan is responsible to the pasha of
that place.

The caimacan and his staff collect taxes and customs
and are responsible for the good order of the promontory. In case of war it would be the governor's duty
to procure aid from the pasha for the protection of the
community; otherwise he simply executes the will of
the Holy Synod and carries into effect the result of
its deliberations.

Until the end of the sixteenth century the supreme
government was entrusted to a single ruler, called
ὁ πρῶτος, 'the First Man,' but since that date it has
been administered by the Holy Synod of Mount Athos
('Η ἱέρα Κοινώτης τοῦ Ἁγίου Ὄρους Ἄθω), which is
thus constituted:

First there are the twenty representatives of the
twenty monasteries (the sketes, or priories, have no
voice in the government of the community) called the
antiprosopoi (ἀντιπρόσωποι).

Each monastery elects its antiprosopos on January
1, being the same day on which it appoints its epitropoi if it be an idiorrhythmic house; of these anti-

prosopoi, or representatives, the one sent by the
Lavra—the monastery regarded as chief in rank—
called the *proedros* (πρόεδρος), is the chairman. Besides these there is a body composed of four *epistatai*
(ἐπιστάται) and their chief, the *proepistates* (προεπι-
στάτης). This latter personage is elected by these five
monasteries in turn : Lavra, Vatopedi, Chiliandari,
Iveron, and St. Dionysius. The epistatai are elected
by the other monasteries, on June 1.

Thus in a full Synod there are twenty-five members sitting. The proedros presides, like the Speaker
in the House of Commons ; the epistatai form a
sort of ministry, their chief, the proepistates, bringing
forward the questions ; and this body also carries
into effect whatever is decided by the whole Synod.
There is a secretary of the Synod (ἀρχιγραμματεύς)
and a secretary of the epistatai (γραμματεύς). The
Synod is not only a legislative body, or parliament,
but also a criminal court and a court of appeal.
For instance, supposing my watch were stolen in
the bazaar at Caryes, and I suspected any person, I
should complain to the caimacan, who would arrest the
man and hand him over to the Synod for trial. If he
were found guilty he would be returned to the caimacan
for punishment, when he would either deal summarily
with him, or, in serious cases, send the criminal to
Salonica for trial and punishment at the hands of the
pasha.

To take another case : A monk at Vatopedi considers himself aggrieved, and failing to obtain justice
from the σύναξις, or governing assembly of his monastery, appeals to the Holy Synod ; in this case its
decision is final, and there is no further appeal open

to him. On the other hand, two monasteries have a dispute, as was recently the case with Xeropotamou and Simopetra ; here they would appeal first to the Synod, and if not contented with its judgment an appeal would lie to the Œcumenical Patriarch at Constantinople.

The Holy Synod meets on an average every second day, and party feeling runs as high as possible in such a grave, sleepy Oriental assembly on the great Russian question, the Slavonic monasteries generally supporting Russico (the Russian monastery) against the Greeks. Each monastery pays a yearly tax to the Synod at the rate of 150 piastres [1] for each monk living within the convent and 130 for each of those living outside. Monks at a skete pay 100 piastres a head. Out of this fund 725*l.* is due to the Imperial Government ; the remainder goes to the support of the Synod's little army of twenty Christian soldiers, the repair of the roads, and other necessary expenses.

To return : Word came at last that the Holy Synod was sitting and was waiting to receive us. So we started from the Vatopedi house and walked through a little street or lane to the place where it was assembled. First of the party walked Pantele with the Archbishop's staff in his hand (silver-stick-in-waiting we named him), then his master with his veil over his hat, then O— and myself, followed by Angelos and a little retinue of monks and lay folk. As we went along pilgrims and monks would run up to our prelate and seize his hand, rubbing their foreheads against it and kissing it ; and it was most amusing to watch the truly Eastern manners of the

---

[1] The pound sterling is usually equivalent to about 120 piastres.

Archbishop, who did not take the slightest notice of
these poor people, but, leaving passively his hand in
their fervent grasp, would all the time be talking
pleasantly to us or else staring straight in front of
him.   Of course every eye was turned on us, and from
every door and window a face peeped forth, anxious to
see the curious Franks that were progressing through
the monastic capital.

In a very few minutes we arrived at our destination,
and entering a courtyard were conducted by a crowd
of servants, monks and lay people, up an outside staircase to an open-air gallery on the first floor, which gave
access to the room where the Synod was assembled.
This was a large, rather long, and low apartment.
Round the room were divans, covered with green
damask, above which the walls were almost bare ; the
divan at the end of the room, opposite to that at which
we entered, was left vacant for us.   On each side of the
room were sitting the members of the Synod, reverend
old gentlemen with long grey beards and tall hats, fifteen
in all, the president being seated in an arm-chair with
a table in front of him, and the secretary at his side.

As we entered the room they all rose, and placing
their hands on their hearts bowed very low, and remained in that position whilst we, following the example of the Archbishop, bowed to the right, bowed to
the left, and then, holding up our heads as if we were
accustomed to visit Holy Synods every day, walked
solemnly down the centre of the room and sat down on
the vacant divan at the end.   Then the members of the
Synod seated themselves, and we all remained with our
eyes fixed upon the floor in a highly proper condition
of gravity and discomfort.

We waited and waited in dead silence, the old men around us looking like the ghosts of departed fathers, until we were relieved by the entrance of one of the soldiers in his gay Albanian dress, bringing to us on a tray glyko, mastica, and water. We each took one spoonful of jam and placed our lips to the little glasses of aromatic spirit, saluting at the same time the reverend assembly on each side of us, our bows being returned by similar inclinations. The soldier then departed with the tray and left us just as we had been before. ' Now,' thought I, ' we shall proceed to business.' But no! still all were looking on the floor, and still not a word was spoken !

In this way nearly five minutes passed, and matters were getting extremely serious. I could feel the divan on which I was sitting giving little convulsive jerks at intervals, and I knew, although I dared not look to see, that O— was on the point of laughing ; fortunately for the dignity of the Anglican Church the representative of her hierarchy managed to keep his countenance. At last the strain was slackened by the reappearance of the soldier with his tray, this time containing little cups of coffee, which we gulped down whilst he waited for the cups and saucers to be returned, although the liquid was so very hot that it brought tears to our eyes. When he had finished his coffee the Archbishop, without rising from the divan, commenced the proceedings by a speech. Opening a small hand bag he produced his letter of introduction from the Patriarch, giving it to the nearest representative, who received it with a bow and handed it over to the secretary, who read it aloud to the assembly. The Archbishop then referred to two or three little matters which the Patriarch had

asked him to look after for him during his holiday, and
made a few polite and complimentary remarks about
the Holy Mountain and its inhabitants.

'And now,' said he, 'I have the pleasure of intro-
ducing to you these two distinguished English travellers,
members of the English Church, of which the Archbishop of Canterbury is the head, who have come to
these sacred shores for the purpose of reporting on the
present state of the Orthodox Church and especially of
the holy monasteries.' Then he told them how we
had brought a letter from one of our bishops to the
Œcumenical Patriarch, and how his Holiness had
received us with great honour and had furnished us
with an introductory epistle to the Holy Synod, in
which they would find that we were most warmly
recommended ; and that, not content with that, his
Holiness had written to him, recommending us to his
charge, and how he had had the good fortune to fall
in with us at Cavalla, and so we had come to Athos
together ; that we were very learned persons who
knew all about Athos even before coming there, and
that we must see all that there was to be seen in the
place, and especially the libraries. 'Donnez-moi votre
lettre,' said he to O—, and the Patriarch's letter was
handed to him, and passed with sundry bows to the
secretary, who read it out as he had done the former
one.

'Now,' continued the Archbishop, 'let me introduce
to you by name these most distinguished Englishmen.
The first is the Most Reverend (σεβασμιώτατος) Arthur
Brisco Owen, Priest of the Anglican Church (τῆς
Ἐκκλησίας Ἀγγλικανῆς ἱερεύς), Professor of Theology
in the University of Oxford ; and the other the Most

Illustrious Kyrios Athelstan Riley, Professor of Literature in the University of Oxford.'

As these sounding titles rolled out we each gave
a little nod at the mention of our names to establish
our identities, the whole speech being accompanied by
little bows and grunts of approval at intervals from
the members of the grave divan.

When the Archbishop had finished, the second
in dignity amongst the representatives made a little
speech—for the president was a Bulgarian and could
not speak Greek fluently—in which he welcomed us
to the Holy Mountain, said that they all felt much
honoured by having amongst them representatives of
the English Church, and assured us that the same
hospitality we had experienced at Vatopedi would be
shown to us all over the promontory.

Then through Angelos, who was sitting beside us
as our interpreter, I addressed a few words of thanks
to the good fathers on behalf of myself and my companion ; told them how I had long wished to visit this
cradle of Eastern orthodoxy, and that I was much
pleased to find that my desire was to be accomplished.

After the low murmur of applause which followed
my little oratorical effort had subsided, the assembly
thawed somewhat ; the Archbishop began to tell stories
about us, and soon the words 'liturgy' and 'Gregory
Dialogos' showed that the proper moment had arrived
for the exhibition of our photographs. So I pulled
them out of my pocket and sent them round the divans,
the photographs of the English chancels and altars
greatly assisting the Archbishop in his description of
what he had seen that morning. The whole Synod
got quite excited over this, and innumerable were the

questions that were asked respecting minute points of
Anglican ritual.

' Do they belong to the Protestant Church ? ' (ἡ
'Εκκλησία διαμαρτυρουμένη), asked one monk.

' No,' said the Archbishop, ' they do not, or at least
not to what we call the Protestant Church ; for Protestants have no liturgies, but only praying and preaching,
whereas this English priest celebrated a liturgy, and
the liturgy of St. Gregory Dialogos,' &c. &c.   Here
followed a fresh description of our rites and customs.

' Perhaps they are Presbyterians,' said another ; ' I
have heard that they are not the same as the Protestants.'

' No,' said the Archbishop ; ' Presbyterians have no
bishops, and there are many bishops in the English
Church.   Owen, show them the photograph of your
patriarch.'

Round went the portrait of the Archbishop of
Canterbury, and our good prelate, who had an excellent
memory and never forgot anything that we once told
him, showed that he had profited by our previous
conversations by delivering himself of what almost
amounted to an apology for the English Church, de-
scribing us roughly as a sort of Latin Church that
didn't believe in the Pope.

All this time the secretary was busily writing out
two circular letters of introduction to all the monasteries,
one for the Archbishop and one for us, and as soon as
they were ready he read them out aloud and stamped
them with the seal of the Synod, a die made in four
parts, each part being kept by one of the epistatai.
The following is a translation of the document given
to us :

To the Twenty Sacred and Reverend Monasteries of
the Holy Mountain Athos.

The bearers of this present letter, sealed with our common seal, the most famous gentlemen Arthur Brisco Owen, priest of the Bishop of Canterbury's English Church, and Kyrios Athelstan Riley, a man of letters, both clever persons and lovers of ancient monuments, coming here from England, are warmly recommended by his Religiousness the Altogether Most Holy Œcumenical Patriarch, as being persons particularly desirous of examining the ancient treasures in our sacred monasteries, and also the libraries belonging to them, for purely learned and scientific purposes. Therefore we also, recommending the said two English antiquaries, exhort in a brotherly spirit the Holy Monasteries to receive them gladly, to afford them all possible courteous protection, to zealously supply them with everything in their power that may be necessary for the easiest attainment of the learned object they have in view, and, moreover, to facilitate their transport from one monastery to another.

We conclude, foreseeing that our fraternal request will meet with a favourable reception.

Caryes : July 29, 1883.

All the OVERSEERS *and* GOVERNORS *of the Twenty*
Sacred Monasteries of the Holy Mountain Athos
in Synod assembled.

A table was placed in the centre of the room, and a book thereon, the Archbishop being asked to inscribe his name in it. When he had finished they said they hoped the Englishmen would do the same. I went up first, amidst profound silence, everybody watching the Frank as if he were a curious and rare wild beast. I turned over the pages, which were covered with wonderfully complicated Greek signatures, but could not find any English ones. Seeing that it was proper to put some remark or Scripture before one's name, I wrote the following :

Agnus Dei, qui tollis peccata mundi, dona nobis pacem,

and added my name and college under it, also in
Latin. O— went up and simply inscribed his name
and style underneath mine. Instantly the book was
removed to the divan to see what we had written ; but
the language in which the sentence was clothed proved
too much for the united Synod until Dimopoulos, who
knew Latin, took up the book and read it out to them
in the vulgar tongue.

'Polycala,' said they, 'polycala. God grant us
unity !' And in several monasteries afterwards we
heard the echoes of the pleasure with which our little
orison was received. 'Ah,' they would say, 'we know
all about you ; you wrote a prayer for unity in the
book at the Synod.'

The business being now concluded the assembly
broke up, and we left the room in the same order and
with the same bowings with which we had entered it,
and went to call on the Turkish governor.

His office was situated at the other end of the outside
gallery, but he was absent at Salonica and his secretary
received us instead, very civilly and courteously. As
soon as we were seated he rang a bell. Coffee and
rahatlakoum made their appearance. We exchanged a
few compliments and took our departure.

We descended into the courtyard. I looked up
and saw all the members of the Holy Synod watching
us. After we had passed through the gateway and
had reached the street I ventured to look up again, and
saw that, like boys on a railway bridge, the reverend
fathers had run round to the opposite side, and two or
three windows were quite full of tall hats, the wearers
of which were gazing at the wonderful Franks with
the utmost curiosity.

Before we left Caryes we visited the new town house which the monks of Vatopedi were constructing. It is a fine large building with a church attached, and commands a beautiful view of the sea. After more coffee we mounted our mules at three o'clock and rode back in about three hours to Vatopedi. The return journey was exceedingly pleasant; it was much cooler than it had been in the morning, and when we had ridden halfway the sun set, so that it was almost dark when we reached the noble convent, where a good meal was awaiting us, to which we did ample justice.

CHAPTER VII.

THE following day we spent in taking photographs, amongst others one of a group of monks in front of the refectory. Over their heads, suspended in the archway, was a large wooden *semantron* (σήμαντρον). This is nothing more than a board of sound and good wood; on being struck with a hammer it produces a resonant noise, which can be heard a very long distance. The semantron is used at Athos instead of bells for calling to prayer, and was formerly universally employed by the Eastern Christians, bells having been first introduced in the year 865 by the Venetians, who presented twelve to the emperor Michael III. There are two sorts of wooden semantrons, the large fixed ones and those carried in the hand.[1] Before each service one of the monks takes a hand semantron, and, standing before the west end of the catholicon, strikes on it three hard and distinct blows with the little wooden mallet. He then proceeds round the outside of the church, playing on the semantron by striking blows of varying force on different parts of the wood at uneven intervals, always winding up the 'tune' with three blows similar to those at the beginning. Every night at twelve o'clock the semantron sounds

---

[1] See the engraving of the group before the phiale at the Lavra (*facing page* 188); one of the monks is there represented in the act of striking a hand semantron.

for the night offices, and although I am not a light sleeper it constantly woke me up. There is another kind of semantron, made of iron, in the form of a half-hoop. This is sometimes hung by chains in the pronaos of the catholicon, but more often takes its place amongst the bells in the tower, and of course somewhat resembles them in sound.

The monk that waited upon us in our rooms, whose name was Eutropius, was in great distress when he heard we had taken a photograph without him, and made us promise to take another the following day. Towards sunset we went down to the bay for a bathe; but the Archbishop took O— off for a walk (much against his will), and so I bathed alone. The sea is shallow for the first twenty feet, gradually deepening so as to be out of one's depth at that distance from the shore.

The cool waters of the Ægean were delightful after the heat of the day, and I sat up to my neck in the calm sea and enjoyed the view. The sun had just set behind the hill, and in the afterglow every angle and corner of the towers and battlements of the lordly monastery stood out clear and distinct. Casting my eyes along the shore, I thought I saw a bundle of clothes lying on the beach, and—yes, it positively was— a monastic tall hat! Presently I caught sight of the owner's head bobbing about in the sea. I swam up to it, and found an old monk blowing and puffing in the water, trying to keep himself up with short, quick strokes, and very red in the face he was by reason of his exertions.

'Calemera sas' (Good day to you), said I.

'Ora calee,' replied the monk.

Summoning up the whole of my remaining stock

of Romaic, I remarked, 'Polycala.' 'Polycala,' returned the old gentleman.   He was indeed a curious
object.   He had on a pair of loose cotton drawers,
from the waistband of which was suspended his string
of beads, for not even in the water could he leave his
plaything behind him.[1]   His beard descended half-way
to his middle, and his long grey hair streamed behind
him on the top of the water.   All my conversation
being exhausted, we parted company, and I swam
back to my clothes and dressed.   Whilst I had been
bathing O— had been engaged in a conversation with
the Archbishop on preaching.   The prelate maintained
that, whilst it was a great and difficult work, it was
especially needed in these days, on account of the
spread of materialism.

'Do the priests in your diocese preach?' inquired
O—.

'No,' replied the Archbishop; 'preaching is a great
work—work for a bishop.'

'Then, Monseigneur,' said O—, 'doubtless you
preach?'

'No,' replied the Archbishop, 'no, not very often.
The fact is, I have not the time.   Still, when I am in
my *métropole* upon the great festivals whilst the Gospel
is being read *je pense*, and afterwards I give the people
a short discourse.'

'On the Gospel for the day?'

'No, not always; I preach on any point of faith or
morals.'

The next day being Sunday, we got up very early
indeed (four o'clock) and went to the catholicon.   The

---

[1] All Easterns, both Mohammedan and Christian, use beads as a
pastime as well as for their prayers.

monks had been in church since midnight, but they seemed wonderfully fresh notwithstanding. We took up our position in stalls next to the Archbishop, and for three long hours we stood listening to the extraordinary sounds that proceeded from the throats of the monks. Byzantine music, which is still used in all *Greek* churches, must be heard to be realized, and, as the clergy of the Greek Church in London have adopted the modern system, the majority of my readers must be content to remain in ignorance of this ancient school. To an European Oriental music is almost unbearable ; no note seems to have any relation to its neighbours, for the scales are totally different from our modern ones, and the quarter tones—inadmissible in our system—grate fearfully upon ears that are unaccustomed to them. If he have the patience to resolutely go through a course of the music he will get used by degrees to the odd scales and intervals, and will begin to detect a tune or melody in what seemed to him at the outset but a jumble of discordant sounds. The Greek clergy invariably sing through the nose, and this adds to the unpleasant effect the strange music produces.[1]

No instrumental music of any kind is permitted in the Eastern Church, but sometimes a sort of voice accompaniment of one note, like the drone of a bagpipe, keeps up a low murmuring sound whilst the other voices are engaged upon the tune.

One old monk, who stood in a stall opposite to us, had a wonderfully piercing voice and sang nearly the whole time, gazing vacantly with a stupid fishy eye at the face of the prompter.[2] In the short intervals of repose he would sink down in his stall and apparently

[1] See Appendix.　　　　[2] See page 55

fall fast asleep, waking up again with wonderful precision when his turn came round. We were told that when young he used to sing in his parish church, and so rich and rare was his voice that people came from a distance to hear him, and that frequently his hat was filled with gold pieces by his wealthy admirers! After an office of psalmody the liturgy began, and lasted about two hours. During the latter a monk came round and censed us all singly with waves of the hand

GROUP OF MONKS AND PHIALE AT VATOPEDI.

censer. After church we bathed, holding white umbrellas over our heads to protect our necks from the burning sun—for it was very hot indeed this day—and then enjoyed a long siesta. Afterwards we took a photograph of the phiale with a group of monks in front; one of them a retired bishop, arrayed for the occasion in a cope, with an episcopal staff in his hand. The Eastern bishop's staff is formed at the top like a crutch, the cross pieces being fashioned into the likeness of serpents. What the signification of the serpents may be I cannot discover; various symbolisms were suggested to me by the Athos monks, none being satisfactory.

As we were sitting in our room this afternoon, talking to three or four of our hosts, we were startled at feeling a prolonged shudder pass through the tower in which we were. On asking what it was, one of the monks replied unconcernedly, ' Oh, it's only an earthquake. Occasionally some of our walls are shaken down ; this is a small one, you see.'

Towards evening we went to the kiosk in the garden with some of the monks, and asked them questions about the monastery.

Tradition asserts that Vatopedi was founded by Constantine the Great, destroyed by Julian the Apostate, and restored by Theodosius the Great. The first two statements are more than doubtful, but it is *possible* that Theodosius may have founded the monastery ; so I will give the story of the way in which the emperor came to be connected with it.

Theodosius (who reigned from 379 to 395) had two sons, Arcadius and Honorius. The former (then a boy, but afterwards Emperor of the East) was on a voyage from Rome to Constantinople, when the imperial trireme was caught in a terrific storm off Imbros. Arcadius, wild with fright, was rushing about the deck imploring the aid of the Theotocos, when, catching his foot in some rope, he fell overboard and disappeared. The next morning the trireme gained the bay of Vatopedi, when the nobles to whose charge Arcadius had been entrusted found the boy asleep under a thorn bush on the shore, to their inexpressible astonishment and delight. On awaking he told them that the

Holy Virgin had rescued him from the water and brought him safely to land.

On the return of the party to Constantinople the Emperor Theodosius sent artificers to the Holy Mountain to build a church in honour of God's Mother where his son was found. Honorius and Placidia joined him in the work, and gave, amongst other things, the four porphyry pillars which support the dome of the catholicon. So the church was finished, the holy table being placed, it is said, on the site of the bush, and Arcadius, now Emperor of the East, came himself with the Patriarch Nectarius to the dedication of the building, and because

Εὗρον τὸ παιδί ἐν τῇ βάτῳ [1]

the monastery obtained its name of Vatopedi, 'The Bush of the Child.'

In the year 862, according to the story,[2] Vatopedi was plundered by Arabs or Saracens, who stripped the gold plate off the roof of the catholicon. This was the occasion of the miracle of the icon and the lamp, already related. After this invasion three rich and noble Adrianopolitans, Athanasius, Nicholas (Nicetas?), and Antony, came to Athos with the object of founding a monastery. St. Athanasius of Athos (of whom more anon) succeeded in persuading them that they had not sufficient means to found a new house, and suggested that they should repair Vatopedi. This they did, and living and dying there were buried in the narthex of the catholicon. It is probable that these three men were the real founders of the monas-

---

[1] 'They found the child by the bramble bush.' Mr. Tozer suggests another derivation, Βατοπέδιον, 'the plain of bramble bushes.'

[2] Of John Comnenus.

tery, and that its previous history is as apocryphal as its subsequent is genuine.

After them came the Servians Simeon and Sabbas, who subsequently founded Chiliandari, and they built six chapels. The Emperors Manuel Comnenus and Andronicus Palæologus were benefactors of the monastery, and the Emperor John Cantacuzenus put on the monastic habit in 1355, and died a monk under the name of Joseph.

Vatopedi is supposed by Leake[1] to occupy the site of the ancient *Charadriæ*, one of the six cities mentioned by Herodotus[2] as existing on Acte. The others were *Acrothoon* and *Olophyxus* (now, according to Leake, represented by the Lavra and Chiliandari), *Dion*, *Thyssus*, and *Cleonæ*.

The number of monks at Vatopedi is 220. Besides these there are 130 laymen; these are servants of all sorts—muleteers, blacksmiths, carpenters, &c. Being an idiorrhythmic convent it is not governed by an hegoumenos, or abbot, but, as I have stated above, by three presidents called epitropoi. At the time of our visit they were the following: First epitropos, the prohegoumenos[3] Joseph; the second, the prohegoumenos Dionysius, who was also bursar (τίμιος); the third, the prohegoumenos Gregory. All were well-informed, dignified men, who commanded respect and seemed admirably fitted for their position as rulers of the chief Greek house on Athos. The epitropoi had two secretaries; the name of the first was Theophilus. Besides these officers there is the assembly

---

[1] *Travels in Northern Greece*, vol. iii. p. 149.

[2] *Polymnia*, c. 22.

[3] The title of *prohegoumenos* is purely honorary in idiorrhythmic monasteries.

called the *synaxis*, composed of twenty or thirty old
men elected for life. This body really legislates for
the monastery, and the epitropoi carry its laws into
effect.

The Holy, Venerable, Royal, and Patriarchal
Monastery of Vatopedi (for this is its full title) possesses much land on the promontory, a small quantity
on some of the islands of the Archipelago, and broad
acres in Bessarabia, from which, however, the Russian
Government only allows the convent to draw two-fifths
of its revenue, for political reasons which will be discussed later on in this book. It had lands in Moldavia,
but these were confiscated by Roumania in 1865. The
yearly income of the Roumanian property was esti-
mated at 4,800*l*.[1] Two *sketes* (dependent monasteries)
belong to Vatopedi, the Seraï, or skete of St. Andrew, inhabited by Russians, and the skete of St. Demetrius ;
the former is only nominally dependent. Besides the
sketes Vatopedi has twenty-three kellia (κελλὶ), each
containing five or six monks, with its own little church
and land attached ; also two cathismata (κάθισμα), inhabited by hermits. The difference between a kelli
and a cathisma is this : that in the former the inhabitants provide their own food, but in the latter they live
on food furnished by their monastery.

Vatopedi possesses sixteen churches within the
walls (*esocclesia*) and twelve without (*exocclesia*). This
seems a great number, but it must be remembered
that the catholicon is the only large church, and that
the others, with the exception of two or three of fair
size, are little more than chapels ; yet each is a perfect

---

[1] I quote from the archimandrite Porphyry's account; see the
Christian Remembrancer for 1851.

little church, with bema, nave, and narthex. The liturgy is always celebrated in the catholicon on Sundays and great festivals, in the other churches on week days.

The following is the list of the esocclesia, or churches within the walls:

1. The catholicon, dedicated to the Four Evangelists, containing four paracclesia, or subordinate chapels—St. Nicholas, St. Demetrius, the Archangels, and the Assumption of the Blessed Virgin.

2. The Holy Girdle (of St. Mary).

3. The Holy Unmercenaries ("Αγιοι 'Ανάργυροι), SS. Cosmas and Damian.[1]

4. The Holy Theodores.

5. The Transfiguration.

6. The Three Hierarchs : SS. Basil, Gregory, and Chrysostom.

7. St. Thomas the Apostle.

8. St. Chrysostom.

9. St. John the Evangelist.

10. The Twelve Apostles.

11. The Nativity of the Blessed Virgin.

12. St. Panteleëmon (the hospital chapel).

13. St. George.

14. St. Andrew the Apostle.

15. The Honoured Foterunner (Τίμιος Πρόδρομος), St. John the Baptist.

16. The Holy Trinity.

These are the exocclesia :

1. St. Modestus (stable chapel).

2. The Holy Apostles (cemetery).

3. St. Charalampes.

4. All Saints.

5. St. Tryphon.[2]

---

[1] Two famous martyrs of the third century. Being physicians they cured the sick without fees and so obtained the title of 'Unmercenary' or 'Silverless.'

[2] St. Tryphon (martyred in A.D. 250) is the patron of gardens. Didron says, 'Au mont Athos les chapelles qu'on voit s'élever au milieu d'une plantation de noisetiers ou d'oliviers, au centre d'un champ d'ex-

6. The Holy Archangels.
7. St. Christopher.
8. St. Artemius.
9. St. Onouphrius.
10. The Prophet Elias.
11. The Five Martyrs.
12. St. Nicholas.

ploitation, sont presque toutes dédiées à saint Tryphon, qu'on repré-
sente ordinairement une serpette à la main ' (*Manuel d'Iconographie
Chrétienne*).

CHAPTER VIII.

In every moment of our lives we should be trying to find out, not in what we differ with other people, but in what we agree with them.— RUSKIN.

Monday, August ¹³⁄₁. We had spent such a pleasant time at Vatopedi that it was with regret we were forced to leave our kind hosts to-day, being obliged to press on, as we wished to visit all the monasteries before leaving Athos.

We had coffee as usual in our room and then went to the dining-room, where we were regaled with glyko and more coffee, whilst our entertainers sat on the divan with us, and we all made pretty speeches. The epitropoi presented each of us with an engraving of the monastery and some carved wooden spoons and beads, and so we chatted pleasantly till a servant brought the intelligence that the mules were laden and were waiting for us outside. The epitropoi and other chief monks escorted us to the gate, and having said our last good-byes we mounted our mules and rode off to Pantocratoros.

It took about two hours to reach this monastery by a route which followed the road to Caryes for some distance and then turned off at a height of about 1,100 feet. When we came in sight of Pantocratoros our soldier fired three shots from his antiquated flint-lock

musket, causing O—'s mule to skip about the path,
to the imminent danger of that reverend divine. The
monks fired a salute in return, and we rode up to the
portal in great state. Here we were received by the
epitropoi, who conducted us to the best room overlooking the sea, where we sat down on the divan and had
glyko, coffee, and cigarettes. Dinner was prepared
meanwhile, and a poor meal it proved to be, everything
swimming in oil, so that we could not eat much. After
it we returned to the divan and extracted information

MONASTERY OF PANTOCRATOROS.

about the convent from the monks as we sat sipping
our coffee.

The Monastery of Pantocratoros, or 'The Almighty,' is, like most of the Athos convents, of doubtful foundation. The epitropoi told us that it was
founded by John Comnenus, brother of the Emperor
Alexius Comnenus (1081–1118). But Alexius had no
brother of the name of John, that I can discover,
although his father was John Comnenus, brother of

Isaac Comnénus, the first of the Comnenian Emperors of Constantinople. Another more probable account attributes the foundation to Alexius Strategopulus, the famous general of Michael Palæologus, who wrested Constantinople from the Latins in the year 1261, put to flight Baldwin II., the last of the Latin emperors, and restored the Greek rule in the person of his master.

The grateful emperor was not forgetful of his faithful servant, and a triumph was decreed to Alexius, such as had before been awarded to sovereigns alone. Clothed in the dress of a Cæsar, riding in a magnificent chariot, he was escorted through the entire city amidst the acclamations of the liberated populace. On his head was an emperor's crown, which he was given permission to wear for the rest of his life, and, in addition to the wealth and honours which were showered on him, his name was inscribed in all public documents after that of the emperor for the space of a whole year.[1]

But this brave soldier was a good man and pious, his affections being set rather on things above than on earthly pomps and vanities, and so, resolving to lay up treasure in heaven, he devoted a portion of his riches to the glory of God by founding this monastery of the Almighty in the year 1263, two years after his brilliant achievement, with the assistance of his brother, John the Primicerius.

Being an idiorrhythmic convent, Pantocratoros is governed by epitropoi instead of by an abbot: their names were Theocritus and the archimandrite Atha-

---

[1] Lebeau, *Histoire du Bas-Empire*.

nasius.   There are now fifty monks and twenty servants belonging to it ; in the archimandrite Porphyry's
time there were only twenty monks ; so that their
numbers have increased by more than double during
the last forty years.   The archbishop Georgirenes,
writing in 1678,[1] says that at that time it contained
300 brethren ; but he is a doubtful authority.   Pantocratoros possesses three cathismata, eleven kellia, and
one skete, that of the Prophet Elias, of which I
shall have to give an account later on.   The convent
also holds lands in Lemnos, Thasos, and Asia Minor.
Seven churches are situated within the walls and two
outside ; the list is as follows :

Esocclesia.

1. The catholicon, dedicated to the Transfiguration of our Lord,
containing one paracclesi, the Assumption of the Blessed Virgin
Mary.
2. The Honoured Forerunner (St. John Baptist).
3. St. Panteleëmon.
4. St. Nicholas.
5. St. George.
6. St. Andrew.
7. The Archangels.

Exocclesia.

1. St. Athanasius the Great.
2. St. Athanasius of Athos.

The catholicon is ancient and curious, though
small.[2]

---

[1] *A Description of the Present State of Samos, Nicaria, Patmos, and
Mount Athos,* by Joseph Georgirenes, Archbishop of Samos, now living
in London.   Translated by one that knew the author in Constantinople.
London, 1678.
[2] Measurements : length from west door to iconostasis, 31 feet ;
breadth of nave, 25½ feet, including transepts 36 feet ; breadth of sanctuary,

The chapel of the prothesis and the diaconicon are small chapels, surmounted by domes, and are situated on either side of the apse of the bema. The diameter of each is 6 feet 9 inches.

The catholicon possesses both an esonarthex and an exonarthex, and has a paracclesi at the north-west corner, dedicated to the Assumption of the Blessed Virgin. As usual, the interior walls of the church are entirely covered with frescoes. Most of these have been repainted, but the monks point out the following as the unrestored work of Panselinus : [1] the *faces* of the three large figures of Christ, the Virgin, and the Baptist, over and on each side of the west doorway in the esonarthex ; also the faces *inside* this doorway on the west wall of the nave.

Thirdly, all the figures in the second row on the east side of the north transept (Old Testament characters) are said to be untouched. The rest of the frescoes were repainted in a creditable manner, on the old lines, fifty years ago. The exceptions of the monks seemed to me to be rather doubtful.

On one of the four pillars of white marble which support the dome is a miraculous icon which was formerly in the oil stores and caused the oil to increase during a dearth. It has been repainted, and the silver work is modern Russian. We afterwards saw the jar connected with this miracle in the oil cellar.

The monastery is situated on a rocky cliff, and has its little port immediately below it. Probably the

or bema, 25½ feet ; length from iconostasis to end of sanctuary apse, 16½ feet.

[1] See below in the description of the Protaton at Caryes.

walls were once battlemented, but now rooms have
been built on them, overhanging in the way already
described at Vatopedi.   There is a tower on the land
side, which contains the library.   The books are well
kept, but there is no catalogue.   Here it was that
Curzon in 1837 found that terrible wreck which he
calls 'indeed a heart-rending sight.'   The tower had
fallen into ruin, and the roof and floors having given
way, the greater part of the library was rotting on the
ground amongst the rubbish.   It is a comfort to think

ANCIENT BOOK AT PANTOCRATOROS.

that now at least the remainder, consisting of 234
MSS. (sixty-six on vellum), are safely stowed away
under a water-tight roof.   We noticed particularly a
curious chronology of the world, about six inches wide
and twenty-six feet eight inches in length; it is kept
rolled round a stick.   The finest book at Pantocratoros
is kept in the catholicon.   It is said to be in the
handwriting of a certain St. John of Kalavita, a fifth-
century hermit; but Curzon considered it to be the

work of the eleventh or twelfth century. He describes
it in these words : ' It is written in a very minute hand,
and contains the Gospels, some prayers, and lives of
saints, and is ornamented with some small illuminations. The binding is very curious ; it is entirely of
silver gilt and is of great antiquity. The back part
is composed of an intricate kind of chainwork, which
bends when the book is opened.' The Crucifixion is
represented on one cover and the Annunciation on the
other. The lettering points to a Slavonic origin. We
had this book brought out into the courtyard, and there
photographed the binding successfully. This had evidently been done before, as faded photographs of the
binding and of the writing were pasted inside the
cover.

The court in which the catholicon stands is picturesque. In the spandrels of the arches, which form
a sort of cloister, pieces of pottery and plates are let
into the brickwork ; this is not unusual at Athos, but I
note it here because it was the first time we observed
this form of ornament. Opposite the west door of the
catholicon is a plate which looks extremely like a piece
of Moorish lustre-ware.

Our supper in the evening was so bad that we were
obliged to draw upon our slender stores and make our
meal off the preserved soup, tinned tunny, and Dutch
cheese which we had brought from Constantinople.
We were a little afraid of offending our kind hosts by
thus casting aspersions upon their entertainment ; so
Angelos was told to explain to them what curious tastes
Franks have, and how they never touch oil (*rancid*) in
their own country. This he did quite to their satisfac-
tion. After supper we had a long conversation with

the epitropoi and the Archbishop about the unity of
Christendom and the English Church. An intelligent
young Greek, a visitor to Athos, took part in the discussion. He was a sub-editor of the Patriarchal organ
the Ἐκκλησιαστικὴ Ἀλήθεια, to which he was
anxious we should subscribe, in order to correct any
misstatements which might appear in it concerning the
English Church ; this is, however, already done by
Canon Curtis, the chaplain of the Crimean Memorial
Church at Constantinople, whose long residence in the
East has given him a considerable acquaintance with
the Eastern modes of thought. A certain Dr. X.,
formerly a Roman priest, then a Lutheran, and now,
for the present at any rate, a member of the Orthodox
Eastern Church, resides in London, and is looked upon
as an oracle by the readers of the Ἀλήθεια ; this person
constantly contributes articles on Anglicanism to the
periodical. Canon Curtis assured us that his contributions are generally full of misrepresentations, and
betray a bitter hatred of our communion. The Canon
is constantly writing to the Ἀλήθεια to correct and
protest, but for the fair play of the editors I am sorry
to say that his letters do not always gain admission to
its columns.

To return to our conversation, which next turned
upon the *Filioque*: This mighty question, the cause
of the Great Schism, is hardly a subject for discussion
by individuals, and I can never see much use in thus
treating it. When, in God's mercy, the time comes for
the Churches to demand mutual explanations with a
view to Catholic unity, everything points to the belief
that there will not be much difficulty in satisfying
the Easterns of our orthodoxy whilst recognising the

validity of their objection to the insertion of the clause in the Creed. Between Easterns and Romans the case is different ; the Oriental fear and hatred of the Papal pretensions and aggression are far weightier considerations than any question of orthodoxy. The Easterns, resolved to join battle upon these issues, seem to have chosen the doctrine of the Procession of the Holy Spirit as an impregnable position for the fight.

We afterwards translated some of the Prayer Book to our audience, and fault was found with our form of private absolution. ' I absolve thee,' said the Archbishop, ' is too strong ; it shows a Latin influence. The absolution in your liturgy is in better form and more in keeping with antiquity.' We asked the Archbishop what he thought of Western baptism, and he replied that the Eastern Church refuses to recognise a baptism as valid unless it be performed with three complete immersions. ' Therefore,' said he, ' when a Roman priest comes over to us we *rebaptize* him, because we do not allow baptism by aspersion, nor, except in cases of sickness, by affusion ; and we *reordain* him, because an unbaptized person cannot be validly ordained.

' According to our doctrine,' continued the Archbishop, ' the Pope of Rome himself is neither more nor less than an unbaptized layman, and if he joined our communion would have to be baptized. Still, supposing the *whole* Latin Church and its patriarch were to submit to us in a body, then the Church by an exercise of the *economy of the Church* would recognise Western baptisms and ordinations, and they would become valid by the mere act of recognition.'

We ventured to suggest that the question was a

simple one : either Western baptisms and ordinations
are valid or they are not valid, and if they be not valid
no amount of recognition by the Church can make
them valid. This ' economy ' has already been exer-
cised by the Russian Church, which is part of the
Eastern Church, in full communion with the Patriarch
of Constantinople, and in this way : Numerous converts
being made amongst the Lutheran Finns and Latin
Poles, and it being extremely inconvenient, not to say
repelling, to have to rebaptize them, the Russian Church
takes them as if they were baptized, and then, having
confirmed them, admits them to the Eucharist and the
other sacraments. Thus if I, as a Western, wished to
join the Holy Eastern Church and went to Constantinople or Athens and craved admittance to her communion, I should be told, ' You must first be rebaptized,
or rather baptized, for you have never received that
indispensable sacrament.' If I rejected this injunction
and travelled north to St. Petersburg I should be told
that the Church received me as if I were baptized ;
that this was quite sufficient ; and I should be at once
admitted, after recanting my heresies, if I held any, to
the sacraments of the Holy Eastern Church. If I then
returned to Constantinople or Athens I should be
received into communion ; for as a member of the
Russian Church I should be necessarily in full communion with the rest of the Orthodox Church. May not
' economy ' be merely a grand name for ' expediency ' ?
Speaking broadly, the Easterns look upon Western
baptisms in the following way, though there are diver-
sities of opinion amongst them : It is not baptism ($Bá\pi$-
$\tau\iota\sigma\mu a$), because the person is not *dipped* ($B a \pi \tau i \zeta \omega$) ;
but it *is* the laver of regeneration (i.e. what the

Westerns do is sufficient to regenerate the person) ; therefore it is *a* sacrament although it is not the sacrament of baptism. This explanation was given me by one of the Œcumenical Patriarch's deacons, who became an intimate acquaintance of mine a few years ago, when he was in Oxford, studying Anglican theology. It does not seem to mean much more than that our baptism is the sacrament irregularly performed.

Although we did not on this occasion discuss the question of the marriage of the clergy, I have frequently done so at other times. Perhaps it is not generally known that our custom of permitting the clergy to marry *after* ordination is one of the greatest obstacles to union with the Easterns. It is true that they have never enforced the celibacy of the clergy, as the Roman Church, but they have retained that discipline, which seems to have been universal from the earliest ages of Christianity, that candidates for holy orders, if they chose the married state, should wed before their ordination. The question of clerical celibacy was raised at the Council of Nicæa in 325, and the proposal to enforce it rejected, the old discipline above mentioned being deemed sufficient. As far as I know, every Church in the world, Eastern or Western, Catholic or schismatical, with the exception of the Anglican, the decayed and feeble remnant of the Assyrian or Nestorian Church, and the Protestant sects, retains the primitive discipline of forbidding clerical marriages ; and although the mediæval abuses probably required a strong remedy, this departure from the practice of antiquity is hard to defend. A foolish and useless restriction, it may be said. In good truth this age is not favourable to high ideals ; and yet the sight of a priest's courtship will sometimes cause even the most thought-less of us to wince a little.   The Archbishop remarked that it would materially assist the cause of unity if representatives could be exchanged between Lambeth and Phanar,[1] even if this were done solely for the pur-pose of mutual study of the doctrines, practices, and thoughts of the two communions.

We spoke of liberalism and infidelity, and the havoc they are making in Western Christendom, pointing out that movements which begin in the West generally advance eastwards, that the Orientals must expect soon to feel their power, and how an united Christendom could easily withstand an onslaught to which divided Churches might succumb.   Wishing to illustrate our meaning in Eastern fashion, I bethought me of the old parable of the strength of the sticks, singly weak, when united in one bundle, and brought out our parcel of sticks and umbrellas for the purpose. Our friends greatly appreciated this *argumentum ad baculos*, and I was concluding my parable satisfac-torily when an unforeseen disaster occurred.   In the heat of discussion I had not perceived the entrance of a monk with our coffee, whose slippered feet tread-ing the soft matting produced no sounds save of the faintest.   Turning hastily round to replace my instru-ments of allegory in a corner, I encountered the coffee tray with considerable force.   Over went tray, cups, and coffee, and the poor monk stood speechless amidst the wreck, whilst I, the unfortunate cause of the mis-chief, began to stammer out my apologies.   But the

----

[1] Phanar is the quarter of Constantinople which was assigned to the Patriarch for his residence after the capture of the city by the Mussulmans.

Archbishop and the epitropoi hailed the catastrophe with delight. ' Polycala !' said they, ' polycala ! God has sent an omen ! Spilt coffee is the luckiest thing in the world. God will give us unity !' And the poor monk joined in the cry, and trotted off for more coffee, whilst the company with beaming countenances made room for me on the divan.

CHAPTER IX.

THE next day we got up at seven o'clock and took a photograph of the monastery. Coffee was brought and we wrote our names in the visitors' book, the Archbishop adding his wonderful signature with a long sentence in Greek, setting forth how the night before we had had a discussion on the Anglican and Eastern Churches and the necessity for reunion, for which he earnestly prayed. Then we took mules to the skete of the Prophet Elias, the Russian dependency of Pantocratoros. The skete is situated about half an hour's ride up the valley, which runs down from the central ridge to the rocky shore on which Pantocratoros stands, and is at a considerable elevation (400 feet) above the monastery. The buildings are all modern, the house having been founded by a monk called Païsius in the year 1753. Païsius was a Russian who first came to Athos in 1746. Cypresses grow round the skete in great plenty, and on an open space near it stands a windmill.

We were received with the clanging of all the bells and semantra in the place. The Archbishop put his veil (ἐπανωκαλυμαύχιον) over his tall black hat (καλυμαύχιον). We all dismounted and were received by the monks in the gateway. Arraying the Archbishop in a cope of purple silk, they accompanied us to the catholicon, two monks with lighted candles walking in front of him and Peter behind holding up the train of his cope. In the church we had a short service, lasting perhaps five minutes, the Archbishop standing in a throne and we in stalls. A priest within the bema and a deacon outside the holy doors conducted the prayers, the latter repeating a litany containing, amongst other things, a petition for 'the most beloved of God Philotheos.' When the deacon repeated the Archbishop's name he turned and bowed to him, and the monks said, 'Kyrie eleison, Kyrie eleison, Kyrie eleison,' after each suffrage. Then the Archbishop said a short prayer from the throne, afterwards descending into the centre of the church, where, raising his hand with his fingers in the Eastern position of blessing, he slowly turned round as on a pivot. The solemnity of this part of the proceedings was somewhat marred by Peter, who, in the act of running round his master with the tail of the cope in his hands, tripped over the folds and very nearly measured his length on the floor.

The service ended, we were conducted to the reception room, which was furnished with chairs as well as a divan and adorned with bright-coloured Russian prints on the walls. Instead of coffee, tea was brought to us, for wherever Russians are 'tchai' is to be found; and I may add that the Russian word for it is used not only in the Levant but throughout the East. Very good this tea was, and very acceptable after the endless little cups of thick Turkish coffee; not that this coffee is to be despised, but when you have it at least five times a day it begins to pall upon the taste. All sketes are cœnobite, and so ruled by an abbot, or, to speak more correctly, by a prior, or *dicaios* (δίκαιος), as he is called. The dicaios of St. Elias and another monk

entertained us over our tea. The latter was a particularly well-informed man, by name Anthony, and
seemed to be the right hand of the dicaios. We
chatted pleasantly about unity and the usual topics,
and also paid many compliments to Russia and the
Russians, which pleased our hosts exceedingly. By-
and-by they brought us their visitors' book, in which
we inscribed our names, and added that we were glad
to be able to avail ourselves of that hospitality which
we had always experienced from Russians ; and this
may have been the cause of our having an excellent
dinner, the best we had yet sat down to at Athos.

During this repast we talked to the monks about
their native country, and told them how we had seen
the new Church of the Saviour at Moscow the year
before, and how magnificent it was; all of which interested our friends greatly. They had a little ship,
the return of which from Russia they were daily ex-
pecting. It was to bring them caviar, tea, and many
other luxuries. After dinner we were shown into a
clean-looking room with iron bedsteads, and, as the day
was very hot and we knew the Archbishop would refuse
to move on until after his nap, we lay down on the
inviting beds for a siesta. Not very long did I remain
in that position. Before five minutes had elapsed, I
sprang up and caught in a twinkling six bugs, that had
just sat down to dinner. O— was more fortunate ; he
was unmolested, but the possibility of a like fate soon
compelled him to follow my example and banish all
thoughts of sleep. At three o'clock we went to
vespers and enjoyed the 'tetraphone,' or part music,
of the Russian Church. Outside the church were
several monks listening to the service at the open.

transept windows, each bending over a sort of crutch, resting his breast on its broad arms. These crutches are universally used by those who attend Divine service in the open air and feel the need of some support.

There is nothing of interest in the catholicon, which is dedicated to the prophet Elias. There are two other esocclesia, dedicated respectively to St. Metrophanes and the Annunciation. The two exocclesia are dedicated to the two Archangels and St. Nicholas. The name of the dicaios was Tobias. We left the skete with the same musical honours with which we had been received, but the ceremonies were rather disconcerted by our discovery at the last moment that my white umbrella was missing (I thought I had lent it to the Archbishop, but he denied the charge) and having to send monks scampering all over the place to find it. However, the bellringers and semantron players stuck manfully to their work, and after five minutes of prolonged leave-taking, the missing article being found, either in the garden, whither we had gone to take a photograph, or in one of the chapels, we mounted our mules and rode off to Stavroniketa.

This monastery is on the sea, a little to the south of Pantocratoros. Our muleteers took a short cut, which, like most short cuts, did not answer; for after they had conducted us along the face of the cliff by a steep path we suddenly found a wall barring farther progress. A careful search revealed no gate, so there was nothing for it but to retrace our steps. With considerable difficulty we turned our mules' heads, the path being very narrow, climbed to the top of the cliff again, and descended to the monastery by another road. Thus it took us nearly two hours and a half to reach our destination. Stavroniketa, or the Monastery of the Conquering Cross, is situated, like Pantocratoros, on a rock overhanging the sea. It is a picturesque building with a tall tower on the land side, the top of which is both battlemented and machicolated, like a Gothic keep. It was either founded or restored by Jeremias I. in 1540 or 1541

VIEW OF A PORTION OF THE EASTERN SHORE OF THE PROMONTORY, WITH STAVRONIKETA IN THE FOREGROUND AND MOUNT ATHOS IN THE DISTANCE.

(Jeremias occupied the Patriarchal throne of Constantinople from 1520 to 1543)—probably restored, both from the appearance of the catholicon and the tradition of the monks ; for they assert that the founder was Nicephoros Stavroniketos, an officer of the Emperor John Zimiskes [1] (969–976); that it was destroyed by

[1] I have adopted the most usual spelling for the Emperor's name Zimiskes is an Armenian word, and is occasionally written, as Finlay remarks, ' in a frightful manner '—Tzimiskes, Chimishkik, and Chumuskik. His native place rejoiced in the name of Chumushkazak or Tchemeschgedzeg.

African pirates, rebuilt by Jeremias, and that its name is derived from its founder. They say also that the present buildings and the catholicon date from the restoration, but I think the latter must be older than the sixteenth century, and Curzon seems to have been of the same opinion. There were six esocclesia, but two have been lately destroyed by fire and are not yet rebuilt. They are as follows :

1. The catholicon, dedicated to St. Nicholas.
2. Assumption of the Blessed Virgin.
3. The Honoured Forerunner.
4. St. Eleutherius.
5. St. George
6. The Holy Apostles } at present burnt.

There is one exocclesi, St. Demetrius, attached to the cemetery. The monastery possesses six kellia, one cathisma, and twenty-two calyvia. A calyvi is like a small kelli, but has no chapel attached to it. The inhabitant of a calyvi is a hermit who pays annually to the monastery half a Turkish lira (equal to nine shillings) for the house and a small plot of ground. By the cultivation of this ground and by begging at the monasteries he supports himself. I have already mentioned the large number of hermits that are fed every day at the great houses of Vatopedi and Iveron.

The chief epitropos, by name Averkius, quite startled us. He had a very red face and a voice like a crow ; he talked prodigiously, in the loudest tones, and ended each sentence with a hoarse laugh. We were positively deafened by the terrific noise he made. The other epitropos, called Gregentius, and another monk sat meekly on the divan, not speaking a word ; the noisy fellow had it all his own way. He told us

about the spoliation of the monastic lands in Vallachia,
and how Stavroniketa had suffered with the rest. 'But
we have enough,' said he, amidst shouts of apparently .
meaningless laughter ; 'we cultivate our lands on Athos
the better.   God gave and God has taken away, and
we must be content.'   Then he related how a short
time ago nearly the whole monastery had been burnt
down, and at this point his mirth became utterly un-
controllable ; peals of laughter followed one upon
another until the tears trickled down his cheeks, and
we began to try how long we could keep the joke up
by putting in a little chuckle of our own occasionally,
being forced at last to desist from very pity!   The
Archbishop looked very much annoyed, and hardly
spoke at all.   We thought he was angry at such an
unseemly exhibition taking place before us, and I
think he suspected, as we did, that the epitropos had
been looking too much upon the red wine.   However,
we afterwards heard that his laughter was a form of
nervousness, and this was proved by the fact that when
we had been in his company for an hour or two, and
his shyness had begun to wear off, the bursts of
laughter became fewer and less uproarious ; but still
to the very last he was, to say the least, exceedingly
merry.

O— at length grew tired of our noisy host, and
commenced a voyage of discovery in the neighbourhood of the supper table, which was spread in an
anteroom outside the place where we were sitting.
Presently he returned and beckoned to me to follow.
I did so, and found myself in an extremely ill-smelling
apartment.

'My dear O—,' said I, 'where does the abominable

odour come from? There must be a drain underneath the window.'

O— made no reply, but, pointing to a bowl full of
a reddish liquid which was gradually cooling on the
table, he said simply, 'Smell it.' I applied my nose
to the bowl and took one sniff.

'Good heavens!' said I; 'what on earth can it
be?'

'Our soup,' replied O— very gravely.

'No, no,' I exclaimed in desperation; 'impossible.
No one could swallow *that.*'

'Yes,' said O—, 'that's our soup, and that is the
reason of the smell you perceived just now.'

At that moment in trooped the Archbishop, the
epitropoi, and Angelos, and we had to sit down to
supper. What a meal that was! Never in the whole
course of my travels have I experienced anything to
equal it. The smell of the soup was so bad that I
really thought several times I should have to beat
a hasty retreat. The bowl was placed before the
Archbishop (O— and I were sitting on each side of
him), and he began to ladle out the stuff on to plates.
It was composed of three parts hot water and one part
hot rancid oil, in which delicious compound lobster and
octopus had been digested. It needs not to be said
that we neither of us ventured upon a trial of it. We
observed that the Archbishop only drank half of his
portion.

'Come,' said O— to me in English across the
table, 'it must be bad if the Archbishop can't
manage it.'

We munched our dry bread (ugh! wasn't it gritty!)
and waited patiently. Second course: octopus boiled

in the same oil.   Again we refused, much to the distress of the merry epitropos ; but the utter hopelessness
of the task of eating the dish lent firmness to our
refusal.   Again the Archbishop took a helping, but
after the first few mouthfuls I saw him beginning to
play with the red tentacles, which were swimming in
the brown oil, and trying to drain off a little of the
latter from the fish.   We remarked in French, ' You
don't seem to have much of an appetite, Monseigneur,
after our ride ; ' but the Archbishop with true Oriental
politeness only answered by a smile.   We ate a little
of our Dutch cheese, for we dared not draw further
on our slender stores, and so went practically supper-
less to bed, and after a hard day's work too.   O—
would contradict me flatly, I know, if I said that he
was as cross as two sticks that evening and left me
to do all the talking, but it would be quite true nevertheless.

The monks spread sheets on the divan for our use
that were too filthy for us to think of using.   How long
it was since they had been washed, and how many
sleepers they had inclosed since that operation, and of
what kind, we shuddered to think ; so, piling them
up in a corner, we brought out for the first time
our ' levinges,' or sleeping-bags, and indeed we were
rarely able to dispense with them afterwards.

A levinge is made of two bags, one of light calico,
the other of muslin, each about six or seven feet in
length.   The open ends of the bags are sewn together,
so as to make one continuous sack, the only entrance
being through a neck projecting from the side of the
calico bag, which can be securely closed by a running
tape ; the whole contrivance, when folded for packing,

being about the same weight and size as an ordinary night shirt.

Having spread the calico portion of the bag (which represents the sheets) on the divan, you tie up the muslin part to a nail or some other convenient fastening on the wall above your head, the muslin having been already distended by a cane hoop (made in three pieces for portability), so as to form a canopy over the pillow at right angles to the calico bag. Then you spread a rug, if it be cold, over the calico, and enter the bag by the neck, already described. Once inside, the strings attached to the entrance are tightened, wound round the end of the neck, and tied; and there you are, snug and comfortable, and can watch with the greatest pleasure your baffled enemies, who, in their futile attempts to force an entrance, run up and down the outside of the muslin and end by ensconcing themselves, as daylight breaks, in the folds at the top of the canopy, where you have the supreme delight of catching and slaughtering them the next morning.

But I am anticipating our bed time. We talked a little to the noisy epitropos, and asked him questions concerning the state of the monastery. There are now forty-five monks, who observe the idiorrhythmic rule. If Archbishop Georgirenes' statement be correct, they have increased since his time by fifteen. There are also fifteen servants.

Soon the epitropoi went to bed, and, the Archbishop and O— being engaged in conversation, I went into the open air to enjoy the fresh breezes of the night. The moon was nearly at the full and her rays were streaming down into the courtyard, so that the catholicon and the surrounding buildings with their domes and roofs were bathed in the silvery light.   The monastery was as still as possible, all the monks having retired to rest in preparation for the great night service.   I stood a long while watching the moonlight, so long that I became too absorbed to notice that the Archbishop had joined me on the balcony.   Suddenly a slight noise startled me, and turning round I found him by my side.   'My Lord,' said I, 'we say in England that the moon is the type of the Panaghia; she is very glorious, and yet but shines with a reflected light.' Probably the Archbishop did not comprehend the astronomy of the remark, but he appreciated its theology, for he replied, 'That is an orthodox statement; and yet do not all Christians love God's Mother?' and I said, 'There are strange things now in Christendom, my Lord.'

CHAPTER X.

THE catholicon of Stavroniketa is very small.[1]   It is dedicated, as has been already said, to St. Nicholas the Wonderworker.   This is the famous father of Nicæa, who in his indignation dealt the heretic Arius in the midst of the council that box on the ear for which he was punished with a temporary suspension *a sacris* by the assembled bishops, who admired his zeal for the truth although they could not overlook his breach of decorum.[2]   No saint has ever been so widely popular as St. Nicholas.   Not only in the East is his name held in the greatest veneration, but in every country in Europe churches have been built in his honour.   He is regarded as the special patron of sailors, and a modern Greek proverb runs as follows :

Καὶ εἰς τὴν θάλασσαν βοηθεῖ,
Καὶ εἰς τὴν γῆν θαυματουργεῖ.[3]

This is how he acquired his reputation, as Adam of St. Victor tells us in one of his beautiful sequences :

---

[1] Size of the catholicon : from iconostasis to east end of apse, 9 feet ; from iconostasis to west door of nave, 24½ feet ; extreme breadth of church, 21 feet ; length of narthex, 24 feet.

[2] Stanley's *Eastern Church.*

[3]   He both assists us on the sea,
And on the land works wondrously.

Quidam nautæ navigantes,
Et contra fluctuum sævitiam luctantes,
    Nave pene dissoluta,
    Jam de vita desperantes,
In tanto positi periculo, clamantes
    Voces dicunt omnes una :

'O beate Nicholae,
Nos ad maris portum trahe
    De mortis angustia.
Trahe nos ad portum maris,
Tu qui tot auxiliaris
    Pietatis gratia.'

Dum clamarent, nec incassum,
'Ecce !' quidam dicit, 'assum
    Ad vestra præsidia.'
Statim aura datur grata
Et tempestas fit sedata :
    Quieverunt maria.[1]

In the catholicon is preserved a miraculous picture of the saint, with the following history attached to it :

---

[1] I append Mr. Wrangham's translation :

'Certain sailors once, when sailing,
And fighting 'gainst fierce waves with struggles unavailing,
    Shipwrecked nigh through stress of weather,
    Hope of life already failing
Amid such dangers set, aloud their fate bewailing,
    Lift their voices all together :

'"Blessed Nicholas, oh, steer us
From the straits of death so near us
    To the haven of the sea !
To that harbour in the distance
Draw us, who dost grant assistance,
    Through the grace of charity !"

'Lo ! while thus they cried, nor vainly,
"I am here," a voice said plainly,
    "To watch o'er you and to aid !"
Instantly blow favouring breezes,
Instantly the tempest ceases,
    And to rest the sea is laid.'

At the time of the iconoclastic heresy this icon was struck and otherwise insulted by a heretic, and then thrown into the sea. A fisherman brought it up in his net, and found an oyster sticking to the face of the picture where it had been struck. This is all the information I could get from the monks. On asking *when* the fisherman found the picture, I received the usual answer, 'Who knows? A very long time ago.' Questions as to how it came to Stavroniketa and what the oyster had to do with the story, or with the sanctity of the picture, shared the same fate. I cannot do more, therefore, than describe the icon. The face is of mosaic, the setting silver gilt of ancient workmanship, but probably more modern than the mosaic. The oyster shell is carved and preserved separately in the church. After we had seen the picture of St. Nicholas one of the monks in priest's orders put on a stole, and certain candles having been lighted the relics were brought out for our veneration. They were the left hand of St. Anne; a few teeth of the Prodromos; a lump of earth and bones, being the relics of the 20,000 martyrs of Nicomedia; a piece of the shoulder of St. Basil, and some myron (μύρον) of St. Nicholas. Myron [1] is an odoriferous unguent which exudes from the relics of certain saints, who are called from this circumstance μυροβλύται, myroblytes. As the monastery was very poor at the time of our visit,

---

[1] Τοῦτο τὸ μύρον δαίμονας συμπνίγει, νόσους φυγαδεύει. (Nathaniel Chumnus.) And possibly Sir John Maundeville is alluding to this *myron* in the following passage (where he is speaking of the relics of St. Catherine on Mount Sinai): 'The prelate of the Monkes schewethe the Relykes to the Pilgrymes. And with an Instrument of Sylver, he frotethe the Bones: and thanne ther gothe out a lytylle Oyle, as thoughe it were a maner swetynge, that is nouther lyche to Oyle ne to Bawme; but it is fulle swete of smelle.

on account of the expense of rebuilding the burnt-out portion, we ventured to make a small offering to the church, this being the only instance during the whole of our visit where we felt we could properly do so, though we used to give presents to the muleteers and occa-. sionally to the monk that waited on us, when we heard that he was a poor man to whom a little gift would be acceptable.

After the relics had been put away, we asked to see the library. It had been burnt, but the books saved, and these were lying in heaps on the floor of a dark room, in such confusion that it was impossible for us to pick out anything of interest. It is not impro- bable that some have been lost or seriously damaged by 'fire, water, and removal.' Anyhow it is to be hoped that they will soon be rearranged in a new library. Curzon found here 800 MSS., of which 200 were on vellum, the best books being a MS. of the 'Scala Perfectionis' in Greek of the tenth or eleventh century, a paper MS. of the Acts and Epistles, both of which had fine illuminations, and eight large folios containing the entire works of St. Chrysostom.[1]

We had breakfast the next morning at eleven, and fared no better than the night before. The kind-hearted monks had done their best by providing special soup for us ροσμπηφοφάγοι καὶ μπλομποντιγγοφάγοι Ἄγγλοι,[2] and a cock to follow. The soup was the liquor in which the cock had been boiled, but they had put rancid

---

[1] I am informed by Professor Spyridion Lambros, of Athens, that when he visited the library three or four years back there were only 169 MSS., fifty-seven being on vellum, some finely illuminated.

[2] 'Roast-beef-eating and plum-pudding-eating Englishmen,' as the Greek newspapers of Constantinople are in the habit of informing their readers at Christmas time, in special articles on our national idiosyn- crasies.

butter into it, and we found it quite uneatable. 'Never mind,' said the epitropos, 'there is a cock to follow; you will like him.' The gallant fowl soon appeared, with his legs and wings sticking out in the most ridiculous way, for the monks of Mount Athos do not take the trouble of trussing fowls for table. He had been boiled in the soup and looked very blue and sodden. By this time, however, our appetites had been sharpened by abstinence, so that we were not going to be put off by the look of the victuals. O— was helped first. 'There,' said the Archbishop, as he tore the poor bird into fragments, 'there is a nice wing for you.' 'Yes,' added the noisy epitropos, with one of his paroxysms of mirth, 'don't mind us ; eat it all yourselves.' O— took a large mouthful (I had waited, as usual, to see what he thought of the bird, for I strongly object to shocks on the palate ; if a thing is nasty I like to be prepared for it) and we all watched him. The instant he tasted the morsel I saw that something was the matter. The tears came into his eyes in the agony of the moment as he strove to swallow it. At last he succeeded and gasped out, 'I'm nearly poisoned. What can they have done to it ?' We discovered that the cock had been dressed with almost putrid butter. Of course we were obliged to send it away, though I am afraid we hurt the epitropos' feelings. We were very sorry, especially as the cock—imported, of course, and therefore valuable [1]—was quite useless to everyone else in the monastery, it being the beginning of the fortnight's fast before August 15. Still there was no help for it, and we could only direct Angelos to make the best

---

[1] It will be remembered that no female animals are allowed on the promontory.

K

apologies to the monks and tell them—what I am afraid
was not strictly true—that we were not at all hungry,
and were doing admirably on bread, fruit, and nuts.

We strove to divert attention from our daintiness
by starting a discussion upon the Roman Church—a
genial topic which soon found plenty of employment
for the monastic tongues.

'Of course,' said the epitropos, when the first burst
of anti-Papal fervour had subsided, 'of course it is a
well-known fact that all Roman priests are immoral.'

'No,' I replied; 'that is not true. You have never
been in Roman Catholic countries, whilst this English
priest and I have seen much of the Roman clergy, and
we know that there are as good men amongst them as
anywhere in Christendom.'

'Well, the greater number are immoral,' urged the
epitropos.

'Few of them,' said I.

'A great many,' said the epitropos.

'Very few,' said I.

'Yes,' interposed the Archbishop, 'this Frank
gentleman is right. All *Catolic*[1] priests are not immoral. Besides, he has visited the Pope's countries,
and ought to know better than you.'

We left Stavroniketa at two o'clock in the afternoon of Wednesday, August $\frac{15}{3}$, and arrived an hour
later at Iveron, or the Holy Patriarchal and Royal
Monastery of the Iberians. This convent is close to
the sea, very little above its level, at the mouth of a
pretty glen, which widens into a small valley where the

---

[1] The peculiar pronunciation by the Greeks of the word *Catholic* when
used with reference to the Roman Church in contradistinction to the
Eastern Church.

monastic inclosure begins. It is surrounded by fine
trees, the side of the hill on the south of the monastery
being especially well-wooded. Just below the convent
is the fortified port which Comnenus calls the Port of
Clement. This is the only evidence I have been able
to find in support of the assertion of Professor Damalas,
of the University of Athens, who told me that Iveron
was anciently called the Monastery of St. Clement.

We were received with great splendour. Under
the portico, which is supported by six marble columns

IVERON.

of rather poor design, was a priest in a *phœnolion*, or
chasuble, holding a richly bound copy of the Holy
Gospels. He was attended by monks with long and
thick wax candles, and two deacons, each dressed in a
stoicharion, or alb of cloth of gold, who censed the
Archbishop on each side with silver censers. Our
prelate was arrayed in a purple cope, and we all moved
in procession to the catholicon amidst the strains of
Byzantine chanting.

K 2

The service of reception being concluded, we went to the principal guest-room and had glyko and coffee ; we were then shown to our room, a large apartment with plenty of windows and a divan, as usual, round three of its walls.

We unpacked, read a little, and took a siesta.   I was driven away from my divan by the enemy that crawls (or rather runs), and took refuge in the middle of the room, lying on the matted floor with an air cushion for a pillow.   In the cool of the evening we walked down to the sea, and did not return until supper time.   The oil was better here than at Stavroniketa, but still far from good, and the viands dressed with it were almost uneatable.   We had a salad of raw onions and tomatoes, stewed octopus, and snails boiled in oil, also a few hard-boiled eggs, which were passable.   All eggs, of course, have to be brought to the promontory ; milk is never seen here.

My companion, dainty as usual, would neither look at the octopus nor the snails.   I took some of both and tried to like them.   Octopus is like tough and insipid lobster, and is quite eatable when you have conquered your repugnance to the tentacles and their suckers. Our table companions made a prodigious noise in sucking the snails out of their shells ; pins are scarce amongst the monks.   I took a few, and promised to eat more the next day if they would boil me some in plain water.

This evening we developed some of our photo-graphic negatives.   There was a tap with a sink con-veniently situated in the passage outside our room, which we used until some enormous slugs, attracted by the unusual flow of water, walked out of the drain and took possession of the developing trays, to our great disgust.

Iveron was founded by three Iberians or Georgians, by name John, Euthymius, and George, about the year 980, under the following circumstances: Romanus Lecapenus (?), Emperor of Constantinople, had given to David, prince or couropalate of Georgia, the country of High Karthli, and David, as a proof of his fidelity to the Emperor, had sent some of the principal personages of his court to Constantinople as hostages.

Among these were Euthymius, or Ewthym, and his maternal grandfather Abougharb, eristhaw of the Ksan. Now Ewthym's father, whose name was John, had embraced the monastic life, and at the time of sending the hostages was in one of the monasteries of Mount Olympus. Hearing that his son had been included in their number, he went to Constantinople to claim him on the ground that he had been taken without his consent, and finally took him away with him to Olympus. Wearied with the homage paid to him as a saint, he quitted this monastery with Ewthym and certain of his disciples, and came to the Lavra at Mount Athos. Here the father and son lived for some time in company with the brother-in-law of the former, one John Grdzélidzé, also called, more euphemistically, Thornic, or Tornicius, who, it seems, was a distinguished warrior. The party next migrated, for the sake of greater retirement, to a secluded spot a mile from the Lavra, where they built a church in honour of St. John the Evangelist. Now the Emperor Basil II. being terribly embarrassed by the revolt of Bardas Sklerus (who had utterly routed the Byzantine general Bardas Pochas), the queen mother, Theophano, having heard

that Thornic was in Greece, sent an urgent letter to
him by a special messenger, begging him to repair
instantly to Constantinople. He complied, and after
consultation with the imperial court proceeded to
his native country to ask the aid of David. The
couropalate thereupon raised a body of 12,000
Georgians and placed them under the command of
Thornic. With these troops the warrior monk, aided
by his lieutenant Dchodchic, a Georgian prince, defeated Sklerus, forced him to fly into Persia, and
returned laden with rich booty. This was in the
year 979.[1] Thornic returned to Mount Athos, resumed
the monastic habit, and with his share of the spoil
founded Iveron, or the Iberian monastery, being aided
by his kinsmen John and Ewthym and by Theophano,
who provided him with workmen and sacred vessels
for the church and endowed the house with farms and
lands. It is said that another relative joined the
monastic family in the person of one Waraz-Watché,
Thornic's brother. After the death of Thornic, John
wished to visit Spain, it being thought at that time that
the Spaniards and the Georgians were of the same
race, but he died before he could carry out his project.
He was succeeded in the government of the convent
by his son Ewthym. Ewthym made the first translation of the Bible from Greek into Georgian; of this
I shall have occasion to speak in the account of the
library. His strict government caused discontent
amongst the monks, chiefly of Greek nationality, and
forced him to go to Constantinople for the purpose of
arranging the difficulties that had arisen. Here he

---

[1] A tattered fragment of the coat of mail which Thornic wore on this
occasion still hangs on the wall of the library, as also his bow, of the
Tartar shape and somewhat battered.

died on May 13, 1028, from an injury caused by a fall from his horse.

Shortly after Ewthym's death the catholicon was built by a monk named George Mthatsmidel, at the expense of the King Bagrat IV. of Georgia (1027–1072). I have little doubt that George Mthatsmidel is identical with St. George of Athos, who succeeded Ewthym either directly or after a short interval as abbot of Iveron, who died in 1066 and who is commemorated in the Georgian kalendar only (on June 27). St. George retranslated the Holy Scriptures into Georgian.[1]

In the thirteenth century Iveron was ravaged by Westerns, whether by the crusaders or by the Catalans is doubtful; the date given is 1260. Shortly afterwards it was again laid waste by the Emperor Michael Palæologus, who, for political reasons, had effected a formal union with the Latin Church at the Council of Lyons in the year 1274 by the aid of the Patriarch Veccus, one of his creatures. This union was never recognised by the bulk of the Eastern Church, Mount Athos being the centre of the opposition to the imperial will, and consequently the monks of the Holy Mountain had a very bad time from 1274 to 1280.[2] Then Pope Nicholas III. died, and his successor, Martin IV., excommunicated the Emperor as a hypocritical heretic, and so cut the one link that had feebly bound the East to the West for six years.

The monastery was restored, but it was again laid low by the Turks about the time of the fall of Constantinople. At the end of the fifteenth century the

---

[1] For the greater part of this history I am indebted to Brosset's *Histoire de la Géorgie*, St. Petersburg, 1849–58. I cannot find any mention of Thornic by Byzantine writers.

[2] See the history of the Monastery of Zographou.

monks appealed successfully to the princes of Iberia
or Georgia to aid in the restoration of their Iberian
house.   It soon afterwards fell again into debt and
decay by reason of the oppression of the infidels, and
it was again assisted by Georgia in 1592.

In 1614 Parthenius of the Morea and Gabriel of
Athos restored the hall at the charges of Radulas,
voivode of Hungaro-Vallachia.   In 1674 another
Georgian prince bestowed gifts on the monastery, and
adorned the refectory with frescoes.   Mouravieff states
that these have all been repainted except the portraits
of this Georgian prince and of Radulas.   I did not
notice these frescoes particularly, so cannot give any
further information about them.

The monastery was completely destroyed by fire in
1865 with the exception of the isolated buildings in
the court (catholicon, Church of the Virgin Portress,
refectory, and certain offices) and, I think, the tower
opposite the gateway.   This disaster has naturally
destroyed much of its interest.   It is now rebuilt on
a more regular plan, with dividing walls at intervals
having iron doors in the corridors, which are supposed
to be fireproof.   We often asked the monks at the
different convents why they did not insure their buildings at some Athenian insurance office, in view of the
frequent fires which attack and sometimes ruin them.
Their reply was always the same, that it had never
been the custom to do so, and they did not wish to try
a new thing.   Truly Athos is the home of conservatism!   The noisy epitropos of Stavroniketa said that
they preferred being in God's hands.   If He willed
that they should be punished by fire, they would be,
and there was an end of it.

The south-east corner of the monastery is still in ruins, but the sea front we found nearly finished at the time of our visit ; a rich old archimandrite, Athanasius, who had been at Iveron for fifty years, was rebuilding this part at his own expense, and very highly he stood in the monastic opinion in consequence of his liberality. A nice set of rooms was to be reserved in the new building for the old fellow's private use.

These are the eighteen churches within the walls of the convent.

1. The catholicon, dedicated to the Assumption of the Blessed Virgin ; containing two paracclesia, St. Nicholas and the Holy Archangels.

2. The Church of the Virgin Portress.

3. The Forerunner (old catholicon).

(The above are situated in the courtyard.)

4. St. Modestus.

5. St. Dionysius, the Areopagite.

6. St. Spyridion.[1]

7. St. Neophytus.

8. St. Eustathius.

9. The Presentation of the Blessed Virgin in the Temple.

10. St. Charalampes.

11. St. Stephen.

12. SS. Constantine and Helen.

13. The Transfiguration of Our Lord.

14. St. John the Divine ⎫
15. All Saints ⎬ burnt, and not yet restored.
16. St. Panteleëmon ⎭

17. St. George.

18. SS. John, Euthymius, and George ;[2] burnt, and not yet restored.

Exocclesia.

1. The Panaghia.

2. Archangels.

---

[1] One of the fathers of Nicæa. His entire body is preserved at Corfu, with the exception of the right hand, which is at Rome.

[2] See above, p. 133.

3. St. Basil.
4. The Presentation in the Temple of the Blessed Virgin Mary.
5. St. Tryphon.
6. The Five Martyrs—Eustratius, Mardarius, Orestes, Eugenius, and Auxenius.
7. St. Demetrius.
8. St. Minas.
9. St. Sabbas.
10. The Forty Martyrs.

Iveron possesses forty kellia and one skete dedicated to St. John the Baptist.[1]   The archimandrite Porphyry (from whom I have quoted before) gives the number of monks attached to this skete as thirty.   Fourteen calyvia belong to the skete of St. John.

The catholicon possesses an esonarthex and an exonarthex, the latter frescoed with the martyrdoms of saints, and a pronaos.[2]

Behind the holy table, on a framework of curious design, made of wood inlaid with ivory, which also supports two candles, is a magnificent silver-gilt and enamelled cross of the finest Byzantine work.   It is set with rubies and turquoises, and delicate little dragons with rubies for eyes project like gargoyles from the main stem.

The interior of the church is covered with frescoes, and the floor is rich with *opus Alexandrinum.*   Outside is a bell tower containing eight small bells, and a large one which was cast at Moscow.

---

[1] This skete is now about the same size as that of St. Demetrius belonging to Vatopedi.

[2] The breadth of the nave is a little over 55 feet (I am not sure from my notes whether or not this is the extreme breadth across transepts) ; length from iconostasis to west wall, 38 feet.   The bema or sanctuary measures as follows : length from doors of iconostasis to end of east apse, 21½ feet ; breadth, 15½ feet, or, including the chapel of the prothesis and the diaconicon, the same as the rest of the church.

On the north side of the catholicon, near the entrance to the monastery, is the Church of Our Lady of the Gate, so called because it contains the famous icon of the Portaïtissa (Πορταίτισσα), or Portress, concerning which the following wonderful story is told.

In the reign of Theophilus, the iconoclastic emperor (829-842), this picture was accidentally discovered in a widow's house at Nicæa by an imperial messenger who had entered to rest. Drawing his sword, he struck the face of the Virgin, when blood spurted from the picture over the insulter, who, terrified by the occurrence, took to flight. The widow, fearing that the matter would be noised abroad, cast the icon into the sea. Seventy years afterwards, at the commencement of the tenth century, Theophilus having been long dead and Theodora having restored the use of images in 842, the picture appeared off the coast of Mount Athos, surrounded by rays of fire. The monks having never before heard of a similar case of fire in the midst of the sea, launched their boats and rowed towards the apparition; but as they approached the fire receded, to their great disappointment. Then a voice was heard, 'Gabriel the Georgian is worthy to bear the icon of the Most Holy Virgin.' So the monks went to the Georgian convent [1] and asked who Gabriel might be. 'A hermit on the mountain,' was the reply. They fetched him from his retreat, and despatched him in a boat towards the fiery apparition. Now the whole aspect of affairs was altered, for as fast as Gabriel approached, so fast did the picture move towards him, until at last the hermit stepped out of

[1] Iveron was not founded at this time, but Georgians seem to have frequented the Lavra.

his boat, and walking boldly on the water met the icon
and conveyed it to the shore. This was on Easter
Tuesday. The monks brought the picture in procession
to Gabriel's convent, and by his advice placed it near
the portal, so that everyone going in or coming out
might have the opportunity of paying respect to it.
Thus it obtained its name of Portaïtissa, and a church
was afterwards built to contain it by a Georgian called
Achothan, Prince of Moukhran.[1]

The patriarch Nicon, Russia's greatest ecclesiastic,
though a jealous reformer of abuses connected with
pictures, had a copy of this icon made and brought it
to Moscow, where it is still held in the highest veneration and is known by the name of 'the Iberian
Mother of God.' Nicon also built a convent in Russia
in imitation of Iveron.

We visited the bakery with its large troughs for
kneading bread and a huge oven. The number of
pilgrims and hermits who are daily dependent on the
monastery has been already mentioned in a former
chapter.

The monks get their commons every day after
vespers. There is a large refectory, now only used,
like that at Vatopedi, on great occasions. A pretty
white marble phiale, of recent construction, stands in
the court at the west end of the catholicon.

Iveron possesses an extremely rich library, containing, amongst others, 1,384 Greek manuscripts. We
had no time to make anything but the most superficial
examination of this Biblical treasury. There are an
evangelistarium, dated 1386, containing some exceedingly fine illuminations, eight or nine inches square ; a

[1] Brosset.

large folio evangelistarium of 312 leaves; a folio patristic work beautifully bound and presented by Dionysius, Patriarch of Constantinople; a fine psalter, and a large number of classics rather rare to find in the Athos libraries. But the chief literary treasure is undoubtedly the Georgian Bible in two very large and thick folios bound in black leather. This is the original manuscript, in the handwriting of St. Ewthym, of the first translation made of the Holy Scriptures into that language, a pious work undertaken by the founder of Iveron, as has been before mentioned.[1]

[1] Whilst Dr. Pinkerton was making inquiries at St. Petersburg as to a Georgian version of the Holy Scriptures, Prince George, son of the last King of Georgia, informed him that whilst reading the annals of his nation he had fallen upon a passage in which it was said that when St. Euphemius (Ewthym) translated the Holy Scriptures into the Georgian language he deposited a copy of it in the Iberian or Georgian monastery at Mount Athos. On receipt of this information Pinkerton asked Prince Galitzin, president of the Russian Bible Society, to write to the Iberian monastery at Mount Athos and ascertain whether such a manuscript still existed. Prince Galitzin complied with his request, and after several months the following answer was returned :

'According to the request of your Highness, I have made proper search in the library of this monastery. I have found different books in the Georgian language, of which some are written on parchment and others on paper.

'For a very long time we were entirely ignorant of their contents, having no knowledge of the Georgian language. It is only between four or five years that a Georgian monk, named Laurentius, visited this monastery, whom we requested to examine these works, and it is from his testimony and explication that the annexed catalogue has been prepared.

'Among the said books there are two large volumes of the Old Testament on parchment. We possess also some other manuscripts in the Georgian language, which are not indicated in the catalogue, and of the names of which we are still ignorant.

'Respecting a manuscript of the Bible translated by St. George, the first apostle of Christianity in ancient Iberia, we are entirely ignorant. The manuscript of the Georgian Bible which we possess in our library is in the handwriting of St. Euphemius, the Georgian, the founder and the patron of the Holy Monastery, the Chrysostom of this nation, and the

We did not find these Iberian monks quite so pleasant as those at most of the other monasteries. They seemed to be of rather a lower class, with the exception of the old archimandrite Athanasius : to him and his attendant monk (who after his master's decease was to slip into his easy shoes) we paid a formal visit. The latter was very fond of watches, of which he had several, and so made great friends with O——, as this happens to be *his* particular hobby. I may here notice in passing

first who translated the Old and New Testament into the Georgian language, and who gave to his countrymen translations of other works, and also composed several himself.

'It is impossible for us at present to transcribe these books, as none of us understand the Georgian language ; and it is equally impossible for us to part with the originals mentioned in the catalogue, as the most terrible excommunication and anathemas have, from time immemorial, been pronounced by the Holy Synod and the Patriarchs against those who should dare to carry away, or in any manner whatever dispose of, a single volume of this library : the preservation of it is due to these sage precautions.

'At different periods learned travellers and others have had permission to read these books ; but none of them were ever allowed to carry a single volume out of the monastery.

'From these circumstances your Highness will observe that the only way to attain the laudable and Christian object in view will be to send some persons learned in the Georgian language, in order to take a faithful transcript of the Georgian Bible, or of any of the other manuscripts which may be found salutary or useful.

'When such individuals shall arrive here they shall be fraternally welcomed by us, and we shall do our utmost to afford them every possible facility in order to obtain the desired object.

'(Signed)　Nicephor,
'Librarian of the Iberian Monastery of Mount Athos.
Mount Athos : October 15, 1817.

Thirty-nine Georgian manuscripts were named in the catalogue, mostly on theological subjects, amongst them the Old Testament in two volumes, the Four Gospels, the Acts of the Apostles, the Psalms, the Gospels in the vulgar idiom, the commentaries of St. Chrysostom on St. Matthew's and St. John's Gospels, the works of St. Gregory the Theologue, the discourses and moral maxims of St. Basil the Great, the autograph works of St. Euphemius the Georgian.

See the *Sixteenth Report of the British and Foreign Bible Society*, 1820.

.that in the clock tower of the monastery is an ancient clock of Venetian or Genoese construction, probably one of the earliest timepieces in existence. It has no pendulum, but an escapement somewhat resembling that of a verge watch ; this, having been broken, was fastened to the beam above by two wires.

O— asked one of the monks how it went, and jokingly suggested it might lose an hour in a week. ' Oh, yes,' replied the monk, not at all astonished, ' quite that.'

The night before our departure from Iveron we devoted the time after supper to extracting information about the monastery from one of the epitropoi. I use the word ' extracting ' advisedly ; it is necessary to use the ' screw ' before you can get statistics out of an Oriental.

Iveron has 200 monks,[1] who now follow the idiorrhythmic rule. There are sixty lay servants. Like Vatopedi, this monastery is governed by three epitropoi, or rather by two epitropoi and a dicaios, or prior, who ranks as an epitropos ; also by a deliberative assembly of the *proestamenoi* (προεστάμενοι). These are the ' aristocracy ' of the place, being the oldest and richest of the monks, and correspond, I presume, to the synaxis at Vatopedi. As at Vatopedi, the epitropoi are the executive of this assembly. The community possesses lands in Macedonia, Thrace, Thasos, and, I believe, in Georgia also. Two monasteries in Moldavia and Vallachia formerly belonged to Iveron, from which it received an annual income of about 2,400*l*. These were lost in 1865.

We somehow missed seeing the relics when we

[1] A hundred and seventy of these are Greeks.

visited the catholicon ; so I asked the chief epitropos, through Angelos, to give me a list of the principal ones. I thought the question harmless, but the old gentleman became huffy and said that all their relics were ' principal ;' there was no difference between them, obstinately refusing to give us any further information. Whether Angelos had misinterpreted my question, or whether the epitropos thought we were going to scoff, I cannot tell.   Seeing that something was the matter, we did not press him further.

I may here mention that in each monastery the key of the outer gate is brought to the superior every evening at sunset, after which hour no one is admitted within the walls except under very special circumstances. The great key of Iveron was brought to the epitropos as we were sitting with him before supper.   It measures nine and a half inches in length.

CHAPTER XI.

Amidst the grove that crowns yon tufted hill,
Which, were it not for many a mountain nigh
Rising in lofty ranks, and loftier still,
Might well itself be deem'd of dignity,
The convent's white walls glisten fair on high :
Here dwells the caloyer ; nor rude is he,
Nor niggard of his cheer the passer-by
To welcome still ; nor heedless will he flee
From hence, if he delight kind Nature's sheen to see.

Childe Harold.

Friday, August $\frac{17}{5}$. We started early for Philotheou,
and had a charmingly pretty ride to that monastery.
It is some distance inland (about three miles), being a
thousand feet above the sea-level, but it commands an
extensive view of the Strymonic gulf with the island
of Thasos in the distance. We reached Philotheou a
little before eleven o'clock, and were received in the
usual manner, i.e. with bells and procession. Having
had nothing wherewith to fortify the inner man that
morning, except some Turkish coffee and dry bread,
we were naturally ravenous, but had to wait a very
long time whilst our dinner was being prepared. So,
much against the will of the Archbishop, who hated
anything like energy, we determined upon visiting the
catholicon and the library beforehand. The former
contains a remarkable picture of the Blessed Virgin,
to my mind the finest specimen of the Byzantine school
on Athos. The Mother is represented in the act of

L

kissing the Child, whose arm hangs down naturally.
It is attributed to the great Evangelist-painter, and
is called the Glykophilousa (Γλυκοφιλοῦσα), or the
Sweetly-kissing One. Like the Portaïtissa, it was thrown
into the sea at the time of the iconoclasts, and being
wafted to Athos was brought ashore by the fathers.
Where it landed a spring gushed forth. This spring
still exists, but we had no time to visit it, as it is some
way from the monastery. It is represented in the print
of the monastery which was given to us by the monks,
as being on the shore, close to the port. This icon
is placed against the north-east pillar which supports
the dome.

The catholicon is dedicated to the Annunciation.
In ancient times the convent itself was called the
Monastery of the Annunciation, and not Philotheou;
at least so the monks say. There are two paracclesia,
dedicated to the Forerunner and the Archangels.[1]

As usual, stalls run round the whole church, including the narthex, and the walls are frescoed. These were
repainted in 1765. In the esonarthex, which is particularly large, is a curious fresco, on the north wall
near a small doorway, representing a monk nailed to a
cross; the Seven Deadly Sins are shooting arrows at
him, whilst an angel appears above holding out to him
a crown of glory. On the breast of the monk is this
inscription: καρδίαν καθαρὰν κτίσον ἐν ἐμοί, ὦ Θεὸς
('Make me a clean heart, O God'). Truly a touching emblem of the monastic life, which even in these

---

[1] The catholicon measures 33 feet from iconostasis to the west wall
of nave; across the nave from north to south, 28 feet, or, across transepts,
39 feet. The esonarthex measures 22½ feet from east to west; the sanctuary is 13 feet in breadth, and 13½ feet from iconostasis to the east end
of the apse.

solitudes is exposed to the temptations of the flesh and the devil, although the world may have been renounced and left behind for ever. In the exonarthex are frescoes representing scenes from the Apocalypse. All over the Holy Mountain one finds that these frescoes have suffered curious mutilations. Whilst the figures of the saints have escaped, those of the devils have been scratched, cut about, and frequently have had their eyes gouged out. This was done by the Turkish soldiers, 3,000 of whom were quartered on the monasteries from 1821 to 1830.[1] These infidels, whilst respecting the Christian saints as holy men or dervishes, who might do them harm if insulted, vented their wrath on the fiends, so that at the time of our visit there was hardly a single devil that had had the good luck to escape with an uninjured face. No doubt all will be gradually restored to their pristine ugliness.

The chief relics preserved in the catholicon are a portion of the True Cross, the right hand of St. Chrysostom,[2] and a bone of St. Marina. The principal books in the library are an uncial manuscript in quarto, containing part of the Gospels (imperfect), of the eighth century, another manuscript of the Gospels with fine full-page illuminations of the Four Evangelists, and one of the twelfth century written in double columns with one or two small illuminations and bound in red velvet. There are also two rolls of the fourteenth century, containing the liturgy of St. Basil.

---

[1] During the War of Independence Athos wavered between patriotism and gratitude to the Turks, who had loyally kept their promises since the conquest. The monks finally determined to remain neutral, but the Turks quartered troops upon the monasteries as a precaution.

[2] This relic was given to the monastery by the Emperor Andronicus II. in the year 1284.—*Muralt.*

Having completed our investigations of the catholicon and the library, we asked for the long-expected repast, but were told that it would not be ready for another half-hour at the least; so we determined to occupy the time by taking a photograph of the monastery. We crossed a pretty little paddock bounded by a rivulet which trickled under the trees, forming a scene which reminded us of a bit of English meadowland. Having ascended the side of the hill and planted our camera

MONASTERY OF PHILOTHEOU.

in a vineyard, we obtained a fair view of the monastery. Carefully focussing the picture, we handed over the remainder of the process to the Archbishop's care, and he acquitted himself nobly, to his great content.

Dinner came at last, and very acceptable it was; for my part I could almost have eaten an octopus alive, but we had nothing to complain of in the fare provided for us. Afterwards we sat on the divan drinking the *epilecanion* (ἐπιλεκάνιον)—literally, 'the wine drunk after the dishes '—and coffee. This epilecanion is generally a strong, sweet wine, different from that which is drunk during dinner; it is brought to the divan after every meal.

The two epitropoi, the archimandrites Eustratius and Simeon, were well-educated and pleasant men; the former had been in England. We had a long and interesting conversation with them, chiefly about unity and the Anglican Church. Our photographs of the Archbishop of Canterbury and English churches were much appreciated, and our prelate of Cavalla described his impressions of the liturgy of St. Gregory Dialogos. Altogether we spent a very pleasant day at Philotheou, and should have stayed longer but that we heard, to our dismay, that this was the very night when the monks of Athos celebrate the liturgy on the top of the Holy Mountain in the little chapel of the Transfiguration. The Feast of the Transfiguration is kept on the same day as in our own Church, i.e. on August 6.

We had timed our departure from England so as to allow of our being present at this special service; but somehow or other, partly through carelessness, partly through the difference between the old and new styles, we had miscalculated the day. We resolved on making a supreme effort to get to the Lavra in time, so at once ordered the mules to be got ready, and started from Philotheou at 2.30 P.M.

Before proceeding, I had better give the particulars concerning this monastery.

Philotheou is an idiorrhythmic convent, containing fifty monks and twenty servants. Some think that the founders were Leo II., King of Kachetia, and his son Alexander II., who succeeded him on the throne. Leo reigned from 1520 to 1574, and was twenty-five years of age in 1531, when the monastery is said to have been founded. Alexander was only four at that time, so he must have finished what his father had begun.[1] The monks informed us that it was founded before the ninth century, when it was called simply the Monastery of the Annunciation, but that between that time and the tenth century it was restored by a certain Patriarch of Constantinople called Philotheos, from whom it derived its present name. John Comnenus says that it was built by three men called Arsenius, Philotheos, and Dionysius before the twelfth century, and repaired by Leo, King of Kachetia (Leo I. ?), and his son Alexander in the year from Adam 7000. On the whole I think we may admit that the monastery was founded in early times,[2] either by Philotheos alone or by the three above-mentioned persons, that Leo II. rebuilt it, or perhaps refounded it, in 1531, and that Alexander I. finished his father's work ; the connection of these two kings with the monastery is an historical fact.

Philotheou was entirely burnt in 1871, with the exception of the catholicon. The restoration is now nearly completed. It possesses lands in Thasos and Cassandra, and fourteen kellia on the Holy Mountain. The following is a list of the churches attached to it :

Esocclesia.

1. The catholicon, dedicated to the Annunciation ; containing two paracclesia, dedicated to the Forerunner and the Archangels.
2. St. Chrysostom.
3. St. Nicholas.
4. St. Marina.
5. The Five Martyrs.

---

[1] Brosset, *Histoire de la Géorgie.*   [2] See second note on page 147.

Exocclesia.

1. All Saints.
2. The Three Hierarchs (SS. Basil, Chrysostom, and Gregory)
3. Nativity of the Blessed Virgin.
4. The Prophet Elias.
5. St. Anthony.[1]

We wished to ride direct to the Lavra, passing by Caracalla in order to save time; but the Archbishop said that it was not the custom to take the mules of one monastery beyond the next convent, and that, as the Lavra was many hours' ride, it would not be fair to ask our kind hosts to break through the ordinary rule. So we arranged to ride to Caracalla, obtain fresh mules from that monastery as soon as possible, and then proceed on our journey.

It took us about thirty-five minutes to reach Caracalla, the road quickly descending through woodlands under the shade of splendid chestnuts and beeches. We had sent on word from Philotheou that we wished to have the mules ready for us on our arrival, but of course they were not forthcoming, so, much against our will, we went upstairs and had glyko and coffee. The room in which we were received was circular with a very low divan round the walls. We told the monks of our anxiety to get to the Lavra in time to make the ascent of the peak that night. This, they said, was impossible, but they would do their best to hasten us on our journey by sending us by sea, which route would save us considerable time. So, telling the

---

[1] The great founder of monasticism. Born A.D. 250 in Egypt, of wealthy parents, at the age of eighteen he sold all that he had and gave to the poor, retiring to the awful solitudes of the Thebaid. After exerting an extraordinary influence over the Christian world, he died at the advanced age of 105 years.

monks that we should return to Caracalla before leaving the Holy Mountain, we mounted our mules and rode down to the port of the monastery in half an hour. We embarked in a tolerably large rowing-boat, putting all our luggage at the bottom to serve as ballast.

The sea was by no means smooth, and the Archbishop was evidently unaccustomed to the billowy deep. He was sitting by my side on one of the portmanteaux, and at each large wave he clutched me tightly by the knee. Angelos having explained to him that I was acquainted with the art of swimming, I felt tolerably certain that in case of a disaster he intended to hang on to my leg. Very soon, however, the prelate had the laugh. Like him, the sea had filled me with apprehensions, though of a different kind, and after about twenty minutes' tossing I withdrew to a more retired position in the stern of the boat. 'Voilà,' said the Archbishop to O—, in great glee, 'il est malade! Ha! ha! la mer n'est pas bonne pour *lui*!' And my unfeeling fellow-travellers joined in giving vent to considerable merriment at my expense.

Between Caracalla and the Lavra there existed formerly a Latin monastery containing orthodox[1] monks, who came originally from Amalfi. Mouravieff says, 'I saw in an Athos deed, bearing the date of 1169, a Latin inscription of the Amalfitan hegoumenos.'[2]

The ruins of this monastery still, it is said, exist.. We heard nothing about it at Athos, but we made no inquiries, not being at that time aware of its having had an existence. O— maintains that as we passed

---

[1] De Vogüé says that this convent, Omorphonô, was founded at the instigation of Pope Innocent III. to latinize Athos (*Syrie, Palestine, Mont-Athos.* Paris, 1878).

[2] See *Christian Remembrancer* for 1851.

along the shore he saw a ruined tower, which the monks said was a ruined monastery, but of which they did not tell him the name. Ruined towers and Latin monasteries had no seductions for me at that time ; the only thing I cared about was to see the port of the Lavra.

At last we reached the port, or 'arsenal,' having been two hours and a half on the voyage. Here it was that Curzon landed on the Holy Mountain in 1837.

PORT OF THE LAVRA.

The landing-place is charmingly pretty. The entrance is very narrow, not more than fifteen feet from rock to rock; below water it must be as narrow as ten. On your right as you enter is a small castle with a massive square tower in the midst. One can easily picture to one's self the stout defence it must have made in days gone by against the pirates who swarmed in these seas, how the valiant monks with their lay brethren would man the walls, and how a shower of arrows, and perhaps ball and Greek fire too, would be directed towards the aggressors from every loophole and battlement. Now all is changed, and though the little drawbridge is still raised every evening, through old custom, everything around has slumbered peacefully for the last hundred years. Projecting rooms with low roofs are built on the top of the walls, as at the monasteries, and the building is inhabited by two or three old monks, who divide their time between prayer, cultivating their vegetables, and fishing in the sea. The little schooner belonging to the Lavra, clean and trim, lies securely at her moorings inside the breakwater, and besides the castle there is a boathouse in which the monks keep their tackling and appliances for fishing.

We landed, and, as I still felt ill, I left the party to go up to the Lavra with the luggage, whilst I sat down to rest under the mulberry trees, which with figs and olives grow down to the water's edge. After about a quarter of an hour I partially recovered, and passing the Byzantine castle walked up a long and steep lane, paved with large stones and planted on each side with trees, the tops of which nearly met over the road. Presently the great monastery appeared above me, stretching for an immense distance along the hillside and surrounded with a high wall flanked with many towers. It was getting dusk as I entered the gate and made my way to the room where the Archbishop and O— were being received. Supper was soon served, but I could not touch a morsel, and so put up my levinge, and not long afterwards fell asleep. All our haste had been thrown away; under any circumstances I could not have made the ascent of the mountain that night. O— tried to start, but the monks said it would be impossible to go until morning, even though a bright moon was shining. As we afterwards found, they were quite right; the path was too difficult to have been attempted by moonlight.

Our room at the Lavra was of considerable proportions, being at least forty feet by thirty, and was a good specimen of the better class of rooms at the Athos monasteries. It projected over the outside walls of the convent for about six feet, this part being constructed entirely of timber and supported by brackets of the same material. Windows through which there was a beautiful view of the sea occupied the whole of the front of this overhanging portion, and two other windows were inserted in the sides of the six-feet projection. There was a divan round three sides of the room, the central portion along the window side being the place of honour. Cushions were placed at intervals along the divan, and the floor was covered with matting. In the centre of the room stood a small table, and I think there were three common chairs. But there was one other feature of this apartment which is so characteristic of Athos rooms that I must not omit to mention it. On the side opposite the windows a portion of the room—say, six feet in width—was cut off by a screen going straight across from wall to wall, having a balustrade at the bottom, with open spaces between pillars above. This forms a sort of anteroom or vestibule; the matting does not begin till you enter the room proper, generally by a step through an archway in the centre of the screen; here it was that Angelos used to pull off my high riding-boots and produce my pair of red Turkish slippers when we entered the reception room of any monastery ; for, as it is customary to put your feet upon the divan, it is considered polite to remove your dirty boots beforehand. The Archbishop used to sit cross-legged on the cushions, a feat which causes the average European excruciating agony, so we used to compromise the matter by lounging on our elbows, after the manner of the ancient Romans at their meals. The walls are usually quite bare, and were so here, plastered and whitewashed. A shelf about six feet from the floor runs round the room, and there is generally a photograph of the Patriarch of Constantinople ; sometimes, though rarely, other pictures.

We were waited upon by the most inquisitive man it has ever been my unhappy lot to fall in with. He was a young and rather good-looking monk, with a pale face and dark hair. None of our possessions escaped his attention. If I went to my portmanteau he would follow for the purpose of scrutinizing its contents, and a dirty hand would undertake a voyage of discovery amongst my clean linen. If I produced any article, such as a tooth brush, for instance, he would ask, ‘ What is it ? ’ and when I explained its use would exclaim, ‘ Kyrie eleison ! ’ [1] in his astonishment at the wonderful Frank inventions. If I took up a book he would come and look over my shoulder and finally take it out of my hand, saying, ‘ What is it ? what is it ? ’ and proceed to read it, as likely as not upside down. For some little time he amused us by his naïve simplicity and childishness, but at last our patience became exhausted and we cast about for some plan to rid us of our

---

[1] This is a frequent exclamation amongst the monks, and exactly answers to the ‘ Lawk-a-mussy ! ’ of our lower orders in England.

tormentor. O— suggested a good dose out of the medicine chest, and I remembered that I had a box of very strong and large pills, covered with gold and silver leaf, labelled ' Native,' which I had had specially made the year before to please and astonish the natives of Persia ; for when you are travelling in the East you are constantly asked for medicine. ' Now,' thought I, ' a nice dose of two, or even three, of those boluses will do our friend a world of good ; he won't know whether he is on his head or his heels the next morning, and he will be for ever cured of meddling with Frankish things. Besides he is quite young enough to be able to learn manners.' So we opened the portmanteaux and searched for the pill-box, our friend taking the greatest interest in the proceedings, little knowing what was in store for him. We could not find the box anywhere, although we pulled out all our things, to the young monk's huge delight, in our efforts to find it. Then we turned to the basket and searched high and low for it, but without success.

'What a nuisance,' said O—, 'to have brought that box so far with us (I am sure I saw it at the last monastery), and then to have lost it just when we wanted it !'

However, we certainly had lost it, and we began to think that our little practical joking was at an end, when I suddenly remembered that we possessed a bottle containing a powerful solution of ammonia, that I had had made of more than usual strength before starting, for the purpose of applying to the bites of mosquitoes and other venomous insects. Being anxious that my friend should fall into his own trap, I took the bottle out of the case, which was lying on the

table, withdrew the stopper, and applied my nose to it,
shutting my eyes and pretending to inhale the marvellous perfume.   Quick as thought the monk was at my
elbow.   '*Ti ene?*' said he, as he snatched the bottle
out of my hand.   I made no reply, but simply gave it
over to him.   He took a prodigious sniff, and I verily
believe thought at first that his head was off!   The
tears streamed from his eyes, while he choked and
gasped for breath. ' Ky-ky-kyrie eleison ! ' how strong
it was!   Angelos, who was present at the time, thoroughly enjoyed the joke and shouted with laughter at
the monk's discomfiture, and the latter joined in the
merriment when he found that he was not seriously
injured after all, and begged me to lend him the
wonderful bottle (which he handled very carefully),
as he wished to play the same trick on some of his
brother monks.   He caught two or three most successfully, but by this time Angelos had spread the story
round the monastery, and I have no doubt the joke
against him was not easily forgotten.

At 3 P.M. on the day after our arrival we took a
walk in the neighbourhood of the convent in the company of Angelos, who carried the photographic apparatus, for we hoped to take a good view of the monastic
buildings from the mountain-side.   The Lavra is some
height above the sea, about three-quarters of a mile
from the shore, and is situated at the south-east corner
of the promontory, at the very foot of the mountain.
We climbed past a mill, which is worked in a manner
sufficiently curious to be described.   There are no per-
manent streams at Athos of sufficient power to work a
waterwheel, so the monks have hit upon the following
device.   A reservoir to contain the water which runs

down from the hills in little rivulets has been built just above the mill. When the latter is to be worked, a sluice is opened in the side of the reservoir, and the water is allowed to escape down a steep gully to the wheel. Thus the extent of the fall is taken advantage of, so as to economise the water, very little of which is spent in driving the wheel.

A short distance above the reservoir is a kelli, and on the verandah of this little house stood an old man,

THE LAVRA.

who, we perceived, was beckoning and shouting an invitation in Romaic. Anxious to see the inside of a kelli, we went up to the old fellow, who said that he was the archimandrite Simeon, expressed himself highly gratified at the honour we were doing him, and showed us what a fine view of the Lavra could be obtained from his verandah. So we brought the camera to this wooden balcony, which groaned and creaked most ominously as we walked over the rotten timbers. ' Don't be afraid,' said old Simeon ; 'if you take care not to stand too close together the balcony won't give way.' Angelos wisely remained inside whilst we arranged the camera and took the photograph. Our cheery old host brought out glyko and coffee, and we talked to him about his little property. He had bought the life tenancy of the kelli from the Lavra, and with it the fifteen stremmata of land attached to it. Three young monks lived with him as his servants, and the vegetables from their garden, added to the fish they caught in the sea, enabled them all to subsist together comfortably and contentedly.

Like most tenants the archimandrite had a grumble against his landlords, and, as we considered, a fair one. ' They won't put my balcony in order,' said he ; ' I am always telling them that it will come down some fine day, for I sha'n't do anything to it.'

However, he thought it might last out his lifetime, and if he does not ask too many young Englishmen with their fat dragomans to call on him I dare say it will. We asked our host if we might see the little church attached to his kelli, and, being infirm and the staircase steep and rickety, he directed his younger brethren to escort us thither. We went into the garden and thence to the church—an offshoot, as it were, from the house. Picking our way through the onions and other vegetables stored on the floor of the narthex, we entered the building, which was dedicated to St. Athanasius (of Athos ?). It had old paintings on the iconostasis, and a few stasidia, or stalls, round the walls. The old archimandrite managed to get down to the garden by the time we left the church, and as a parting gift presented us with two large and ripe pears. So we bade adieu to our new friend and returned to the monastery, which I will here describe as best I can.

It is surrounded, like Vatopedi, by high and strong walls, with towers at intervals, several of which have escaped the levelling process. These towers and part of the walls are battlemented ; the rest of the walls are built upon, with overhanging rooms, as at the other

COURTYARD OF THE LAVRA.

monasteries. There is but one entrance, defended by several iron doors ; and a porch, consisting of a dome supported by four marble columns, stands in front of the outer gate. I may here mention that only very great people ride up to the gate of a monastery ; you descend from your mule at a longer or shorter distance from the entrance, according to your rank.

Inside the Lavra is a confused mass of buildings of every shape and size ; even those which surround the court are built of various heights and patterns, with roofs of different pitch and level ; here a balcony pro-

M

jects, there a verandah or an arcade breaks the surface
of the wall ; and in the centre of the quadrangle (if
one may apply that word to an inclosure which is
made up of angles) are churches, domestic offices,
trees, and fountains, dotted about in picturesque con-
fusion. There are no blank walls or pavements; all
is cut up into little courts and nooks and corners,
casting well-defined lights and shadows under the
Eastern sky, enough to make this ancient monastery
a very paradise for artists. It has never been burnt,
and this accounts to a great extent for its picturesque
irregularity.

The name of the monastery is derived from the
word λαύρα, meaning a *lane* or *street between houses*.
Readers of ecclesiastical history will remember that
this was the ancient name for a monastery, signifying
that it was but a collection of separate houses or cells,
where individual monks lived, a sort of town of
hermits. Whether this was the first monastery, properly so called, on Athos, in which the independent
monks were gathered together between four walls,
and so received the name of *the* Lavra, or whether it
was dignified with the title on account of its superior
size and wealth, is a disputed point amongst travellers.
Some think that its founder, St. Athanasius of Athos
(of whom more presently), was the first who ever built
a monastery on the Holy Mountain. As he lived in
the tenth century, this would falsify many of the early
traditions of the place ; and since the Monastery of
Xeropotamou is known to have been *restored* by the
Emperor Romanus Lecapenus in 924,[1] about forty
years before St. Athanasius founded the Lavra, this

---

[1] Tozer's *Highlands of Turkey*, vol. i. p. 133.

fact proves that at least one convent existed before his time. Probably the early history of Athos will never have much light thrown on it, and we must be content with going back only so far as the tenth century for our earliest historical character of whose existence and connection with Athos there can be no manner of doubt.

St. Athanasius the Athonite was a Georgian by nation, who came from Trebizonde to Mount Athos about the year 950, and founded the Lavra in 963 or 964, chiefly at the expense of the Emperor Nicephorus Phocas, to whom the saint had foretold a victory over the Saracens. It is said that Nicephorus had some thoughts of retiring to Athos himself, but the purple proved to have superior attractions for him. In other respects this emperor, though he seems to have been a religious man in spite of Gibbon's insinuation of insincerity, was an enemy to the monasteries, forbidding their foundation and enacting a sort of Byzantine Statute of Mortmain. He also had a weakness for keeping bishoprics and other preferments vacant for a considerable time, during which he enjoyed their revenues, a trick not uncommon with temporal rulers of the Church. But the founder of the Lavra died with a prayer for pardon on his lips (' O God, grant me Thy mercy') when he was foully assassinated on December 10, 969—'a brave soldier, an able general, and, with all his defects, one of the most virtuous men and conscientious sovereigns that ever occupied the throne of Constantinople.'[1] John Zimiskes, the murderer of Nicephorus and his successor on the imperial throne, is said to have

[1] Finlay's *History of Greece*, vol. ii. p. 334.

enriched the Lavra, and long afterwards Neagulus, Hospodar of Moldo-Vallachia, bestowed benefactions upon it.

Many are the stories told of the illustrious St. Athanasius the Athonite, of the wonders that he wrought and the visions vouchsafed to him, and how the Virgin Mother used to appear to him and aid him in his work. Once, when disheartened at his difficulties and despairing of the welfare of the monastery, he resolved to abandon his design and resume his old hermit's life ; so turning his back upon the house he set out to seek some retired spot, where he could devote his time to religion, undisturbed by worldly cares and temporal affairs. But God barred his way, as He did the path of Balaam, for as he went the Mother of God herself appeared to him, demanding of him why he had fled the Lavra ; and when Athanasius replied that he and his monks lacked the necessaries of life, she told him to return and all should be supplied. The saint, astonished at this command from a woman, inquired who she was. ' I am the Mother of Jesus Christ,' replied St. Mary. But St. Athanasius, having had already not a few dealings with the old enemy, that ' *tortuosus serpens*,' answered, ' Pardon me, O Lady, if I do not believe before I see a sign ; for many are the snares of Satan.' So the Holy Virgin bade him take his staff and strike a rock at the side of the path in the form of a cross and in the name of the All Holy Trinity, that so, by the grace of her Son, water would gush forth. He did so, and from the stone poured streams of water, clear as crystal, which since that day have never ceased to flow. Then St. Athanasius, perceiving the finger of

God, was not disobedient unto the heavenly vision, but turning back again remained at the Lavra till the day of his death.[1]

One hundred and seventy monks belong to this monastery, who follow the idiorrhythmic rule : their numbers seem to have increased by thirty during the last fifty years. There are also a hundred lay servants. It possesses land in Lemnos, Imbros, Scyros, Thrace, and Macedonia. There are three sketes attached to it—St. Anne and the Prodromos, both of which will be described later on, and the Capsocalyvi (καυσο-καλύβι), dedicated to the Holy Trinity. This skete acquired its odd name, literally ' The Burnt Cottage,' in this manner : Long ago there lived on Athos a certain holy man, by name Maximus, who, not being content with the ordinary hermit's life, used to construct a little temporary hut or booth, in which he would spend a year, and then setting fire to it would migrate to another place, where he would build himself another. The skete was founded in the year 1745, on the site of one of the temporary habitations of this good hermit. We did not visit it, but were informed by the secretary of the Holy Synod, Dimopoulos of Vatopedi, that the Capsocalyvi was larger than the skete of St. Demetrius, which contains fifty monks and will be hereafter noticed.

The monastery possesses five cathismata and forty kellia, besides the calyvia attached to the three sketes. The government is entrusted to the assembly of the proestamenoi and two epitropoi, who at the time of our visit were the monks Gabriel and Nicandros. There

---

[1] John Comnenus, Προσκυνητάριον. Georgirenes, *Present State of Samos, &c.*

are nineteen churches within the walls and five without, as follows :

Esocclesia.

1. The catholicon, St. Athanasius of Athos; contains two paracclesia, the Forty Martyrs and St. Nicholas.
2. St. Athanasius of Athos.
3. St. Nicholas.
4. The Holy Unmercenaries.
5. The Assumption of Our Lady.
6. St. Stephen Protomartyr.
7. The Panaghia Coucouzelissa.
8. The Holy Trinity.
9. The Forerunner.
10. St. George.
11. St. John the Divine.
12. St. Basil.
13. All Saints.
14. St. Michael, Bishop of Sunadon.
15. St. Modestus.
16. St. Charalampes.
17. St. Theodore.
18. The Archangels.
19. St. Onouphrius.

Exocclesia.

1. St. Gregory.
2. The Prophet Elias.
3. St. Paraskeue.[1]
4. The Holy Apostles.
5. The Holy Unmercenaries.

This last church is about half an hour from the Lavra, and is said to have been built by St. Athanasius

---

[1] St. Paraskeue, or St. Friday, to translate her name into English, called after the day of the week upon which she was born, suffered martyrdom by decapitation in the year of our Salvation 140, on her refusal to worship idols. She is reported to have employed to the heathen the answer recommended by Jeremiah : ' The gods that have not made the heavens and the earth, even they shall perish from the earth and from under these heavens.'

in the space of twenty-four hours, after it had been repeatedly destroyed by devils during the nights of its construction. A picture representing this miracle is in the church of the Panaghia Coucouzelissa.

The catholicon [1] is remarkable in that the central dome is not supported by the usual four pillars. The narthex is divided by two columns into a quasi-esonarthex and exonarthex. All the frescoes in the narthex were repainted in the worst possible taste in 1852. The brazen doors, however, leading from the narthex into the church are worthy of notice. There is a pronaos, the arches of which are filled with glazed windows. The floor of the church is paved with various marbles. In the transepts above the stalls the walls are decorated with tiles of a blue-green pattern on a white ground. These tiles are continued for four feet above the backs of the stalls; then come the old frescoes, untouched, but almost obliterated by damp and age. Many old icons hang on the walls of the sanctuary, and the apse is furnished with a stone seat round the wall, with the synthronos, or throne of the bishop of the diocese. Over this throne is a painted figure of St. Athanasius, given by John Blantis, a Vallachian prince. At the east end of the apse too is a small marble table which covers the place where St. Athanasius and four workmen fell from the roof and were killed during

---

[1] It measures 35 feet from the iconostasis to west wall of nave, and 55 feet across the transepts. The sanctuary is 20½ feet from iconostasis to east end of the apse, and 17½ from north to south, not including the chapel of the prothesis and the diaconicon. The narthex measures 26½ feet from east to west, and 36½ from north to south, exclusive of the two paracclesia of the Forty Martyrs and St. Nicholas, which are situated, the former on the north, the latter on the south side of the nave and narthex of the central church. The total width of the narthex, including the paracclesia, is 79 feet.

the building of the church. I cannot find any account
of St. Athanasius's death besides this, which the monks
affirmed to be the true story. An ancient cross of
silver gilt studded with precious stones stands behind
the holy table. The metal work is plain, with medallions
of saints at the extremities of the arms and one representing Christ in the centre. It measures three feet
eight inches in height (not including the staff), and two
feet four and a half inches across. Its metal surface
is inscribed with the verse from the Psalms :

Through Thee will we overthrow our enemies, and in Thy Name
will we tread them under that rise up against us.'[1] Ps. xliv. 6 (Sept.
Ver. xliii. 6).

On each side of the holy doors is an icon, one of
Christ, the other of the Blessed Virgin. These pictures,
with the exception of the faces, which are painted, are
composed of worked silver set with precious stones of
large size and are particularly fine. They were presented to the monastery by the Emperor Michael
(Andronicus ?) Palæologus. First amongst the relics
preserved in this church is a large piece of the Holy
Cross, measuring no less than seven inches in length ;
it is arranged in the form of a double cross,

and is contained in a truly magnificent reliquary. This
splendid case, oblong in shape, measuring $17\frac{1}{2} \times 11\frac{1}{4}$
inches, is of gold set with rows of precious stones,
rubies, pearls, emeralds, and enamelled medallions ;

---

[1] 'Εν σοὶ τοὺς ἐχθροὺς ἡμῶν κερατιοῦμεν, καὶ ἐν τῷ ὀνόματί σου ἐξουδενώσομεν
τοὺς ἐπανισταμένους ἡμῖν.

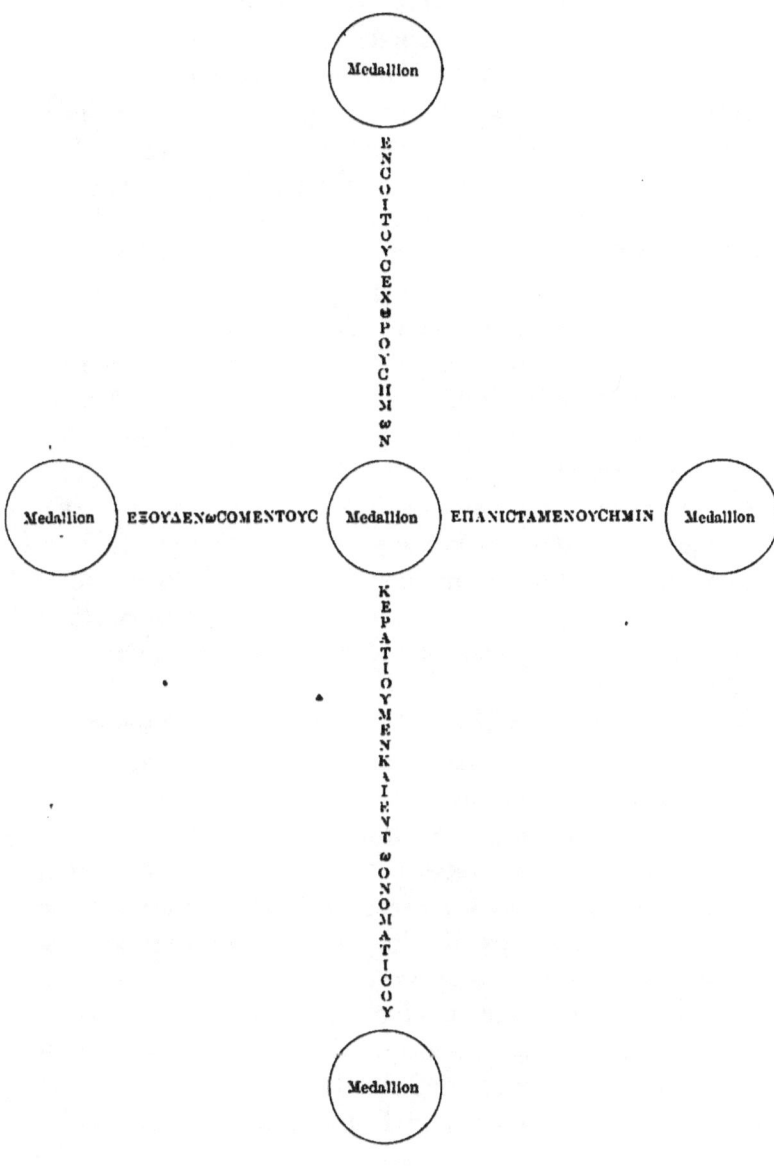

eight rows one way and twelve the other, making
ninety-six jewels and enamels in all. Four enormous
heart-shaped pearls are disposed amongst the rest
towards the corners; the two largest measure respec-
tively $1\frac{1}{2}$ and $1\frac{5}{8}$ of an inch across. This priceless
shrine, well worthy of the precious relic on which the
Christian cannot gaze without emotion, was given by
the Emperor Nicephorus, the patron of St. Athanasius
and co-founder of the monastery.

Here also are preserved the head of the great St.
Basil and the left hand of St. Chrysostom;[1] also an
icon of the Holy Child set in a fine enamelled frame,
said to have belonged to the Empress Theodora,
and an icon of St. John the Divine, painted on a composition of wax and resin, and mounted in a rich
frame with ten medallions of saints round it; this
was presented to the monastery by the Emperor John
Zimiskes. In the north-west corner of the paracclesia
of the Forty Martyrs is the tomb of St. Athanasius
the Athonite.

From the catholicon and the tomb of St. Athanasius
we were taken to see the church dedicated to his
honour. Here are preserved two staves and a cross,
all of which belonged to him. The latter is a thick
and solid piece of wood, cut into the shape of a cross
and mounted in silver; it is attached to a massive iron
collar, and must weigh altogether about five pounds.
The staves are plain iron rods; one, crutch-topped,
measures 4 feet $1\frac{1}{2}$ inch in length; the other, which ends
in a small cross, is rather larger, 4 feet $7\frac{1}{2}$ inches; with
this the saint commanded devils.

There is another church in the courtyard near the

[1] See p. 147.

gate, into which we strolled with our attendant monks. Seeing an icon in it which, from the offerings suspended from it, I knew to be looked upon as miraculous, I pointed it out to the company and asked them if this were not the case. '*Malista*,' said they, 'it is indeed miraculous; that is the holy icon of the Panaghia Coucouzélissa, to whom this church is dedicated.'

'Panaghia *what*?' said I, taken aback by the strange epithet.

'Coucouzélissa,' replied the monks.

'Oh, indeed!' said I. 'Well, how did it get that extraordinary name?'

'That was the holy icon,' said a monastic spokesman, 'before which the great John Coucouzele[1] used to sing.'

'And who was he?'

'What!' replied the monks in the greatest astonishment; 'what, not know John Coucouzele!'

'No,' said I with great diffidence, for the good monks looked at me so reproachfully. 'I'm quite ashamed of my ignorance : of course I ought to know all about him; but I really never heard of him before.'

'Well,' quoth the chief spokesman in a compassionate tone, 'I will tell you the story. This holy man was the chief singer at the emperor's palace at Constantinople.'

'When?' asked O—.

The good monk looked slightly put out at this interruption, and some conversation ensued amongst the brethren, all of course speaking at once, which ended in the reply that they didn't know—how should they?— and nobody knew, but that it was certainly a very, very

[1] Pronounced as if it were written in English *Coocoozdylee*.

long time ago, *palia ! palia !* and that the date was of
no consequence whatever to the story.   So the narrative proceeded.

'As I was saying, Coucouzele was the chief singer
to the great emperor, for he had a very beautiful voice.
Now one day he was singing a *canon* before the holy
icon of the Panaghia in the chapel of the palace, when
the icon spoke and said, 'You do very well, John
Coucouzele, in singing before my picture ; sing on, John
Coucouzele, and here is a medal for you ;' and lo ! the
hand of the icon moved towards John and dropped
into his palm a coin, with which the singer worked
many miracles, and when he died he was numbered
amongst the saints.'

'But,' said I, 'how did the picture come here ?   You
say that the miracle took place at Constantinople.   Did
John Cou-cou-cou—'

'Zele,' said Angelos, prompting me.

'Yes, Coucouzele.   Did he bring it here himself ?
What has he to do with the Agion Oros ?'

Nobody knew much about this point, but the majority thought that he did come to the Holy Mountain
with his picture ; at any rate there *was* the picture, and
what did it matter how it got there ?   O— asked if they
had the wonderful coin, but the monks said no, that was
a great pity, but unfortunately the coin had been lost.

Nothing more could be got out of the monks respecting the saint and his wonderful picture, and on
my return to England I completely failed to find any
mention of him in any book until one day I was turning
over the leaves of a musical primer given to me at the
convent of St. Gregory, when to my great joy I discovered at the end of the book ' The Story of the Life

of the Great Master of the Musical Art, Mr. John Coucouzele,'[1] which occupies four closely printed pages. As this quaint account differs somewhat from that of the monks, at the risk of wearying my readers I will give a short version of it.

'Come hither,' so the story begins, 'come hither, all ye people of the Priests, and listen, all ye of the Rulers, come. and I will tell you things concerning the life of John, surnamed the Coucouzele.' Then it goes on to tell us how John was born in Dyrrachium 'of the first of Justinian' (τῆς πρώτης τῆς Ἰουστινιανῆς)—that is, in the ancient diocese of Justiniana prima,[2] the modern Durazzo, in Albania, on the coast of the Adriatic. No clue is given to the century in which he lived, but it is said that, his father having died, his mother sent him to be educated in religion. Now John, having a very beautiful voice, obtained admission to the imperial school, for such boys as showed promise were educated at the expense of the emperor. Here he surpassed his fellows in knowledge of the musical art and in singing, so that he became the wonder of all that knew him. One day his schoolfellows asked him what he was going to have for dinner, and he, being a poor provincial who only knew the Greek of Dyrrachium, like Chaucer's Prioresse, who spoke French

After the scole of Stratford atte Bowe,

replied ' *Coukia* and *zelia*' (κουκία καὶ ζέλια) ; whence the boys nicknamed him ' Coucouzele.' At last it came to the ears of the emperor that Coucouzele

---

[1] Διήγησις εἰς τὸν βίον τοῦ Μεγάλου Μαΐστορος τῆς Μουσικῆς τέχνης Κυρίου Ἰωάννου τοῦ Κουκουζέλου.

[2] Concerning this diocese, see Bingham, *Antiquities of the Christian Church*, book ix. chap. iv. sec. xii.

was a prodigy of musical learning ; at which he was
delighted, and when he had heard him sing he loved
him, and as a proof of his regard—*compelled him to
marry!* Poor John seems to have been exceedingly
dubious as to the bliss of matrimony, and answered, ' I
pray and beseech your Majesty give me leave to go
home to see my mother, and then the will of God and
the Emperor be done.'

Here the story becomes very obscure. John goes
home and finds his mother weeping and lamenting ;
why, is not clear, for, as she too speaks the Greek of
Dyrrachium, the cause of all her woe is unintelligible.
However, for the benefit of the curious, I will give her
words :

' Μύα δὲ μίλο Ἰωάννῃ γδέμησεν,'

with the assurance that they need not take the
trouble of looking them out in a lexicon. ' I am here,'
cries John, and then they fall upon each other's necks
and there is great rejoicing. After several days Coucouzele returns to the Emperor, who makes him a great
feast. But John cannot get out of his head those words
of his mother, and on thinking over things resolves to
become a monk. Now the abbot, or hegoumenos, of the
Lavra happened to be in Constantinople on business,
and when he left to return to the Holy Mountain,
Coucouzele put on old clothes, and taking a staff
followed him at a distance, having escaped apparently
from the impending marriage, for we hear nothing more
about the wife. When he arrived at Athos he watched
the abbot safely into the Lavra, and then went up to
the door and sat down under the porch. In answer
to the questions of the porter he said that he was very
anxious to be a monk, and that if he were admitted

he would work hard, for he knew how to tend goats. Fortunately for Coucouzele the monastery was in great need of a goatherd, so away runs the porter to the abbot and tells him that there is a goatherd sitting at the gate who craves admission to the order of the monks. The abbot was overcome with joy at the godsend, and bade the porter bring Coucouzele into the Lavra. So our friend John attained his object, and after having been instructed in religion by the hegoumenos was sent to watch over the flocks on the mountain. Meanwhile the Emperor at Constantinople cannot make out what has become of his musician, and searches for him throughout the length and breadth of the empire, but no Coucouzele is to be found.

But one day our friend goes out as usual to tend his flock, and is suddenly seized with a violent desire to sing a psalm; so he looks this way and that, and seeing no one, he breaks forth into one of the ancient melodies of the Church. He was sitting on the top of a high rock, whence he could see a long distance, but, as ill luck would have it, a hermit dwelt in a cave just below him. This old fellow, roused by the ravishing strains which proceeded from the rock above him, thought he heard an angel singing, but on coming out of his cave and looking up he saw the goatherd carolling on his rocky perch, and the goats not straying, but listening, as if spell-bound, to the entrancing music. Coucouzele's fame seems to have reached the hermit, for he immediately made up his mind that this wonderful singer could be no other than he for whom the Emperor had been searching far and wide, so he rushed off to the hegoumenos of the Lavra and brought him to the spot. The abbot taxes Cou-

couzele with his identity, which the goatherd is forced
to acknowledge, and the end of the matter is that the
hegoumenos himself goes to Constantinople and obtains
from the Emperor permission for Coucouzele to remain
as a monk at Athos.   The Emperor accompanies the
hegoumenos back to the Lavra, spends a few pleasant
days on a visit to Coucouzele, and then returns to his
capital.   After this John devotes himself in earnest to
the monastic life, and at last employs his whole time,
night and day, in nothing else but singing psalms and
praying.

Now comes the story of the picture.   One day
during Lent, having been singing, as his custom was,
the praises of the Theotocos, after completing his vigil
he fell asleep as he stood, when the Theotocos appeared
and gave him a gold coin, saying, 'Sing to me, and I
will never leave you.'   Coucouzele awoke, found the
coin in his right hand, and, weeping tears of joy, burst
forth in a hymn to the Mother of God.   He placed
the coin in the church, where it did many wonders,
and he himself from that time forward never left the
church, but remained standing in it, so that one of his
feet mortified and his hand melted away until the
marrow from it dropped to the ground.   But the
Theotocos cured him, saying, 'From henceforth be
thou healed.'   And so he remained till the day of his
death, blessing the Mother of God in hymns and
spiritual songs.   Moreover this man of God foresaw
his death, and made preparation for it, desiring to be
buried in the Church of the Archangel, which he had
built.   Early one morning he departs.

' This is the life of the great Master of Music
and Melody, John the Coucouzele, the second John of

Damascus, whose foot the Theotocos healed and to whom she gave the coin;' so the legend ends with a rhapsody about well-tuned cymbals and loud cymbals, strings and pipes, and the divine David, winding up with a doxology and εἰς τοὺς αἰῶνας τῶν αἰώνων ἀμήν. This seems to be the proper place to discuss the questions which naturally arise in the minds of Western and especially of English travellers. What are we to think of these legends? What attitude are we to take up with regard to them?

Let us take, for instance, the story of John Coucouzcle. It seems clear that there is a mistake somewhere. It is *very improbable*, though not *impossible*, that Our Lady should have given him that coin or medal, the reward of his devotion to her. This episode at least appears to bear the impress of the fabulous. And, again, in the legend of the Gorgoÿpecoös at Docheiariou it is almost incredible that the Blessed Virgin should have made the apparently senseless remark that is attributed to her, those words which are the very foundation of the whole story. Are we, then, to reject altogether legends and miracles such as these?

As a preliminary consideration, I think we may admit that the Greeks are peculiarly given to credulity and superstition, as we Englishmen are prone to unsupernaturalism and scepticism, and also that the virtues of the former are the evangelical virtues—faith, obedience to ecclesiastical authority, and reverence: of the latter, the natural virtues—truthfulness, honesty, and a certain moral integrity, which may, perhaps, be best expressed by the word *uprightness*. The tendency of a Greek is to believe implicitly any supernatural story, however great the demand it makes upon his

N

faith, however absurd it is in its details ; the ordinary Englishman, on the contrary, is likely to reject as superstitious the story of any Divine interference, however trifling, with what he calls the Law of Nature.

The true position lies somewhere between the two extremes, and to reach this mean I would urge the old philosopher's advice on both Greeks and Anglicans, ' Resist your natural tendency and lean towards the opposite extreme,' in the case of an alleged miracle advising the Eastern (maintaining all due respect for authority) to question before believing, and the Western (without abandoning his love of truth) to believe before questioning.   A few words will, I trust, not be thought out of place in consideration of the line a faithful English Churchman ought to take with respect to ecclesiastical miracles and relics in the case of—

    a. One known to be false ;

    b. One probably false ;

    c. A doubtful miracle upon which no additional light can be thrown.

    a. As an example of the first, let us take the alleged miracle of the holy fire at Jerusalem.   An English traveller visits the Church of the Holy Sepulchre on Easter Day.   He sees the fire brought out of the Sepulchre, and knows that it has just been kindled by the Patriarch, and yet sees the enthusiasm of the populace, who believe it to have been sent down from heaven.   What is he to do ?   Clearly he is not bound to treat the circumstance with respect as a Divine interposition, as he knows that the Patriarch himself would admit that the popular belief was false.   Is he, then, to address the people and to endeavour to dissuade them from treating the fire as miraculous ?   Surely not, because not being in authority he has no responsibility in the matter, and would be even totally unable to rectify the popular error ; for the poor people would look upon him very much in the light of a heretic, to whom no credence could be given. Secondly, we are apt to exaggerate the importance of errors such as these. Faith in our Lord and in the doctrines of His Church, coupled with the fruit of good works, will save a man, but the mere knowledge of the truth or falsity of a miraculous story is a matter of curiosity, and not of spiritual life or death. Therefore the exposition of the falsity of the holy fire is not of such importance as to warrant the interference of a Western stranger, who by rooting up this tare is in great danger of pulling up with it the wheat of their respect for religious authority —nay, even of their saving faith—so that the last state shall be worse than the first. If this weed is to be removed at all, it must be done by the tender hands of those labourers who have been called to work in this vineyard of the Lord,• not crushed by the rude foot of the trespasser. Still there is a certain course open to us, which indeed amounts to a duty, and that is to make use of any opportunities that may be afforded us of privately remonstrating with the ecclesiastical authorities and representing to them the mischief such a proceeding causes to the whole Christian world.

b. To illustrate this let us consider the proper attitude with regard to the relic of the gold, incense, and myrrh of the Magi, some of which is said to exist at the Monastery of St Paul. This on calm reflection all must admit to be an extremely doubtful relic, and yet we cannot *prove* its falsity or deny the possibility

of God having ordained that these holy gifts should
have been piously preserved to be a source of edification to His faithful servants throughout these centuries.
I stand before this relic at St. Paul's, and the Church
of the country, whose jurisdiction I recognise, says to
me in the person of the abbot, ' These are the gifts of
the Three Kings.'   Have I a right to refuse reverence
to them, and thus scandalize those who, being convinced of their authenticity, will look upon my action
as a dishonour of holy things ?   Surely charity forbids
such a course.

c. Lastly, in the case of a miracle or relic which
hangs in the balance, and there is no sufficient evidence
obtainable to cause this or that scale to turn ; as is
usual with the majority of relics, the chain of evidence
having been broken in the course of long years : here,
it is clear, we must accept the ruling of the Church
and throw our responsibility upon her.   On the other
hand, if we were in a position of authority we should
never *encourage* a devotion to a doubtful relic or
miracle ; still, if people really believed in it, and it were
impossible to disprove it, we should have no right to
quarrel with them or to forbid what was generally
credited through motives of piety.

To conclude : All miracles and stories of the
supernatural must fall under one of these three
heads :

1. True.
2. False.
3. Partly true, partly false.

Under the last we are probably justified in placing
such a story as that of John Coucouzele.   What is
untrue in such cases we may ascribe to three causes—

1. Exaggeration and accretion in the course of ages ;

2. Excess of faith in attributing all wonderful things to the direct interposition of the Deity ;[1]

3. Absolute falsehood.

The last is, of course, responsible also for those miracles under the second category. And in the case of these it is not the poor people who accept them, or their rulers, who in good faith ratify them, that deserve contempt or blame; but those bad men who for private ends, through pride and covetousness, carried away by the snares of the arch-deceiver, have invented these tales, imposed upon Christ's little flock, and worked a wrong which still cries against them, it may be for centuries after they have crumbled away in the tomb. Verily they have their reward.

---

[1] This excess seems nearer to the mean than the denial to Him of all interference in the natural government of the world He has created.

CHAPTER XII.

THE library of the Lavra is kept in a building situated in the middle of the court, so as to be completely isolated in case of fire, and the books are well cared for ; altogether we felt obliged to commend the monks for having of late years appreciated the value of their books. The inhabitants of Mount Athos have not yet got beyond a recognition of the *value* of their literary treasures ; nobody seems to take any interest in them, and except at Vatopedi and Russico I could not discover that it even entered anybody's head to read the books.

The following are some of the principal manuscripts ; the librarian being away and no one else knowing anything about the contents of the library, we had to take the books down at random, judging of them by their backs, and thus some important ones may have escaped us, for we had not time to go through the library systematically :

An evangelistarium in uncial characters, once a fine manuscript but now much damaged ; this is not the uncial evangelistarium mentioned by Curzon. Another fine copy (quarto) of the Holy Gospels, in a curious binding of crimson silk, covered with elaborate patterns in silver thread; it has two clasps in front and one top and bottom, making four in all, composed of plaited leather with brass mounts; it contains illuminations of the Four Evangelists. Another beautiful evangelistarium, a folio in good preservation, written in parallel columns with fine miniatures; at the end of this book, on the last two pages, is an inscription in a large sprawling hand which says that it was presented by the Empress Irene.[1] We found one palimpsest.

There were no early manuscripts of the liturgies that we could discover, and we were ever on the watch for them. All the manuscripts of the liturgies that we saw at Athos were of the same date—fourteenth or fifteenth century, I think. They are always written on rolls of great length.

The refectory is in its usual position, i.e. on the opposite side of the court, in front of the west door of the catholicon; it is about the same size as the refectory at Vatopedi; like it the interior walls are covered with frescoes, and it contains twenty-three marble tables.

This evening (Saturday, August $\frac{18}{6}$) Michael, ex-Metropolitan of Belgrade and Primate of Servia, arrived at the monastery. He was a clean-looking, well-bred old man, with a gentle face and silky beard, and did not look at all like a man who had recently mixed himself up with political intrigues to the extent of defying his sovereign. Into the history and the rights and wrongs of this dispute I will not take my readers; suffice it to say that, King Milan subjecting himself and his infant kingdom to Austrian instead of Russian influence, the Primate and bishops of Servia,

---

[1] Irene governed the Empire of the East from 797 to 802.

fearing the consequences of a Latin instead of an
Orthodox ally, violently opposed the King, who finally
deposed the whole bench with a stroke of his pen and
obtained fresh prelates from the Orthodox Church in
the Austrian dominions. The Patriarch of Constantinople did not suffer himself to be drawn into the
quarrel, and simply recognised the new bishops without
condemning the old ; and thus it was that Michael was
wandering about the East in exile, waiting for a turn of
Fortune's wheel to throw him up again into his metro-
political throne. How far he had acted from purely
religious in opposition to political motives, and whether
or not he was a mere puppet in the hands of intriguing
Russia, I am not sufficiently well acquainted with the
quarrel to say, but will merely repeat that his manner
and appearance impressed us favourably. A monk
from the Servian Monastery of Chiliandari had been
deputed to act as his chaplain and attendant during
his sojourn on the Holy Mountain : he was possessed
of a most wonderful head of hair, which stood out
like a thatch all round. We all had supper together,
and the conversation turned entirely on the English
Church and the unity of Christendom. Our theological remarks had first to be translated into Greek
by Angelos to the Servian monk, and then from Greek
into Slavonic by the monk to Michael ; so what they
were like by the time they reached the latter I shudder
to think.

We afterwards found that the ex-Primate understood French, so we might have spared ourselves and
him a great deal of trouble. Our discussion lasted
till a late hour, and as we rose to separate *our* Archbishop, as we always called him (for we had become

such great friends that we looked upon him quite
as one of ourselves) turned to O— and inquired
whether he proposed to celebrate the Eucharist on
the morrow, as it was Sunday. O— replied in the
affirmative, and the Servian prelate immediately expressed a wish to be present.

The next morning we rose before seven o'clock,
and found that the Archbishop of Cavalla had been up
two good hours already, and had been looking after
the arrangement of a temporary altar in the large
chamber adjacent to our sleeping-room. The monks
had procured an Old and a New Testament, for which
I had asked the night before, so that the archbishops
might follow the Scriptural portion of our services.
Our hosts had unearthed them from the library, and
they proved to be two immense folios which required a
desk to sustain them. By the time I had found all
the places and marked them with slips of paper I discovered that the room—a very large one—was as full as
it would hold of monks. The morning was already
hot, and the atmosphere of our temporary chapel consequently stifling. O— wished the Archbishop to
dismiss the greater part of the assembly ; but the monks
begged hard to be allowed to be present, and suggested
that the altar might be moved outside to a sort of
gallery which runs round the side of the monastery on
the first floor, open to the air on the courtyard side by
reason of an arcade. So this was done, and seats for
the archbishops and a desk for the great books were
placed on the north side of the altar, whilst all the rest
stood behind on the west of it. O— had resolved to
say the daily service before celebrating the Eucharist,
because the Greeks invariably have long offices before

the liturgy, and as of course he would have to say his offices either publicly or privately, it seemed advisable to follow the Greek, and, indeed, a very general English custom, of amalgamating the whole.

I cannot tell how many were present at the service; certainly a great number, composed of monks, hermits, pilgrims, and here and there amongst the sombre crowd a white fustinella peeped out, denoting the pre-sence of a muleteer or other lay servant. The whole gallery was full to the very end, and some were even standing on the parapet and on the sills of the windows which opened on to the passage. Before the service began, our Archbishop, at O—'s request, came to our room (which we used as a vestry) and gave him his blessing. Mattins was said, without note, then the litany, the archbishops following the psalms and lessons in the big folios, and then, with as little interruption as possible, O— commenced the Eucharist. At the con-clusion of the prayer of humble access the archbishops rose from their seats and there occurred a slight con-fusion, caused by the monks in front passing word to some of those behind, who, owing to the press, had sat down on the parapet, that all were to stand; but it almost instantly subsided and the service proceeded.

As we knelt before the rude altar in the early morning under the bright and sunny Eastern sky, the familiar English rites and English words in that strange land, and the English priest pleading the One adorable Sacrifice in the presence of that weird and old-world company, all seemed to me inexpressibly solemn; for were not the blessed angels now with us, and around our humble table, the same that had veiled their faces for centuries before the Holy Mysteries in the ancient church in the court below, and were they not joining us in our cry, ' O Lamb of God, that takest away the sins of the world, grant us Thy peace ' ? Yet sad it was that we, children of One Father, could not join together in the same Eucharistic feast, because there is still that mountain between us, cast up by pride and misunderstanding, by arrogance and schism, that lofty barrier never to be removed until the Voice shall say, ' Be thou removed, and be thou cast into the sea.'

' Remember not, Lord, our offences, nor the offences of our forefathers ; spare Thy people, whom Thou hast redeemed with Thy most precious blood, and be not angry with us for ever.'

' Be not angry with us for ever ! ' May God hasten the time of our separation, and may He again unite His Holy Catholic Church to be glorious and triumphant over the powers of darkness which are brooding so ominously over the world ! ' Spare us, good Lord, and be not angry with us *for ever* ! '

After breakfast the Servian archbishop departed for Caracalla. We took two photographs of the interior of the Lavra, one of them showing the west end of the catholicon with the phiale and a group of monks standing about it.

The marble basin, which measures 7 feet 8 inches in diameter, is carved with its pedestal out of one block of white marble. It contains a real fountain of gilt metal, of which the monks were very proud and insisted upon making it play during the taking of the photograph. I made one of the monks fetch a hand semantron and put on the cloak which they use when performing any distinct official act connected with Divine service. This cloak is of thin black material,

gathered at the neck ; descending thence in pleats, it
sweeps the ground behind to the length of about four
inches, being somewhat shorter in front.   On the opposite page is an engraving copied from the photograph.
The monk is represented in the act of striking the
semantron with the mallet, and the position is exceedingly natural.   The columns and carved parapet of
the fountain are of white marble.   The boughs which
overshadow it on either side belong to two ancient
cypresses of great size, said to have been planted by
St. Athanasius, the founder, in the tenth century.   The
trunk of the largest measures fourteen feet in circumfe-
rence just above the ground, before it begins to spread.

Towards evening I went to the little port and took
a photograph of the castle, and returning sat down in
the pretty lane to enjoy the stillness of the evening.
Meanwhile O— had been talking to the Archbishop
of Cavalla about our English difficulties, and as I
joined them in the monastery they had just got on
to the subject of that unpleasant young woman, the
Deceased Wife's Sister.

'Of course,' said the Archbishop, ' it is a most monstrous proposal to allow a man to marry his wife's
sister, and your Church is deserving of the sympathy
of all Christians in the struggle upon which she is engaged.   We are still more strict than you, prohibiting
all marriages within the sixth degree of relationship.'

Then he proceeded to tell us a rather funny story
of a marriage case that had lately occurred in his
diocese.

A young man fell in love with a young woman of
the same village, but unfortunately his sweetheart was
some sort of a distant cousin to him, within the pro-

THE LAVRA, FROM A MONASTIC ENGRAVING.

hibited degrees, and therefore no priest would marry
them. They appealed in vain to the Archbishop,
who told them that the Church knew of no dispen-
sations, and that therefore they must make up their
minds that the marriage was impossible. 'But,' said
the Archbishop to us, 'they were a most obstinate
couple ; for the space of four years did they pester
me to allow them to be married, coming out to meet
me as I made my yearly visitation of the village,
and hanging with tears and supplications on my
horse's bridle. Altogether it was very embarrassing.
But this was not the worst, for in their despair they
tried to make away with themselves, and so determined
were they that on four several occasions the man threw
himself into the sea, but was happily observed and
dragged out before life was extinct, and three times
the girl tried to poison herself, but she also was rescued from suicide. At last the young man's father,
who was a priest, took compassion on them and married them.'

'Well,' said we, 'and what did you do ?'

'I suspended the priest for three months,' said the
Archbishop, 'and I excommunicated the couple.'

'And are they still excommunicate ?'

'Yes,' replied the Archbishop, 'they are, and have
been so for the last two years, ever since they de-
fied the authority of the Church. They never cease
imploring me to remove the sentence, and when I
go back perhaps I shall do so. You see it was a
difficult case.'

The Archbishop told this pitiful tale with much
hilarity, evidently quite appreciating its comic side.
But after all it was no joke for the unfortunate couple,

who were undergoing all the spiritual and temporal
disadvantages connected with their punishment in their
remote village, whilst we were laughing over their
misfortunes on a comfortable divan at Mount Athos.
Still they were lucky in being under the jurisdiction of
a prelate who seemed disposed to take a merciful view
of the case, and look upon their offence as a sort of
youthful folly; otherwise, in a Church which still retains her ancient discipline, such a flagrant act of disobedience to her laws might have met with a far
heavier and more lasting penalty.

We supped this evening chiefly on large black
snails. Half the fortnight's fast was now over, and we
began to look forward to the improvement in our fare
which the festival of the Assumption would bring ; for
then the monks would go out fishing again, and provide the table with something more delectable than
these slimy creatures.

We had intended to make the ascent of Athos the
next morning, but the weather proved too stormy ;
showers fell at intervals during the day, whilst thick
clouds enveloped the summit of the mountain. A
monk was brought to see us who spoke English, and
very fairly too ; he had been a sailor on both English
and American ships, and knew the principal ports of
both countries. Now he had retired to end his days
in peace on the Agion Oros. He was between forty
and fifty years of age. This was by no means the
only instance we came across of English-speaking
sailors who had left the sea, sometimes in the prime of
life, to find a monastic home on these peaceful shores.
What a change from the rude and bustling life before
the mast on board an English ship to the life of retire-

ment and prayer on the quiet slopes of the Holy Mountain! Very few of the Athos monks have been brought up to the monastic life; the majority of them have embraced it after a longer or shorter experience of those delights which the world can offer. My readers will ask what it is that thus attracts them. I think there are two prominent motives, and first comes the wish to save their souls. The life of a consistent monk is looked upon as a sure passport to the heavenly country, and the Paradise of the Mother of God [1] is considered to be the best place for fostering monastic virtues. This I believe to be the paramount consideration which weighs with these men. Secondly, there is that love of rest and quietness—call it idleness, energetic Western, if you will—that is the lodestar of the Oriental mind.

Now, whilst I am fully alive to the evils of Quietism, it appears to me that in our England of the nineteenth century we are in danger of underrating the value of the contemplative life. In modern Europe we live so fast, there is so much to be *done* every day of our lives, that we are apt to give up *thinking* altogether, except so far as it aids us directly in our work. And yet both Christian and pagan philosophers have looked upon the contemplative life as the highest life possible to man ; for the nearer we approach to pure contemplation, the nearer we are to that life which is to be our highest reward hereafter, in which our supreme happiness will consist in the contemplation of the attributes of the Deity. Of course it may be validly urged that so long as man is in the world there is

---

[1] Athos is called Ὁ Παράδεισος τῆς Θεοτόκου on account of the frequent appearances of the Blessed Virgin to its inhabitants.

definite work for him to do therein, that he is put into it to act as well as to meditate, and this is the true answer to the Quietist. Still, as we may not give our lives to mere contemplation (for even monks perform manual labour and devote themselves to prayer, which according to the Christian doctrine is a mighty work and does more good to the world than any art or science),[1] so if we occupy ourselves entirely with actual labour we shall proportionately lose by thus cultivating only one part, and that not the highest, of our nature.

And this truth forces itself most vividly upon a man when, restless, busy Europe being left behind, he finds himself on the peaceful shores of the Holy Mountain. It is as if he had been navigating some mighty river, and having battled long against the rushing current, the whirling eddies, and the hissing water, had just turned some projecting point of land and shot at once into a little tranquil pool, where the still waters scarcely moved the rushes and the tiny wavelets hardly rippled on the bank. For here on this hallowed ground, trodden for centuries by the feet of saints and men of God, all seems to breathe tranquillity and peace; there is no hurrying to and fro, no business, no labours beyond what is necessary to till the fruitful earth, to ply the net in the teeming waters, and that labour of love the offering up of prayer and praise to the Divine Creator of all the matchless

---

[1] A hermit on his knees is surely benefiting his fellow-men at least as much as an astronomer peeping through his telescope; yet how differently are the two judged by the world! Not that the pursuit of purely speculative science is to be condemned. The attempt to fathom the purposes of God, and to make ourselves masters of His secrets, is probably quite lawful, provided all is done for the advancement of His glory, and only the legitimate result of the reason with which He has furnished us.

beauty of rock and tree, of sea and mountain, that enchants the eye at every turn on this most favoured spot. Fascinating surely is this picture even to an English mind ; what wonder if it prove an irresistible allurement to the impressionable Oriental ?

Of the abuse of the contemplative life no better example can be found than that of the celebrated controversy concerning the Uncreated Light, which arose in consequence of the practices of the Quietists of Mount Athos in the fourteenth century.

A certain abbot of a monastery at Constantinople, whose name was Simeon and who lived in the eleventh century, was the author of all the mischief. Following instructions which he had laid down, certain of the monks of Athos devoted themselves wholly to contemplation, and maintained that by this means, after long fasting and prayer, with their heads bent down upon their breasts and their eyes looking into their stomachs, they saw within their bodies a wonderful light, which was the light which shone at our Lord's Transfiguration on Mount Tabor, and they further asserted that the light which appeared on the Mount of Transfiguration was not a created but an uncreated light. I will give Simeon's instructions in full,[1] although I do not pretend to thoroughly understand them.

When thou art alone in thy cell, shut the door and seat thyself in a corner ; raise thy spirit far above all vain and transitory things ; then rest thy beard on thy belly, turn the eyes with all possible concentration of thought towards the middle of thy stomach—that is to say, towards the navel —then holding thy breath and taking no respiration either through the mouth or the nose, search thy entrails for the place of the heart, which is the seat of all the powers of the soul.

[1] See Fleury, *Hist. Eccl.* 95, 9; also Gibbon, *Dec. of Rom. Emp* chap. lxiii.

O

At first thou wilt find there nought but thick shadows and darkness hard to dispel, but if thou dost persevere, continuing this practice night and day, thou wilt find a marvellous thing, a joy without interruption, for as soon as the spirit has found the seat of the heart it will see that which it has never known before; it will see the air which is in the heart, and it will see itself, luminous and easy of discernment.

Now a certain monk of Calabria, Barlaam by name,[1] happened to be on a visit to the Holy Mountain in the year 1341, and during his stay heard the story of the light which the monks saw in their stomachs. Barlaam, being a profound theologian as well as a philosopher, tried to laugh the monks out of their conceit, saying first of all that he did not believe they saw any light at all in their stomachs; secondly, that, even if they did, it had nothing whatever to do with the light on Mount Tabor; lastly, that the light of the Transfiguration itself was not an uncreated but a created light; wherefore he solemnly warned them to desist from such follies, which were nothing else but the revival of the old Massalian heresy. He ended by nicknaming them ὀμφαλόψυχοι, 'the navel-souled ones.' The monks were furious at being called heretics, and found a champion in a certain Gregory Palamas (a

---

[1] Barlaam was sent by the Emperor Andronicus in 1339 on a fruitless embassy to Pope Benedict XII. to suggest a basis for the union of the Eastern and Western Churches. He was tutor to Petrarch and to Boccaccio, and by the influence of the former, after having conformed to the Latin Church, he was promoted to the bishopric of Hieracium, in Calabria. Gibbon says of him, 'Barlaam was the first who revived, beyond the Alps, the memory, or at least the writings, of Homer. He is described by Petrarch and Boccace as a man of a diminutive stature, though truly great in the measure of learning and genius; of a piercing discernment, though of a slow and painful elocution. For many ages, as they affirm, Greece had not produced his equal in the knowledge of history, grammar, and philosophy; and his merit was celebrated in the attestations of the princes and doctors of Constantinople.' (*Rom. Emp.* chap. lxvi.)

monk of Mount Athos who afterwards became Archbishop of Thessalonica). Gregory defended the monastic theory by maintaining that the essence of the
Deity was distinct from His effluence or operation,
that the latter was eternal and uncreated, and that the
light which shone on the Mount of Transfiguration
was this uncreated effluence, though not the substance
of the Deity. Barlaam appealed to Constantinople,
and, after no less than four councils had been held, he
was finally condemned and the doctrine of the Uncreated
Light was declared to be a Christian verity. This took
place in 1351. The Eastern Church, however, was
almost torn to pieces by the violence of the controversy,
which lasted for nearly a hundred years before the
matter finally dropped ; but long before this Gregory
Palamas had been honoured with a commemoration in
the services for the Second Sunday in Lent, and the
opinions of Barlaam had been added to those heresies
which are solemnly anathematized on the First Sunday
in Lent, or 'Orthodoxy Sunday.'

Dr. Neale, in his learned work on the 'Holy Eastern
Church,' says that although the controversy has died
away it must not be forgotten 'that the Church
of Constantinople stands pledged by an unrescinded
Council to the absurd and erroneous doctrine of
Palamas. It is true that the movement was as much
a political as a religious one, and may as fitly be named,
as it was named, Cantacuzenism [1] as Palamism.
Still the office of Gregory Palamas and the anathemas
against Barlaam remain in the Triodion ; these surely
should be removed. At present, however, in the city
and immediate neighbourhood of Constantinople (as I

---

[1] The Emperor John Cantacuzenus supported Palamas.

am informed), the office is forbidden.'[1] He then goes
on to show that the patriarchate of Constantinople is
the only part of the Eastern Church responsible for
the doctrine of the Uncreated Light.

At the risk of being tedious I will close the account
of this curious dispute with the translation of one of
the anathemas read on Orthodoxy Sunday.

> To them that think and say that the light which shone from our
> Lord in His holy Transfiguration was either an appearance and a
> creature, and a vision that appeared for a little time, and was forth-
> with dissolved, or else the very essence of God ; as wholly, and to
> the loss of their souls, throwing themselves into two contrarieties and
> impossibilities, and, on the one side, holding the madness of Arius
> (who divided the One Godhead and the One God into things created
> and uncreated), and, on the other, carried away with the impiety of
> the Massalians (who say that the Divine Substance is visible); and
> confess not, according to the inspired teaching of the saints and the
> pious belief of the Church, that that most Divine light was not a
> creature, nor the essence of God, but an uncreated and physical
> grace, and forth-shining, and energy, which ever inseparably pro-
> ceedeth from the Divine essence itself—

> Anathema, Anathema, Anathema.

During our journey we endeavoured to ascertain
whether any traditions of this mighty controversy still
existed in the land of its birth ; but, although we
mentioned the Uncreated Light to the leading monks
at several of the monasteries, no one seemed to know
anything about it, and the name of Barlaam, which
once would have been sufficient to have raised the
fiercest religious enthusiasm, only produced the answer,
' Barlaam ? No, we have never heard of him. Who

---

[1] I verified this at Constantinople last year. Dr. Neale was right ; the
office is not used. My informant, curiously, was the archimandrite
Gregory Palamas, a descendant of the famous author of the theory. The
archimandrite said, ' The Uncreated Light is a true and orthodox belief,
but not a dogma.'

was he ?' No monk now expects to see the light of
Mount Tabor in his stomach, and we may hope that
the Church of Constantinople has, so far as lies within
her power, blotted out from her history a page which
contributes not to her glory but to her shame.

At four o'clock in the afternoon we left the Lavra
for the skete of the Prodromos, the epitropoi and principal monks accompanying us to the gate. Amongst
the latter was a fine old man with a snowy beard and
a figure which must have been once tall and commanding, now bent with age and leaning upon a staff.
This was the archimandrite Benjamin, who had fought
in the Greek war of independence. He had only one
eye, a singularly bright and piercing one ; the other,
over which he wore a black patch, had been lost in
the service of his country in 1821. This ancient
warrior was eighty-two years of age.

Our path for the first half-hour lay over flat and
stony ground amongst low bushes, consisting of bay,
Turkey oaks, and arbutus. Afterwards we met with
different vegetation, and crossed several beautiful
glens, amidst picturesque rocks and shady trees. At
last, as we rode over the brow of a hill, we suddenly
caught sight of the skete, a regularly built convent of
considerable size, with the domes of the catholicon
rising above the roof of the buildings. It is situated
on a plateau between the mountain and the sea, half
a mile from the shore, at the elevation of about 700
feet, and belongs to the Roumanians. The monks
were on the look-out for us, and the instant our cavalcade appeared in sight all the bells began to ring, and
after being received in the usual manner we were
taken up to a beautifully clean room for our glyko and

coffee. The dicaios (or hegoumenos, as he is called *inside* the skete) was absent, having gone to Bucharest, so we were received by an old man named Esaias, the second in command, and a well-bred and not very elderly monk called David. Esaias was one of the politest men I have ever met; at every opportunity he would place his hand on his breast and bow to us. He was seventy-three years of age and had never once tasted meat since he embraced the monastic life at seventeen; for, as we were told at supper, which shortly appeared on the table in cœnobite monasteries they never touch flesh food. Nevertheless our meal was an excellent one, served on a clean table-cloth, and almost for the first time on Mount Athos clean napkins were given to us. Instead of the ordinary brown and gritty bread the good monks had provided each of their guests with one of the cakes (προσφορά) made for Eucharistic use. They are composed of fine flour, stamped with a cross and the words 'Jesus Christ conquers' ('Ιησοῦς Χριστὸς νικᾷ).

The evening was a stormy one, and Esaias on looking out of the window remarked, 'Glory to God! it is going to rain!' and soon the patter of the drops outside confirmed the old man's forecast. We talked long and earnestly about unity. 'There is but one Gospel,' said Esaias; 'we ought all to be one.'

The monk David gave up his room to O— and myself. It was positively luxurious—two clean beds, bright little pictures on the snowy walls, including photographs of David's friends and relatives, a carpet on the floor, and certain other luxuries which betokened the presence of European civilization. Here we did not think it necessary to put out our levinges, and the

result justified our expectations, for although a few
fleas fastened themselves upon O— in the course of
the night the greater enemy did not take the field.

We had another excellent repast the next morning,
the monks being very good in trying to suit our palates
by the omission of the abominable oil from the dishes.
Afterwards we were taken to see the cave of St.
Athanasius the Athonite.   A short walk brought us to
the edge of a lofty cliff, and we descended by a rather
steep path along the face of it to the cave   This is
several hundred feet (probably between 400 and 500,
but the distances are deceptive) above the sea, which
here runs into the land and forms a little bay with the
high cliffs on three sides of it.   It would be difficult to
choose a more lovely spot for retirement.   The cave
has been enlarged by the erection of a small cottage at
its mouth, below which a few terraces keep up enough
earth to form a little garden, in which the hermit (for
one still lives here) grows his herbs and vegetables.
An olive tree or two and a few vines and fig trees,
growing in wild luxuriance under the sheltering cliff,
furnish him with oil and fruit, whilst creeping plants,
and shrubs, and flowers spring up and flourish wherever
there is sufficient earth to cover the rock.   Down far
below, at the foot of the cliff, is the tiny bay with the
blue water sparkling in the sunshine, beyond the open
sea.   Inside the cave are two little chapels ; the inner,
which is the smaller, was the one used by St. Athanasius, and measures six feet three inches across the
iconostasis, five feet four inches from the iconostasis to
the west wall, and only eight feet four inches in its
extreme length from east to west, including both nave
and sanctuary.

The altar, or holy table, is formed by a little hole
being scooped out of the rock above it; it measures
three feet in length.　Notwithstanding its extreme
minuteness this little chapel is perfect in all its ritual
parts and necessary appliances, having an iconostasis
with the holy door and its curtain in the centre, and a
second door to the north of it, and being also provided
with a stall or two.　Besides the chapels the hermit had
two rooms, one of which he used as a sort of kitchen,

CAVE OF ST. ATHANASIUS, WITH THE HERMIT.

the other as his sleeping and living room.　Both were
about seven feet square, and so low that we could only
just stand upright in them; they were almost destitute
of furniture and domestic utensils.　A short time back
there were two hermits living together in this place,
but one died, and a plain wooden cross in front of the
cave marks the spot where he lies.　Here he lived,
died, and was buried, and now his brother sits under
his fig tree alone with God on the face of that silent
rock.

It was a difficult place to photograph, as one naturally could not get far enough away from the subject; but at last, at the risk of my neck, I managed to obtain a tolerable picture of the cave itself with the hermit standing in his little garden.   Of course it conveys no idea of its romantic situation.   The good man gave us some grapes and figs, and so, bidding him adieu, we scrambled back to the top of the cliff and left him to his solitude.

Returning to the skete, we occupied the remainder of the day in examining its buildings.   The catholicon was built between 1857 and 1860, and has three domes —one over the sanctuary, another (the largest) over the nave, between the transepts, and a third over the narthex.   There are no divisions behind the iconostasis, but bema, chapel of the prothesis, and diaconicon form as it were one large room.   The narthex too is only divided from the nave by an archway and two pillars. The pronaos extends on either side of the church for some distance beyond the north and south walls of the nave.[1]   There is nothing of interest in the church beyond a very beautiful picture of the Virgin with the Holy Child in her arms, which, I think, was on the north-east pillar which supports the central dome. Many offerings were suspended round it; for monks and pilgrims had vied with each other in decking the picture of the fairest among women, and had made her cheeks comely with rows of jewels and her neck with

---

[1] The measurements are as follows : *Sanctuary*, from north to south, 26½ feet ; across chord of apse, 13½ feet ; from iconostasis to end of east apse, 20 feet.   *Nave*, across transepts, 40 feet ; from iconostasis to narthex, 36 feet.   From this point to the west end of the narthex is 21 feet, and as the narthex is not architecturally divided from the nave it may be counted as part of it, which will make the total length of the nave 57 feet.

chains of gold. This was pointed out to us as being a miraculous icon. 'But,' said we, 'it looks like a modern picture.' 'So it is,' replied Esaias; 'it was painted in the year 1860. Moreover we have often tried to take a copy of it, for many people in Roumania would like to see it, but we cannot manage to do it.' Here at last was a miracle of our own time, and, eager to hear the story from the lips of one who was acquainted with all the circumstances and who appeared to be a man of true piety, we begged old Esaias to proceed. And this was the story he told.

This Roumanian skete was founded in the year 1853 by a few monks, of whom Esaias himself was one. Now when the church was built, seven years later, the dicaios, or hegoumenos, was anxious to obtain some celebrated icon to place within it, and so he searched through the length and breadth of the Orthodox Church to find one that he could buy. But, as might have been expected, no monastery could be found willing to part with one; so the hegoumenos gave up the idea in despair. He went, therefore, to his native country, Roumania, and commissioned the best artist he could find—an old monk—to paint him an icon for the new church on the Holy Mountain. The monk commenced his work, but before he had proceeded far he came to the hegoumenos and told him that he was afraid he should have to give it up, because his hand trembled so much through age and infirmity; 'for,' said he, 'I shall never be able to do justice to such a subject.'

'Well,' replied the abbot, 'you can but do your best, and then God will excuse all shortcomings. Nevertheless, my son, this shaking of your hand may be the result of your sins : go therefore to the church and there recite the canon ; pray to God to help you, and then go back and finish the picture.'

The old man did as he was advised. Covering up the picture, he went to the church and prayed. When his devotions were finished he returned to his easel and lifted off from the face of the icon the handkerchief which covered it. The picture had been painted by the angels.

CHAPTER XIII.

And there is another Hille, that is clept Athos, that is so highe, that the Schadewe of hym rechethe to Lempne, that is an Ile; and it is 76 Myle betwene. And aboven at the cop of the Hille is the Eir so cleer, that Men may fynde no Wynd there. And therefore may no Best lyve there; and so is the Eyr drye. And Men seye in theise Contrees, that Philosophres som tyme wenten upon theise Hilles, and helden to here Nose a Spounge moysted with Watre, for to have Eyr; for the Eyr above was so drye.—SIR JOHN MAUNDEVILLE.

THE refectory at the skete of the Prodromos is much like a Western one. We visited it whilst the monks were taking their evening meal, which consisted of a wineglassful of coarse rum, an allowance of wine, and two very nasty-looking dishes of vegetables cooked in strong-smelling oil. During supper a monk reads aloud from some spiritual book. Behind the door hangs a long string of knots called the κομβοσχοίνιον (if this be made of beads, like a Western rosary, instead of knots, it is called a κομβολόγιον); its use is the following:

If a monk has committed any fault, such as disobedience to the orders of the hegoumenos, whilst the rest are at their meal he has to take this string of knots or beads from off its peg and go into the middle of the refectory. Here he stands, repeating at each knot the prayer called the εὐχή, with a prostration each time, until the meal is over. This prayer is the ordinary form used by the Greek Christian, and is

therefore called ' *the* prayer.' If he wants any temporal
or spiritual blessing he will not pray directly, ' grant
this ' or 'give me that,' but he will simply repeat the
εὐχή slowly and with devotion for the length of time
he wishes to be at prayer. It is as follows :

O Lord Jesus Christ, Son of the Living God, have mercy upon
me.

This use of the rosary is called the canon (κανών).

A κομβοσχοίνιον also hangs in the church, and is
thus used: If during the long services a monk is observed
to be slumbering in his stall, one of his brethren takes
a small wax taper, and lighting it at a lamp goes up
softly to the culprit and affixes it to the arm of his
stall. When the monk awakes out of his nap he
stands self-convicted by seeing the lighted taper at his
elbow, and instantly taking the string of knots from
its place he performs the canon in the midst of
the church for the space of half an hour. This
quaint custom only exists where the cœnobite rule is
observed.

Before our supper the sound of a very skilfully
played semantron announced the service of *apodeipnon*,
or compline, which I attended, and welcomed as a
relief the change from the nasal ' Kyrie eleison ' to its
Roumanian form, ' Dómne milueste ; ' the chanting too
seemed to be rather more tuneful than that in the
Greek convents.

We had a long conversation after our meal with
Esaias and David. The Roumanians first came to
Athos in 1820, when they rented a kelli from the
Lavra. The little church belonging to this kelli
(dedicated to St. John Baptist) still exists just outside
the walls.

In 1853 a few monks founded the skete on the site of the kelli. They pay to the Lavra an annual sum, equal to about 15*l*. sterling, for the privilege of cutting wood on the mountain, besides the amount of money they paid down when the contract enabling them to found the skete was made. The name of the dicaios is Damianus. There are now ninety monks and ten servants, all Roumanians. They have a small farm in Thasos, from which they obtain their oil, eggs, &c., and a little property in Roumania. When the Roumanian Government took possession of the lands of the monasteries it agreed to pay as an equivalent a certain fixed sum each year to every monk, but the number of the monks was not to be increased.

Esocclesia.

1. Catholicon, dedicated to the Epiphany.
2. Assumption of the Blessed Virgin.
3. The Annunciation.
4. The Holy Unmercenaries.

There is one church outside the walls, that which has been already mentioned as having been the chapel of the original kelli, dedicated to the Prodromos, or Forerunner, St. John the Baptist.

At the time of our visit the monks were actively engaged in the erection of new buildings to complete the south side of the quadrangle.

In connection with the catholicon I ought to have mentioned that, as we were examining the interior, my eye caught a fresco on the wall, representing St. Christopher, in all respects conventionally drawn, with the Child on his shoulder and the pine tree in his hand, except that instead of an ordinary head the artist had given him the head of a dog with two great tusks

sticking out of his jaws.   I could not believe at first
that it was intended for the saint, until the sight of
the words ἅγιος Χριστοφόρος beneath the figure removed all doubt.   I called to the monks and asked
them what made them give St. Christopher such a
monstrous head.

'Don't you know,' said they, 'that St. Christopher
had a dog's head?'   'No,' replied I ; 'we have no such
tradition in the West—at least I never heard of it—and
we always represent him, though a giant, with a proper
head.'   'Oh, yes,' said they, 'he had a dog's head and
tusks; you will see one of his tusks at the second
monastery from here, and it has a fine smell.'

And sure enough we did see the tusk at St.
Dionysius, and it *had* a fine smell.   But I am anticipating.

Esaias furnished me with the following scheme of
an ordinary day at the skete : The monks rise a little
before midnight and go to the church.   Then they
say Mattins and the offices of the First, Third, and
Sixth Hours.   These last until about 4 A.M., except on
Sundays and festivals, when they do not terminate
till six o'clock.   After the hours comes the liturgy ;
celebrated in the principal church on Sundays and
festivals, in one of the smaller churches on week days.
Then they drink a little coffee and have a meal at
eight.   After this repast they pursue their ordinary
avocations, and have at least an hour and a half's sleep
before 3 P.M., when they sing the Ninth Hour and
Vespers.   This service lasts till about half-past four.
Then comes supper at six and then Compline, which
lasts an hour, after which they retire to rest at about
8.30 P.M.   But on the festivals called ἀγρυπνία they

are in church the whole night, since Great Vespers and the night offices begin immediately after Little Vespers and last from twelve to fifteen hours. These festivals occur on the average rather more than once a week. On three days in the week—namely, Mondays, Wednesdays, and Fridays—the monks have only one meal, and this is eaten in the middle of the day. Besides these weekly fast days there are the four Lents[1] and several other particular occasions. On these days eggs, cheese, fish, wine, and oil are forbidden. In idiorrhythmic monasteries flesh meat is eaten on feast days ; in cœnobite ones the monks never touch it.

Wednesday, August $\frac{22}{10}$. This morning Angelos came to us early, with the news that, although it still looked cloudy, the muleteers thought that we might as well attempt the ascent of the peak. We had kept the Lavra mules, with their attendants, since the skete was badly provided with riding animals. As a matter of fact we knew perfectly well that these idle muleteers had been putting stumbling-blocks in the way of going up the mountain, hoping that we should think better of our project and so spare them the trouble of the climb ; it was only when they found us quite determined that they began to think that they had better get the unpleasant job over as soon as possible.

We rose instantly, packed up our portmanteaux, and ordered the mules to be laden. After taking some coffee we stuffed our saddle bags with the good bread of the skete, took leave of our hospitable friends at about half-past eight o'clock, and rode towards the west.

---

[1] I.e. the Forty Days (as ours) : the Fast of the Apostles Peter and Paul, from the first Sunday after Pentecost to June 28 ; the Fast of the Mother of God, August 1–14 ; the Fast of Christmas, November 15 to December 24.

We ascended rapidly, the mules scrambling like
cats amongst the rocks and bushes.   At this end of
the promontory, between the peak and the sea, the
land is cut up into rugged rocks and cliffs, and as a
rule the forest trees are only to be found occasionally
in sheltered situations.   Soon after passing a fearful
precipice at a great height above the sea we arrived
at the kelli of Kerasia, about two hours and a half
after leaving the skete.   This house is situated on a
small plateau, or break in the descent from the mountain to the sea, and is sheltered on each side by high
spurs of the mountain, being open only to the sea in
front.   Its height above the sea-level is about 2,200
feet.   Georgirenes says of Kerasia that it is a 'plot of
Ground, all strew'd with such Hermitages as are at St.
Anne.'   This well describes the position of the kelli,
although the writer seems to infer that it is a skete
like St. Anne, which is not the case.   All around it are
little cottages and huts, some on comparatively smooth
ground surrounded with gardens, others on the rugged
slopes ; and one is situated on the point of a stupendous
and hardly accessible rock, the sides of which descend
almost perpendicularly for at least 3,000 feet into the
sea.   We much wished to visit this hermitage, but time
forbade us to loiter ; so we were obliged to be content
with the view of it from above, as we ascended the
mountain, when we could plainly see this kelli with its
little chapel, a most ideal place for a hermit.   Probably a week devoted to the visitation of the hermitages
situated on the point of Athos would amply repay the
trouble and difficulty the expedition would entail.

The principal kelli of Kerasia, at which we dismounted, is a good house, having been built by some

P

itinerant church painters, who lived in it for about three years and then sold it to the Lavra. They have left traces of their handicraft, for the walls of the principal room are decorated with two large frescoes, well executed but in a realistic and bad style of art; representing on the one side the story of Susanna, and on the other, if I remember aright, David's first view of Bathsheba: rather odd subjects for the walls of a hermitage.

It is now tenanted by a solitary old monk, who evidently lives in the most frugal way, for all he could give us for luncheon was eggs (half of which were uneatable), raw tomatoes and cucumbers; these, with our Dutch cheese and some of the bread we had brought from the Prodromos, formed our repast—not very satisfying after our rough morning's ride, nor particularly appropriate to the work that was to follow, the ascent of a mountain 7,000 feet high.

At a quarter to twelve we started, leaving Angelos behind, to his great delight, for his burly frame was not at all suited to mountaineering, giving him instructions to do the best he could for us in preparing a supper for our return. Peter also stayed at Kerasia, for he protested that his head would not stand great heights, and he felt convinced that if he tried to go up the mountain he should break his neck! So away we rode, the Archbishop, O— and myself, the faithful Pantele in front with his master's stick, and two muleteers to show us the way.

Up we went, past the region of forest trees, over the rocks and loose stones, which afforded but treacherous foothold for the mules; but these wonderful beasts never once came down. Our prelate was in merry pin. The keen mountain air seemed to have raised his spirits to the highest pitch. He had provided himself with a long and thick stick, and as he rode behind O—'s mule he devoted himself to accelerating its pace by the most vicious prods and blows. 'Thwack, thwack,' went the stick, 'Hi! hi!' shouted the Archbishop, and the unfortunate animal would bound up the mountain side with sudden jerks which momently threatened to shake its rider from his seat.

'I wish the Archbishop would lose that stick,' said O—; and presently he did, and a pretty fuss there was until it was recovered!

At last we reached a rocky platform overhanging a precipice, on which stands the little Church of the Panaghia, 1,000 feet below the summit of the mountain. Attached to this chapel is a hut, in which the pilgrims rest on the night before the festival of the Transfiguration. Nobody lives here, and the place is only used on this one night of the year.

Beyond this point the mules could not go; so we dismounted, and having looked into the little church went inside the hut. A wooden sleeping-bench formed its only furniture, upon which I lay down to rest for a few minutes before we recommenced our ascent. Meanwhile O— had converted another part of the bench into a temporary observatory, and was engaged in taking the readings of the aneroid and the thermometer, so as to calculate the height of the mountain. We had not been more than two minutes in the hut when I saw O— hastily investigate his dress. 'Why, here's a flea!' said he, 'and another! and another! and another!' He caught a dozen straight off, and then snatching up his scientific apparatus dashed out of the

P 2

room. I was not slow to follow him, before the fleas had time to turn their attention to me. They had evidently been left behind by the pilgrims five days before, and were naturally exceedingly hungry. After a few minutes' rest on the grass outside we started for the summit, to the Archbishop's great disgust, for he wanted to take an hour's nap. We were soon past the pine trees, climbing up the steep side of the white marble peak by a zigzag path. Very soon the Archbishop became exhausted, and, as we feared he would never reach the top, whilst we were determined to finish our climb, we left him sitting on a rock, and gained the summit of the mountain in exactly one hour after leaving the Panaghia. We found ourselves in a cloud, and it being very chilly we took refuge in the little Chapel of the Transfiguration, lighted the lamps of the iconostasis (with great difficulty, for the wicks, like everything else in the chapel, were as wet as they could be), and sang *Magnificat*.

This chapel is of the most primitive construction. It has no windows, and a dome built of loose stones forms the roof, through the holes in which a few rays of light penetrate into the church. It measures nine feet from the west wall to the iconostasis, and five beyond to the east wall. At the west there is a shed, which might be called a narthex, containing a little well scooped out of the rock to hold the rain water from the roof. On the iconostasis are four icons of brass, those next the holy doors representing the Transfiguration and the Blessed Virgin, the others St. Athanasius and St. John the Baptist. On coming out we found that the clouds were no longer round the peak, but were floating beneath us. The rocky platform at the top of the mountain is very small; there is only just room for the chapel and a small path round its south and west sides. On the north the mountain descends abruptly in a tremendous precipice; on the remaining sides the platform slopes a little before breaking away. Just as we had sat down to rest and O— had lighted a pipe, the clouds cleared off and disclosed the land and sea below us. To the north the promontory stretched away to the mainland, twisting itself into little bays and gulfs, looking like some snaky monster floating on the sea. We could distinguish several of the monasteries on the east side of the promontory, lying peacefully by the sea shore. On the west of us was the Gulf of the Holy Mountain sparkling in the sunshine, and, beyond, the peninsula of Longos, or Sithonia; on the north-east the blue waters of the Strymonic Gulf, with the island of Thasos in the distance; on the south the open sea, with Lemnos on the horizon. It was indeed a glorious sight.

Whilst we were thus enjoying ourselves a cheery voice broke the stillness of the air, and round the corner of the chapel wall appeared the Archbishop, with the faithful Pantele bringing up the rear. The prelate threw himself down beside us, exhausted by his unwonted exertions but yet immensely pleased with himself. 'We are all *hadjis* now,' said he, using the Turkish word for a pilgrim. And, indeed, a visit to the Holy Mountain, including the ascent of the peak, is looked upon by the orthodox world as a pilgrimage second only to that of a visit to the Holy Land. When he had recovered his breath he bethought himself of the perpetual cigarette, but the papers had been left behind.

'Donnez-moi votre tchibouque,' said he to O —, who thereupon handed to him his pipe, and the Archbishop began to console himself with the fragrant weed.

No wonder he was tired; in addition to his ordinary grey cloak lined with ermine he had put over all another enormous cloak, also lined with fur, from which his head alone appeared. Fancy climbing a mountain in two long fur cloaks and a cassock!

We left the summit at a quarter to four o'clock, after having picked up some loose pieces of marble as memorials of our pilgrimage. When we had descended a short distance, O—, finding his stone heavy, handed it to the Archbishop to be passed on to Pantele, for him to carry; but the prelate in his excess of good spirits tried to throw it to his cavass, which of course resulted in its flying wide of its mark and rolling down the slope until it was lost at the bottom. Whilst the Archbishop was giving vent to his merriment at the catastrophe, his foot slipped and he very nearly met with the same fate, and there was something extremely comical in the sight of the Archbishop lying flat on his back with his high hat bounding down the side of the mountain and taking a short cut of its own to the bottom. However, we all reached the Panaghia in safety at 4.45. We instantly mounted our mules, for we observed to our dismay that the blackest of clouds was descending from the top of the mountain, and that a great storm was evidently brewing. We rode down as fast as we could, and reached Kerasia at six o'clock.

Angelos had concocted some fair soup with haricot beans, onions, and some of our cakes of preserved soup; thus, with some cheese, and vegetables from the garden, we made a fair meal. The Archbishop would not share our soup or our cheese, on account of the fast, so he came off second best. We had to eat our food off a low table about a foot high, the old-fashioned Eastern table for use with divans.

The old monk had only two thin tapers and no oil, so we were forced to make the greatest haste over our supper and sleeping arrangements, so as to avoid going to bed in the dark. We spread our rugs on the wooden divan, put up our levinges, and went to bed; and although the boards were hard, our rugs thin, and the fleas innumerable, we soon fell asleep amidst the flashes of lightning, the peals of thunder, and the patter of the rain outside, for the great storm had broken at last.

CHAPTER XIV.

More blest the life of godly Eremite,
Such as on lonely Athos may be seen,
Watching at eve upon the giant height,
Which looks o'er waves so blue, skies so serene,
That he who there at such an hour hath been
Will wistful linger on that hallow'd spot ;
Then slowly tear him from the 'witching scene,
Sigh forth one wish that such had been his lot,
Then turn to hate a world he had almost forgot.
                              Childe Harold

WE rose at 7 A.M., packed up our things, breakfasted off dry bread, a couple of meat lozenges, and some spring water—for there was no coffee to be had—and started for the Monastery of St. Paul.

The storm of the previous night had completely passed away, and it was as pleasant a morning as one could wish for. We had heard that the roads on this part of the promontory were very bad, but we never expected to find them half so bad as they proved to be.

As a rule they are merely narrow paths on the face either of the precipice or, what is just as bad, an almost perpendicular slope, covered with loose stones, except where steps of rock wind and twist backwards and forwards over the depth below. It is really marvellous how the mules manage to keep their footing, especially as in some places these paths are almost as steep as a staircase.

After we had gone some distance the road became

MONASTERY OF ST. PAUL

worse, not only on account of its ruggedness and its enormous height above the place where one would eventually land if one's mule happened to slip, but also because the shrubs and bushes which overhang the path tore and scratched us nearly out of our saddles. So we all dismounted except O—, who stuck manfully to his beast and arrived safely at the bottom of a very awkward bit.

'Vous vivez encore?' were the first words of the Archbishop as we joined each other and remounted our mules.

After about two hours of this hard work we crossed a spur of the mountain, and the Monastery of St. Paul burst upon our view. I do not think any scene at Athos so much impressed me with its beauty as this first view of Agios Pavlos. A French traveller has remarked that it reminds one of Gustave Doré's weird and majestic conceptions; and Mr. Jerningham [1] says: 'To describe its grand aspect, its wonderful position, or the magnificence of the scenery above, below, and around it, is wholly impossible. Indeed, the same remark may apply generally to the whole peninsula. Its varied beauty defies description and baffles any attempt of the kind.'

Between us and the monastery lay a deep ravine, the dry bed of a torrent which ceases to flow in summer. This ravine or gorge descends from the very top of the mountain to the sea. Not only is the position of the convent romantic, but its buildings are indescribably picturesque, with the rows of balconies and overhanging rooms and the great tower and battlemented wall behind them. We were not long in

[1] *To and from Constantinople.*

descending into the torrent-bed and ascending on the farther side to the monastic portal.

We were received with the accustomed honours and taken upstairs to be regaled on rahatlakoum and coffee—not very satisfying, as we had practically had nothing to eat that day. We deluded ourselves with the belief that breakfast would be ready in a short time, but the monks took *two hours* to prepare it, so when it did at last make its appearance we were almost too hungry to eat, although what was provided was not bad. After breakfast we all took 'kef' till three o'clock, when the deputy hegoumenos (the superior of the convent was absent) escorted us to the library. Here are over ninety MSS., but only five on vellum ; one of these a quarto, written in the year 800. But it is most extraordinary that the 200 Bulgarian and Servian manuscripts that Curzon saw in 1837 have absolutely disappeared ; not a single one was to be found. And not only have the books gone, but apparently every remembrance of them also, for nobody had ever heard of them. ' Perhaps the Russians have taken them,' said the monks, ' or perhaps they have been destroyed.' The monastery has never been burnt, and, as I cannot believe that the books could have entirely vanished without leaving a trace of their existence, I think that during some repairs they must have been carelessly thrown into some corner of the rambling old monastery. And it is rambling indeed. We were taken over the buildings by the deputy hegoumenos through the heavily timbered galleries, which run in all directions. How it would burn if it once caught fire ! On the land side there is a high battlemented wall and a tower ; for here the monastery needs most protection, on account of the nature of the site.   The courtyard, which contains the catholicon, is small and confined.

Towards evening we went down to the sea, about a mile distant, to bathe.   On the way I endeavoured to take a photograph of the monastery.   There was a walled vineyard lying on the opposite side of the ravine between the convent and the sea, from which I calculated a good view might be obtained.   Whilst the others went towards the shore I walked round the vineyard until I found a place where I might scramble up the wall.   At last I forced an entrance, and, after trying several places, selected a spot on the edge of the wall, from whence there was a capital view of the monastery.   I had just arranged the legs of the camera when I heard a shrill voice calling out to me, and on looking round saw that a little old man had emerged from the kelli in the vineyard and was coming towards me as fast as he could, shouting and gesticulating as if he were afraid I was going to steal all he possessed. When he came close and found that I was a foreigner he suggested that perhaps I was a Russian.   'No,' said I, 'I am an Englishman.'   On hearing that, the old hermit changed his tone in an instant, and we became great friends.   He helped me to arrange my 'microscope,' as he called it, and after I had taken the photograph of the monastery I showed him how he might look through the camera and see the view. This idea pleased him immensely, and he was already peeping through the back when I made signs that he must put his head underneath the black cloth, which I was holding over the apparatus, so as to shut out the light.   On this, with a look of terror and surprise, he stepped back about four paces. 'Ochi! ochi!' said he, 'no! no!' and all my endeavours to bring him back were useless. Evidently he was fearful of magic, thinking that the black cloth had some connection with the fiend; and I dare say to this day he tells his cronies of the narrow escape he had, and how near he came to losing his soul for the sake of a trumpery peepshow!

However, if he entertained a suspicion that a devil was lurking in the camera he thought none the worse of its owner, for he escorted me to the end of his vineyard and filled my hat with grapes. I afterwards joined O— and bathed.

This evening we talked to the deputy hegoumenos about the monastery. These are the particulars he gave us.

St. Paul's contains eighty monks and twenty servants. It has lands on the mainland near Salonica, on Thasos, and on Cassandra; also a small quantity in Moldavia, in which country it formerly possessed two monasteries, but these have been taken away. Two sketes belong to it, the Nativity of the Blessed Virgin and St. Demetrius;[1] also thirty-two kellia, besides the calyvia belonging to the sketes. The cœnobite rule is observed, and the name of the hegoumenos is Sophronius.

Esocclesia.

1. Catholicon, dedicated to the Purification of the Blessed Virgin, containing two paracclesia—St. George and St. Nicholas.

2. St. Anthimus.

3. St. Gregory.

4. St. Nicholas.

[1] This is probably the skete which, according to the archimandrite Porphyry, contained thirty monks.

ST. PAUL'S, FROM A MONASTIC ENGRAVING OF 1850.

5. St. Constantine.
6. St. George.

Churches without the Walls.

1. St. Demetrius.
2. All Saints.
3. The Panaghia.
4. St. Constantine.
5. St. Spyridion

The early history of the convent is obscure, but it seems probable that it owes its origin to St. Paul, a son of the Emperor Maurice[1] (582–602), who lived here an ascetic life and built a chapel on the site of the future monastery. This seems to have been dependent on Xeropotamou until the year 1404, when it was sold to two Servian nobles, Gerasimus[2] and Anthony, who founded the independent Monastery of St. Paul. John Constantine Biancobano, hospodar of Hungaro-Vallachia, repainted and enlarged it, and added the tower and the refectory in the year 1700.

We occupied the next morning in visiting the catholicon, which is a fine church but new (1845). Like that of the Prodromos there are no divisions behind the iconostasis, and the nave is not separated from the narthex by a wall but by pillars and an archway, on each side of which is an icon. There is a pronaos and two paracclesia—St. George and St. Nicholas—and it is remarkable that these paracclesia are not separated from the main body of the church, but in their open arrangement more nearly resemble Latin side chapels. The walls are not frescoed.[3]

[1] According to Du Cange, Maurice had a son of this name.
[2] The daughter of Gerasimus became the wife of Mahomet II., the conqueror of Constantinople.
[3] Measurements : Sanctuary : from north to south, 43½ feet ; from

After we had measured the church a priest put on a stole, and candles being lighted the relics were brought out from behind the iconostasis. First we were shown a piece of the True Cross, about eight inches long, of this shape,

showing the hole made by one of the nails; it is preserved in a large silver shrine, ornamented both outside and inside with large enamels on porcelain. There is a second relic of the True Cross almost as large as the first; this was presented to the monastery by Elizabeth, Empress of Russia, 136 years ago. We were then shown the gifts of the Magi, said to have been brought to this monastery by a mysterious woman called Cala Maria, or Mary the Beautiful. The incense is contained in a sort of basket made of the gold, through the interstices of which it can be seen; the handle of the basket is formed of the beads of myrrh. There are three distinct relics of these gifts, and each of them has a different form. Besides these most valued relics are the skull of St. Panteleëmon and a leg of St. Gregory the Theologue; also an icon said to have belonged to the Empress Theodora, which escaped unhurt from the flames into which it had been thrust by certain iconoclasts. The church also contains the following treasures :

(a) A magnificent cross, used as an altar cross, of

iconostasis to end of east apse, 18 feet ; across chord of east apse, 16 feet. Nave : across transepts, 50½ feet ; from iconostasis to archway leading to narthex, 32½ feet ; from this archway to the west end of narthex, 24 feet.

wood overlaid with fine silver-gilt work and studded all
over with precious stones. The great beauty of this
cross, however, consists in the miniatures, painted in the
earliest Byzantine style, which cover both its back and
front. There were originally twenty-eight miniatures
on each side, making fifty-six in all ; of these the twenty
large ones are intact, but eight small ones are missing
on one side and five on the other. They represent
scenes from the life of Christ, being painted in gold
and colours on vellum and encrusted with seed pearls ;
each is covered with a small piece of glass. The cross
is altogether in very bad repair, and appears to have
been shamefully used. It has a stand of Persian brass
work, which of course does not belong to it.

(*b*) A book cover (probably belonging to a book of
the Gospels) of similar workmanship. In the centre
is a plaque of ruby-coloured glass, on which is painted
in gold our Blessed Saviour, with outstretched arms ;
beyond this is a border of illuminations on vellum,
from $1\frac{1}{2}$ to 2 inches wide, the groundwork of which
is composed of seed pearls ; then comes an outer
margin of silver-gilt, studded with jewels, on which
were originally fourteen small medallions, painted like
the centre plaque ; of these only six now remain.

(*c*) A diptych, also of the same workmanship, representing on the one side the Crucifixion and on the
other the Annunciation ; surrounded by a border of
lozenge-shaped medallions, with square medallions at
the four corners of each side.

All the inscriptions on the illuminations are in
Latin, and the monks assert that these three magnifi-
cent objects were presented by Pope Silvester to the
Emperor Constantine the Great when he baptized

him in A.D. 315. Truly a most startling statement for Athos monks to make, of all people; for this story of the baptism of Constantine is an ancient, though now somewhat decayed, support of the claims of the Papacy. As a matter of fact Constantine was baptized by Eusebius, Bishop of Nicomedia, in A.D. 337.

After examining these treasures we breakfasted, and then, bidding farewell to our hosts, ordered our luggage to be sent down to the port to meet us at a certain hour, and set out for the skete of St. Anne.

We had passed this place on our way from Kerasia the preceding day, but at a considerable height above it, so we had partially to retrace our steps. We soon, however, branched off on to another road. It was quite as bad as that of the day before, if not worse, for the last part of this terrible path winds up the face of a precipice overhanging the sea; in one place it is tunnelled through a projecting piece of rock. We were all very glad when we found ourselves safe in the valley of St. Anne. This is shut in between three mountain-sides and the sea, and is a charmingly retired spot. The skete itself is situated on the rocky ledge of a great slope, at the height of 1,000 feet above the sea; and all about the valley, from the mountain-side far above the skete down to the shore, are dotted the calyvia belonging to it, sixty in number,[1] each with its garden and little church. In these calyvia live during the week the 150 monks. Every Saturday night they assemble in the skete and pass the night together in the kyriacon (or principal church, which answers to the catholicon of a monastery),

[1] John Comnenus gives the same number.

returning on Sunday to their homes. In the calyvia they live a common life, two or three together, and occupy themselves with cultivating their gardens, carving little crosses to sell to the pilgrims at Caryes and stamps for the Eucharistic bread. Besides these manual labours they have to attend, of course, to their daily devotions.

Georgirenes thus describes the life of the monks of St. Anne's : ' Here Hermits live most retired and melancholly, being not above two or three, sometimes but one in an House. And they do imitate the Lives of those antient Monks in Ægypt, about Thebaïs, that were imitators of St. Anthony, who did himself, as did all his followers, live and maintain themselves by hand labour and manufactures, though of a very mean sort, yet enough to earn them Food and Raiment.'

This is the true life of a skete monk, and St. Anne's is the type of the real skete, those of St. Elias, the Seraï, and the Prodromos being merely monasteries without the name.

The skete itself is surrounded by gardens and vineyards, watered by mountain streams, which either flow in little rivulets along the paths or are carried along the wooden troughs formed of the hollowed-out trunks of trees; these are extensively used on Athos, especially in the neighbourhood of Caryes, where the water is frequently carried overhead across the roads.

It consists of the kyriacon, a bell tower, and a few domestic buildings, inhabited by two or three monks during the week and used as a sort of club and refectory on Sundays. Several monks were waiting to receive us and to offer us the usual refreshment ; they seemed to be poorer than the regular monastic religious.

Q

The kyriacon is dedicated to St. Anne and contains two paracclesia, St. Charalampes and the Zoödóchos Peeghee (ἡ Ζωοδόχος Πηγή), or Life-giving Fountain.[1] The sanctuary measures 21 feet from iconostasis to end of east apse, and 40 feet from north to south, across the bema and the two side chapels. Nave : across the transepts, 60½ feet ; from iconostasis to west wall of nave, 30 feet ; narthex from east to west, 19½ feet.

There is no pronaos and no west door to the narthex, the entrance to the church being by a door in the south wall of the narthex. There is a small library on the north side of the narthex, containing six-and-forty manuscripts, only three of which are written on vellum and none of any interest. We did not see the relics; they include, according to John Comnenus, the left foot of St. Anne.[2] The history of this skete is obscure. 'Perhaps as old as 1007, historically founded in 1680;' so says Porphyry,[3] and the information we obtained on the spot does not throw much light upon it. According to the monks there was originally a monastery close to the sea, dedicated to St. Eleutherius, and they pointed out to us some ruined buildings on the distant shore as being

---

[1] A tender and graceful title of the Blessed Virgin. Under this invocation she is represented as sitting in the midst of a basin filled with water, in which fish are swimming. Her hands are extended, and before her is the Infant Christ in the attitude of benediction. Sometimes He bears on His lap an open book, in which is written, 'I am the Living Water.' Around the fountain men of all conditions, from princes and bishops to the beggars and the impotent, are crowding to bathe and to drink.

[2] 'At Costantynoble lyethe Seynte Anne oure Ladyes Modre, whom Seynte Elyne dede brynge fro Jerusalem.'—*Maundeville*.

[3] *Christian Remembrancer*, 1851.

the remains of this place. They further informed us that 400 years ago, owing to the monastery being repeatedly attacked by pirates, the monks determined to abandon it; they first built the Church of St. Panteleëmon on the mountain-side, a little way above the present skete, and afterwards moved to St. Anne's. The Church of St. Panteleëmon still exists. Comnenus affirms that the present kyriacon was enlarged by Dionysius Andrius, the ex-Patriarch who paved the Athos roads. The skete and all the land about here belongs to the Lavra.

It was very hard to rouse the Archbishop from his kef, but at last we succeeded in making a start and left the skete at half-past three. In an hour we arrived at the port of St. Paul, after having scrambled down an almost perpendicular bank. The mules have a peculiar way of descending a steep place; they plant their fore feet firmly, and then allow their hind legs to slip down the hill. At first the rider fancies every moment that the mule.is falling, but he soon discovers that, although the mule often slips heavily, *it always manages to keep two feet firm;* this is of course the secret of these animals' wonderful performances on the mountain paths.

Our luggage was waiting for us, but the Archbishop's had not arrived from the monastery, and to our great disappointment he told us that he was not coming with us; we were going too fast for him, he said, and, as time was no object whatever to him, but of great consequence to us, he feared we must part. So we kissed his hand and very regretfully bade him farewell, assuring him that we should meet again at another monastery—in fact, that we should take care to do so.

Q 2

'No,' said the Archbishop, 'I fear we shall never see each other again.   Good-bye.'

We pushed off from the little port, and two monks rowed us over the smooth surface of the sea towards a point of rock.   The Archbishop stood upon the shore with the faithful Pantele and Peter, and waved his handkerchief, which we answered by waving our hats until the little rocky promontory hid him from our view.

The Monastery of St. Dionysius was now in sight, and in about half an hour we reached the harbour beneath the rock on which the monastery stands, with its lofty walls and rows of overhanging balconies.   We tried to take a photograph whilst our luggage was being landed, but the sun was setting and the light too bad ; so, thinking that Angelos had already heralded our arrival, we climbed up the 200 feet which is the height of the ascent from the sea to the portal of the monastery.   We were received by a monk at the gate and led through the gloomy courts and corridors to a dark, low, and rather dirty room.   Angelos now arrived with our baggage, and we set him to work to scold our monk and to demand where the hegoumenos was and why we had been taken to such a miserable place.   So away he went to announce our arrival to his superior and to prepare our meal.   It did not take long to get supper ready, for it was not a very grand meal, and our tempers did not improve our appetites, our churlish reception having put us into the worst of humours.   There were no chairs, so we sat on a very low divan round a table which was perhaps a foot high.   Nearly the whole of our dining-room was built out from the wall over the precipice ; the floor sloped outwards as if the supports had slightly given way, and looking out of window made one's blood run cold.

Supper being ended, we again asked after the abbot's health, and gave our monk to understand that we had no intention of sleeping where we had supped. We were presently taken, therefore, to a large room on the other side of the convent; but still no hegoumenos appeared. Then we sent word to him that we wished to see him, and the answer was returned that he had gone to bed, and hoped we would excuse him till the morning. This being an *ultimatum* we disposed ourselves for sleep.

We rose about seven, and accompanied the monks who had been sent to conduct us to the hegoumenos.

My lord abbot was very apologetic and conciliatory over the glyko and coffee, but O— thought proper to look like thunder, and I received his apologies rather coldly; however, as he was very civil and conducted us in person to the catholicon, we finally forgave him. This church,[1] dedicated to St. John the Baptist, is a fine building, pinched in between the domestic buildings which surround it, so that it will infallibly be burnt if the monastery ever catches fire again, as it did on October 21, 1523. In that great conflagration the whole of the convent was gutted; it was restored with this church—which was rebuilt on a larger scale— about the year 1580, by Peter, the voivode, authentes of Hungaro-Vallachia. It possesses an esonarthex, an

---

[1] The nave measures 29 feet from west wall to iconostasis, and 41½ feet across the transepts. The sanctuary is 13 feet from iconostasis to end of east apse, and 13 feet across, or, including the two side chapels, 41½ feet.

exonarthex, a sort of pronaos—a wooden balcony over-looking the sea—and a curious cloister on the south side of the church. On the north of the nartheces is a paracclesi of the Panaghia, containing a small picture said to be by St. Luke, now utterly ruined. Finely carved doors lead from the esonarthex into the nave. The frescoes, with which the walls are covered, date from the rebuilding of the monastery by the voivode Peter; when Mr. Tozer was visiting St. Dionysius he found a young monk engaged upon their restoration.

The chief relics are the right hands of St. John the Baptist and of St. John, Patriarch of Alexandria (St. John the Merciful?), a piece of St. Peter's chain, a portion of the True Cross, and the tusk of St. Christopher to which we were referred when at the skete of the Prodromos. I produced my tape and found that it measured about two inches in length from the point to where it had been broken off above the root. A piece of the head or forehead of St. John Baptist is said to have been here. If it be still preserved I cannot say ; we did not see it. In addition to these there are the bones of St. Niphon, confessor to Neagulus, voi-vode of Hungaro-Vallachia, who gave the magnificent casket in which they are preserved. Of this saint Georgirenes gives the following account in his descrip-tion of the convent :

Besides these they show the Bones of one Nymphus, once Patri-arch of Constantinople, who being weary of publick employment retir'd hither, unknown to any who he was ; so they, looking upon him as a poor Vagabond that wanted work, employ'd him as their Muleteer to fetch in their wood ; in which employment he continued with great humility and faithfulness many years, not offering to ride any of the Mules going or coming, and kept all the Church Fasts strictly in the midst of all his drudgery. At his death bed he dis-

cover'd to the Superiour who he was, and that he chose that manner
of Life to mortifie his proud flesh. Whereupon, looking upon him as
a Saint, they keep his Bones as a sacred Relique.

St. Niphon is commemorated on August 11. The
casket or shrine—containing all his bones with the
exception (so Comnenus says) of his head and right
hand, which were preserved in the Monastery of
Argiesius in Hungaro-Vallachia—is very elaborate and
interesting. It takes the form of a church, modelled
in silver-gilt, and measures 1 foot 11 inches long by
1 foot broad and 2 feet in its extreme height. The
architecture of this church is a curious mixture of
Byzantine and Gothic ; for instance, it possesses four
small domes and one large one in the centre ; between these are small spires ; the roof is gabled and
the windows are filled with semi-flamboyant tracery.
Round the church are medallions of saints in niello
work. Curzon says of this extraordinary reliquary :

'It is altogether a wonderful and precious monument of ancient art, the production of an almost
unknown country, rich, quaint, and original in its
design and execution, and is indeed one of the most
curious objects on Mount Athos.'

The only other thing of interest in the catholicon
is an icon of the Baptist, which escaped the general
conflagration in the sixteenth century. The library is
a small room over the church, approached by a very
steep and narrow staircase in the wall, up which
Angelos threaded his way with extreme difficulty
There appeared to be at least 500 manuscripts. The
principal ones are a quarto evangelistarium in uncial
letters, consisting of 474 leaves, imperfect, probably of
the seventh century; another uncial book of the Gospels,

also of the seventh century. Both these manuscripts are in good preservation. Besides these two there are a thick octavo New Testament of the twelfth century, with full-page illuminations ; a folio evangelistarium with a large illumination at the beginning, and several rolls containing liturgies, but all late. The books seemed well cared for.

Besides the catholicon with its paracclesi St. Dionysius possesses the following churches within the walls :

> The Archangels,
> St. Nicholas,
> St. Chrysostom,
> St. George,
> St. Niphon,
> The Holy Unmercenaries,
> St. John the Divine ;

and outside the convent :

> All Saints,
> The Holy Apostles,
> St. James the brother of God,
> St. Demetrius,

making twelve churches in all. Six kellia belong to it, likewise four farms in Chalcidice and two in the island of Thasos. The community, numbering 100 monks, follows the cœnobite rule ; these monks have ten servants, and their old abbot's name is Kyriacos.

Now for the history of the monastery.

The founder was a certain Dionysius, a native of a village called Corussus, in Castoria. This man came to Mount Athos and lived as a hermit on the spot where the monastery is now built. Having for several nights seen the apparition of a great torch burning in that place, he resolved to found a monastery there, and for that purpose went to Trebizonde, of which city his brother was archbishop. By his influence he succeeded in interesting the Emperor of Trebizonde, Alexius III. Comnenus, in his project, and returning to Athos he built, in 1380 or 1385, a church in honour of St. John the Baptist at Alexius's expense. The chrysobull of the Emperor relating to the foundation of the monastery is still preserved, and I much regret that we did not ask to see it, being unaware of its existence. It is described in Finlay's 'History of Greece,' on the authority, I believe, of Fallmerayer, as 'one of the most valuable monuments of the pictorial and caligraphical art of the Greeks in the Middle Ages. This imperial charter consists of a roll of paper, a foot and a half broad and fifteen feet long, surrounded by a rich border of arabesques. The imperial titles are set forth in capitals about three inches high, emblazoned in gold and ultramarine; and the word "Majesty," wherever it occurs in the document, is always written, like the Emperor's signature, with the imperial red ink. This curious document acquires its greatest value from containing at its head, under a half-length figure of our Saviour with hands extended to bless the imperial figures, two full-length portraits of the Emperor Alexios and the Empress Theodora, about sixteen inches high, in which their features, their imperial crowns, their rich robes and splendid jewels are represented in colours with all the care and minuteness of the ablest Byzantine artists. Immediately under the imperial titles, below the portraits, are the two golden *bullæ*, or seals, each of the size of a crown piece, bearing the respective effigies and titles of the two sovereigns.   The seals are attached to the bull by chains of gold.'

Later on the voivode Neagulus, who gave the shrine of St. Niphon, built the tower and an aqueduct ; and after the fire of 1523 the voivode Peter restored the monastery and rebuilt the church, Silvanus, a monk, being Peter's 'clerk of the works.'   Roxandra, this good voivode's daughter, built an infirmary and the fine refectory, and her husband, Alexander the voivode, became a monk under the name of Pachomius.   Other benefactors were Macarius, metropolitan of Heraclea, and two pairs of brothers, about whom I can discover nothing, named respectively Lazarus and Boïus, Manuel and Thomas.

CHAPTER XV.

WE left St. Dionysius at about half-past ten, after having again taken glyko and coffee with the abbot Kyriacos, who now could not do enough for us.

Our luggage was put into a boat, and two stout monks rowed us round the point which shuts out the

MONASTERY OF ST. GREGORY.

view of St. Gregory from St. Dionysius. The voyage did not take much more than a quarter of an hour. On the way we stopped to take a photograph of the convent from a rock; on reaching the port, much to our annoyance we found that we had taken its least picturesque side. It is situated, very much like St.

Dionysius, on a rocky promontory which forms one side of a narrow gorge running down to the sea.

On the little quay stood a pleasant-looking, quiet-mannered monk, who received us very courteously, as if he were accustomed to perform the duties of hospitality, and took us up to the monastery. Here the hegoumenos was waiting for us in a bright and clean chamber overlooking the sea. We sat for a long time chatting over our coffee to these two most intelligent and gentlemanly men. They were much interested in hearing about the Anglican Church, and discussed the possibilities of unity thoughtfully and without prejudice. Soon breakfast was announced, and we were conducted along the corridor to another part of the monastery, where, on a table covered with a snow-white cloth, a capital meal had been prepared. We had not sat down to such a repast since leaving the skete of the Prodromos, and, odds-trenchers-and-knives, how we ate! The abbot having some business to transact, his courteous deputy, who had met us at the quay, entertained us right nobly, although he would not join us in eating and drinking. After breakfast we returned to the reception room and had coffee, for the fourth time this day, and it was only half-past twelve.

Having indulged in a short siesta we were taken to the catholicon. There is nothing of any particular interest about this church [1] except a good iconostasis of

---

[1] But Didron noticed a curious fresco, I suppose somewhere in the catholicon. 'Au couvent de Saint-Grégoire, dans le mont Athos, j'ai vu un Adam et Eve sans nombril.' How this would have pleased Sir Thomas Browne, who wrote a whole essay in support of his favourite conceit !

The measurements of this catholicon are as follows : Sanctuary : from north to south, including chapels, 23 feet ; from iconostasis to east end of apse, 12 feet. Nave, across transepts, 38 feet ; from iconostasis to west wall of nave, 25 feet.

carved wood ; there are a few relics, but, as vespers was just going to be sung, we had no time to see them.

There are both nartheces, and on the south side is a paracclesi dedicated to St. Gregory. The library contains about 150 manuscripts ; among them a paper octavo of the fifteenth century, consisting of six leaves, curious on account of the extremely minute characters in which it is written; the subject is the Shepherd of Hermas. There are four vellum MSS., one being of the ninth century, consisting of a collection of sermons. There are also several late (seventeenth and eighteenth century) classical MSS., containing various works of Homer, Plutarch, and Hesiod. All the old books were burnt, and the present collection only dates from the last hundred years.

The refectory is small and poor. In it we had a lesson in Byzantine music; a monk singing to us from the notes in the musical primer which I have before described, and which he finally gave me. We returned to the reception room to take our farewell cup of coffee. As we passed the catholicon a monk with a censer coming through the doorway censed us and other persons who were standing outside.

The Monastery of St. Gregory contains eighty monks and ten servants. The community has lands in Macedonia and Chalcidice, having lost two small farms in Vallachia in 1865. The following is a list of the churches :

Esocclesia.

1. The catholicon, dedicated to St. Nicholas, containing one paracclesi, dedicated to St. Gregory.
2. The Zoödóchos Pceghee, or Life-giving Fountain.
3. St. Demetrius.
4. The Holy Archangels.
5. St. Anastasia.

Exocclesia.

1. All Saints (cemetery church).
2. The Blessed Virgin.
3. The Holy Fathers of Athos (i.e. all the⎫ All these have
saints that the Holy Mountain has produced).   ⎬ cathismata
4. St. John the Divine.   ⎪ attached to
5. St. Stephen.   ⎬ them.
6. St. Tryphon (at Caryes).   ⎭

Besides the five cathismata there are four kellia
belonging to the monastery. The monastery seems to
have been founded about the year 1260 by St. Gregory
the younger, who, according to the monastic tradition,
was a missionary from Mount Sinai. It was restored
by Alexander, Hospodar of Moldo-Vallachia, in 1497.
On November 30, 1761, it was destroyed by fire.

Vespers was still being chanted when we left the
convent, but the good abbot, Simeon, came out of the
catholicon to bid us farewell and accompanied us to
the gate.

'We are much disappointed,' said he, 'at your
leaving us so soon; you ought to have stayed the
night at least; but perhaps you will come back to us
again before you leave Athos?'

We said that we should do our best to return, so as
to spend a few days under their most hospitable roof;
and we fully intended to do so, thinking that we should
have some time on our hands after having completed
the circuit of the monasteries. But, alas! our sojourn
on the Holy Mountain was all too short, and we did
not see again the kind abbot and his courteous lieutenant.
The latter escorted us to the boat.

Our crew consisted of a couple of monks and two
servitors. One of these cosmicoi was a well-built

ST. GREGORY'S, FROM A MONASTIC ENGRAVING OF 1819.

(In the upper portion of the plate is St. Nicholas, the Patron of the Monastery, habited as an Eastern Bishop.)

youth of nineteen, with an ugly but honest and good-
natured face, who chattered incessantly during the
whole voyage.   Being curious to get an insight into
the habits and thoughts of these Athonite lay-folk, we
entered into conversation with him and asked him a
good many questions, which he answered with the
accompaniment of wry faces and grimaces, as is
usual with the lower orders of Greeks when under
cross-examination, to express, I suppose, the mental
torture such a proceeding causes them.   He told us
that his home was in some obscure island of the
Archipelago, and that he had come to Athos to make
a little money by his calling, that of fisherman and
sailor.   He had worked at St. Gregory's for a year,
and in that time had amassed a small store of savings,
with which he had embarked in a little schooner,
hoping to work his passage back to his island home.
Hardly had they set sail when a storm came on, and
before they left the Gulf of the Holy Mountain they
were wrecked in the Bay of Daphne (which is the
safest anchorage at Athos and lies under the Monastery of Xeropotamou).   Our unlucky friend barely
escaped with his life, all his worldly possessions being
lost, and he sorrowfully pointed out to us the remains
of the wreck (for we were just passing the place), where
twenty-five as good mejidiehs as ever were coined were
lying at the bottom of the sea.

We tried to cheer him up, suggesting that another
year would produce another crop of mejidiehs and that
Athos was as pleasant a place as one could wish for.
But he said he was very anxious to go home and he
didn't like being at Athos at all.   Was it, then, the
monks that he disliked, or was the food bad ?   Oh, no ;

the victuals were good enough and the caloyers all
very well, but he particularly wished to get back to
his island.

'Ah,' said we, 'you want to get married!' It was
quite ridiculous to see how the broad, good-humoured
face blushed under this indictment. And with many
grimaces he was obliged to own that there *was* a
young lady in the case, who was anxiously awaiting
his return. At this news all on board joined in
chaffing him unmercifully, and told him that by this
time his sweetheart had certainly married somebody
else; but this he stoutly denied, although he admitted
that, as neither of them could read or write, he had
had no tidings of her since their parting. Then, much
to the edification of our two monastic oarsmen, I proceeded to deliver a little homily on the advantages
of a celibate life and on the number of bad wives
there are about, ending by quoting the advice of the
Apostle: 'He that marrieth doeth well, but he that
marrieth not doeth better;' a text which was received
in the bows of the boat with shouts of 'Polycala,' but
the devoted lover remained unmoved alike by taunt
and precept.

So the time passed cheerfully enough, although it
took us nearly three hours to reach Russico. The
Gulf of the Holy Mountain was as smooth as glass,
and we thoroughly enjoyed the splendid scenery on
our right as we skirted the western side of the promontory. We passed two monasteries on our way, intending to visit them later on—the wonderful Simopetra on
its lofty crag, joined to the side of the mountain by an
aqueduct, and Xeropotamou on the slope above the
Bay of Daphne.

With few exceptions the sea washes the rocky bases of the precipices all the way from Cape St. George (the ancient Nymphæum) to the other side of Simopetra, and these exceptions are the little bays or creeks where the valleys, in which the monasteries are inclosed, run down to the sea. Thus the Monasteries of St. Paul, St. Dionysius, St. Gregory, and Simopetra are almost completely isolated from each other, and for this reason it is customary to go from one to the other by boat, unless the weather be stormy, so as to avoid the dangerous paths which are the only other means of communication. Soon after passing Simopetra the mountain begins to fall away, and by the time one reaches Xeropotamou the frowning cliffs have given place to gentle slopes.

The white walls of Russico can be seen a great way off; we seemed to be a long time getting there, and, as the sun was near the ridge of Longos, we began to get impatient, fearing lest the gates should be shut. Several ships were lying in the little bay, which is secure enough except when south winds blow, and amongst them the steam launch belonging to the monastery : for Russico is a go-ahead colony; the inhabitants pride themselves upon being the subjects of a first-class European Power and despise the Greek civilization as a relic of Oriental barbarism. The whole place is more like a small town than a monastery, although the convent itself, which is of considerable size, is inclosed and can be entered only through a gateway; for all around it and down to the water's edge are workshops, and storehouses, and dwelling houses; and still the monks are building more, so that the great monastery is increasing in extent year by year.

R

It cannot be disguised that Russico has more concern with politics than religion, and that unless the Russian colonization of Athos receives a check the greatest political complications will ensue. As I have just said, I am fully persuaded that Russico is mainly a government affair supported by government money, and indirectly, if not directly, under government control.

But it will be asked, What interests other than religious can Russia have at Mount Athos? From a political point of view the possession of the Holy Mountain is of the highest importance to Russia in furthering her schemes for the extension of her territory to the shores of the Mediterranean. The eyes of Russia and of Austria are both turned covetously upon Salonica, a town second to Constantinople alone in political importance, on account of the power it would confer on its possessors over the destinies of European Turkey, and the acquisition of the Athonite peninsula would enable Russia to give checkmate to the schemes of her rival; for the whole promontory may be looked upon as one gigantic natural fortress, practically unassailable by sea and connected with the mainland by an isthmus only a mile and a half in breadth, which a few earthworks would render impassable,[1] whilst, owing to the dangerous nature of the coast and the frequency of storms, a successful blockade would be impossible. Each monastery, too, is defended by strong walls and gates, able to afford a stout resistance to any attacking body destitute of artillery, which, from the extreme ruggedness of the country, could be only partially employed by a land force.

---

[1] I am told that the Russians have founded a settlement (Chormitza) near here, containing 100 monks.

The history of the Russian colonization of the Holy Mountain is one dismal story of abuse of confidence, hypocrisy, bribery, and machination, and yet a tale with an amusing side to it, for at last the sharp and crafty Greeks have been outwitted by the χονδρο-κέφαλοι Ρῶσσοι, *the Russian numskulls.* Soon after reaching Athos we discovered that great ill-feeling existed between the Greeks and their northern co-religionists, the former complaining that the Russians had firmly established themselves on the Holy Mountain by false pretences. The danger which they fear is that Russia will claim the promontory as her own when sufficient Russian subjects have been imported to outnumber the Greeks, and that thus a great blow will be struck at the authority of the Œcumenical Patriarch and at the pre-eminence of the Greek Church, the ultimate aim of the Russians being to remove the patriarchate to Moscow, or in some other way to subject the mother to the daughter Church and both to the Czar and his ministers. This may be one motive for the Russian colonization of Athos, and it is true that the Greek Church, coextensive with the Greek *nation*, would prove a great obstacle in the way of the Muscovite appropriation of Constantinople or other parts of the Turkish Empire where the Greeks form the larger part, or even a considerable minority, of the population. Appreciating this fact, the Russians may well wish to break the power of the Church, a task of such magnitude that even the conqueror Mahomet II. shrank from undertaking it. And there are not wanting other signs besides the colonization of Mount Athos to show that the Russians are pursuing this policy. Turkey is at the present time at the feet of

R 2

her conquerors and completely under her influence. The recent conflict between the Phanar and the Porte, which has resulted in the resignation of the late Patriarch, Joachim III.[1] (by whom we were received before going to Athos), has been almost certainly the work of Russian intrigue, as was the late Bulgarian schism, not yet healed. The weakening effect of such troubles as these to the Church of Constantinople may be easily realized.

As Russico is the head-quarters of the Russians, has been for centuries connected with their country, and was the starting-point of the present Russian colonization, it may be as well to give in this place the history of the monastery, and then to discuss the events of the past fifty years in connexion with it.

The convent was founded, it is said, by St. Lazarus Knezes of Servia, and dedicated to St. Panteleëmon of Thessalonica. In the year 1169 it was given by the authorities of Athos to certain Russian monks, who had been living from the end of the eleventh century in the Monastery of the Assumption, on the east side of the promontory. After this it seems to have changed hands several times, and to have been occupied successively by Servians and Greeks. Up to 1765 the monastery was situated farther inland, at a place called Xilourgon (though it was certainly called Russico as early as the sixteenth century,[2] and probably took that name in 1169); in the year 1765 the monks moved nearer the sea, where they erected some new buildings. The monastery was almost entirely rebuilt

---

[1] 1884.

[2] See Belon, *Les Observations de plusieurs Singularitez*, 1555.

in 1812 by Greek monks at the charges of Callimaki, Hospodar of Moldavia.

Probably at this time there were no Russians at all in the monastery ; Curzon, who was there in 1837, does not seem to have come across any, and he mentions that the hegoumenos then ruled over 130 monks. Now there are 800 attached to Russico, of whom 450 live within the walls, together with 150 servants, and all are Russians, with the exception of a very few Greek monks of the lowest and most ignorant type and one or two Bulgarians.[1] This extraordinary change requires some explanation. I will give my readers the Greek account, of which they can believe as much as they please. I will not vouch for its accuracy, but from what we saw and heard at Russico I believe it to be in the main facts true. My informant was a well-known professor of the University of Athens whom we met at Athos, and his story was corroborated by the Greek monks.

In 1839 the Russians asked permission of Gerasimus, the abbot of St. Panteleëmon or Russico, to bring eighteen Russian monks to the convent, promising in writing that their number should never be increased beyond fifty, the Greek monks numbering at that time 150 ; but afterwards, by means of bringing servants from Russia and then making them monks, they increased their numbers until in 1869 they had reached 400. By this time, having got simple old Gerasimus completely into their power, they tore up the compromising document limiting their numbers, and through the abbot expelled all the monks who opposed their

[1] Amongst them we came across several retired officers from the Russian army, still in the prime of life.

schemes,[1] Eutropius, our guest master at Vatopedi,
being the last of the original Greek monks.   Finally,
to make matters quite sure—for in cases of dispute such
as these an appeal lies to the Patriarch of Constantinople (as has been more fully explained in a previous
chapter) — Macarius, the present abbot, bribed the
last Patriarch in 1876 to support the Russian interest
with 20,000 liras in hard cash and a cross worth
another 5,000, besides the little *douceurs* distributed
amongst certain of the Holy Synod of Constantinople
to make them 'vote straight.'   Altogether a very
pretty little business, not much to the credit of either
party.   And, remember, I am giving the Greeks' account, and they would not be likely to invent stories
to their own discredit.

Having thus obtained a firm footing at Russico,
the Russians turned their attention to other parts of
the promontory, and in 1837 took a kelli on the site
of the Prophet Elias, turning it into the present skete.
The inhabitant of a kelli is, of course, only a life
tenant, and at his death the cottage and land revert to
the monastery, which relets it to another monk : in the
case of the Prophet Elias this ought to have occurred.
But the old house had been pulled down and a skete

---

[1] The Greeks have a grand story about Gerasimus's terrible fate, which
I will give as an example of the tales they told us concerning their enemies.
When this abbot died he was buried as usual and dug up, in the ordinary
course, at the end of three years.   To the horror of the Russians the
corpse was entire ; for it is the universal superstition in this part of the
world that if a body is not decomposed its late owner has gone to a bad
place.   So they popped the old gentleman back again into the hole and
tried to keep the matter quiet.   At the end of another three years they
again uprooted him, and again found him in his former condition.   Then
they tried another spot of ground, thinking that the soil might be at
fault, but with no better result.   At the time of our visit the Greeks
assured us that poor Gerasimus had just been buried for the fourth time !

created on its site.   So the Russians established themselves in the possession of what is practically a monastery ; for in a true skete the mother monastery appoints
the superior, but in this case the monks elect their
own ruler and are only theoretically dependent on the
mother house.

In precisely the same way was the Seraï, or skete
of St. Andrew, founded out of a kelli belonging to
Vatopedi by a certain Russian monk named Bessarion,
who (so it is said) ingratiated himself with the monks
of that house by his good fellowship and merry dis-
position ; so that, completely thrown off their guard
by one whom they looked upon as a half-witted
buffoon, they never suspected any sinister designs
until they awoke one fine day to find that the Russian
fool had set up a monastery of his own.[1]

Besides these new foundations the Russians have
also endeavoured to possess themselves of Iveron, until
1830 entirely inhabited by Greeks, although in its
early days it was frequented by Iberians or Georgians.
In that year a Georgian monk called Benedictus
arrived with one servitor and took the cathisma of the
Prophet Elias from the monastery.   In 1872 another
Benedictus arrived with two fellow-countrymen, took a
kelli, and afterwards, without the permission of the
convent, brought thirty-five other Georgians.   Now
these Georgians in the interests of Russia, to whom
Georgia belongs, claim the monastery as their own by
reason of its foundation and name as against the 170
Greek inmates, but as yet unsuccessfully.

---

[1] After the Gerasimus *fiasco* the Russians were not going to stand any
more nonsense from contumacious bodies, so they boiled Bessarion.—
Græcia mendax.

Lastly, the skete of St. Andrew having no port, that community has been for some time endeavouring to buy the arsenal of Stavroniketa ; and the Monastery of Coutloumoussi is also greatly coveted by the Russians, who have been bidding for it since 1863. But now the original inhabitants of the Holy Mountain, being fully roused, have entered into a solemn compact never again to sell a foot of ground to the intruders ; and to this resolution they have adhered, so that for the last three years the Russians have not been able to buy any land whatever, although they have offered enormous prices for it—as much as 30,000 liras for a kelli worth 2,000. Thus they are obliged to make the most of what they have already, and consequently at their two great stations, Russico and St. Andrew's, they are hard at work with stones and mortar. Many are the tales told of lights seen at night on the mountain moving between these two communities, the evidence of secret communications carried on under the cover of darkness. The bitterness of feeling between the two parties may be imagined from the fact that the Greeks attribute the frequent fires which have taken place in their monasteries during the last fifty years to Russian incendiaries. The real mainspring of all these Russian plots is said to be not the abbot Macarius, but a certain ghostly man ($\pi\nu\epsilon\upsilon\mu\alpha\tau\iota\kappa\acute{o}\varsigma$) who lives in great retirement at Russico. To this man the Russian pilgrims apply for spiritual if not temporal advice, and he is accused of acquiring influence over them and of enhancing his reputation for sanctity by the following means : Nearly all the pilgrims pass through Constantinople, and during their stay in that city are interviewed by this man's secret agents, who transmit to him the names of the pilgrims, with certain particulars about each which they have gained from them. On their arrival at Russico they are introduced to this *pnevmaticos*, who, to their great astonishment, enters at once into their family affairs. 'Ah, Ivan, how is your wife, Nadejda?' 'And you, Nicholaïevitch, did you leave Katinka in good health?' Thus, say the Greeks, has he acquired his reputation as a prophet and one directly inspired by God.

As I said before, I give these stories chiefly for the sake of showing the bitterness of the struggle now undoubtedly going on at Athos, though there is great reason for believing that these tales are only exaggerations of the truth. It is quite possible, and even probable, that the Greeks are jealous of the greater number of Russian than of Greek pilgrims to the Holy Mountain (caused by the deeper religious feeling that exists amongst the lower orders of Russians than amongst the Greeks),—pilgrims who make the journey, I believe, entirely from religious motives. Yet that the Russian authorities both at home and at Athos are scheming for important political ends I see no reason to doubt; but that munitions of war are being stored up at Russico, as has been asserted, is very improbable, and I saw nothing to confirm this statement.

I am no hater of Russia. On the contrary, I see much to admire in a great Christian empire filled with ambitious schemes, having for a backbone a vast peasant class blindly devoted to their sovereign and enthusiastically attached to their national Church. In some respects I go further than the most zealous Russophile, for I can even appreciate the Russian

Government—in *theory* the only government worth the name in Europe, though in *practice* enfeebled by the worst of political diseases, widespread official corruption. This, with the licentious selfishness of the upper classes, unworthy of their humbler countrymen, will be the means of destroying the empire, if Providence shall have decreed its destruction.

But no unprejudiced traveller in Russia or her dependencies can fail to see that she is the enemy of England, and that her thirst for territory gravely threatens the peace not only of this country but of Europe. There are statesmen and journalists who tell us that we are all fools, frightened by a shadow, and that Russia is the most peaceable and friendly country in Europe. I hope it may be so, for I should be glad to see England allied to a religious and monarchical country such as Russia, if such an alliance were possible. Russia may be working simply in the interests of civilization and humanity. We shall see.

CHAPTER XVI.

He
Lodg'd in the abbey, where the reverend abbot
With all his convent honourably receiv'd him.—*Henry VIII.*

ON arriving at the port of Russico we bade our crew farewell, taking care to place a mejidieh in the rough palm of the devoted lover, to form a nest-egg for the other twenty-four.

At the gate of the monastery we presented our circular letter for transmission to the abbot, and were then shown to our rooms, on the east side of the convent. It being Saturday night the greater part of the monks had gone to bed, including the abbot, who sent word to this effect, adding that a monk would represent him that evening and that he hoped to see us after the liturgy in the morning. Accordingly the guest-master, whose name was Heliodorus, soon appeared, was very polite and civil, and arranged a bedroom (with beds in it!) for us at the end of a long passage, with a dining-room, in which Angelos slept, opposite to it. Then he bade us good-night, and leaving us in charge of an ignorant but honest Greek monk called Conon, so took his departure.

Sunday, August $\frac{26}{14}$. We got up at seven o'clock. The bells were still ringing as they had been when we went to bed. Close to us was one of the churches, and the monotonous chanting of the monks had soon lulled me to sleep, whilst the perfume of the incense came in at the window and filled our bedchamber. When I awoke the same chanting greeted my ears and the same scent of incense pervaded the air. O— asserted that both bells and chanting had been going on since he went to bed, and of course he hadn't had a wink of sleep—no, not the whole night through, &c. &c., his usual complaint when it is time to get up in the morning !

We reached the principal church (not the catholicon) about eight o'clock, were taken to three stalls which had been reserved for us next the iconostasis on the south side, and remained there until nearly ten. This church is a long narrow room at the top of the north or highest side of the monastery, which is built on the slope of the hill. Its walls are whitewashed, but on them are several well-executed icons. The iconostasis is rich, and above the holy doors is suspended a small icon covered with pearls and diamonds ; the usual stalls are round the walls. Here the service is always in Slavonic, and the music the reformed Russian in four parts. The quire was not very good, but, as the monks had been singing the whole night, one must excuse them for having been slightly out of tune. Afterwards we paid a visit to the abbot Macarius. He was sitting at the top of a long narrow room with chairs all round it, on this occasion occupied by guests and monks. Macarius is a fine-looking, middle-aged man, with a long beard just beginning to grow grey ; not unlike a Western abbot in his manners. The expression of his countenance is shrewd, his presence dignified, and his air commanding ; altogether the sort of man one would expect to find at the head of the

1,600 Russian monks of the Holy Mountain. Over his habit he wears a pectoral cross.

He rose to receive us and shook us warmly by the hand, saying he was much pleased to see us. Glyko and 'tchai' were served, and we conversed, through two interpreters, about the Anglican and Oriental Churches, the monastery, and other kindred topics. However, he could not stay long with us, as the monks required his presence in the refectory; so courteously wishing us good-bye he took his departure.

Heliodorus conducted us over a portion of the monastery, and first of all to the refectory, which was quite full of monks eating their dinner. About 300 of them were thus engaged; the rest, with some pilgrims, were waiting outside till their turn should come. A monk was reading from a pulpit some spiritual book in Russian or Slavonic ; the abbot Macarius presided. The food was very scanty, consisting only of a few vegetables. All were provided with wooden spoons, and the quietness with which these 300 monks ate their food was most remarkable. After walking up the gangway from end to end we left the hall and went back to our own repast. The afternoon was spent in visiting different parts of the monastery—the room where they paint icons, the place where these are stored up, and the little shop outside the walls where they are sold.

We were taken to the burial ground, about twenty yards square, and to its little church. It is just outside the monastery, at the south-east corner, and is apparently a favourite place for profitable meditation ; for from our windows we could see monks constantly going up the little hill which leads to it. In the church

are the bones of the monks whose three years in the
cemetery are over. On one side of the church are
long shelves of a considerable depth, clean and nicely
painted, and on these skulls of departed brethren are
neatly arranged, to the number, we were told, of 1,500.
On another side arm and leg bones are stacked, and
at the entrance stand two great boxes about half full
of the smaller bones, the lids being propped open and
perforated zinc let into the sides of the chests to air the
contents.

At seven o'clock the great service for the festival
of the Assumption began, which was to last until ten
the next morning. We went at eight to the upper
church, already mentioned, and stayed there two hours.
The singing was good, and the vestments of the clergy
very costly, most of the ministers being clad in red and
gold damask. On the head of the abbot Macarius
was a crown covered with enamels and blazing with
diamonds and other precious stones. Contrary to the
usual rather slovenly performance of the complicated
Oriental rites, everything was done in the most exact
manner, and went smoothly and with dignity. We
were especially struck with two deacons, fine tall men,
who wore albs of cloth of gold, over which their beards
descended in front and their long wavy hair behind.
Each with one hand supported on his left shoulder
an incense boat in the form of a silver-gilt church, and
in the other held a silver censer. And so they passed
slowly up and down the church, censing icons and
people, keeping time exactly both in their steps and in
the swinging of their censers. Close in front of us, in
a detached stall, stood an old Russian in the long black
coat and high boots of his nation. He was, we were

told, a merchant of enormous wealth, though his coat was rusty and all his garments threadbare, who, mindful of that Scripture which warns the rich of the difficulty of their salvation, had made this pilgrimage to the Holy Mountain, there to pray, to fast, and to do alms for the good of his soul. And, as far as another can judge, he did pray indeed! At every service at which we were present there was this ancient pilgrim in his stall, and on this particular night during the whole of the fifteen hours he never left the church, although his devotions were of the most laborious kind. According to the Russian custom he bowed and crossed himself almost continuously, never allowing more than half a minute to elapse without a lowly reverence and that holy sign, sometimes varied by a prostration on the floor, before which exercise he would cross himself convulsively twelve times in quick succession. Long before we left, the perspiration was dropping from his forehead on to the floor.

We returned to our room, added the Anglican vespers to our devotions in church, and so to bed; but, as the soft breezes of the night wafted into our chamber the perfume of the incense and the chanting of the monks, I could not help pondering over the old man keeping his vigil in the church above, and how that the kingdom of heaven suffers violence and the violent take it by force.

Heliodorus came to us in the morning and conducted us to the guests' dining-room, where breakfast was prepared. Afterwards, although he had been up all night, he insisted upon taking us to the library, a separate building in the courtyard. It is in capital order, containing a great number of modern works and about 500 MSS. on paper, with fifty on vellum, none of any particular interest. There are twelve Bulgarian MSS. Could these have come from St. Paul's ? Amongst others was a small psalter of Western origin—French or German, if I remember aright. Matthew, the librarian, showed us the various sections of subjects into which the modern books are arranged, and said that they possessed a copy of one of William Palmer's [1] works in Greek, but he could not find it at that moment. As he said that the monks here used their library—and indeed there were evidences of the truth of his assertion—we left one of the four Greek copies of the other William Palmer's 'History of the Church,' which Canon Curtis had given to us to distribute at Athos.

We spent the day rather idly in preparation for our work on the morrow, for we proposed to ride back to Caryes and see the monasteries on that side of the promontory which we had omitted. So we wrote our diaries, and also a long inscription in the visitors' book. After supper we took a short walk, returning just as the gates were closing for the night ; then developed several negatives and prepared the slides for our journey to the east side of Athos.

I have already given the history of Russico and other particulars concerning the monastery ; it only remains to insert a list of its churches.

---

[1] Of Magdalen College, Oxford.

Esocclesia.

1. The catholicon, dedicated to St. Pantelcëmon, containing one paracclesia, the Assumption of the Blessed Virgin Mary.
2. St. Metrophanes.
3. The Protection of the Blessed Virgin.
4. St. Alexander Nevski.
5. The Holy Archangels.
6. St. Demetrius.
7. St. Sergius.
8. St. Nicholas.
9. St. Sabbas.
10. St. Charalampes.
11. The Prodromos.
12. All the Saints of the Holy Mountain.
13. St. Joachim and St. Anna.
14. The Presentation of the Blessed Virgin.
15. The Nativity of the Blessed Virgin.
16. The Holy Apostles Peter and Paul.
17. All Saints.
18. SS. Constantine and Helen.
19. The Ascension.
20. St. John the Divine.

Exocclesia.

1. The Holy Trinity.
2. St. Demetrius.
3. The Holy Unmercenaries Cosmas and Damian.
4. St. Sabbas.
5. The Zoödóchos Peeghee.
6. The Annunciation.
7. St. George (1).
8. St. George (2).
9. The Three Hierarchs, Basil, Gregory, and Chrysostom.
10. St. Catharine.
11. St. Barbara.
12. The Forty Martyrs.
13. St. Gregory.

S

Russico possesses one skete, dedicated to the Blessed Virgin, containing twenty Bulgarians ; no kellia or cathismata ; but I believe there are several colonies of Russian monks belonging to Russico on the promontory, though of what sort I am ignorant.

Tuesday, August $\frac{28}{16}$. Started at ten o'clock and rode to Xeropotamou in about thirty-five minutes. We were received at the gate by the epitropoi; and soon provided with breakfast. The conversation turned upon the old subject, the unity of the Church, and these two presidents, by name Agathangelos and Paul, with a certain archimandrite called Nathaniel, were much interested in hearing about the Anglican Church and in the exhibition of our ecclesiastical photographs.

At breakfast we were given meat in the shape of kebabs,[1] the first flesh food we had tasted since leaving Stavroniketa ; for whilst we were amongst the idiorrhythmic convents on the east side of Athos the great fast was going on, and on the west all the monasteries are cœnobite with the exception of this house and Docheiariou. The meat looked suspiciously like mule, but, as the good monks assured us that it was the best mutton, we consumed it in faith. Afterwards, whilst the monks slept, we photographed the courtyard and the outside of the convent, and then roused some of them to take us over the place.

Xeropotamou is built over the side of a torrent bed, dry in summer, whence the name of the monas-

---

[1] Kebabs are small pieces of lamb or mutton toasted over the fire on a skewer. To prepare to perfection this most delicious of Oriental dishes first place on your skewer a piece of meat, then a piece of fat, then meat again, a kidney, meat, and so repeat the process until the skewer is full.

tery. It is some little distance from the sea, above
the Bay of Daphne, which it overlooks. The north-
west side of the monastery has just been rebuilt—in
fact, it was not quite finished at the time of our visit—
and the rest, including the catholicon, was almost
entirely rebuilt about a hundred years ago on account
of its ruinous condition.

It is said to have been founded in the first half
of the fifth century after Christ by the Empress
Pulcheria, and therefore claims to be one of the oldest
foundations on the Holy Mountain. From some
cause it was apparently in a ruinous condition in the
tenth century, for it was restored in the reign of the
Emperor Romanus Lecapenus,[1] and possibly under
his patronage, by a monk named Paul, who was the
son of Michael III. In the time of the Sultan Selim,
the second after the conqueror Mahomet II., the
monastery was burnt. It is said that the Forty
Martyrs of Sebaste, to whom the catholicon is dedicated, appeared in a vision to the great Mohammedan
ruler, and told him that if, on an appeal from the
monks, he would rebuild the monastery they would
help him in his wars against the Arabs. Selim
obeyed, and not only rebuilt the monastery but also
remitted the head tax levied on its inhabitants. So
to this day the monks of Xeropotamou pay taxes for
their farms alone. Shortly afterwards it again fell
into decay, probably through the depredations of
pirates, and this time Alexander, voivode of Vallachia,
repaired it in 1600. At the end of the last century
the catholicon required rebuilding, which was done in

---

[1] The chrysobull of the Emperor still exists.

S 2

1763, and at the time of the Greek revolution this unfortunate monastery was again ruined. Since then
it has been gradually repaired, and now presents a
flourishing aspect ; a wonderful example of vitality.
The catholicon, standing, as usual, in the middle of the
courtyard, is a fine church.[1]   There is a pronaos, and
two paracclesia, dedicated respectively to SS. Constantine and Helen and the Taxiarchs, Michael and Gabriel.
On the iconostasis, to the right of the holy doors, is an
icon of the Forty Martyrs, before which six lamps are
suspended, constantly burning, according to the wish of
the Sultan Selim.   The relics include a large portion
of the Holy Rood, of the shape given on page 222,
measuring 1 foot 1 inch in length and 6 inches across
the longest transverse piece.   It is mounted in gold
set with precious stones, emeralds, and diamonds.   At
the foot of the cross is the following inscription :
Κωνσταντίνου Εὐφροσύνης καὶ τῶν τέκνων.   Besides
this there are portions of the relics of the Forty
Martyrs and of St. Niphon.   We were next shown a
patera said to have been presented by the Empress
Pulcheria.   The material is probably of ivory, stained
green.   It is carved in high relief, the figures, which
are beautifully executed, representing the Virgin and
Child surrounded by apostles and prophets.   Two
curious properties are claimed for this cup—one that
water placed therein will boil in twenty-four hours ;
the other that if this water be drunk by any person
who has taken poison, or has been bitten by a snake,

---

[1] It measures 47 feet across the transepts and 35½ feet from iconostasis to west wall of nave.   The narthex is large, measuring 28 feet from
east to west, and 57 feet from north to south.   The sanctuary is 15 feet
across the chord of east apse ; from iconostasis to end of east apse, 15½
feet ; from north to south, including side chapels, 33½ feet.

he will recover. We were assured that two years ago a monk who had been bitten by a venomous serpent was cured in this way. As it takes twenty-four hours to procure the dose, a supply is kept ready to hand in a bottle. We were anxious to make trial of this water-boiling patera, but, as we were leaving in an hour, the experiment would not have been satisfactory, and when we returned to Xeropotamou some days afterwards we had forgotten all about Pulcheria's wonderful gift. We asked to be allowed to photograph this interesting work of art, but the monks seemed to be afraid that we should extract its boiling and curative properties in the operation and objected to this being done. The library contains about 300 manuscripts, over 100 being on vellum, one of them a quarto of the Gospels beautifully illuminated but much injured ; there were no others of any particular interest. An archimandrite of the monastery, lately deceased, has left the monks all his modern books—a very miscellaneous collection—which will form a nucleus for a modern library if the monks take the trouble to collect any more. Amongst these books were the works of Voltaire.

Xeropotamou contains ninety monks and thirty servants. About 150 people are fed by the convent every day ; this number includes guests and hermits. It possesses four kellia and five churches without the walls—i.e.

The Annunciation,
St. Artemius,
St. Tryphon,
All Saints,
The Zoödóchos Peeghee—

and eight churches within the walls—

The catholicon, dedicated to the Forty Martyrs, containing the two paracclesia above mentioned ;
  The Prodromos ;
  The Panaghia ;
  The Holy Cross ;
  St. George ;
  St. Theodosius ;
  The Holy Apostles ;
  St. Demetrius.

When we had explored the monastery we took glyko and coffee with our hosts, were by them escorted to the gate, and then jumped into the saddle and rode off to Caryes.

It took us about two hours to reach the metropolis of Athos, the road rising to the top of the ridge or backbone of the promontory by a rather steep ascent. On our way we passed several parties, chiefly lay folk, walking beside their mules, which were conveying goods of various kinds to the Bay of Daphne, the chief port of Athos, which lies below Xeropotamou, as has been before mentioned. Occasionally we met hermits, —some old, some young—with their gowns tucked up for active exertion, each with his wallet to carry the food distributed to them at the monasteries. After crossing the ridge, which is thickly wooded, we caught sight of the Strymonic Gulf, and descended rapidly to Caryes through the luxuriant vegetation which clothes the eastern side.

The streets of Caryes are narrow and the impediments to riding many, so that, after having been nearly decapitated by the awnings and the network of ropes with which they are suspended from house to house, we dismounted and proceeded on foot to our old quarters, the town house of Vatopedi. But nobody was here, and on the recommendation of several monastic loiterers we went to the Seraï, or skete of St. Andrew, the great Russian house just outside Caryes, on the road to Vatopedi. The Russian monks received us most hospitably, and allotted to our use a clean bedroom well furnished in the European style, close to a grand *salon* containing sofas, tables with tablecloths, chairs with crochet chair-backs, &c., looking as if it had been brought bodily with all its contents from St. Petersburg.

We had an excellent dinner (though of course it was *maigre*, as we were amongst cœnobite monks), retiring to rest about eleven o'clock; and having had a few skirmishes with the enemy, who was not, I am glad to say, in force, we put up our levinges and slept soundly after our hard's day's work.

We had sent word to Coutloumoussi that we proposed to breakfast there the next morning, this monastery being situated at Caryes, like the Seraï, only on the opposite side of the town. So we started from the Russian skete at half-past nine, and walked into Caryes to explore the place at our leisure; for when we were last there the visit to the Holy Synod had taken up all our time. Nearly all the shopkeepers are monks, and everything seemed to be very dear except our old friend the octopus, who might be seen in a dry and withered state hanging up in every doorway, looking very tough and nasty, loathsome reptile that he is! If you, my dear reader, had lived on him for a fortnight, then only would you be able to enter into our feelings towards him. Before being cooked he must

be treated in a peculiar way to make him tender. You
find a large flat stone—a paving stone is best—and
then taking up your octopus, you dash him down with
all your force on the stone. This must be repeated
forty times to prepare him for human teeth and diges-
tion.[1]

We did not buy anything, although we fixed upon
the things we wanted to purchase, and made our first
bids, just to show that time was no object to us and
that we could afford to wait until prices came down. It
is always difficult in the East to know the value of the
various goods, and whether octopus was 'quiet,' incense
'dull,' or felt hats 'lively' I cannot say; all I know is
that we were asked much more for the different articles
than we finally gave on another day.

Coutloumoussi is reached from Caryes by a narrow
lane. It presents a somewhat dirty and decayed appearance, and its inhabitants were not particularly
bright specimens of the monastic order. It was founded
by a Turk, the son of Aseddin, of the family of Cout-
loumoush, related to the Seljuk sultans. His mother,
Anna, was a Christian, and after her death in 1268 he
became a Christian at Constantinople, and was baptized
by the name of Constantine. He embraced monasticism
at Athos, and founded this monastery in the reign of
Andronicus II. (1282–1328).[2] Constantine narrowly
escaped being sultan of Iconium. John Comnenus
puts the foundation of the monastery 200 years earlier,
in the reign of Alexius Comnenus, and says that it was
destroyed by 'the Pope of Rome.' He does not, how-

---

[1] Πολύπους τύπτεται πολλάκις πρὸς τὸ πέπων γένεσθαι.—*Suidas.*

[2] In 1334 the monastery of Philadelphia was incorporated with
Coutloumoussi.

ever, endeavour to explain the curious Turkish name, and is almost certainly wrong. The monastery has been restored at various times by Neagulus, Hospodar of Vallachia, and the voivodes Radulas, Myrtzas, and Vintilas. In Curzon's time the buildings were in good repair, and he describes them as being the most regular on Mount Athos, but adds that they were almost uninhabited. In 1845 a fire destroyed a great part of it; in 1875 another conflagration ravaged it again, and this time the catholicon only just escaped. Consequently one side of the court is still in ruins, it never having been completely rebuilt since the catastrophe of 1845. We were told that the restoration was to commence next year. The library contains 500 manuscripts, ninety-five being on vellum. Owing to the entire absence of catalogue or order we were unable to find much of interest during our short visit. There was one uncial evangelistarium with one leaf missing (replaced), several other manuscripts of the Gospels and of the Psalter with illuminations. The monastery is cœnobite, it having tried the idiorrhythmic rule for a time (according to Mr. Tozer, who saw it under both governments), but having returned to the old form, as being better. It now contains eighty monks and fifteen servants, ruled over by an abbot, eighty years of age, by name Joseph. He has been a monk for sixty years and abbot for thirty. By reason of his rheumatism and other infirmities he cannot leave his room, so that we were entertained by his lieutenant, whose name was Chariton.

Coutloumoussi possesses a few farms in Thasos and Macedonia and the following churches :

Esocclesia.

1. The catholicon, dedicated to the Transfiguration, containing one paracclesi, the Panaghia.
2. SS. Basil, Gregory, and Chrysostom.
3. The Holy Unmercenaries.
4. The Archangels.
5. The Panaghia.

Exocclesia.

1. St. Nicholas.
2. St. Tryphon.

It has one skete, dedicated to St. Panteleëmon, and twenty kellia.

There is nothing particular about the catholicon,[1] either in the building or its contents. The diaconicon and chapel of the prothesis are almost circular chapels, at the north-east and south-east corners of the church. There are a narthex, a pronaos, and a paracclesi of the Blessed Virgin on the north side of the narthex. No relics or treasures of any importance, so the monks told us, although I find from John Comnenus that the church formerly boasted of the head of St. Alypius the Stylite, the hand of St. Eustratius, a portion of the True Cross kept in a reliquary of silver gilt, and the foot of St. Anne, ' the Ancestress of God ' (Θεοπρομήτωρ), as her Greek title runs. Surely the latter relic cannot have been lost ? But perhaps the monks were suspicious of us, and feared that, like too many Englishmen, we only asked after the relics to scoff at them.

Our breakfast proved anything but a success, although we had given the monks the minutest injunctions how to cook it.

---

[1] It measures 12½ feet across the chord of east apse, 12½ feet from iconostasis across the sanctuary to east wall of apse ; from iconostasis to west wall of nave, 28 feet ; across transepts, 43½ feet.

'Mind,' said we, 'there are two things that we Englishmen never eat. We never touch oil and we never touch butter. We are aware this is a curious custom of ours, but we are Franks, you know, and all Franks have odd tastes.' So the cook promised faithfully that he would carry out our wishes.

When the soup made its appearance we tasted it and put down our spoons in disgust.

'There is oil in it,' said I.

'Of course there is,' said O—. 'How very provoking!'

'No,' said the attendant monks, 'there is no oil in the soup.'

'Then if it's not oil it's butter,' replied we; 'anyhow it's uneatable.'

But the monks stoutly denied that there was either oil or butter in the compound, and at last the cook was called up and strictly interrogated.

'Oh, no,' said he; 'the soup was made with neither butter nor oil, but when it was done it was so tasteless that I put a *little*—such a *very* little—butter into it, just to flavour it.'

'Why couldn't you do as you were told?' said O— in the best English; 'as it is you have just spoiled our breakfast.'

And so it turned out. Every dish had *just a little* rancid butter in it and had to be sent away. However our hosts gave us some good wine and some coffee, and we tried to make ourselves as agreeable as possible to them under the circumstances.

After this delectable meal we had a curious example of the state of the medical science at Mount Athos.

Angelos, who had been suffering all the morning

from earache, asked the monks if they could help his case. So away went some of them to fetch the doctor, who was nothing more than one of the community, an old monk with a long grey beard. He peeped first into one and then into the other of our dragoman's ears and departed for his drug. He returned with a small bottle of rather thick yellow oil, a stout twig, and a lump of cotton wool.

'What kind of oil is that ?' we inquired.

'Oh, it's rat oil,' said Angelos, 'capital stuff. We always use it in Greece.'

'*Rat oil* ?' said O—, always eager to acquire the latest scientific knowledge, 'rat oil ? How is it made ?'

'Why,' replied the leech, 'it is a very simple remedy, and quite easy to make. You take a young rat from the nest—when it is just born and pink, you know—and you put it into a bottle of oil and place it in the sun. At the end of a few weeks you will find the rat quite gone, dissolved in the oil. Then you cork up the bottle and keep the oil for use.'

'Good heavens, Angelos !' cried O— in alarm, 'you are surely not going to put that stuff into your ear ?'

'Of course I am,' replied Angelos ; 'everybody knows how good rat oil is. It is a well-known remedy not only for earache but for all sorts and kinds of diseases.'

So saying he held up his right ear for the dressing, and the old monk began pouring the oil into it and stirring it about inside with the twig, and afterwards plugged up the orifice with a large piece of wool. Then came the turn of the other ear, and that was treated in the same way.

Angelos declared he felt better already, and expressed his pleasure at having fallen in with a doctor that knew his business.

'Well,' said O——, 'if science teaches me anything your ear will be much worse to-morrow. I can't think how you can be so foolish as to put filth of that sort into it.'

But Angelos would not hear anything against the treatment, and we began to talk to the old man about his art. He appeared to have quite a practice in the monastery and neighbourhood.

We asked him what he could cure. 'Supposing I were to break my leg,' said I, 'could you mend it for me ?'

No, the old leech didn't think he could manage that. Anything in a small way he would undertake— headaches, or earaches, or toothaches, or stomachaches ; oh yes ! he was a wonderful hand at such complaints and knew of all sorts of sovereign remedies for them. But a broken bone—no, that was a serious matter ; he didn't think he could undertake *that*.

So we joked and gossiped till it was time to depart.

On our way through Caryes we made inquiries for a certain Gregory the son of Demetrius, who we had been told was the best worker in inlaid woods on the promontory. The old art of inlaying in ivory, mother-of-pearl, and tortoiseshell has completely died out at Athos—if indeed it ever existed, as I suspect the splendid inlaid work of this kind which one sees in all the churches here came from farther east—but there is still excellent work done in wood inlay. Beautiful modern doors of this kind in various monasteries had frequently excited my cupidity, and on my asking who made such doors the answer was invariably the same —'Gregory the son of Demetrius.'

We hunted high and low for the said Gregory, and at last ran him to earth in the new Vatopedi house, where he was engaged in the carpentry work. He brought us to his own little house in the town, a pretty vine-clad cottage overlooking the street, and there we struck a bargain with him to make a door for a little chapel in a house I was building in London. He was to make it and transport it to the consulate at Salonica, and was then to receive fourteen liras (Turkish pounds, worth about 18s.) in addition to the five liras which I advanced to pay for the woods necessary for the work. Gregory went back with us to the Seraï, and a contract was drawn up, which he sealed.

I left him perfect liberty to design the door as he pleased, and when it arrived in England at the expiration of about six months it thoroughly justified the trust I had reposed in him. I had feared that it would have been rather *rococo* in style, for the old Byzantine forms have been largely influenced by this corrupt Italian period ; but, on the contrary, it proved to be as chaste in design as excellent in execution, and when Gregory pleaded, in a most touching letter, for a present, I gladly sent him an additional five liras as a reward for his honesty and skill. Gregory the son of Demetrius was an Albanian by birth, and had come to reside on Athos, though not, I believe, permanently. He could not speak or write Greek correctly ; in fact, he could only read or write with difficulty.

We had a capital dinner this evening at seven o'clock, and chatted with our hosts till nine, when they went to bed. We were not long in following their example.

CHAPTER XVII.

To-day you may be alive, dear man,
 Worth many a thousand pound ;
To-morrow you may be dead, dear man,
 And your body be laid underground.

With one turf at your head, O man,
 And another at your feet,
Thy good deeds and thy bad, O man,
 Will all together meet.—*Old Carol.*

Thursday, August $\frac{30}{18}$. No Angelos appeared this morning to prepare our bath as usual, and so soon as I had dressed I hastened to his room to discover the reason. Here I found him groaning on his bed, unable to eat or drink or lift his head from the pillow. We had intended to ride to Caracalla to-day, but I saw clearly that we should have to give it up under the circumstances, and I returned to O— and told him how matters stood,

' Of course,' said he ; ' it is exactly what I knew would happen. If a fellow will put putrid rat into his ears what can he expect ? '

So we had breakfast and about noon sallied forth towards the town. First we went to the post office, where by good luck the postmaster spoke French and several other languages besides. We sat and talked to him for more than an hour, smoked his cigarettes, and consumed rahatlakoum and coffee. He was a

very intelligent young Greek who had been sent here
from Constantinople to take charge of the post station,
and very dull he found it.

'I have not a soul to speak to,' he complained;
'there are no educated people in Caryes except a few
monks, and I soon get tired of them. And no women
of any kind. Ah, *c'est affreux, messieurs, c'est affreux!*'
And the poor fellow begged us to sit and talk to him
a little longer. This we did, and amused ourselves
by sending a telegram to the telegraph clerk at
Salonica, wishing him a very good day, a wire having
been recently laid from that place to Caryes.

'For,' said our friend, 'we may just as well use
it, for nobody else does. Perhaps fifty telegrams
are sent in the course of a year, chiefly about the
steamers which call here, for who would want to telegraph to Athos? So when I feel very dull I just ring
up the clerk at Salonica and ask how the world is
going on.'

We laughed at his troubles, telling him that it was
a capital thing for him, because there was no chance
of his getting into mischief at Caryes, and went away
feeling that our forced stay had at least been the means
of giving a little pleasure to somebody.

We walked back towards St. Andrew's, visiting the
Protaton, or chief church of Caryes, on our way. Finding
it closed, we sat down on the shady side of it to rest,
as it was very hot. Presently a monk arrived, who
explained to us, with some difficulty, that the church
would soon be opened; this shortly occurred and we
were admitted.

It is dedicated to the Assumption of Our Lady, and
is one of the most curious churches on Mount Athos,

unlike any of the others, and is probably the most ancient.   Comnenus says that it was founded by Constantine the Great and burnt down by Julian the Apostate.   But the connexion of the first Christian emperor with Athos rests entirely upon vague traditions.

The ground plan is as nearly as possible a parallelogram, there being only internal transepts, of which the chapel of the prothesis and the diaconicon are continuations in the same line farther east, and into which they open by the usual doors in the iconostasis; this is carried straight across the church.   A slightly pointed arch of 22½ feet span divides the quasi-transept on each side from the nave; between these transepts there is no central dome, as is universally the case in the other Athos churches, but the whole building is covered like a basilica with a flat wooden roof, beneath which are quasi-clerestory windows.   The width of the church is 50 feet; the extreme length (not including a division at the west end which may be considered either as an exonarthex or a pronaos) is 63½ feet, of which 22½ feet is the length of bema from iconostasis to east wall of apse.   The sanctuary is 22 feet across, not including the side chapels, which are each 14 feet from north to south and make up the breadth of the parallelogram, 50 feet.   The 41½ feet which is the length of the church west of the iconostasis is divided into two almost equal portions of nave and narthex.   As has been said before there is a pronaos, or exonarthex, on the west; there is a similar excrescence on the north side of the church, between the west end and the false north transept, and here is the principal entrance.   The present iconostasis is placed about one foot in front of the old marble one.

T

In the east apse is what was formerly the *synthronos,* or bishop's seat. It is now used as a support for an icon. On the north side of the church (if I remember aright, under the arch of the north transept) is a picture ascribed to St. Luke. It had an immense number of candles before it and a canopy like an umbrella over it. The monks who were our guides showed it the greatest reverence by innumerable prostrations.

Not only will this building interest the architect and antiquary, but the student of art will find it the best place for studying the Athos frescoes, for here they have been apparently untouched (though much injured by age and damp), and there is but little doubt that many of them are the work of the great master Manuel Panselenus, of Thessalonica : one in particular, representing the infant Saviour, is of great merit; it is to be found on the west wall of the church. This painter is believed to have flourished in the twelfth century, in the reign of Andronicus I., and thus to have lived long before Cimabue and Giotto. The Italian artists are said to have learned from the Greeks, and Giunta Pisano was the pupil of an unknown Byzantine artist in 1210. Possibly this famous Athos painter may have contributed to the revival of the art in Western Europe; at any rate he was the founder of the school of painting which has existed, in unbroken descent, though feebly, to the present day. His name Πανσέληνος is said to have been given him because he was compared, on account of his brilliant talents, to the moon in all her splendour. Many of the frescoes attributed to him may be the work of his immediate pupils. As his school of painting decayed, and all invention perished, the monks of Mount Athos became copyists instead of painters, and so servile were they that definite instructions on the most minute points were handed down in writing from generation to generation, giving exact directions as to how each saint and subject should be portrayed.

Didron,[1] visiting Mount Athos about 1840, found monks thus painting by absolute rule, and he has translated the book by which these artists worked.[2] There are now signs of the approaching annihilation of the native school that has existed in this odd way for so many centuries, for Russian influence is grafting modern European art on the old stock ; a process which, far from revivifying it, is raising a strange and unpleasing hybrid.

According to the old rules, before mixing his colours the painter was directed to fall on his knees and recite the following prayer :

O Lord Jesu Christ, our God, Who wast endowed with a Divine and incomprehensible nature, Who didst take a Body in the womb of the Virgin Mary for the salvation of mankind, and didst deign to limn the sacred character of Thy immortal Face, and to impress it upon a holy veil, which served to cure the sickness of the satrap Abgarus and to enlighten his soul with the knowledge of the True God ; Thou Who didst illuminate with Thy Holy Spirit Thy Divine Apostle and Evangelist Luke, that he might represent the beauty of Thy most pure Mother, who carried Thee, a tiny Infant, in her arms and said, ' The Grace of Him Who is born of me is poured out upon men : ' Do Thou, Divine Master of all that exists, do Thou enlighten and direct the soul and heart and spirit of Thy servant N— ; guide his hands that he may be enabled worthily and perfectly to represent Thy image, that of Thy most holy Mother, and those of all the Saints for the glory, the joy, and the embellishment of Thy most holy

---

[1] See his *Manuel d'Iconographie Chrétienne*, 1845.
[2] Ἑρμηνεία τῆς ζωγραφικῆς.

Church. Pardon the sins of all those who shall venerate these icons, and of those who, piously casting themselves on their knees before them, shall render honour to the models which are in the heavens. Save them, I beseech Thee, from every evil influence, and instruct them by good counsels, through the intercessions of Thy most holy Mother, of the illustrious Apostle and Evangelist St. Luke, and of all Thy Saints. Amen.

Attached to the Protaton is a library containing eighty MSS., forty of which are on vellum, several being of the ninth, tenth, and eleventh centuries, and one, a book of the Gospels, of so early a date as the seventh. We returned to St. Andrew's and found Angelos still very ill and very humble and submissive. Would *we* doctor him and give him something out of our medicine chest? But, alas! we had no remedies for his complaint, though I ran through our list of drugs—rhubarb pills, blue pills, opium pills, arnica, chlorodyne, sal volatile, ginger, quinine, mustard plasters; no, there was nothing that could by any possibility cure earache! But our unfortunate drago-man implored us for *something*; he was sure it would do him good, whatever it was, so long as it was medicine. So we finally gave him an opium pill from a supply we had brought in case of cholera (which was very prevalent in the East in 1883), thinking it could not do him any harm and might send him to sleep; and then ordered hot onions to be applied to his ears, a good old-fashioned remedy for earache which I suddenly remembered.

I was getting really alarmed about him, for O—, whom I always regard as the representative of science, commenced the most gloomy forebodings, giving it as his opinion that he had an abscess in his ear, that naturally enough the rat had disagreed with it, and that the probable result would be blood-poisoning.

This afternoon we photographed the Seraï. As usual, after we had clambered over walls and through hedges, and had gained a position whence we thought the best view was obtainable, we discovered to our chagrin that on walking quietly back to the skete by the road there was an infinitely better view to be had, taking in the whole of the buildings.

Afterwards we went to vespers, which was followed by some sort of service for the dead, but of what kind we could not exactly discover, and Angelos being *hors de combat*, and the monks talking nothing but Russian, we could not inquire. In the middle of the church, on a table, were placed a candlestick holding three candles, and a plate of boiled rice, with a cross marked over it, with raisins and a candle stuck in the middle. We all had little tapers given to us, which at a certain point in the service we lighted one from another. Three or four priests and two deacons with censers stood round the table, and each in turn read through long lists of names, which they evidently were not well acquainted with, as they stumbled over them and hesitated dreadfully, and had to be prompted by a monk who was in the next stall to us. This service lasted for about an hour, when we all put out our tapers and departed.

A monk named Philemon, who was in priest's orders, took us over the skete. This man would come and sit with us in our grand *salon* continually, and would talk to us in Russian for an hour together, although he knew we could not understand a word of what he said. He seemed to us to be a particularly good specimen of the monastic order. There are some faces which unmistakably bear the impress of piety ; such a countenance had the priest Philemon. He was somewhat beyond middle age and looked rather delicate, almost consumptive. Apparently he was in some authority in the skete, and although he was a simple and, I should say, unlearned man (though it was difficult for us to judge under the circumstances) yet he was more refined in manner than the majority of his brethren.

The Seraï or skete of St. Andrew contains 230 monks and sixty servants, who, as in all sketes, follow the cœnobite rule. The name of the superior is Theodoretus. It has no land except the garden round it, and *theoretically* belongs to, or is dependent on, Vatopedi. Nevertheless it is apparently of great wealth, so that there is not much doubt as to where the money comes from.

It was founded, I believe, in 1849. I have already given all I know about its origin.[1]

Esocclesia.

1. St. Andrew.
2. The Panaghia.
3. Protection of the Blessed Virgin Mary.

Exocclesia.

1. All Saints of the Holy Mountain.
2. St. Nicholas.

The principal existing church (the foundation of the new central church has just been begun) is of the orthodox Russian pattern, built, like a Western church,

[1] P. 247.

with an elongated nave ; not, as a Greek church, in the form of a cross with equal limbs. It presents nothing of interest. The principal relic is the head (or portion of the head) of St. Andrew the Apostle. This was originally at Pantocratoros ; how the Russians obtained the relic, and whether they have possessed themselves of the whole or only a part of what was at the Greek monastery, I am unable to say, as I did not obtain information at Pantocratoros. It is contained in a magnificent silver-gilt shrine with a canopy over it, of modern Russian workmanship. As this receptacle is of full size, one supposes at first sight that the monks claim the entire body of the Apostle ; this, however, is not the case. The custom of placing a portion of a relic in a reliquary large enough to contain the whole frequently gives rise to mistakes on the part of travellers. As, for instance, you may see two silver skulls, each said roughly to contain the head of the same saint. On inquiry you will find that they each inclose only a small part of it, perhaps only just the piece that you see through the little opening in the silver skull.

Philemon took us first to the refectory, where the monks were having their supper. It is a miserably low, dark room, little better than a cellar. A new refectory is being built. Then we went to view the foundations of the great church, and afterwards were taken to the cemetery. Here we observed several holes somewhat resembling shallow graves, and so guessed that they had been uprooting some dead monks, which we presently found to be the case, as we came upon some pieces of the garments in which they had been buried and two or three locks of hair.

A friend of mine who recently visited Mount
Athos was shown some newly dug-up skeletons,
those of the cosmicoi, or laymen, being yellow and
discoloured, whilst those of the monks were white and
glistening. ' See,' said his attendant monk, ' see the
effect of prayer.'

In the cemetery chapel the skulls of the deceased
were neatly piled in rows, all labelled with the names
and ages of their owners and the dates of their deaths.
Some were placed in little wooden boxes with lids ;
one of these skulls Philemon took out of its receptacle and handled lovingly. He gave us to understand that it belonged to a great friend of his, who
had died three years back ; and there upon the
bleached forehead was written his name. The good
priest heaved a little sigh, put the skull back into its
box, crossed himself, and led us out of the chapel.

Barbarous are these bone houses, perhaps, but yet
they have their uses. It is the fashion to labour to
forget death and to live as much as possible in the
present ; but to call before our eyes our own death-
beds each time we hear a passing bell, to cultivate
the thought of our own dissolutions whenever we hear
of a friend's departure or look upon a sepulchre—these
are not dangerous and morbid exercises, but rather
pious and laudable customs, full of possible profit to
that part of us which is immortal. And when we
cast our eyes around such a charnel-house as I have
described, and are tempted, as we gaze upon the
mouldering remains of poor mortality, to cry out with
the prophet, ' *O tu quid fecisti Adam !* O thou
Adam, what hast thou done ! for though it was thou
that sinned, thou art not fallen alone, but we all that

come of thee;' and with a horrible dread to add,
'For what profit is it unto us if there be promised us
an immortal time, whereas we have done the works
that bring death?' the answer of the Archangel will
banish all vain lamentations and infuse into our quaking
hearts fresh courage and fresh hope. 'This is the
condition of the battle which man, that is born upon
the earth, shall fight: that if he be overcome he shall
suffer as thou hast said, but if he get the victory he
shall receive life. Choose thee life, that thou mayest
live.'

We dined this evening, as usual, with a few of the
chief monks, the principal dish being cutlets of pink
caviar, which I commend to epicures.

Our hosts were most hospitable, and in addition to
the decanter of wine—and good wine too—which was
placed before each person insisted upon our drinking
a fresh supply. As we could not talk to them we
tried to make ourselves agreeable in other ways, and
proposed the health of the Czar, which was drunk
with much monastic enthusiasm. After dinner we
received in our *salon*, and three or four monks, including Philemon, came and talked to us until we went to
bed.

Friday, August $\frac{31}{19}$. Angelos better, to my relief;
so we determined to push on to Caracalla. He was
able to go with us to the bazaar at Caryes to help us
make a few bargains. We bought some Eucharistic
bread stamps, and chose from a number of copper
plates, curiously engraved by native talent with icons
and other sacred subjects, such as we wished to have
prints from, ordering them to be ready for us in a fortnight's time, when we calculated we should be passing

through the little metropolis again, before our departure from the promontory.   These prints were exactly
similar in execution to those rude representations of
the monasteries given to us on leaving each as sou-
venirs.   Meanwhile Angelos had the good fortune to
fall in with some sort of lay doctor ; perhaps he was
the Athenian maintained by Vatopedi.   He prescribed
an application of oil and laudanum for his ears, and
Angelos managed to get the laudanum from a monk
who kept a chandler's shop.   Before we left Caryes we
attempted to take a photograph of the one street which
forms the bazaar.   This naturally caused a prodigious
commotion, and a crowd immediately collected in front
of the eye of the camera.   Of course when they discovered what our machine was, and it was noised
abroad that in some vague way they were going to have
their portraits taken, everybody within eyesight or
hailing distance rushed to the scene of action.   So we
made Angelos harangue the assembly and tell them
that unless they gave the poor camera fair play nobody
would have his picture painted, but if they would implicitly obey the Frank's instructions he held out good
hopes that the likenesses of the majority of them would
get into that box and be forwarded to England.   So
whilst O— manipulated the lens I walked some little
distance down the bazaar, marshalling the crowd into
two lines on each side, thus leaving a way clear down
the centre to the camera.   Angelos hushed the crowd
for an instant, O— whipped off the cap of the lens,
and the view, such as it was, was taken.   Here is the
engraving of it ; it is at least a collection of types of
countenances, monastic and lay.

    We returned to the Seraï, and having packed up

our baggage took a farewell cup of 'tchai' in our *salon*. Some interesting conversation was going on between Philemon and Angelos, the former speaking very seriously and earnestly, the latter pooh-poohing him and evidently giving vent to scoffs, at which the good priest looked so pained and troubled that I could not help inquiring what was the subject. 'Oh,' said Angelos, 'this foolish old monk is trying to persuade

HIGH STREET, CARYES.

me to go to Caracalla by way of Iveron, to pray there before the icon of the Portaïtissa to get my earache cured ; but I am not so ignorant as the stupid monks, and I am telling him that at Athens we are giving up all that sort of thing.'

Here Philemon turned round to me and in his simple way appealed to me in Russian. I requested to have his words translated.

He was asking me if I did not think it worth Angelos's while to go to Iveron. 'It is almost on his way,' said he ; 'it will not take him more than half an hour to go there and back, and he will return cured of his earache. Surely it is well worth his spending another half-hour on his journey for the sake of getting rid of his pain.'

I was much struck with the absolute confidence of the man. Clearly he could not understand anyone disbelieving the miracle which he was convinced would be worked. It was the case of Naaman over again. If Angelos went there he would be cured ; there was no doubt about it. Surely he would not be so foolish as to refuse to go to be relieved ? But, alas! I knew more of the world than Philemon, and so I said gravely to our dragoman—

'No, Angelos, we will not diverge from our road ; there is no manner of use in your going to Iveron : *you* will never get cured.'

'Tell the good priest,' added I, 'that I say no prayer is answered, no miracle is worked, without faith, and that you acknowledge that you have no faith, so that it is waste of time for you to go to the Portaïtissa.' And when Philemon heard my reply he turned round to me and sorrowfully signed his assent. 'Surely,' I hear my reader say, 'surely you do not believe that anyone could be cured by such means under any circumstances ; it only proves how grossly superstitious the monks are ; ' and my answer is, 'Yes, I do believe it.' Have you ever thought how difficult it is to fix the point where true religion ends and superstition begins ? Not that I wish to deny that there was a leaven of

superstition in Philemon's advice; that may be so;[1]
but I know there was more faith in it than you or I
have ever had, or ever will have, thanks to the atmosphere in which we live. Call it childish faith if you
will; it is the sort of faith that God loves to answer.
Because we have been blinded to supernatural things
by modern enlightenment, shall we be angry that a
poor monk still feels the hand of God in his? Surely
as Christian men we dare not deny that miracles may
be, and sometimes are, obtained by prayer. Listen to
a little story.

There was an old woman who lived in a cottage
at the bottom of a hill, and a good old woman too;
for, although the hill was steep and her legs had seen
their best days, she never omitted to go on Sundays
to her chapel, which lay on the other side of it. One
day the minister she sat under preached a sermon on
prayer, taking for his text the words, ' If ye shall say
unto this mountain, Be thou removed and be thou
cast into the sea, it shall be done.' The discourse
made a great impression upon this ancient dame; for
she could not help thinking how nice it would be if the
hill between her and her chapel were done away with,
and how it would save her old legs. So before she
went to bed that night she included in her prayers a
petition that the hill might be removed and cast somewhere on the other side of her garden.

---

[1] I have heard of three other cases of Oriental superstition, so much
resembling the one in question that I cannot help alluding to them.
One was the restoration to life of a dead man on accidental contact with
the relics of a saint; the second, the cure of sickness by the *shadow* of a
holy man; the third, a similar case of recovery by contact with the
garments of a saint. The cures in two at least of these cases are well
authenticated (2 Kings xiv. 21; Acts v. 15, xix. 12).

Next morning she rose, went to her window, and looked out ; and there sure enough was the obnoxious hill, looking as big and as steep as ever.

'Ah!' cried the old woman as she shook her fist at the offending obstacle, '*I thought you'd still be there!*'

CHAPTER XVIII.

She was the purest Virgin,
  And the cleanest from sin ;
She was the handmaid of our Lord
  And Mother of our King.
                    The Carnal and the Crane.

DURING the conversation related in the preceding
chapter the caimacan, or Turkish governor, arrived to
call on us, and fresh cups of tea were ordered.   Unfortunately he could only speak Turkish, and, as there
happened to be no one present who understood that
language, we were unable to exchange any remark, so
drank our tea in silence, mutually admiring each other.
All this took a long time, for the caimacan had a nice
cool room to sit in and some refreshing *tchai* ; and what
were minutes and hours to him ? He had nothing
better to do, whilst we, on the contrary, were very
anxious to get to our destination before nightfall, but
of course could not with any courtesy leave our guest ;
so we had to wait until the governor rose, when we
exchanged salaams and departed.

As we passed through the gate we met a bishop
coming in. He was introduced to us as the Lord
Nilos, and he spoke French fluently. We had no
time to improve our acquaintance then, but we met
him again afterwards, as I shall relate. Two horses
with European saddles had been provided for us for
the first time on Athos. We mounted, and at four

o'clock were actually on the march. We rode through Caryes, a piece of presumption at which our muleteer was perfectly appalled, it being a crime visited with the utmost rigour of the law ; but, as the afternoon was hot, instead of ignominiously tramping beside our steeds, we preferred to exercise our privileges as the distinguished persons we were, friends of the Œcumenical Patriarch and Holy Synod, not to mention the caimacan ! On our way a Turkish official ran up to us and seizing our hands saluted them with his forehead and lips in the orthodox manner. What the poor man wanted I cannot say ; perhaps backsheesh (which he did not get) ; perhaps he was overcome by the magnificent spectacle of the illustrious Englishmen riding through those sacred streets.

We descended to Iveron (which we did pass after all) in two hours and a half, crossing the most lovely country on our way, pretty little glens and valleys and hill slopes, all covered with arbutus and olives and vines and forest trees, enlivened by the charming little monastic retreats dotted over the smiling landscape, white and trim, with their picturesque verandahs and tiny chapels with domes of rough-hewn stones. There before us was the sparkling sea, and the islands beyond rising out of the waters ; behind us the great mountain ridge we were descending, ever increasing in height towards the south until the great marble peak suddenly shot up far above the pine trees, and catching the setting sun showed itself clear and distinct in rosy whiteness against the evening sky.

By the time we reached Iveron it was getting dark, and some of the monks, who were sitting outside in their kiosk, enjoying the cool breezes from the sea,

tried to persuade us to stay the night at their house ;
but, as we had already lost a day at St. Andrew's, we
feared to yield to their temptation, and passing the
marble portico of the monastery without dismounting
gained the shore.

Our road now lay along the sea, sometimes on the
very shore itself, sometimes rising a little distance
above it and winding round the corners of the projecting rocks. Twilight is of short duration in these
countries, and it soon began to get really dark, and
the horses, not so sure-footed as the mules, stumbled
painfully over the uneven path. Angelos too delayed
us considerably. He had begun a new method of
treatment for his complaint, and by putting on every
coat and waistcoat he possessed, one over the other,
and a thick pilot coat over all, had improvised a sort of
Turkish bath, walking the whole distance from Caryes
and leading his mule. Consequently he soon began to
lag behind, and O— was continually inquiring of me,
' Where is your great ox ? ' ' Behind, I suppose, as
usual.' ' Well, of course we shall never get to Caracalla
to-night,' &c. &c.

However at last we saw lights inland above us,
and so knew that we must have arrived at the little
harbour from which we had embarked on that miserable
passage to the Lavra just a fortnight ago. And this
proved to be the case, for we immediately turned away
from the sea and rode up a steep path towards the
lights. About three-quarters of an hour after leaving
the shore we reached the monastery and rode round to
the gate.

All was now dark ; not a light was to be seen in the
windows, and of course the gate of the monastery was

U

closed.   We dismounted and shouted several times as
loudly as we could, but no answer came from within.
Evidently the monks had all gone to bed and were
by this time sound asleep.   So in desperation I
picked up a big stone and hammered at the great iron-
bound door.

After I had indulged in this exercise for some little
time O— declared that he saw a light going up
inside the tower over the gateway,[1] and presently a
head appeared, very cautiously, from a window at the
top.

We hailed the head with fresh shouts.

' Who are you ? ' said the head.

' Englishmen,' we all replied together.

' *Englishmen ?* ' answered the head in a tone of in-
credulity, as much as to say, ' Don't think you're going
to gammon *me !* '

' Yes, two Englishmen,' we replied.

' But I see four,' said the head.

' Oh, they are our servants—our dragoman from
Athens and a muleteer from the Seraï, both good and
true men.'

' Yes,' added Angelos, ' we are attendants on these
noble Englishmen.'

' *Where* did you say you came from ? ' said the
head.

' From the Seraï,' we shouted all at once again.

The head surveyed us for a moment or two and
then disappeared with the light, and we were left, as
before, in darkness.

Just as I was picking up my stone to recommence

---

[1] ' The gate of the monastery is adorn'd with an exceeding high
Tower.'—*Georgirenes.*

the attack on the door a light appeared at another window, this time not in the tower, but in the wall, and a lantern being hung out, two monks, shading their eyes from the light, took a careful survey of us.

'Unbar the door!' cried O——.

No, they replied; they never opened their gates at this time of night, and besides the hegoumenos had the key and he had gone to bed.

'Then you must wake him up,' said we; 'we can't stay here all night.'

But who were we? said they, and where did we come from? and where were we going? and why did we knock at their gate so late?

So we had to answer all these questions over again, and added that we had been benighted on our way from Iveron, having been delayed at starting; that we were not brigands come to sack the monastery, but two peaceable travellers with our two servants, four in all, and that we should be exceedingly obliged to them if they would open the door as soon as they could.

'But I see *five* horses,' said one of the monks, craning his head as far as possible out of the window and peering down upon us with the aid of the lantern. So we had to explain that one carried our baggage and that we had no friends in ambuscade. Then the light and the monks departed, and after a few moments we heard the welcome sound of the unfastening of bolts and the clanking of chains, and finally the great door creaked on its hinges and we were admitted, just twenty minutes after our arrival before the gate.

Now the good monks could not do enough for us, and although it was so late they cooked us a modest supper of eggs. The abbot being in bed we were

entertained by two subordinate monks, one of whom
was a bit of a wag and kept us in roars of laughter.
He would address O— as *pappa*, beginning every
sentence with this word.

After supper a mattress was put for each of us on
the divan (we supped and slept in the same circular
room in which we were entertained on the occasion of

CARACALLA.

our former hasty visit); we put up our levinges and
were soon lulled to sleep by the tinkling of the mule
bells on the hills.

Caracalla is beautifully situated some distance from
the sea, of which it enjoys a fine view, being at a considerable height above it. Its high irregular walls
and lofty gate-tower give it a very feudal and picturesque appearance. When it was founded, and by
whom, is not certain, but most probably the founder
was a prince of the name of John Antonius Caracalla,
who is said to have lived in the reign of Romanus

Diogenes (1067–1071), that brave emperor who was rewarded for his noble and partially successful attempts to check the inroads of the Turks by a cruel death at the hands of his countrymen.   Anyhow there is evidence that Romanus bestowed certain privileges upon the monastery in 1070.[1] If we accept this origin all difficulty vanishes with respect to the name of the convent.   Otherwise there seems to be no alternative but to derive its name with Mr. Tozer from Κάρυαι Καλαί, 'fine hazels,' on account of the nut trees amidst which it is situated (and readers of Mr. Curzon's 'Monasteries of the Levant' will remember how the abbot of Caracalla speculated in nuts), or else to accept M. Langlois's suggestion, 'Cara, cala,' two Turkish words, one signifying 'black' and the other 'earth.'   But I think the evidence in favour of the word being derived from the founder's name is too strong.   The tradition is at least as old as the time of Archbishop Georgirenes, 1678.   The archimandrite Porphyry, a trustworthy man who, spent some time in Athos about forty years ago, examining the charters and other historical documents, attributes the foundation to a certain Antonius, son of a Roman prince called Caracalla, in the reign of Romanus Diogenes, and *all* accounts give Caracalla as the name of the founder, although some speak of him as the Emperor Caracalla, who reigned from A.D. 211 to 217, a manifest absurdity.

There is no doubt as to the connexion of the voivode Peter, Hospodar of Moldavia, with the monastery, and the story of its rebuilding I will give from John Comnenus.

---

[1] Muralt, *Chronographie Byzantine.*

This voivode, wishing to restore it, sent his proto-spatharius, or chief swordsman (a high military title), whose name was also Peter, with a large sum of money for the purpose, as it seems, of rebuilding the monastery or of founding another in its place. But the chief swordsman, greedy of gain, only built a tower near the sea and returned to Bogdania. The voivode having discovered the trick that had been played him, was naturally furious, and determined to cut off Peter's head. The latter, to save his life, promised if he were let off to build the monastery at his own charges, and this the voivode allowed him to do. Coming to Athos, he erected the monastery on the place where it now stands,[1] and then returned joyfully to Bogdania, where his master received him with all honour.

Finally the voivode and his protospatharius re-solved with one consent to go to the Holy Mountain to embrace the monastic life, and as they had borne the same names in the world so they determined to bear the same in religion, and both Peters were called by one name, Pachomius. And they piously passed their lives in this monastery, where also they now rest in the Lord. Comnenus says that in his day the cell of the chief swordsman existed outside the monastery. Perhaps it is still there?

The catholicon is a fine church with a beautiful carved iconostasis.[2] It contains an interesting icon of

---

[1] It seems probable from this story that the original monastery had been so far destroyed that there was a question as to whether it should be rebuilt on a new site or not, and that finally the latter counsel pre-vailed.

[2] Measurements: Sanctuary: from north to south, including side chapels, 25 feet; across chord of east apse, 11½ feet; from iconostasis

a monk of this monastery named Gideon, a Turk who was converted to Christianity. He finally won the crown of martyrdom at Turnavo, being chopped to pieces by order of the Pasha of Thessaly because he refused to deny Christ. This happened in the year 1818, and there is one old monk still living who remembers him.

The principal relics are a piece of the True Cross, part of the skull of St. Bartholomew, a lump of earth mingled with bones of the Forty Martyrs of Nicomedia, and the body of St. Gideon in a beautiful silver shrine. There are no interesting reliquaries.

On the roof of the narthex are queer representations of the Flood. In one fresco Noah is inviting the animals to enter something which looks like a railway signal-box by beating a semantron. This signal-box is the ark, but Noah and the animals are so much bigger that there seems to be considerable doubt as to whether they can get into it, and an adventurous camel that has made the attempt has apparently got into difficulties with his neck.

The library is contained in a small room on the ground floor close to the catholicon, used also as a lumber room for old guns and other objects of little interest to the monks. It is not isolated, but forms part of the domestic buildings, so stands a good chance of being burnt. Sometimes the Athos libraries are separate buildings in the courtyard, as at the Lavra; sometimes they are placed over the narthex or porch

---

to end of east apse, 12 feet. Nave: across transepts, 37 feet; from iconostasis to west wall, 26½ feet. Esonarthex (which opens into the nave by three doorways), from east to west, 21½ feet, nearly the length of nave. There is also an exonarthex.

of the catholicon, as at St. Dionysius; in these cases they are tolerably safe in case of fire attacking the monastery. But usually they occupy some room in the buildings themselves, and when a general conflagration occurs some get burnt, others suffer terribly from being thrown out of window or otherwise hastened to a place of comparative security. We always tried to impress upon the monks the importance of having separate buildings for their books.

The librarian, so the monks said, was away (we were beginning to look upon this officer as a fabulous being; he was *always* away); nobody else knew anything about the books, and of course there was no sort of catalogue. So we had to rummage for ourselves amongst the dusty shelves. O— found a fine manuscript of the New Testament and an illuminated evangelistarium, and I a splendid folio of the Gospels in uncials of the seventh century. We calculated that there were about 250 manuscripts in all, on vellum and paper.

Besides the books an old *epitrachelion*, or priest's stole, which was hanging up on a nail, attracted my attention. It was a fine specimen of Byzantine embroidery of considerable antiquity, and, as it had evidently been disused on account of its age and worn-out appearance, I much wished to become its possessor; but Angelos was afraid to ask the monks to sell it, lest they should be offended; and, indeed, we found it everywhere impossible to offer to buy anything from the monasteries. There was another old stole in the library, but not of such fine workmanship as the former.

After taking an unsuccessful photograph of the

monastery (two of the younger and more agile monks running up to the top of the tower and standing on the parapet to make themselves prominent) we had breakfast, and then tried to extract some information respecting the monastery from its head, the abbot Stephen. But the old gentleman had apparently the greatest possible objection to answering questions or taxing his memory in any way, and literally writhed under his examination. At each interrogation he looked this way and that, any way but at us, as if he were trying to find a means of escape, wriggled in his seat until I thought he would have fallen off the divan, repeated our question, and declared his inability to answer in the most provoking way.

Asked how many monks there were in the monastery, after writhing like an eel on a spear, and making several unsuccessful attempts at parrying the question, he at length replied that he had no idea.

'Are there a hundred?' asked O—.

'No, not so many as that,' replied our victim.

'Are there twenty?' said I.

'Yes.'

'Thirty?'

'Yes.'

'Are you quite sure there are not seventy?'

'Yes, quite sure.'

And finally by the process of exhaustion we managed to fix the number at fifty, with the help of two rather more intelligent monks whom we called in as their abbot's assessors. Really we were, perhaps, a little formidable, Angelos asking the questions and we two outlandish fellows, sitting each with pocket-book and pencil in hand, waiting for the answers! It

required the greatest perseverance on our part, but
we were determined not to let him go until we had
obtained full particulars of everything, and although
we succeeded at last I will undertake to say that the
poor abbot never spent such a miserable morning in
his life.

As to the subject of foundation, of course we could
get no information. Founded by an imperial family,
perhaps Caracalla, but he didn't know, was all that the
abbot could tell us, although we put the question in
every possible form a dozen times.

Besides the fifty monks there are twelve servants.
The rule is cœnobite. The monastery has lands in
Cassandra and Thasos, and formerly possessed a farm
in Moldavia.

The churches are :

Esocclesia.

1. The catholicon, dedicated to the Holy Apostles (to all, or, as
Georgirenes says, to SS. Peter and Paul ?).
   2. The Annunciation.
   3. The Assumption.
   4. The Panteleëmon.
   5. St. John the Merciful, Patriarch of Alexandria.[1]

---

[1] St. John the Merciful, or the Almoner, furnished, according to Neale,
the name to the famous order of Hospitallers. He was a native of
Cyprus, being the son of the governor of that island. He devoted himself to God and was distinguished for the liberality of his alms. In 609
he became the 35th patriarch of Alexandria. Soon afterwards, in 614,
Chosroes, King of Persia, overran Syria and took Jerusalem. 90,000
Christians were massacred, principally by the accursed Jews, who
bought them from the Persians for that purpose; the Patriarch
Zacharias and an immense number of the inhabitants were carried into
captivity, and the True Cross fell into the hands of the infidels. In this
fearful calamity John fed the refugees, redeemed captives, and rebuilt the
churches that had been thrown down. Whilst the Patriarch was thus
taxing all the resources of the Church of Alexandria a famine broke out

6. St. George.

7. SS. Barlaam and Joseph.[1]

Exocclesi.

All Saints (cemetery chapel).

There are ten kellia attached to Caracalla.

The monastery has suffered considerably from fires, the last of which took place in 1874.

By the time we had asked all our questions and had obtained satisfactory replies the mules were ready, so we descended to the gateway and mounted them. When we were in our saddles and just moving off the good abbot heaped coals of fire on our heads by presenting each of us with a splendid bunch of grapes as a parting gift. I really believe he was sorry to lose us, although we had plagued him so!

The first part of our ride took us past Philotheou,

in Egypt, owing to a deficiency in the rise of the Nile : the treasury of the Church was exhausted, and he borrowed until he could find none to trust or lend. Every day he fed 7,500 poor folk, besides the alms he sent to Jerusalem. Referring my reader to Neale's *History of the Holy Eastern Church* (*Pat. of Alexandria*) for further particulars concerning the life of this good man, I will conclude by giving one of the stories about him.

He discovered that during the celebration of the Eucharist many persons left the church after the Gospel, without waiting for the Oblation (this seems to be an old abuse). On one occasion St. John followed them, and when they expressed astonishment at such an occurrence the Patriarch replied, ' My sons, where the sheep are there should the shepherd be. It is for your sakes that I go to church, for I could celebrate at home.' After applying this quaint remedy twice it is said that he cured his flock of their bad habit.

He died in 620, at the age of sixty-four, at his native city of Amathus, in Cyprus, and was there buried. His relics were translated first to Constantinople, then to Buda, and finally to Posen in the year 1530. His festival is November 12. Such an admirable character deserves this long note.

[1] St. Joseph, or rather St. Josaphat, was a holy king of India. Concerning these saints see the *Legenda aurea*, ' De Sanctis Josaphat et Barlaam.'

by the road we had gone over before.   Leaving that
monastery on our right, for the next four hours we
rode through a beautiful forest, our path winding
through the shrubs and the trees, which not only shielded
us from the hot sun but also intercepted our view, so
that only once or twice did we see the peak of Athos
through the wood, and only occasionally caught sight
of the blue sea beneath us.   We had to ascend a considerable height, so as to cross the backbone of the
peninsula.   Two hours after leaving Caracalla we
reached the top, and as we rode along the ridge had
for a short time views of the sea on either hand, both
of the Strymonic and Singitic gulfs, before plunging
again into a wood on the other side.   Shortly after
three o'clock we drew near Xeropotamou, and at four
found ourselves back again in our old quarters at
Russico.

Here was our friend the metropolitan Michael,
very pleasant and courteous, as before ; we were sorry
that he left Athos that evening, when, owing to our not
understanding that he was going, we missed saying
farewell to him.   A good dinner greatly refreshed us
after our ride across the promontory, and we retired to
bed soon afterwards, having spent a most enjoyable
day.   I ought to have said that Angelos was much
better—in fact, his earache had nearly gone, although it
had left a little deafness behind.   He much appreciated
getting back to Russico, for last night at Caracalla he
was driven from his divan and had taken refuge in the
middle of the room ; and whilst we were snugly tucked
up in our levinges, he was occupying himself with
picking off the intruders that crawled on to his burly
person and throwing them away to the extremities of

the room. Rather poor fun, I should think, but we told him that, being a native of these parts, he ought to be accustomed to all such discomforts!

The next day being Sunday, O——, by permission, celebrated the Holy Eucharist in our room. We afterwards discovered that the monks were rather annoyed at having been asked leave for this; why I know not. It was the same with everything at Russico. Although the Russians could not have been more hospitable than they were, yet underneath all their civility there existed an unpleasant sort of feeling, which it was hard to account for unless it were political jealousy of Englishmen. Thus they were unwilling to show us their treasures or their relics, objected to our going behind the iconostasis in the churches, and showed suspicion of us in many other little ways—so different from all the other monasteries, the Russian skete of St. Andrew not excepted, where we were received with what I can only call brotherly affection. And yet, as I say, with it all they were scrupulously civil and kind, pressing us to stay with them and giving us the best of everything.

We passed the day in thoroughly Oriental fashion, lying for the most part on our beds, half asleep, half awake. At three o'clock we went to the principal (Russian) church for vespers, and much enjoyed the 'tetraphone' music. At the conclusion of the office a richly jewelled icon of Our Lady, which hung near the top of the iconostasis, was slowly let down in front of the holy doors. The abbot Macarius stood before it on the platform, or *soleas*,[1] of the iconostasis; two priests stood on each side of him towards the picture, facing

---

[1] The sanctuary step, which projects outside the iconostasis, usually to the breadth of several feet.

each other, and two deacons, with silver censers in their
hands, also facing each other, nearest the picture. Then
the abbot, taking a book and holding it up close to his
face, commenced to intone a long litany, each petition
being about four times the length of those in the litany
of the English Prayer Book, and the burden of it ' Hail,'
a word which occurred, say, six times in each petition,
and the only word we could understand, as the language was Slavonic. At the end of each of these
sentences the abbot and his two priests crossed themselves and bowed very low, whilst the deacons turned
and censed the icon, the quire meanwhile chanting
a threefold ' Lord, have mercy,' a doxology, or an
' Alleluya.' This curious service lasted for the best
part of an hour, without any variation, and then two
monks advanced and supported the picture in their arms
between them, leaning it on their shoulders ; and first
the abbot and then the priests and the deacons, after
prostrating themselves thrice, touching the ground
with their foreheads each time, advanced and kissed
the icon and prostrated themselves again. All the
monks and lay people followed, and the poor old
Russian merchant, who was still in his stall by us,
knocked his head upon the ground so often and so
vehemently that we began to fear that each prostration
would be his last. The icon, a modern one, was, we
were told, miraculous and came from Jerusalem.

And can I defend this, or must I admit that such
devotion comes at least within measurable distance of
idolatry ?

Let me say at once that I am not prepared to defend
every Oriental position, far from it, and that I should not
like to see a service of this kind in our English churches,

though quite ready to admit my judgment wrong. But even though we may think it to be our duty to reprehend a devotion or a practice, I do plead most earnestly for an unprejudiced consideration of the question before we venture to judge our brethren of the Catholic Church. I entreat that we may put the best construction possible on their actions and attribute to them the best motives ; that we may indulge in a little wholesome self-examination, to see whether the particular doctrine or practice which obtains amongst them, and to. which we object, is wholly devoid of good or has not been, by the mercy of God, a means of preserving them from some pitfalls into which we have fallen ; and finally, since their peculiar position and history may have been favourable to the growth of certain spiritual flowers, as ours to the growth of others, that we may try to cull these for our own benefit. Thus, if we must have controversy, we may at least endeavour to make it profitable to ourselves. Now, as we understand the feelings of the Greeks no better than they understand ours, it is just as unfair for us to call them idolatrous and their rites and customs superstitious as for the Greeks to speak of the English (as a friend remarked to me not long since) as *an admirable people, with pre-eminent virtues but no religion.* It is just as difficult for us Anglicans to throw ourselves into an Oriental way of looking at things as for an Eastern to view theological questions through Anglican spectacles.

Again, ' people that live in glass houses should not throw stones.' If the Greek Church has exaggerated the honour due to the Blessed Virgin, how far have we erred in the opposite direction ? In England we may adorn our churches with the similitudes of patriarchs and prophets, of apostles, nay, even of martyrs, confessors, and virgins; but there is *one* Saint that may seldom be represented in picture or in sculpture, and there is *one* name which may scarcely be mentioned in this Christian land but with an apology and bated breath, the name of Mary, the Virgin Mother of God.[1]

And if you would have the Oriental opinion on this our strange Anglican custom, hear the answer of the Easterns to the nonjuring English bishops, who laboured, to their eternal honour, for peace in the early part of the eighteenth century.

They were ready, so said the Anglican divines, to call the Mother of Our Lord blessed, and magnify the grace of God which so highly exalted her; yet were they afraid of giving the glory of God to a creature, or to run into any extreme by blessing or magnifying her.

'Here,' wrote back the Eastern prelates in reply, 'here we may fairly cry out with David, *There were they in great fear where no fear was!*' And that the Oriental Church does not intentionally teach her children to pay idolatrous worship to pictures and to images is clear from her formularies.

I believe and confess, according to the understanding of the Holy Eastern Church, that the Saints in Christ who reign in heaven are worthy to be honoured and invoked, and that their prayers and intercessions move the All-merciful God to the salvation of our souls; also that to venerate their incorruptible relics, as also the precious virtues of their remains, is well-pleasing to God.

---

[1] A divine of the English Church not long ago edited a hymn book in which the words of a well-known hymn, 'Jesu, Son of Mary, hear,' were altered to 'Jesu, Son of *David*, hear,' for no other reason, apparently, than because the name of Mary was offensive to English ears.

I admit that the pictures of Christ our Saviour, of the Holy Virgin, and of other saints are meet to be had and to be honoured, not for the purpose of worship, but that by having them before our eyes we may be encouraged to devotion and to the imitation of the deeds of the righteous ones represented by the pictures.[1]

If it be said that it is all very well to talk of the Church not teaching idolatry, the poor and ignorant of the laity at least do, to all intents and purposes, pay to the Holy Virgin and to her icons the worship due to God alone, it may be replied that in England, where we boast of education and enlightenment, the doctrine of the Communion of Saints is to the ordinary layman simply a dry dogma, absolutely without meaning to him and certainly bearing no fruit; so that he is in great danger of substituting the material world for the spiritual, and even of losing his belief in the supernatural altogether; and that one result of the suppression of all teaching with regard to St. Mary has been that half the Anglican Church is, through ignorance, semi-Nestorian.[2]

The true doctrine of the Orthodox Church of the East, as distinguished from the Roman teaching respecting the Blessed Virgin on the one hand and the Protestant on the other, is so well put in an essay on

[1] Catechism of the Russian Church.

[2] I recently had a conversation with a person of the lower middle class which opened my eyes. She was a pious Churchwoman, a regular communicant, a supporter of 'Gospel temperance' (whatever that may mean), and took a real interest in all religious matters. I had made use of the expression 'the Blessed Virgin or any other saint,' when she pulled me up with the remark, 'Surely, sir, you don't think the Virgin Mary was a saint? I have always looked upon her as a sinful woman just like any of us.' Words, indeed, to make one shudder.

And yet another illustration. About six months ago I came across a little book on abuses in the English Church, written by two beneficed. clergymen and addressed to the Anglican episcopate. One chapter

X

the dogma of the Immaculate Conception by Andrew Nicolaievitch Mouravieff, sometime procurator to the Holy Governing Synod of Russia,[1] and describes so excellently the Catholic position, that I cannot refrain from quoting an extract from it.

There is nothing contrary to orthodox doctrine in the assertion that the Blessed Virgin was without *actual* sin. Grant that St. Mary was, in a manner peculiar to herself, freed from *original* sin, and that she thus became, as Liguori affirms, the restorer of the human race ; and what do you teach but that the Passion and Death of our Lord were not indispensable for the salvation of mankind ? See to what a blasphemous conclusion the new dogma leads. See how it detracts from the expiatory merits of the Redeemer. They affirm that it is necessary for the glory and honour of the Blessed Virgin herself to have her conception immaculate. We are far from the idea of Protestants, who, while they respect in the person of the Mother of God her virtues, her humility, her submission to the Divine Will, see not, and will not see, her exaltation above all creatures, celestial and terrestrial, and her mediation between her Son and the faithful. We agree entirely so far as this : that our duty is to glorify, by every possible means, her whom the Almighty has invested with majesty, and whom, according to the Gospel, all generations must call blessed. We agree that this is a holy work and the duty of every Christian. This the Orthodox Church does : since the earliest ages of Christianity she has glorified the Blessed Virgin, naming her more precious than the cherubim and infinitely more glorious than the seraphim ; supplicating her as the most powerful Mediatress with the Lord and the mightiest advocate of the Christian world. In commemorating the principal events of her life the Orthodox Church glorifies them by particular feasts, as the Nativity, the Presentation, and the Assumption. Under the conviction that the Blessed Virgin, as Mother of

---

was headed 'Mariolatry,' and spoke of the great heresiarch as the 'faithful Nestorius' who opposed 'the heretical Cyril' (I think the word was 'heretical ;' at any rate it was equivalent to it) in his attempt to establish the 'blasphemous title of the Theotocos.'

[1] Translated from the Russ by Neale, *Voices from the East.* Masters 1859.

the Most High God, always enjoys a maternal access to her Son and
to God, and prays incessantly for the Christian world, the Orthodox
Church terminates nearly all her prayers by 'commemorating the
most holy, undefiled, excellently laudable Mother of God and Ever-
Virgin,' as a proof how powerful is her intercession with God and
how capable of propitiating His favour. But while thus glorifying
St. Mary the Orthodox Church has never entered on the question
whether her conception was immaculate, and has even considered
the question itself unsuitable to the dignity of the Queen of Angels.

CHAPTER XIX.

Monday, ^{*September 3*} ^{*August 22*}. We had arranged to visit Simopetra to-day, as it will be remembered we had omitted
this monastery on our way from St. Gregory's to
Russico. The monks kindly offered to send us by
their launch, so steam was got up and we went on board
at nine o'clock. She was a nice little craft, having been
built at Constantinople by English engineers. All the
crew were monks, and very curious it was to see the
skipper at the wheel in full monastic dress and the
fireman stoking the engine in a tall hat.

The dial marked the extreme pressure of steam,
and we went through the water at a great pace, taking
only three-quarters of an hour to reach the port of
Simopetra. On our way we passed a little boat rowing
close in shore and going towards Xeropotamou. On
investigation it proved to contain the metropolitan of
Cavalla, sitting in the stern, with his white umbrella
over his head and the faithful Pantele and Peter in the
bows. They were too far off for us to hold any verbal
communication with them, but we waved our hats and
handkerchiefs and were pleased to find that we were
recognised.

I am utterly unable to describe the wonderful

SIMOPETRA.

position of the monastery of Simon the Anchorite,[1] and
although we tried to photograph it from no less than
four different places we could not get one negative that
did it justice.

From the mountain-side a deep valley or cleft
descends to the sea. Perched on the very point of an
isolated rock in the midst of that ravine is the monastery, at the height of between 900 and 1,000 feet above
the sea. As you stand on the little quay, which is
defended by an ancient fortress, the monastery towers
right above your head, standing out against the sky,
only connected with the mountain by an aqueduct,
consisting of two rows of thirteen or fourteen arches.
With great labour a terraced garden has been scooped
out of the rock and built up below the aqueduct, much
of the earth having been brought thither, and in it the
monks grow their fruit and vegetables, the produce
being hauled up by means of a basket and a pulley.
On this side the walls come down almost to the garden,
and here is the entrance to the monastery; but on the
other sides the rock is steep and rugged; the walls
rise from it straight and bare, pierced at intervals by
small windows, and then wooden balconies commence,
bracketed out from the wall one above the other, overhanging the precipice. In one place there are no less
than *seven* rows of these balconies. Usually, however,
there are from two to four. The mules which had
brought down the Archbishop's party were still standing
at the port; so we had no need to make use of the
speaking-trumpet which is kept below as a means of
communication with the monastery. However, one of

[1] 'Romance has not figured a situation more wild and picturesque.'
—*Sibthorpe.*

the monks, who lived in the old tower at the port, applying his mouth to one end of the trumpet and raising the other to heaven, shouted through it a warning of our approach, and presently a voice that seemed to come from the clouds responded to the call.

The road up to the convent is indeed what Ricaut quaintly calls it, 'a craggy and asperous ascent.' It winds and twists up the side of the mountain, and although the path is good the ascent is extremely rapid, and at the turns of the road the mules frequently put their heads over an abyss, wheeling slowly round as if they were contemplating the propriety of suicide.

After three-quarters of an hour of this climbing we reached the gate of the monastery, where the principal monks were waiting to receive us. They held our stirrups (if you can call two rope nooses stirrups) whilst we dismounted, and then conducted us through a long winding passage, evidently so constructed for purposes of defence, into the courtyard. This is so small that the catholicon almost fills it, and the few apertures that exist between the roof of the church and the surrounding buildings are, for the most part, covered with glass. This curious pinched-in arrangement is due, of course, to the peculiarity of the site.

The catholicon is dedicated to the Nativity of Christ.[1] As Mr. Tozer remarks, it possesses more windows than is usual with a Byzantine church, owing to the darkness caused by its being so squeezed between other buildings.

---

[1] Measurements: Sanctuary: from north to south, including chapels, 24½ feet (this is the extreme width of the church, not including transepts) ; across chord of east apse, 9¾ feet ; from iconostasis to wall of east apse, 11½ feet. Nave: from iconostasis to west wall, 26 feet ; across transepts, 33 feet. The esonarthex measures 15 feet from east to west.

There is a very low, dark esonarthex. The exo-narthex is somewhat irregular, having its north-west corner cut off, owing to the contraction of the court-yard.

The frescoes which cover the walls of the church have, unfortunately, been repainted. The iconostasis of carved wood is fine and well executed. We did not see the relics, which are of St. Modestus, St. Barlaam, and St. Mary Magdalen. The last is probably that mentioned by Georgirenes. 'They shew here an hand for a sacred Relique of St. Mary Magdalen's body, but the Fingers of it are extraordinary great.'

In the west gallery of the church, over the narthex, is the small room which forms the library. There are nearly 250 manuscripts, rather over forty of which are written on vellum; none of any interest that we could discover. They are not arranged in any order and are not particularly well cared for.

LIST OF CHURCHES BELONGING TO SIMOPETRA.

Esocclesia.

1. Catholicon (the Nativity).
2. The Archangels.
3. St. George.
4. St. Mary Magdalen.
5. St. Charalampes.

Exocclesia.

1. The Nativity of Our Lady.
2. The Assumption of Our Lady.
3. St. John the Divine } attached to two cathismata.
4. St. Simon }

The monastery possesses four kellia, in addition to the two cathismata mentioned above; also two farms in Cassandra and one in the island of Lemnos. Being a poor convent, it has suffered severely from the loss of its lands in Moldavia.[1]   There are seventy-five monks attached to it, who follow the cœnobite rule, and about twenty servants.   The abbot's name is Neophytus.

The monks gave us a good meal, and afterwards we sat in a room situated in the topmost story, facing the sea.   Here the abbot told us the history of the monastery.

He said that it was founded by John Unglessi, King of Servia and Moldavia, about 1250 (I believe the real date is 1363[2]).   His daughter being ill, he besought the intercession of St. Simon, who had lived on this rock as a hermit and had died five years previously.   His daughter recovered, and the King founded the monastery as a thank offering.

Comnenus gives the same account, but adds further particulars concerning St. Simon.   He says that he was a hermit, who lived near here and saw a bright star descending and resting on the point of rock.   God revealed to him the meaning of the vision—that he was to build a church on that site.   This he did, and called it the New Bethlehem.   Afterwards John Unglessi founded the monastery, as has been said, and finally himself became a monk.   This story is referred to in a print of Simopetra presented to us on leaving, which, besides a view of the monastery, gives several scenes from the life of St. Simon.   In one the saint as he prays sees the star upon the rock; in another the church is being built, and St. Simon is removing a great stone by the sign of the cross; in a third John

[1] It seems to have lost a revenue of 3,850*l.* from a monastery at Bucharest, which had been its property since 1594.   See *Christ. Rem.* 1851.

[2] Muralt, *Chronographie Byzantine.*

Unglessi is praying before the icon of St. Simon, whilst his daughter writhes upon the floor ; and the fourth is an extremely funny picture. A monk is lying on his back, two venerable persons with glories round their heads are holding up his feet, whilst a third, who is standing in a cloud, administers the bastinado. Most of the other pictures, all quaintly delineated, are unintelligible.

MONASTERY OF SIMOPETRA.

We went out upon the balcony in front of the room in which we were sitting. What a glorious view it was! —beneath us the little port where we had landed that morning, and the Gulf of the Holy Mountain, with the sister promontory of Longos on the farther side. The balcony upon which we stood was the highest, four others being beneath us. Clarke[1] says of Simopetra, 'The view from its external gallery is one of the most awful and terrific that can be conceived. The

[1] Professor Clarke was at Athos in 1801.

spectator looking down feels as if he were suspended over a gloomy abyss.'

There was a speaking-trumpet lying on a seat, of the same size and shape as the one at the port. So, taking it up, I roared through it, 'God save the Queen!' to the great amusement of the monks who were standing beside me, and to the astonishment of the good people at the harbour beneath, who told us on our return that they wondered what could be happening up above!

Before we left the monastery we took two photographs of it from the mountain on different sides. I have given both views here, as they give a good idea of the building, although they do not do justice to its position.

As the abbot escorted us through the tortuous passage to the gate he told us of the terrible calamity which befell Simopetra in the sixteenth century. The monastery caught fire, unfortunately close to the entrance, thus cutting off the means of escape. The unfortunate inhabitants were driven gradually to the side which faces the sea, and so there was no choice left but that of the precipice or of the fire. Some of the younger monks succeeded in letting themselves down by ropes, but the great majority were either dashed to pieces or burnt to death. With the exception of the catholicon, which must have had a marvellous escape, the whole convent was destroyed—that is to say, it was completely gutted and everything that could burn was burnt, the great stone walls alone remaining intact. Even now, though three centuries have passed since that awful catastrophe, the monks can hardly speak of it without a shudder.

We mounted our mules soon after three o'clock and

reached the port at four. Here, after some delay, we embarked in a rowing boat and directed our monastic oarsmen to pull us to Xeropotamou ; for we had heard from the abbot of Simopetra that the metropolitan of Cavalla had gone thither. On our arrival at the little bay and harbour of Daphne we found mules awaiting us, for we had sent word that morning overland from Simopetra that we were coming. We mounted them, and riding for a little way up 'the Dry River'—the mountain torrent, dry in summer, which gives its name to Xeropotamou—we struck up the hill to our left, reaching the convent in the course of half an hour. Here we received a most cordial welcome both from the Archbishop and the monks ; the former absolutely fell on our necks and kissed us, and made us promise not to part company again.

'Stay here to-night,' said he, 'and to-morrow, as time is precious to you, we will go to Russico together.'

We had left all our luggage at that monastery, as we had not intended staying away for a night, and this we explained to the Archbishop.

'Never mind,' said he. 'Send Angelos back to Russico and order him to forward your luggage here to-night by the mule which takes him. He can stay at Russico until we come ; meanwhile I will be your dragoman !'

So this course was agreed upon, and Angelos departed.

The monks provided us with an excellent repast, which we much enjoyed, and after some pleasant conversation with our old friend, our portmanteaux having arrived, we retired to separate bedrooms, the Archbishop superintending the suspension of the curtains of our levinges and otherwise taking the most fatherly care of us.

The next morning I was awakened by a most terrific uproar in the corridor, several persons all talking at the same time, and that in no gentle manner, and the voice of the Archbishop rising high above the din, conveying the impression that its owner was considerably ruffled. After lying awake for a few minutes and finding that the noise rather increased than lessened, I got out of bed and opened my door a little to see what was happening, as I did so encountering O—, also with his head through his doorway, on the opposite side of the passage.

'What is the matter?' said I.

'I can't conceive. The noise awoke me, and I thought that the monastery was on fire at the least.'

There were about six monks, Pantele, and our prelate; and whether the monks and the Archbishop were together storming at the unfortunate cavass, or the Archbishop and Pantele at the monks, and what the bone of contention was, we never exactly discovered, but they were certainly all very much out of temper, and the Archbishop of Cavalla was not the man to be crossed.

As soon as they saw us looking out of our rooms they seemed to think we were in want of something, and one of the company advanced with two very dirty towels and two jugs of water for our baths. These were the identical towels that all the company had used in washing their hands after dinner the previous evening, and we had remarked at the time how filthy they were. Perhaps the dispute had been about these, for our archiepiscopal dragoman interposed and told the monk to take them away and bring us fresh ones. The Englishmen, he said, were accustomed to have clean towels for their baths.

'Very sorry,' said the monk, 'but we have no others.'

'Then you must get some,' replied the Archbishop. 'I am not going to allow them to have these.'

And it was all in vain that our hosts protested that these were the only two towels in the monastery, and that as everybody, even the Archbishop, used them, why could not we?

'No,' said he, 'they must have clean towels.'

So after another long discussion they finally brought two new pieces of very coarse and thick linen with the dressing still on, having never been washed, as stiff as boards, which proved to be quite useless, as the water ran off the dressing like rain off a duck's back; thus we were constrained to use our handkerchiefs (you have no idea what can be done with a pocket-hand-kerchief till you try) and the fringes of the dirty towels.

We expected to start for Russico at once, but instead, at the Archbishop's pleasure, we managed to waste the day very well until three o'clock, when we at last got off, and reached our destination in three-quarters of an hour. The customary little service of reception was performed in the church, on account of the Archbishop in Greek, which caused a slight confusion. the Russian monks on one side of the quire being unable to sing 'Kyrie eleison.'

Poor Conon was delighted to see us, and repeated over and over again like a parrot the one sentence of English that I had taught him—'I am a fool!' 'I am a fool!' I was not able to refrain from the joke, as he was certainly one of the most ignorant and childish monks we had met. He was always laughing, so that it was impossible to be angry with him for long, as the more you scolded him the more he laughed. He told us this evening that he had run away from his native place to Mount Athos, and that his mother did not know where he was, which conduct we severely reprimanded and bade him write home at once.

The next day we tried to move on to the next monastery, St. Xenophon's, but the Archbishop wished to remain at Russico until the following day. We employed the time therefore in a fresh exploration of the buildings. O— visited the printing press, the rooms where the books are bound, and afterwards we both paid a second visit to the library. Last evening O— had asked for the music of a certain Kyrie we had heard in the church, which for some reason or other the monks were unwilling to give him; but now the Archbishop suddenly remembered the circumstance, and on hearing that he had not received the music ordered our hosts to send the book which contained it to our room, which they did. Then we went to a room were they painted icons, and after a deal of talking arranged to have an icon of St. Laurence painted 'in the Byzantine manner,' as the artist said, to distinguish it from those he was engaged upon, which I am sorry to say showed a sad falling off from the traditional art in the direction of the worst European taste.

To-day we made the acquaintance of a most intelligent old Bulgarian monk named Magistrion, who spoke French fluently. He told us that he was a widower and had had eleven children. When the last was married, some three years ago, he resolved to devote himself to religion· (I think he had been a merchant), and so joined this monastery, where he was engaged in translating the sermons of numerous Russian divines into Greek. This was the only instance we came across of an Athos monk being engaged in distinct literary work. I do not mean to say that other cases could not be found, but I should think that outside Russico there are very few. Magistrion also knew something about the English Church, and brought us from the library a small book, written by one Gatte, formerly a Roman Catholic clergyman, but now in charge of the Orthodox church at Paris, giving some account of all Christian denominations, and consequently discussing the Anglican Church, and that very fairly. Magistrion said that he was prevented from doing as much literary work as he wished owing to the frequent and lengthy services, and gave us the following description of an ordinary day at Russico ; it does not differ much from the account of the monastic obligations furnished us at the skete of the Prodromos : The monks go to church at midnight and recite the night offices until five A.M., when they repose for an hour. At six o'clock, after singing terce and sext, they commence the liturgy, which on ordinary days lasts till eight o'clock, but on Sundays and festivals till nearly ten. On days when they have more than one meal they now breakfast, and then work and sleep until three P.M., when they once more go to church, this time for none and vespers, which last until five. At this hour they sup, and from six to half-past seven recite compline in church ; after which they go to bed until eleven, when the bell summons them to private prayer before the midnight service. On festivals the midnight service lasts ten hours.

Magistrion was full of a wonderful flower which he grew, and upon which he prided himself exceedingly. He promised to give us the means of producing this plant in England, and later on in the day brought *one* seed, carefully wrapped up in paper. 'Ah,' said he, expatiating on its rare qualities, 'quelle belle fleur ! quelle belle fleur! Je vous assure, messieurs, une fleur excellente !' And most exact were the instructions we received respecting this ' fleur excellente '— how it was to be sown in March, how it loved the sun, and many other matters relating to its cultivation.

We also again came across the Bishop Nilos, to whom we had been hurriedly presented as we were leaving the Seraï.

Nilos was a man not only of education, but also of considerable knowledge of the world. He had travelled a great deal, chiefly for the purpose of interesting the European Governments in the question of the Roumanian spoliation of the monastic lands, and had been to London nine times. Here he had come across Bishop Blomfield, and consequently thought he knew all about the English Church. He began to talk about Anglican theology, especially with reference to the Holy Communion, and supported his low opinion of our doctrine by the assertion that after the communion of the people the priest had for his own secular use whatever was left over of the *Sacrament*! It was not difficult to see how the mistake had occurred, and it only proves how true the proverb is that 'a little knowledge is a dangerous thing,' and shows how easily we may misunderstand rites and customs that are foreign to us. Of course we contradicted the monstrous assertion, but Nilos was obstinate.

'Ah, mes chers,' said he in a patronizing way, 'I know better!' To tell us that we were unacquainted with the customs of our own Church was a little too provoking. But our friend the Archbishop of Cavalla, who was sitting on the same sofa with us, came to the rescue, and explained to the bishop that, having both read and seen our liturgy, he could tell him that he was mistaken, and insisted that an English priest like O— probably knew more about his own Church than an outsider, the result being that Nilos was completely routed by our archiepiscopal ally. And, to our great amusement (for Nilos understood French perfectly), our prelate turned to O—, who was sitting on the other side of Nilos, and said in a tone of compassionate superiority, 'Cette ignorance est très triste ; il se mêle!'

There was not much love lost between these two dignitaries, I fancy; for all the Greeks detested Nilos, and, if the stories told about him were true, not without reason. We heard that a few years back he aimed at the patriarchate of Alexandria, and, being a man of property, by a judicious use of his money he very nearly obtained what he wanted, for he was actually elected to the see.[1] But unfortunately for him his monastery (Esphigmenou) refused to give him a character by withholding what we should call at Oxford his 'grace;' thus Nilos lost his prize. He had

---

[1] A great and terrible abuse in the Greek Church. The Turkish rulers of Constantinople compelled the Patriarch to buy his appointment, and the evil practice has descended to other appointments in the Church. Yet this custom does not altogether date from the conquest ; it unhappily obtained to a considerable extent long before. Thus Maundeville says

been tried, I believe, before the Synod of Constantinople, and incapacitated from holding any ecclesiastical benefice, though he was allowed to retain his episcopal rank.   He lived on Mount Athos in a kelli, and having been 'sent to Coventry' by his countrymen, had 'taken up' with the Russians, spending his time chiefly in their houses.

What his crimes were I cannot say ; his character was represented, truthfully or falsely, as that of a desperate intriguer.   But I am unwilling to blacken his reputation on the authority of his enemies ; possibly his unpopularity was due merely to his political sympathy with Russia—an unpardonable offence in Greek eyes—and I should be sorry to judge him without hearing the other side.

In the afternoon we visited several churches.   In some of them a monk would be found reading aloud to himself from a desk in the centre of the building.   On inquiry we found that in one church it is the custom for the monks to take turns of two hours each in read· ing the Gospels, so that there is always one at this devotional exercise day and night; in another the Psalms are read in the same manner.

We paid a state visit to the Abbot Macarius, who lived in a little cell, barely furnished, but with a splendid view of the gulf.   Of course we partook of the usual refreshments, but, as we consisted of Russians, Greeks, and Englishmen, owing to the difficulties of language, conversation flagged somewhat.   The Archbishop

---

of the '*Men of Greece*,' 'Thei sellen Benefices of Holy Chirche : And so don Men in othere places : God amende it, whan his Wille is. And that is gret Sclaundre.   For now is Symonye Kyng crouned in Holy Chirche : God amende it for his Mercy.'   Well may we say *Amen* to the prayer of the pious old traveller.

hardly uttered a syllable, and after a long silence
O—, feeling that he ought to say something, remarked,
' Hot day.'

This was translated, and also the abbot's reply,
'Not so hot as yesterday.'

Five minutes having elapsed, I tried my hand.
' Polycala,' said I, pointing out of the window at the
view.   ' Polycala,' replied the abbot ; and after this we
gave up all attempts, took our departure, and went to
vespers.

The Archbishop came too, and ensconced himself
in a stall in front of the iconostasis.   Whilst the service
was going on we observed that he was busily engaged
with a small volume, apparently reading some passage
over and over again, like a schoolboy getting his task
by heart.   Presently the mystery was explained, for
the deacon, coming to a prayer which the highest
ecclesiastic present ought to read, stopped, and the
officiating priest, who was ' in the altar,' as the Greeks
say, and the Archbishop began the prayer together.
The priest having a stentorian voice, and of course
knowing Slavonic perfectly, would have overmatched
a less resolute prelate than ours, who was naturally
severely handicapped.   But Philotheos, who was not
going to be done out of his prayer after having taken
all the trouble to get it up, stuck manfully to his
rights, stumbling heavily over the consonants of that
wonderful language until the priest, thinking that
something was wrong, turned round and saw how
matters stood.   Thus the Archbishop had the end of
his prayer to himself ; but I am sorry to say I saw
several of the monks laughing at his pronunciation.

There is a little shop outside the walls of Russico,

where icons, crosses, and other religious goods of Russian and native manufacture can be purchased. We invested in a large supply of these, completely clearing out the stock of wooden crosses made by the hermits of Athos.

At midnight, after the development of some negatives, we went to the service for an hour, and then retired to rest, so as to get up for the Archbishop's mass the next morning.

CHAPTER XX.

The liturgy began very early; when we arrived at half-past seven the monks were just about to sing the Gospel.

Philotheos looked magnificent in his saccos,[1] or dalmatic, of the richest crimson silk, stiff with gold; he wore also the crown we had seen on the head of the abbot. The service was gorgeous in the extreme, and lasted for several hours. It was different from any service we had taken part in, for a bishop's mass entails distinct and more elaborate ceremonies. How difficult it is to follow these Oriental rites! The services consist of a series of surprises, and sometimes even the monks seem to be at a loss as to what is coming next.

As we went to the great chamber for coffee the Archbishop said in an aside to us, 'If we had been in my *métropole* I should have taken you behind the iconostasis to see all the rites; here the Russians are so superstitious and bigoted that they would have been offended.'

About three o'clock we paid another visit to the abbot, to take leave of him, the conversation being as desultory as it had been the day before. He accompanied us to the gate, and amidst the ringing of bells

---

[1] Worn by metropolitans when celebrating the liturgy, instead of the *phænolion*, or Eastern chasuble, the Eucharistic vestment of priests.

we walked to the beach, where we found a nice rowing-boat, into which our luggage had been packed, and two excellent rowers. We started at half-past three, and reached Xenophou in half an hour, after a pleasant transit over the smooth waters of the gulf, in the company of one or two of the Russian monks, including Magistrion. Our friend chatted to us in French the whole time, chiefly about his native country, Bulgaria, which he lauded in his pet phrase, 'Ah! quel beau pays!

MONASTERY OF ST. XENOPHON.

Je vous assure, monsieur, un pays *excellent.*' All the while those two devoted friends Pantele and Peter were sitting together on the top of the luggage in the bows, the latter improving the occasion by giving his gossip a theological lecture, to which Pantele was listening with becoming reverence, having the greatest admiration for his friend's clerkship; for was not Peter going to be a holy man and a deacon, and sing litanies in the church ?

The Monastery of Xenophou, or St. Xenophon, is
quite close to the water, there being only a little strip
of garden between the walls and the sea.   The usual
reception being over, we went out with the camera
to take a photograph before the light faded.   After
dragging the apparatus up and down hill, and over
walls and fences, trying to find a good position, we
were at last obliged to content ourselves with one
from the end of the breakwater, giving the sea front of
the monastery, which O— took whilst I joined a monk
and two labourers to make a foreground.   Then we
had a delicious bathe, which much refreshed us, as the
day had been very hot, and afterwards joined the Archbishop and the abbot in the garden by the sea.   It
was the very ideal of a garden ; everything growing
most luxuriantly, lemon trees and oranges, figs, pome-
granates, and vines, all laden with fruit, down to the
very edge of the water.   As we sauntered along the
paths the fresh salt breeze mingled with the scent of
oranges, and limes, and flowers—all those sweet per-
fumes which in the evening the weary earth sends
forth as thank offerings when the oppressive day-heats
have departed.   For

Jam sol recedit igneus,

that red orb had begun to disappear behind the promontory of Sithonia, and the shadows were already
gathering over the waters of the gulf.   All was calm
and quiet; the insects had ceased to hum, and only the
rippling of the wavelets and the sound of distant mule
bells broke the stillness of the air.

I had been reading a little pocket edition of Bacon's
Essays that morning, and as I strolled through the

orange trees his quaint words came into my mind :
' God Almightie first planted a Garden, and, indeed, it
is the Purest of Humane pleasures.'

Xenophou contains within its walls nine churches—

1. The new catholicon, dedicated to St. George ;
2. The old catholicon, St. George, containing two paracclesia,
St. Demetrius and St. Lazarus ;
3. The Presentation of the Blessed Virgin ;
4. The Holy Apostles ;
5. St. Stephen ;
6. St. John the Divine ;
7. The Assumption of the Blessed Virgin ;
8. The Holy Unmercenaries ;
9. St. Euphemia :

and eight exocclesia—

1. St. Philip ;
2. St. Theodore Tyro ;
3. St. Tryphon ;
4. The Holy Trinity (cemetery chapel) ;
5. St. Anthony ;
6. The Prophet Daniel ;
7. St. Nicholas ;
8. St. Nicholas.

The monastic buildings form three sides of a very
large square planted with orange trees, the fourth being
a high wall. In the centre of this courtyard is the new
catholicon, which was commenced in 1819 and finished
in 1836, the architect being an Ephesian. To this we
were taken first, on the morning after our arrival.

It is a fine large church, as the measurements in the
note will show.[1] The dome over the nave is about

---

[1] Sanctuary : across chord of east apse, 17½ feet ; from north to south,
including chapels, 57½ feet ; from iconostasis to end of east apse, 23 feet.
Nave : across iconostasis, 45 feet ; across transepts, 57½ feet ; from icono-

22 feet in diameter, and is supported, as usual, by four columns. The narthex also has a corresponding dome, but the supporting pillars are closer together, the dome itself smaller and flanked by four small domes. There is a pronaos, which returns for a short way north and south.

The iconostasis is very handsome and in good taste, being built of grey Athos marble, relieved with gilding ; the bishop's throne is of the same material. The walls of this church have not yet been painted, owing to want of funds ; they are left rough and un-plastered ; only one of the domes, the central one in the narthex, contains the usual frescoes. Two old Byzantine mosaics of St. George and St. Demetrius are placed on the two west pillars of the narthex, and between the narthex and the nave are two splendid old doors, made of walnut inlaid with mother-of-pearl, which came originally from Constantinople.

The following relics are preserved in this church : a drop of the blood of St. John the Baptist ; part of the head of St. Stephen Protomartyr ; the skull of St. Tryphon ; the jaw of St. Arcadius (son of the founder) ; two pieces of the True Cross, prettily mounted in silver filigree crosses. In the pronaos we noticed two Y-shaped instruments, one of wood, the other of iron, used for beating the semantra with double strokes on Easter Day.

The old catholicon, also in the courtyard, is a small but interesting church. Neyrat[1] says he saw the date

stasis to west wall of nave, 40½, or to west wall of narthex, 82½ feet. Thus it will be seen that, allowing for the thickness of the dividing wall, the narthex is the same length as the nave.

: [1] *L'Athos.* Paris and Lyons, 1880.

976 over the door ; but it cannot be earlier, I think,
than the thirteenth century.　Like the new catholicon
it is dedicated to the Patron of England.　The walls
are covered with paintings in a bad condition, and there
are some fine marbles in the floor and the door jambs.
On the south side of the sanctuary is a tiny paracclesi
dedicated to St. Demetrius, entered by a low door from
the nave ; on the south side of the narthex is another
paracclesi of equally small proportions, dedicated to the
Lazarus whom Our Lord raised from the dead.

A stream of water runs under the marble floor of the
church across the transepts ; two holes covered with
wooden plates communicate with the watercourse.

The refectory is small.　Both this and the narthex
of the old catholicon are said to have been painted at
the charges of the voivode Mataies Bassarabas, and
Comnenus says that he is represented with his wife on
the walls of the refectory.

After seeing the old catholicon we were taken up a
rickety wooden staircase to the library, a small, dark,
unsavoury room.　It contains 160 manuscripts, nine of
which are on vellum, one of these being an evangelistarium of the twelfth century.　There is a service book
with music, well written, on paper, with four fine illuminations of late Byzantine work, these being in good
preservation ; also three rolls of liturgies, probably
the same that Curzon saw, not very ancient or
interesting.

I should mention that this traveller's name is handed
down as that of a thief, and the monks declared that
he had stolen two of the best manuscripts.　So O—
defended our countryman by making Angelos translate
for their benefit the amusing passage from his book ;

but whether he convinced them that Curzon had fairly purchased the manuscripts I cannot say.

We went through the list of books given in the 'Monasteries of the Levant,' and asked for the quarto evangelistarium, bound in red velvet with silver clasps. This book they denied all knowledge of.

'What are you saying?' asked the Archbishop.

We replied that we were asking for a manuscript of the Gospels mentioned in one of our books.

'What have you done with it?' said the Archbishop, turning to the monks.

'We never had it,' replied they.

'Then how could it have got into the Englishman's book?' said he. 'I believe you have sold it. I shall write and tell the Patriarch.'

'Tell anybody you like,' was the rejoinder; 'we never had the horrid book.'

Words got higher and higher, the Archbishop storming at the monks, and I don't know how the matter would have 'ended unless they had thought of a happy expedient.

'Oh,' said they, 'is it a book of the Gospels you are asking for, an old book?'

'Yes,' replied the incensed prelate, 'a very old book.'

'Bound in red velvet?'

'Yes.'

'With silver clasps?'

'Yes,' said he, 'that is the book I want.'

'*That* book? oh, *that* is in the church, in the new catholicon,' said they.

'Very well,' replied the Archbishop, 'then we will go and see it.'

'At this the monks' countenances fell, and after trying to put him off with several lame excuses they finally declared that since we had left the church the key had most unfortunately and mysteriously disappeared, and they feared they should be unable to gratify the Archbishop's curiosity.

'Ah,' said he, 'ah, a capital story, no doubt, and I suppose you expect me to believe it? It is quite plain, however, that you have sold it.'

We discovered long afterwards, to our annoyance, that we had made a mistake about this manuscript, as it was one of the two that Curzon took away with him. But no great harm was done, as the Archbishop in all probability soon forgot the whole matter.

We returned to our room and obtained information about the monastery. It was founded about the year 1081 by St. Xenophon, a noble of Constantinople, assisted, it is said, by the Emperor Nicephorus Botaniates and Alexius Comnenus. Readers of Mr. Curzon's book will remember that one of his purchases at this monastery was a manuscript partly in the handwriting of the latter emperor. St. Arcadius, whose jaw is preserved amongst the relics, was the son of St. Xenophon and lived at Jerusalem. A monk named Symeon seems to have had some connexion with the foundation; he had been of high rank under the Emperor Nicephorus. In 1545 the monastery was restored by Ducas Bornicus and his brother Radulas, Hospodars of Hungaro-Vallachia. There are at present 105 monks and twenty-five servants; the cœnobite rule is observed. The abbot's name is Stephen.

Xenophou possesses lands in Cassandra. The revenue from the lands lost in Roumania was over

1,440*l.*[1] Perhaps this may account for the unfinished state of the catholicon. It has twenty-three calyvia,[2] one kelli, and seven cathismata, which are attached to seven out of the eight exocclesia above mentioned, the eighth church being the cemetery chapel.

From our window we could see a heavy storm was brewing, the head of the gulf being black with clouds which were rapidly approaching. We made frantic efforts to get off, knowing that Docheiariou was quite close, so that we could easily reach our next resting-place before the rain came. Our luggage was all packed and on the landing-stage, and the boat and rowers ready, but for some reason the Archbishop chose to dawdle, as I believe on purpose, for we had roused him after only three-quarters of an hour's *kef*, and he wished to show that he was not to be hurried. After about half an hour he at last started from the divan and sauntered leisurely down to the beach, stopping every now and then to talk to the monks, whilst we were doing our best to urge him on, for the sky overhead was looking as black as pitch. But a just retribution overtook him.

We got into our boat, the luggage following in another, just as the storm broke. The rain came down in sheets, and the sea, which had been perfectly calm, was suddenly lashed into fury by the vehemence of the squall. Our little boat rocked like a nutshell on the crested waves, and the spray dashing over the boat, added to the rain, saturated everybody except me; for I had fortunately provided myself with my

---

[1] Archimandrite Porphyry.

[2] Perhaps attached to the skete of the Annunciation, which, according to the author of 'O Ἄθως, 1885, belongs to Xenophou. I did not hear of this skete.

great waterproof riding-cloak, which kept me quite dry. The Archbishop, who, as I have said before, was by no means fond of the sea, began to get seriously alarmed, muttering what I suppose were prayers under his breath. ' Nous avons mal fait,' said he, ' très mal fait.' He was steering, and in his anxiety to be close to the land in case of swamping he began to point the boat's head towards the shore. We had to pass a little headland before reaching the port, which was on the other side of it, in fair weather not more than a quarter of an hour from the port of Xenophou. The monks who were rowing our boat looked round and saw the danger, for we were going straight upon the rocks, indeed there were isolated rocks all along by the shore. They motioned to the Archbishop to keep us out, but he still steered in the direction of the rocks, muttering, ' A terre ! à terre !' Seeing that the position was desperate, I was obliged to reach behind the prelate, and I am ashamed to say that for some moments there was a little struggle for the mastery, the Archbishop pulling one way and I the other ; but this was a case in which I ventured to oppose episcopal authority, and it ended in my being master of the tiller. The rowers toiled at the oars ; the boat laboured heavily through the waves, and we appeared to be rather going back than advancing, for the squall was right in our teeth. The Archbishop still shouted, ' A terre, Riley ! à terre !' The thunder roared and the lightning played around us. Altogether I was not sorry when we gained the breakwater and shot into the little harbour. Here the rest went into shelter whilst I superintended the landing of the baggage.

The storm passed away as quickly as it came, and

the usual procession greeted us at the gateway of the monastery. The Archbishop, however, being very wet, was for not going through the usual ceremony, but the entreaties of the monks prevailed ; he consented to don the cope over his streaming garments, and we went to the catholicon. But the service was conducted with maimed rites, the Archbishop, to save time, saying his portion whilst the priest was singing his, and finally, throwing off his cope, made his exit before the chanting was half finished. Once seated on the divan, with a dry cloak and a cup of hot coffee, his good humour returned, and we were soon deep in conversation with the epitropoi, Antonius and the deacon Synesius ; both being particularly courteous and kind, and the latter a man of superior education from the college at Chalki.

Docheiariou is built on the side of a hill, and the buildings are thereby rendered the more picturesque in their irregularity as they ascend from the shore. Our lodgings were situated in the upper part, which is protected by a wall and a strong tower or keep, doubtless designed to defend the convent from any attack from the rising ground on the hill above. Here is a little terrace, from which you may look down into the confined courtyard, where grow orange trees and one of the few palms to be found on the promontory ; over the roofs of the conventual buildings you may see the blue waters of the gulf. Two castellated buildings, one half ruined, both on the shore to the right, add to the view. And that afternoon we saw it at its best; for even as we stood upon the terrace the sun burst through the storm clouds and lighted up the surface of the sea.

The catholicon,[1] dedicated to the Holy Archangels, possesses two nartheces. There is nothing of any particular interest in the building or in its contents, but as we managed to take a very fair photograph of its interior. and it is a good specimen of an Athos catholicon, I have had the photograph reproduced as an illustration. The camera was placed in the doorway between the nave and the narthex ; thus the chief feature in the picture is the iconostasis, which stretches across it. In the centre are the holy doors, which, being open, disclose the holy table immediately beyond, with its cross and candlesticks. The doors leading to the diaconicon and chapel of the prothesis are concealed behind the pillars. On the right of the holy doors is the icon of Our Lord, on the left that of the Blessed Virgin ; beyond these on either side are other icons, and it will be observed that a small copy of each icon is placed underneath the original to receive the kisses of the faithful ; this is done partly for convenience, partly for the sake of the better preservation of the icons. The two eastern pillars of the four that support the central dome are of marble ; affixed to that on the right is the icon of the Holy Archangels. Many lamps and candelabra are suspended in front of the sacred pictures, and tapers in massive brass candlesticks burn before them. The great corona, with its innumerable candles, lamps and ostrich eggs dependent from it, hangs under the central dome ; the pretty finely inlaid desk for the icon of the saint of the day, with its four slender columns supporting a canopy, stands in its

[1] Measurements : Sanctuary : across the chord of east apse, 13½ feet ; from north to south, including side chapels, 35½ feet. Nave : across transepts, 43 feet ; from iconostasis to west wall, 30½ feet ; esonarthex, from east to west, 38½ feet.

INTERIOR OF CATHOLICON AT DOCHEIARIOU.

almost invariable place, a few feet from the iconostasis on the right of the holy doors. A few of the *stasidia*, or stalls, come into the picture.

The library contains about 300 manuscripts, sixty-two on vellum. We saw a ὑπομνήματα τῶν ἁγίων, or memoir of the saints, with illuminations ; not a particularly fine book, but probably the one alluded to by Mr. Tozer. None of the manuscripts are of any great age ; I saw no uncials. The porch of the monastery contains a fresco of the parable of the good Samaritan, who is depicted in the act of conducting the stranger to the inn, which is represented by Docheiariou.

The refectory is ancient and its walls are frescoed. Here the monks still dine on feast days, the cœnobite having been exchanged for the idiorrhythmic rule some 120 years ago. Close to the refectory is a little oratory containing the renowned icon of the Gorgoŷpecoos. Originally this oratory was merely a passage leading to the refectory, and the sacred picture but a representation of the Blessed Virgin painted on the wall.

In the year 1654 the chief butler, a monk called Nilos, was passing through the passage in the discharge of his duties, carrying for the purposes of light a flaming torch. As he passed the picture he heard a voice saying :

Ἄλλοτε νὰ μὴ διέλθῃς ἐντεῦθεν μὲ δᾳδία, καπνίζων τὴν ἐμὴν εἰκόνα

(Never again pass through hence, fouling with smoke of thy link my image).

But Nilos took no notice, thinking that one of his brethren was playing him a trick. Not many days after he was again proceeding through the passage, when he was again addressed, in severer terms.

z

Ὦ μοναχὲ ἀμόναχε, ἕως πότε ἀνευλαβῶς καὶ ἀτίμως καπνίζεις τὴν ἐμὴν μορφὴν ;

(O monk, unworthy of the name, how long impiously and irreverently foulest thou with smoke my image ?)

And this time blindness fell upon Nilos, and the brethren found the chief butler on his face before the picture. At his entreaty, however, the Theotocos healed him, speaking to him the third time.

Ὦ μοναχὲ, εἰσηκούσθη ἡ δέησίς σου πρός με, καὶ ἔσο συγχωρημένος, καὶ βλέπων ὡς καὶ πρότερον· ἀνάγγειλον δὲ καὶ τοῖς λοιποῖς ἐνασκουμένοις πατράσι καὶ συναδελφοῖς σου, ὅτι ἐγὼ εἰμὶ ἡ μήτηρ τοῦ Θεοῦ Λόγου, καὶ μετὰ Θεὸν τῆς ἱερᾶς ταύτης μονῆς τῶν ἀρχαγγέλων σκέπη καὶ βοήθεια καὶ κραταιὰ προστασία, προνοουμένη ὑπὲρ αὐτῆς ὡς ὑπέρμαχος κυβερνήτης· καὶ εἰς τὸ ἑξῆς οἱ μοναχοὶ ἃς καταφεύγωσι πρὸς ἐμὲ διὰ καθέτους ἀνάγκην, καὶ γοργῶς θέλω ὑπακούω αὐτῶν, καὶ πάντων τῶν μετ' εὐλαβείας καταφευγόντων εἰς ἐμὲ ὀρθοδόξων χριστιανῶν, ὅτι Γοργοϋπήκοος καλοῦμαι.

(O monk, thy prayer hath been heard in mine ears, and thou shalt have thy desire and shalt see as heretofore. And tell the rest also, the fathers and thy brethren, that I am the Mother of the Word of God, and next to God I am of this holy monastery of the Archangels the stay, and succour, and strong patroness, providing for it as its Ruler and Champion. And henceforth let the monks fly to me when in distress, and I will *listen* to them *readily,* and to all orthodox Christians that have recourse to me religiously, for that I am called the *Ready Listener.*)

Such is the legend of the Gorgoÿpecoos, as related in a book presented to me by the epitropoi of the monastery.[1]

One of the doorways into the passage has now been blocked up, and as there is no window the place is very

---

[1] ΠΡΟΣΚΥΝΗΤΑΡΙΟΝ ΤΟΥ ΒΑΣΙΛΙΚΟΥ, ΠΑΤΡΙΑΡΧΙΚΟΥ, ΣΤΑΥΡΟ-ΠΗΓΙΑΚΟΥ ΤΕ, ΚΑΙ ΣΕΒΑΣΜΙΟΥ ΙΕΡΟΥ ΜΟΝΑΣΤΗΡΙΟΥ ΤΟΥ ΔΟΧΕΙ-ΑΡΕΙΟΥ, ΤΟΥ ΕΝ ΤΩι ΑΓΙΩΝΥΜΩι ΟΡΕΙ ΤΟΥ ΑΘΩΝΟΣ. Bucharest, 1843.

dark, but by the light of the lamps and candles which
burn continually before the icon one can see part of
the old picture peeping through the glistering metallic
cover, which, we were told, was added ten years ago
at the cost of 60,000 piastres.

One more legend must I mention, for it is a famous
story and has given to the monastery its patron saints.
Old Archbishop Georgirenes shall tell the tale.

He says that the convent is called ' Archangeli,
which had before another name, but changed to this
upon this occasion. A young Caloir, that was tilling
the Ground abroad, found a Treasure in an old Urn,
and brought the news of it to the Superiour of the
Convent; he sent with the young Man two other
Caloirs, who finding the Treasure, agreed between
themselves to kill the Boy, and share it betwixt them ;
and so they ty'd a Stone about his neck, and cast him
into the Sea, and hiding the Treasure, came to the
Superiour, and told him the Boy had deceiv'd them,
and was run away. Next morning the Sexton found
the Boy and the Stone about his neck in the Church,
who discover'd all, and told that the Angels Gabriel
and Raphael[1] brought him thither. The two Caloirs
thus convicted, were banish'd, and the Stone set up as
a Monument to this day.'

Another account gives the name of the boy as Basil,
and states that the treasure was found at the foot of
a pillar on the promontory of Longos, opposite to
Docheiariou. On this pillar was an inscription,[2] the
sense of which none could discover until Basil inter-
preted it, and digging where the shadow fell when the

---

[1] All accounts except that of Comnenus agree in substituting *Michael*
for *Raphael*. See below.

[2] Ὁ κρούσας με κατὰ κεφαλῆς εὑρίσκει πλῆθος χρυσίου.

sun rose, he found the hidden treasure. *Three* monks are tempted by the devil to drown the boy, who is rescued by Gabriel and Michael, and found in the bema of the catholicon by the abbot, St. Neophytus.

On another occasion the Holy Archangels are said to have preserved this monastery from the attacks of the Saracens.

There seems to be no reason for doubting that Docheiariou was founded in the tenth century by St. Euthymius, bursar (δοχειάριος) of the Lavra and friend of St. Athanasius of Athos, assisted by his kinsman St. Neophytus. This was in the reign of Nicephorus, not Nicephorus Botaniates, as some accounts allege, for he lived a century too late, but Nicephorus Phocas. An hegoumenos of Docheiariou is mentioned by name in a document of the year 1092.[1]

The pious couple, Alexander the voivode and his wife Roxandra, restored the monastery in 1578, after its destruction by pirates; they are said to have rebuilt and adorned the catholicon at this time.

Besides the catholicon, dedicated to the Holy Archangels, there are eight esocclesia, under the following patronage :

> The Forty Martyrs,
> The Gorgoÿpecoos,
> The Holy Unmercenaries,
> The Three Hierarchs,
> St. George,
> The Assumption of the Blessed Virgin Mary,
> The Annunciation of the Blessed Virgin Mary,
> The Archangels (at the top of the tower) ;

and without the walls—

> St. Peter of Athos,

---

[1] Muralt.

St. Onouphrius,[1]
The Transfiguration,
St. Nicholas (cemetery chapel).

No sketes are attached to the monastery, and although it possesses a few cottages and vineyards it has no proper kellia or cathismata. A few farms belong to it near Erisso and Cassandra. The total number of monks is sixty, and they have ten servants. I have already mentioned that they follow the idiorrhythmic rule.

We had intended to leave Docheiariou the day after our arrival, being Saturday, but at the Archbishop's request we put off our departure until the Sunday.

On Saturday morning our prelate produced a gigantic hook from his travelling bag and proposed a fishing expedition. Accordingly we put out a little way into the gulf in two rowing-boats, and amused ourselves with the lines for nearly a couple of hours. At the end of that time we compared accounts, and found that whilst I had caught two or three fish about the size of a large minnow, and O— had taken nothing, the descendant of the Fishermen had landed a good basketful of fish, which proved an acceptable addition to our midday meal. After vespers we took a walk in the garden up the hill, and saw a water-mill of curious construction, and two cypresses of such a size that they overtopped the tower, far finer than those at the Lavra.

In the kitchen garden were growing vegetables in great luxuriance ; chiefly tomatoes, aubergines, onions, garlic, cabbages, and baniahs.

---

[1] An Egyptian hermit who lived in the fourth century, about the time of the Council of Nicæa.

After supper the conversation turned upon ecclesiastical music, and the monks asked us to give them a specimen of English Church music, which we did.

Nobody seemed to think much of it, and the Archbishop suggested that if one of the epitropoi would favour us with 'Macarios áneer' ('Blessed is the man,' Psalm i.) we might hear something worth listening to. But the epitropoi protested, with becoming modesty, that they did not feel themselves qualified to sing in such exalted presence, and hinted that the Archbishop himself should chant the psalm.

For the first few minutes we tried to look interested and pleased, but then the strain became unbearable. The Archbishop, usually the very type of Oriental languor, had worked himself up to the highest pitch of excitement. His eyes sparkled, his body swayed from side to side, semitones and quartertones poured forth from his throat; he was singing at the very top of his voice. Soon we discovered that he was still engaged upon the last syllable of *áneer*, and O— whispered to me that unless the chant ended speedily he should be obliged to leave the room; indeed, it was all I could do to prevent his departure. At the end of a quarter of an hour the Archbishop was exhausted. We never mentioned the subject of music again.

CHAPTER XXI.

WE left for Constamonitou at a. quarter to ten the next morning. The others had already mounted their mules, and I was just about to follow their example, when one of the polite epitropoi ordered my saddle cloth to be removed and a fresh one to be procured.

'For,' said he, 'we cannot let you depart on an old cloth.'

'Indeed, it is good enough,' said I.

'No,' said the epitropos.

'Please let me go without it,' said I.

'That is not to be thought of,' replied the monk.

By this time the others were well on their road, which winds up the hill through a forest, and so, resigning myself to the delays of ceremony, I sent the baggage after them, only retaining Peter behind with me. Nearly ten minutes elapsed before a Turkey rug of gorgeous hues made its appearance, which I bestrode, and, doffing my hat to the assembled community, at length took my departure. Soon we came up with the baggage, and found that one of the mules' burdens had fallen, the muleteers being busily engaged in replacing it. This accomplished we proceeded up the forest path, but before another three-quarters of an hour had elapsed I saw signs of the pack-saddle again giving way. One of the men on foot also perceived this and ran forward to save it, but too late, for the basket, which was slung on one side, turned a somersault over the mule's back and fell heavily on the top of the Archbishop's 'pragmata,' which were slung on the other. Again another delay of ten minutes occurred. When at last we gained the crest of the hill beneath which Constamonitou lies in a charming valley away from the sea, we were full half an hour behind the other four members of the party; already, methought, must the Archbishop and O— be sipping

CONSTAMONITOU.

their coffee within the little monastery whose white towers peeped out from the trees in front.

Having reached the gate I soon made my way upstairs, and was greeted by O—, who hastily demanded what had detained us.

'Why?' said I, noticing that the Archbishop was not in the best of tempers, ' has anything happened?'

'Yes, indeed,' replied he, 'something *has* happened, and a nice fuss there's been about it too.' In a few words he told me what had occurred.

It seems that when they had surmounted the hill, and had come in sight of Constamonitou, the bells of the monastery began to peal forth ; but before they had gone far the Archbishop, remembering that he was riding in his undress cloak of grey cloth lined with ermine, turned to Pantele and demanded his black cloak. Pantele replied that Peter had it, behind with the baggage.

'Then go back and look for Peter,' said the Archbishop.

Away went Pantele to the top of the hill, whilst the little party halted on the road.   The cavass, after scanning the country towards Docheiariou, returned with the dismal news that no Peter was to be seen, and he feared that he must be some distance behind.   The Archbishop looked very cross at this intelligence, for, finding that nobody arrived, the monks had ceased to ring the bells, and those of them who had come down to meet the prelate with cross, and candles, and incense began glancing round the corner of the gateway to see what had become of him.   O— ventured to suggest that perhaps, all things being considered, it might be better to go on without waiting for Peter.

'No,' said the Archbishop, 'I shall not stir without my cloak.'

Presently the abbot of the monastery was seen advancing towards them.   He came to inquire the reason of the delay, and on being informed said that he felt sure that he was expressing the sentiments of his brethren in saying that they were too much honoured by the visit of the Archbishop to think anything of the absence of his proper dress.   But Philotheos was not to be persuaded.

' No,' said he, ' I shall not move from this place without my cloak.'

Finding that his words produced no effect, the abbot departed, and Pantele was again despatched to the hill-top, and again returned without any tidings of the missing Peter. Meanwhile the archiepiscopal mule, which had been snorting and pawing the ground, and otherwise giving signs of uneasiness, was discovered to be bleeding violently from the mouth, and on examination it was found that a leech had managed to attach itself to the poor animal's palate whilst it had been drinking at some wayside fountain. O— eagerly seized upon this circumstance as an excuse for urging an immediate move in the direction of the monastery, where the mule could be properly attended to, and remarked that they might have to wait an hour for Peter.

' No matter,' replied the incensed prelate, looking as black as thunder. ' No matter if we have to wait here three hours. I shall not stir a step without my cloak.'

At this juncture the abbot was seen again approaching. This time he came with an offer. If his Holiness would deign to wear *his* cloak for the ceremony of reception it was at the disposal of his Holiness. The Archbishop gave one more glance at the hilltop, and finding no prospect of Peter's speedy advent, accepted the compromise, moved somewhat, I make no doubt, by the mental comparison of the delights of a soft divan and a cup of hot coffee with the hard packsaddle of a restive mule. Again the bells pealed forth, the candles in the porch were relighted, and at last he was safely landed within the walls of Constamonitou.

But the innocent cause of all the trouble did not escape. As Peter entered the guest chamber Pantele whispered something into his ear, which was doubtless Greek for ' *You're going to catch it* ; ' and later in the day I heard something about a staff—a *pœmántike ravdos* I think it was—and a pair of sore shoulders !

Breakfast was a long time coming, and when it did appear at half-past twelve it was quite uneatable, owing to the bad oil and rancid butter with which everything was cooked. The hegoumenos, by name Ananias, and the pro-hegoumenos, Simeon, an intelligent, kindly old man, but without much learning, entertained us after breakfast with an account of the monastery. Its early history is involved in obscurity. The tradition of its foundation by Constantine the Great and his son Constans in the fourth century cannot be entertained, although its rejection suggests a difficulty in the derivation of its name and compels us to choose one of three theories—that its original name was changed when the legend of its remote foundation came to be received as genuine ; that the part taken by the great Emperor in bringing the relics of its patron from the Holy Land to his capital suggested the connexion of Constantine with St. Stephen's monastery ; or that its unknown founder bore the name of Constantine or of Constans. Some think it was founded about the middle of the eleventh century, but, be its early history what it may, it is certain that Manuel II. Palæologus (1391–1425) benefited it, for the chrysobull of that emperor was noticed by Curzon, and I believe it still exists amongst the monastic documents, although we did not see it. The convent has passed through many vicissitudes and has been ruined more than once, and an obscure Servian princess called Anna Philanthropiné once restored it, but when she lived I have not been able to make out. For eighty years before 1852 it remained utterly decayed and ruined, and in that year the old pro-hegoumenos Simeon and his master, Joseph, who came from the convent of Mount Sinai, found only two monks left amongst the ruins.

Joseph and Simeon were fired with zeal for the restoration of the monastery to its ancient splendour, and the former went to Russia to raise money for the purpose. In 1866, at the age of eighty-four, Joseph went the way of all flesh, having laid up treasure, like King David, for the building of the temple which his eyes were not to see, and in the following year his spiritual son Simeon commenced the work. It was built on the site of the old ruined catholicon, which was much smaller, and was completed in 1869. In 1881 Simeon, feeling that his life's work was at an end, laid down his authority, having been abbot for thirty years. He is now seventy-five years of age, and has never once tasted flesh meat since he was fifteen, at which age he first embraced the religious life. Though now old and infirm he insisted upon conducting us in person over the church, the crown of his earthly labours.[1] It possesses a beautiful iconostasis of marble, partly from the native quarries, partly from those of Tenos.

There is a pronaos, which returns slightly on the northern and southern sides of the narthex ; in fact the

[1] The measurements of this church are : Sanctuary : from north to south, including side chapels, 30 feet ; across chord of east apse, 13½ feet ; from iconostasis to end of east apse, 14 feet. Nave : across transepts, 42 feet ; from iconostasis to west wall of nave, 30 feet ; from iconostasis to west wall of narthex, 58 feet.

church is built on the same plan as the new catholicon at Xenophou.   At present the interior walls are
merely whitewashed, the monastery not being yet in a
position to afford frescoes.

First amongst the relics comes a piece of the True
Cross, mounted in an exquisite reliquary, a cross of
silver gilt richly enamelled and set with turquoises,
rubies, pearls, and coral, ornamented at the top with
two small movable birds.   It is in three pieces—cross,
stem, and stand—and is altogether a very fine work of
art.   The catholicon also contains portions of the
relics of St. Stephen, patron saint of the convent, to
whom the church is dedicated, of St. Andrew, of St.
Luke, and of St. Panteleëmon, the skull of St. Blaise,[1]
and a piece of Our Lord's coat.   The number of monks
at Constamonitou is now fifty, with six servants ; they
follow the cœnobite rule.   The convent owns two farms
in Longos.   One of them was recently bought by the
two restorers ; the other is said to have been presented
to the monastery by the Emperor John Palæologus.[2]
The convent lost but little land in Moldavia.

Esocclesia.

1. The catholicon, dedicated to St. Stephen.
2. St. Nicholas (in ruins).
3. All Saints.
4. St. Constantine.
5. The Panaghia Portaïtissa.

Exocclesia.

1. The Holy Archangels (cemetery chapel).
2. St. Meletius (attached to a cathisma).
3. St. Anthony ⎫ (both attached to kellia).
4. St. Nicholas ⎭

---

[1] Bishop of Sebaste ; commemorated in our kalendar on Feb. 3, in
the Greek on Feb. 11.   [2] I. or II. ?

The convent possesses one cathisma and two kellia, as above. The monastic buildings are mostly new, but those on the north side of the courtyard are ancient.

There are rather over a hundred manuscripts in Constamonitou, mostly service books of late date, but there are fourteen on vellum, among which is a palimpsest, the new writing consisting of the Gospels (fourteenth century) over a Latin martyrology (of the twelfth). I suspect that the convent originally possessed a large library, but that during its periods of ruin the books were either destroyed or dispersed; probably some may have found their way to Russico, during the last period of poverty and ruin, before the restoration by Simeon and Joseph. For to such a low level had the fortunes of Constamonitou fallen that at one time even the monastic virtue of hospitality was neglected. In the first year of the present century, so the story goes, there knocked a beggar at the convent gate— perhaps a poor pilgrim returning to his home laden with spiritual but destitute of earthly treasures; or possibly a hermit, of whom one sees so many when riding over the rocks or through the forests of the Holy Mountain, each with his gown tucked up, his staff in his hand, and a wallet, to contain the dole he goes to claim, hanging across his back. The porter, answering to the poor man's supplication, bade him go elsewhere, for, owing to the present poverty of the monastery, further distribution of alms, whether in money or in kind, had been prohibited. Thereupon the beggar upbraided the monk with the foolishness of his fellows in allowing themselves to lose two brethren who had long dwelt within the venerable walls of Constamonitou, and whose presence had ever been essential to its prosperity ; for one of the brethren having been short-sightedly expelled, the other, inseparable from his companion, had instantly taken his leave.

'Indeed, I know of no such circumstance,' said the porter. 'Pray what might have been their names ?'

'Well,' replied the beggar, 'the name of the first, whom you expelled, was Dídoté (Δίδοτε), of the second Dothésetai (Δοθήσεται).'[1]

The monastery stands at the head of a well-wooded glen which winds towards the gulf of the Holy Mountain. It is quite out of sight of the sea, and indeed is some distance from it ; Zographou and Chiliandari are the only other monasteries which have no sea view.

After dinner this evening O— caught an enormous bug, which was advancing towards him from a corner of the divan, evidently bent on a predatory excursion. Of such fair proportions was he that a threepenny bit would hardly have covered him. Warned by this and other specimens of the same breed which we came across before going to bed, we entrenched ourselves in our levinges ; and it was well we did so, for the enemy made an attack in force that night, as was proved by the number of well-developed prisoners we made the next morning in the folds of the muslin. The mosquitoes also kept up a busy hum all night ; in fact without levinges a night in Constamonitou would have been intolerable.

[1] 'GIVE and IT-SHALL-BE-GIVEN unto you.'

CHAPTER XXII.

Monday, $\frac{September\ 10}{August\ 29}$. We rose at six A.M. because for once the Archbishop was in a hurry to start, and, after some final conversation with old Simeon over our coffee, we took our departure at half-past eight.   The weather looked rather threatening, and indeed a few drops fell, but it cleared up and soon the sun shone brilliantly. We struck further inland, and crossed several ridges and valleys, thickly covered with every kind of vegetation.   At last we came in sight of the stern and massive walls of Zographou, which is finely situated in a beautiful glen on the slope of a hill, with a quick descent from its western side to the bottom of a ravine. It is surrounded by numerous kellia, and on its northern side, where is the gateway, the cottages cluster so thickly together as to form a little village.   This charming valley is full of every kind of tree and shrub, and tall cypresses stand here and there in dark outline against the lighter green, or raise their pointed tops above the foliage of the woods.

On our arrival we were taken upstairs to a large room at the north-west angle of the building and entertained with glyko and coffee.   Then we had breakfast ; but the dishes proved quite uneatable, and we were obliged to ask for some boiled eggs.   During the monks' siesta we occupied ourselves with the camera, dragging it up to the other side of the valley, and succeeded in obtaining a very fair view of the exterior of the monastery. On our return we found the Archbishop sitting under the walnut trees on the low wall outside the gateway, and proposed an inspection of the monastery.

First we went to the catholicon,[1] which is only eighty years old, and although a fine church has nothing of interest about it except some beautiful doors of tortoiseshell and mother-of-pearl. It has a pronaos and is frescoed throughout, but in bad taste.

It contains the following relics : portions of the Holy Rood, contained in two or three old and pretty crosses ; the jaw of St. Stephen ; relics of St. George, St. Andrew the Apostle, St. Barlaam, SS. Cosmas and Damian, St. Cyril, and the Six-and-Twenty Martyrs. But what the monks prize most of all their treasures is the picture τοῦ Ζωγράφου, of the Painter, and this brings us at once to the history of the monastery.

It is said to have been founded in the reign of Leo the Philosopher[2] (886–911) by three princes[3] named John, Arsenius, and Alexander, or, according to Comnenus, John, Moses, and Aaron, who came from Ochrida, the ancient capital of Bulgaria. When they had built this

[1] Measurements : Sanctuary : from north to south, including chapels, 38½ feet ; across chord of east apse, 15 feet. Nave : across transepts, 54 feet ; from iconostasis to west wall of nave, 37½ feet ; from iconostasis across nave and narthex to the west wall of latter, 71½ feet.

[2] This was the emperor who contracted a fourth marriage in the face of the absolute prohibition of the Oriental Church. Thereupon the brave and upright patriarch Nicholas excommunicated him. 'Neither the fear of exile, nor the desertion of his brethren, nor the authority of the Latin Church, nor the danger of failure or doubt in the succession to the empire, could bend the spirit of the inflexible monk' (Gibbon). One cannot help digressing to notice this brilliant exception to the servile Erastianism of the Byzantine Church.

[3] One tradition says they were nephews of Justinian, another that they were of the family of that great emperor. If they lived in the reign of Leo the Philosopher the former legend is manifestly absurd.

A A

monastery the three founders quarrelled over its name. One wished to dedicate it to the Virgin Mother, the second to St. Nicholas, the third to St. George. So they agreed to prepare a panel of wood, such as icons are wont to be painted on, and having placed it in the church, to lock the doors and pray that the image of the saint to whom the monastery should be dedicated might be imprinted on the wood. When they entered the church they found the image of St. George on the panel, and from a belief that the great martyr had painted his own portrait the monastery acquired its name.

The above is the story of the picture as told to us by the monks. John Comnenus, however, after saying that it was not made by mortal hands, but painted by the saint himself, makes no mention of the founders' dispute, but says that it was formerly in a certain monastery of St. George in the Holy Land, and changed its abode of its own accord, coming to Zographou.

The picture is placed on the south-eastern pillar of the four. On the side of the nose there is a slight excrescence ; this—so the monks said—is either the mark made by the finger or the top of the finger itself (for opinions differed) of a certain Bishop of Erisso, who, to show his disbelief in its supernatural origin, ran his finger contemptuously into the face of the picture, where it instantly stuck, and as it could not be withdrawn the bishop was obliged to have it cut off !

There is another icon of St. George preserved in this church, which the monks told us was thrown into the sea by the iconoclasts, was wafted by the waves to Vatopedi, and from thence was transported to Zographou ón a mule. Comnenus gives an enlarged account of this. He says that having left Arabia and crossed the sea of its own accord, the icon came ashore at Vatopedi. When the fathers of the other monasteries heard of this they went to Vatopedi, and a dispute arose as to which monastery should possess the picture. At last with one consent they agreed to place it on a wild mule and send away the animal to wander whither it would. The mule stopped before the gate of Zographou, and the monks joyfully coming out to meet it, escorted it with candles and incense to the church. Some time after this occurrence certain fathers from an Arabian monastery came on a pilgrimage to the Holy Mountain, recognised their old picture, and giving thanks to God and St. George remained at Zographou to the day of their death.

Lastly, Archbishop Georgirenes makes mention of a third picture of St. George. ' There is a little church not far from the Monastery, that stands alone, and now is useless; but having a fair picture of St. George in it, the Monks thought fit to bring it into their own church; but to no purpose, for so often as they brought it, so often it takes its leave, and is found the next day in the Church.'

This monastery has always belonged to the Bulgarians, and at the present time the large majority of the 120 monks belongs to this race, but amongst them are a few Servians, Greeks, Russians, and Roumanians. They follow the cœnobite rule. There are besides 150 servants.

It is asserted that in the year 1276, when Michael Palæologus was emperor and John Veccos patriarch, the Latins made a descent upon the Holy Mountain and destroyed half the Monastery of Zographou.[1] This was during the first few years after the overthrow of the Latin and the re-establishment of the Greek empire at Constantinople in 1261, when the whole of the Levant was in a turmoil and Michael Palæologus was wresting one by one the islands of the Archipelago from the dominion of the Franks. On this occasion twenty-six of the monks were burnt 'by order of the Pope of Rome,' and a monument of stone which stands in the north-west corner of the courtyard marks the place of their victory. In the catholicon are two frescoes, one representing the burning of the Six-and-Twenty Martyrs, the other the Pope at Doomsday being drawn down into horrible flames by the Fiend. In this church also is preserved an icon of the Blessed Virgin, which they say was cast into the fire with these monks, but was afterwards found unconsumed.

Michael Palæologus restored the monastery, but it was again ruined—burnt by pirates, it is said—and its reconstruction was undertaken by Stephen, Voivode of Moldavia, in the year 1502. All that remains of Stephen's work is the small refectory at the west end of the catholicon; the arsenal or port by the sea also dates from his time. The rest of the monastery is of modern construction, having been built since 1858, except the catholicon, which goes back as far as the beginning of the century, and, though I cannot speak with certainty, the church of the Panaghia, also situated in the centre of the courtyard. Since the time of Stephen, Zographou has continued prosperous, and, whilst it must have lost a revenue of nigh 4,000*l.*

---

[1] The monks of Mount Athos were persecuted by the Latins in 1275 See Muralt.

from the lands in Roumania, it is one of the wealthiest convents on the Holy Mountain. The new buildings, though plain and destitute of detail, are yet built with great solidity and give the monastery an aspect of security and massive strength, which to some degree compensates for the loss of the picturesque. A large portion of the centre of the west front was under construction during our visit.

It contains nine churches within the walls—

1. The catholicon, dedicated to St. George,
2. The Assumption of the Panaghia,
3. St. Nicholas,
4. The Holy Archangels,
5. The Prodromos,
6. The Transfiguration,
7. St. Demetrius,
8. The Six-and-Twenty Martyrs,
9. St. Cosmas ; [1]

and outside—

1. The Annunciation of the Panaghia,
2. St. Nicholas,
3. St. Spyridion,
4. St. John Chrysostom,
5. The Protection of the Panaghia,
6. SS. Peter and Paul,
7. The Nativity of the Panaghia, containing two paracclesia, dedicated respectively to St. Anthony and to St. John of Ryllo.[2]

We were told that the monastery does not boast of a library; this is not quite correct. I have since discovered that there are a few manuscripts, chiefly Greek music books of late date, and only two Greek

---

[1] A Bulgarian hermit of Athos.

[2] Monk of the monastery of that name, which still exists on the slopes of Mount Rhodope, in Roumelia.

manuscripts on vellum, one being an evangelistarium of the twelfth century. There may be, and probably are, some Slavonic manuscripts. The monastery has no sketes, but three kellia; also one farm in Thasos and four in Chalcidice.

The supper this evening was so bad that we were forced to draw upon our slender stores; indeed the oil was worse than that in any other monastery except Stavroniketa, and the smell in the corridor into which the kitchen opened, near our rooms, was quite unbearable. After the meal we had a short conversation with our chief host, a pleasant Bulgarian, whose name I have forgotten; as he had to go to church at twelve o'clock for the long night service he soon left us to have a few hours' sleep. We retired early. The monks provided us with iron bedsteads; but as, on making a minute investigation, we discovered several intruders (not, however, of the threepenny-bit breed), we put up our levinges and slept securely.

We left Zographou the next day at two o'clock for Vatopedi, the Archbishop having promised to celebrate the liturgy for the monks on their great festival of the Holy Girdle. Starting from the monastery, we mounted the hill by a winding path through fine forest scenery, and then, having reached the top of the ridge, proceeded through rather stunted vegetation until, catching sight of the eastern waters, we descended to the bay of Vatopedi.

On the way I resolved to devote one of our few remaining dry plates to a photograph of our party, which was soon to be broken up. It was easy enough to focus the group, but a difficulty arose as to who should manipulate the cap. Finally I selected

the most intelligent-looking of the two muleteers and
got the Archbishop to explain his duty to him, which
he did, telling him that at the first word ' Tora ' the
cap was to be removed and at the second replaced.
Having drilled my man by repeating the process two
or three times, I opened the slide and mounted my
mule.

'Attention !'   Everybody tried to look his best.

' Are you all ready ? '

' Malista,' said the Archbishop.

OUR CAVALCADE.

' Tora !' shouted I.   Off came the cap.   ' Tora !'
The muleteer replaced it cleverly.

Here is the result.

Two hours after leaving Zographou we arrived at
Vatopedi, and the kind monks seemed as pleased to
see us as we certainly were to find ourselves back in
this most hospitable monastery ; they vied with each
other in making us as comfortable as possible.

After bathing in the sea we amused ourselves by
strolling through the courts and watching the crowd
of pilgrims, monks, and hermits that had come up to
the feast from all parts of the promontory and the mainland.   Immense cauldrons of rice and other food were

being prepared for them, some in the kitchen and bakehouses, others over fires kindled in the court-yard ; the flicker of the flames, lighting up the faces of monks and laymen, pilgrims and ascetics, gave striking Rembrandt-like effect as the evening shadows fell and the crowd gathered in little companies about the fires, whilst the monastic cooks, with sleeves tucked up and aprons over their gowns, stirred the contents of the cauldrons with poles or served out the smoking food to their guests.

We had dinner with our old friends the epitropoi and chief monks, and immediately afterwards went to the catholicon for the commencement of the great service. The gorgeous ceremonial of that night beggars all description ; it was far more elaborate than anything of the kind that we had seen before on the Holy Mountain. The space in the centre of the quire under the dome was the only part of the church that was not crowded with worshippers, and here the sacred relics were displayed on tables covered with rich hangings. At one part of the service, just before an endless procession of priests and deacons, in the most splendid vestments, started from the bema to make a station before the holy doors, two monks advanced with tapers and kindled every lamp and candle in the church ;[1] and as these are not only in standards on the pavement and burning before the pictures, but are also suspended in great numbers at various heights, and even close to the very ceiling of the church, the ancient building was lighted up with extraordinary brilliancy. When the last of the multitude of candles had been lighted in

---

[1] See the description of the *Polycleos* in the account given below of a similar service at the skete of St. Anne.

the great coronas under the domes, the monks fetched
long poles ; with these they pushed out the candelabra
to the full extent that their suspending chains permitted
and then let them go, the result being that in a few
moments the whole church was filled with slowly
swinging lights. The effect was indescribably weird.
We remained standing in our stalls for two hours and
a half, watching the endless change of the mystic
ceremonies, and then, overcome by the unaccustomed
strain, retired to our rooms, had a cup of coffee, and
went to bed.

We rose very early the next morning and went
down to the catholicon. The crowd of pilgrims was
too large to allow of all worshipping in the church, and
not only were both nartheces and the pronaos full of
them, but some were following the service in the court
outside. So densely packed was the crowd that it was
as much as two soldiers could do to force a pathway
for us to the quire. Finally we gained our stalls (next
the Archbishop's throne), which had been reserved
for us through the night. The liturgy had already
commenced. The early light was only just beginning
to dawn through the windows, and the church was still
lighted by lamps and tapers. We remained until the
service (or rather services) ended, at nine o'clock, after
having lasted close upon fourteen hours, the Archbishop
himself, as he told us afterwards, not having left the
church for thirteen.

As we attended this great service in a very frag-
mentary manner my reader will pardon me for inserting
in this place the description of a similar one from the
pen of the late Mr. William Palmer, of Magdalen
College, Oxford, almost the only Englishman, save

Dr. Neale, capable of writing on the subject with accuracy.   Mr. Palmer spent a few weeks at Athos with
his brother, the present Archdeacon of Oxford, over
thirty years ago.

The day is Tuesday, July 25th (old style), being the festival of
S. Anne, in the year 1850.   The scene is the scete of S. Anne, an
aggregation of hermitages dependent on the Lavra of S. Athanasius.
On Monday afternoon, the eve of the festival, at about twenty
minutes past one P.M. they began the Ninth Hour and the Little
Vespers, upon the conclusion of which they went almost immediately
into the refectory (which in a scete like this exists only for such
occasions) and took their meal, which was accompanied by a long
reading.   When this was over it wanted but half an hour of the time
which was fixed for the commencement of Great Vespers, in which
they sang the introductory psalm (Ps. civ.) so slowly (the latter part
of it, too, with the insertion of a short hymn to the Trinity after
every half-verse) that before they had come to the end of it it
wanted only ten minutes of seven.   At ten minutes before nine they
went out into the narthex for the Liteia, which on such occasions is
inserted into Vespers.   While they were singing the last Sticheron
of the Liteia a few of those present, and in particular the ex-Bishop
of Trajanopolis, who had been invited here from his retreat near the
Lavra to officiate, went out for a few minutes and took a cup of
coffee in the nearest dwelling.   The Liteia was over at twenty
minutes to ten.   Then they returned into the body of the church
singing the Aposticha of the Vespers, which lasted about an hour
longer, and were followed by the Benediction of the Loaves—another
adjunct of the Great Vespers on such occasions—for which the
Bishop robed in his stall (it being then five minutes to eleven), and
unrobed again immediately afterwards.   Then followed, between the
Great Vespers and the Matins (the Nocturn being omitted, or rather
being superseded by the Great Vespers on such occasions), a reading
at the lectern in the middle of the church, about the Departure or
Rest of S. Anne.   At twenty minutes past eleven they began the
Matins, at which there was a reading of a homily (from a MS. collection by Macarius of Patmos), after the second of the two Cathisms
of the Psalter.   About twenty minutes past twelve they began to
light up the church for the Polycleos, the singing of which was drawn

out to a great length and accompanied by insertions after each half-verse, like those of the introductory psalm in the Vespers. It was finished at a quarter to two A.M. At a quarter past two the Gospel was read. The singing of the Canons, broken by two readings, one after Ode III. and the other after that of the Synaxarion, which followed Ode VI., lasted from twenty-five minutes past two till nearly four o'clock. At half-past four, or thereabouts, the Matins ended, and so did the First Hour at five o'clock. There was then a pause of one hour or rather more, during which some sat down in the stalls of the church, some went out and stood about the doors and walls of the church, or dispersed to the neighbouring hermitages, where they might lie down and rest for half an hour or three-quarters. But at six o'clock A.M. we were all again in the church, and, the Third and Sixth Hours having been read, at half-past six the Bishop came down from his stall and was robed for the Liturgy in the middle of the church. In this Liturgy a monk-deacon was ordained priest, which scarcely made any difference in the length of the service. At ten minutes to nine the Liturgy was finished, the Bishop had blessed two large dishes of Collyba (memorial cakes), and was distributing the Antidoron (i.e. the blessed bread, which is given to those who are present at Liturgy without communicating) from his stall, while they read the two psalms preparatory for the refectory; and thereupon followed the final dismissal, and they left the church. After a very short interval they all met again in the church, and went thence, preceded by lights, to the refectory, where about 300 dined together, of whom nearly two-thirds were strangers from other parts of the Holy Mountain. The Bishop and five or six others dined apart, but at the same time, at the house of the controller (δίκαιος) of the scete, who was also the chief priest of its church. The table in the refectory was blessed before, and thanksgiving made after the meal, as usual. A reading was going on about half the time we were there, and during the rest there was no noise nor conversation, except it may be a word or two here and there in an under tone. When we first sat down portions were set at each place of soup, fish, bread, and wine. There was a second entry, consisting of portions of rice made savoury; and a little later some better wine (though there was no great difference) was carried round to be drunk without water; and the contents of the dishes of Collyba, which we had seen blessed in the church after the Liturgy, were distributed. Before the last grace the father who seemed to have the superintendence of the refectory made an appropriate oration or address to the company at some length : he thanked God for having granted them so to meet this year again, and to keep with due honour their festival ; expressed pleasure at the sight of so many strangers, and hoped they might see the same festival return, and take part in its celebration on many more anniversaries ; and with all this he mixed proper religious allusions to its associations.

Lastly, there was the elevation of the bread in honour of the Blessed Virgin, and each received a morsel of it, holding it over the incense before he ate it. Then we all left the refectory, preceded as before by the lights, and at the foot of the stairs, as we turned to go into the church, we passed by four brethren, the three cooks and the reader, lying prostrate on the ground. In this posture they remained till all had gone by, in compliance with a monastic custom, which enjoins them on such occasions to ask forgiveness in this fashion for any fault or deficiencies in the manner in which they have performed their respective duties towards the company. In the church we were not detained more than a minute or two, and then separated, each going in what direction he pleased. Most, however, of those present by this time stood in need of some repose, and sought a place to lie down in some one or other of the neighbouring hermitages. Plenty of these were scattered all about among the rocks and trees, while underneath the mountain bore down almost perpendicularly into the sea, which was, however, at a considerable distance, as S. Anne stands on a far higher level than most of the seaside monasteries. When we finally left the church it wanted about a quarter to eleven A.M. Thus the whole series of services and readings, with one interval only of an hour, and one or two other inconsiderable pauses, lasted twenty-one hours and a half. And the Vigil service alone (consisting of Great Vespers with its adjuncts, Matins, and First Hour) took up twelve hours and forty minutes. Such festivals (πανηγύρεις) are of course comparatively rare, though every monastery or scete would have one such in the course of the year, and some two or three. But on all the festivals of the first rank on which they make a solemn Vigil (ἀγρυπνία) the same order is followed ; and the Vigil service lasts, not indeed, as in this case, twelve or thirteen hours, but yet not less than eight or nine, being nearly half as long again as on an ordinary Sunday. Of such festivals there may be on an average in each monastery about two in every month, or twenty-four in the course of the year. On the whole the length of the services on festivals is increased chiefly, though not exclusively, by a difference in the style of singing and by the appointment of a greater quantity of matter to be sung. In Lent, on the contrary, the services are lengthened beyond the practice of other seasons, and in winter, ordinarily, beyond the use of summer, not so much by additional singing as by very large additions to the quantity of prayers and psalms and readings, the Psalter being appointed to be said twice through weekly instead of once, the Great Compline being added to the other daily services, and the ordinary monastic readings being at once more than doubled in number and considerably increased in length.

The liturgy being ended, the Archbishop crossed the courtyard, preceded by torch-bearers and wearing a magnificent cope, the train of which was borne by Pantele, to the refectory, where, seated at the high table and surrounded by the presidents of the monastery, he dined in state with all the monks and those of the pilgrims that were fortunate enough to find places. We were advised not to dine with them, as the food would be all cooked with oil, and the monks had therefore provided an excellent cock for our consumption. So after we had taken one turn up and down the refectory to see the commencement of the feast we retired to our rooms and fell upon the bird and part of a large *collyva*, covered all over with sweetmeats, which had been solemnly blessed in the church in commemoration of the departed.

In the afternoon we arranged to visit the neighbouring skete of St. Demetrius. The Archbishop was too tired to join us; so at three o'clock we mounted our mules and started alone, with a soldier going in front to show the way. The path to the skete leads through a narrow glen, where flourishes every kind of tree and shrub. The afternoon was deliciously cool. We enjoyed our ride exceedingly, and thought that the road was, on the whole, the prettiest on the Holy Mountain. Emerging from under the leafy shade of the glen, the skete comes into view on the side of the hill, above the vineyards. Like St. Anne's it consists of a few central buildings and numerous little calyvia, dotted about in all directions on the surrounding slopes.

The monks of St. Demetrius, a poor uneducated set, received us most cordially and entertained us with glyko and coffee. The kyriacon [1] dedicated to St. Demetrius, possesses nothing of interest; its frescoes were repainted eighty years ago. There is a narthex, a pronaos, and a small paracclesi, dedicated to St. Nicholas. There is also another church, dedicated to the Assumption of Our Lady. Fifty monks belong to the skete, and they live in twenty-five calyvia, fourteen of which have chapels attached to them; these monks meet at the skete on Saturdays for the Sunday services, as at St. Anne's. The dicaios is elected annually; his business is to look after the church and central buildings. The skete is under the government of Vatopedi.

I could find out nothing certain respecting the foundation of the monastery. It is said to have been founded by some descendant of St. Demetrius of Salonica. As we left the skete the monks presented us with bunches of grapes of a very large and delicious kind. We rode back to Vatopedi, which we reached shortly after sunset, just as they were closing the gates. Another cock was cooked for our supper this evening.

[1] Measurements: Sanctuary: from north to south, including chapels, 28 feet; across chord of east apse, 11 feet; from iconostasis to end of east apse, 14½ feet. Nave: across transepts, 39½ feet; from iconostasis to west wall, 26 feet, or to west wall of narthex, 49 feet.

Thursday, September $\frac{13}{1}$. Rather late in the day
we started with the Archbishop for Chiliandari ; but
shortly after leaving Vatopedi we resolved to stop on
our way at Esphigmenou, fearing lest we should be
benighted if we ventured upon the longer ride. The
road lies along the shore of the bay, and then turning
a little inland mounts to higher ground. Angelos was
riding a little ahead of us on a large white mule. As
we turned a sharp corner we saw the laughable spectacle
of our dragoman seated on the ground and the mule
quietly trotting off. Now Angelos was particularly
proud of his riding, and used to exhibit various methods
of sitting on the mule ; in this case he had been riding
side-saddle, and the beast having given a slight jerk he
had slipped off. Of course the Archbishop was not slow
to take advantage of the circumstance to pay off old
scores against him ; for there was not much love between
them, owing to the delight which Angelos used to take
in annoying the prelate by the utterance of pestilent
opinions.

'What!' said the Archbishop, looking round, '*you*
fallen off, Angelos! How *could* that have happened ?'

Our unfortunate dragoman muttered something
about his saddle having slipped.

' Indeed!' said his tormentor ; and then calling to
O—, who was behind, he asked if he found that *his*
saddle slipped.

' No,' replied O—.

' Nor do I,' said the Archbishop, and he roared
with laughter at the jest.

Presently he turned to me.

' Does your saddle slip, Riley ?'

'No,' said I.

'Dear me,' said the Archbishop, 'how very unfortunate it is that only Angelos's saddle should give
way, and he so heavy too. I am afraid he must have
hurt himself, sitting on the stony road.'

Angelos looked as sour as vinegar as renewed
peals of laughter proceeded from the Archbishop; in
fact our dragoman's discomfiture caused such exquisite
pleasure to our merry prelate that he chuckled the
whole way to Esphigmenou, ever and again looking
back over his shoulder at Angelos and then indulging
in fresh merriment.

The vegetation on the road partook, as a rule, of
the stunted character of that on the west side of Athos.
We reached Esphigmenou a little before dusk, having
sent on Pantele to announce our arrival. This monastery occupies a retired position on the sea, the waves
of which absolutely wash its walls, and at the time of
Mr. Tozer's first visit (in 1853) had thrown down part
of them. It is closely shut in by the surrounding sides
of a little valley; hence, according to some authorities,
its name, from σφίγγω, to squeeze, because it is com-
pressed between the hills and the sea. But others
derive its appellation from a certain abbot called
Theoctistos, who lived in the ninth century. From
motives of asceticism he is said to have perpetually
worn a cord very tightly bound round his waist; thus
the house came to be called the *Monastery of the
Squeezed One.*

Esphigmenou during the last two centuries has
been steadily increasing in size and importance.
Georgirenes says, 'It is the poorest of all the
monastery (*sic*), not for want of Lands, but of Men to

cultivate them. For the soil about, is the best in all the Mount. It bears Olives of a singular largeness, and wants no other sort of Fruit Trees. But the number of Monks in it amount but to eighty, who being not able to make the best advantage of so much good ground continue poor in a plentiful Soil.'

Curzon found but thirty monks in the place, who, he says, were 'cleaner and kept their church in better order and neater than most of their brethren on Mount Athos.'

In 1760, between the times of Georgirenes and Curzon, it was in ruins, having been gradually restored from that date; and some time back the present abbot, the archimandrite Luke, went to Russia for the purpose of raising funds for the restoration; returning with 8,000*l.*, with which he completed the new buildings. There are now 120 monks, of whom ten are priests and three deacons; they observe the coenobite rule.

The brethren claim Pulcheria and her brother Theodosius the Less as the founders of Esphigmenou in the fifth century. Gass believes it to have been founded in the eleventh, but probably it was only restored in the beginning of that century, having been destroyed by a landslip or falling rocks some time previously. It also suffered at the hands of the crusaders or other Latins. The first notice I can find of Esphigmenou is in the year 1095.[1]

We had a poor supper, and although we prepared some of our concentrated soup the cook managed to spoil it by flavouring it with butter. After the soup boiled eggs were served for our benefit. O— being very particular about their being well cooked, com-

[1] Muralt.

B B

plained they had not been long enough in the pot. Whereupon the serving monk insisted that that could not be ; 'for,' said he. ' I said a *Pater* and a *Pistevo* whilst they were boiling.' It seems that on the Holy Mountain they boil eggs in this manner : They put them on the fire and then commence the recitation of the Lord's Prayer ; this being finished they commence the Nicene Creed, at the end of which the eggs are taken out of the pot and are supposed to be properly cooked.

This is a curious but very characteristic instance of the way in which religion engrosses the minds of the inhabitants of Athos. With them religion is *distributed* ; it is not reserved for special days or certain places, but mixes, sometimes in odd and quaint manners, in the ordinary actions of their lives. Do you speak to a monk ? He will answer in the language of the Scriptures. Do you write him a letter ? He will reply in the style of St. Peter or St. Paul. You demand a cup of cold water. He will bring it you fresh from a holy fountain brimming over with legends of the Blessed Angels or the Saints. Compared with the religion of the West this is not so much a question of degree of piety as of kind.

After supper we had some conversation with Luke the abbot, who we found was a painter, like his great namesake, and then putting up our levinges slept securely on the divan of a room overhanging the sea, the noise of the waves lulling us to sleep as they broke upon the shore underneath the windows.

CHAPTER XXIII.

We rose betimes, for a long day was before us, and after some tea of our own brewing paid a visit to the catholicon. This was built in 1810[1] on the site of the old one, which was in ruins; from the number and size of the windows it is a very light church. The frescoes were painted in 1841. As in most churches of late date the narthex shows signs of disappearing, the old reasons for its retention having become partly obsolete; in this instance a curtain instead of a solid wall divides it from the nave. There is, however, a regular exo-narthex and a pronaos. In the centre of the east apse is the *synthronos*, or throne of the bishop of the diocese. There are two paraclesia on each side of the narthex, that on the north being dedicated to the Archangels, that on the south to the Assumption of the Blessed Virgin.

Of the relics first comes a piece of the Holy Rood (said to have been presented by Pulcheria), in a cross of gold round which run rows of pearls on both sides. Four diamonds are set on the extremities of the arms on one side. Three large emeralds are set transparently at the two ends of the cross piece and at the top; the

---

[1] Measurements: Sanctuary: from north to south, including chapels, 30 feet; across chord of east apse, 12 feet; from iconostasis to end of east apse, 13½ feet. Nave: across from north to south, 30 feet; across transepts, 45 feet; from iconostasis to pseudo-narthex, 34 feet—to west end of narthex, 54 feet.

latter jewel has, however, come away from the reliquary, but is preserved. Between the arms are four red jewels, perhaps rubies. The other relics are the head of St. James the Less, foot of St. Mary Magdalen, part of the hand of St. Chrysostom, and the head of St. Agathangelos, who won the crown of martyrdom in Smyrna about the commencement of the present century. Agathangelos had apostatized in his childhood, but at the age of nineteen, overcome by remorse, he fled to Mount Athos and embraced the monastic life in Esphigmenou. Here he devoted himself to penance for his fall and adopted the Great or Angelic Habit. But all his mortifications were powerless to assuage his deep remorse, and finally, being warned of God in a dream that he should seal his contrition with his blood, he resolved to return to Smyrna, where he had formerly denied his Master, and then openly publish his return to Christianity. He went, accompanied by a priest, whom his convent sent to comfort him in his last hour with the Holy Sacraments, for all knew that he was going to certain death. Standing before the governor of Smyrna, he announced his rejection of the Mohammedan religion and declared that he would die in the faith of the Crucified One. For days the furious infidels employed every means to turn him from his purpose, but in vain ; and finally he suffered death by decapitation.

Pœnas cucurrit fortiter
Et sustulit viriliter ;
Pro Te effundens sanguinem
Æterna dona possidet.

Esphigmenou claims another martyr saint as one of her children, St. Timothy, who had also denied

Christ, but having returned to the faith was living at the
Lavra when the event described above took place.
Fired by the bright example of Agathangelos, he went
to the abbot of Esphigmenou, and announced his intention of going to Adrianople, the scene of his apostasy,
that there he might die for Christ ; with him too a priest
was sent. After divers tortures he also was beheaded.

The refectory is at the west end of the catholicon ; it is an old building frescoed inside, but chiefly
remarkable for its ancient and beautiful inlaid doors.
The buildings on this west side of the monastery are
old ; the rest date from the recent restorations. Passing up a narrow staircase in the thickness of the
wall of the catholicon, we gained the library, which
is situated over its west end and commands an interior view of the church. Here are 325 separate
volumes of manuscripts, some containing two or three
bound together ; seventy-two of them are on vellum.
There is an interesting martyrology of the eleventh
century, containing numerous illuminations on blue and
purple vellum. The uncial Slavonic manuscript of the
Gospels mentioned by Curzon has apparently disappeared ; although we hunted for it all over the shelves
we could not find it. In this library is kept a very
magnificent piece of embroidery, which the monks
assert to have formed part of the tent that Napoleon I.
used during the Russian campaign. An enterprising
member of the community seems to have purchased
it in Vienna in the year 1812, though for what purpose
he bought it I cannot conceive ; it is certainly a very
odd thing to find buried in an Athos monastery. It
measures 10 feet by 9 feet 4 inches, and consists of
cloth of gold covered all over with delicate needle-

work ; in the centre are three medallions, representing
Minerva, Hercules, and Diana ; it is lined with crimson
velvet and purple silk, and the whole is in perfect preservation.

Seeing that we were pleased with this embroidery,
the abbot went to one of the bookcases and pulled it
forward. To our surprise the shelves moved on hinges
and disclosed the entrance to a little room beyond.
This chamber was perfectly full of church plate and
gorgeous vestments. Two large vessels to contain the
agiasma stood on the floor, one being about 4 feet high,
both of massive silver but of modern workmanship
(probably Russian) and in bad taste. There were innumerable sets of altar vessels and censers, more than
we could possibly examine in the time at our disposal,
some of very handsome design ; also two bishops'
crowns, one of solid gold plate and one of crimson
velvet, both covered with precious stones and enamels ;
on the top of the gold one was a beautiful medallion of
the Holy Trinity, enamelled on mother-of-pearl. There
was also a cross, the exact copy of the old one in the
church, made forty years ago. Besides these treasures
there were some rich modern vestments, heavy with
gold and pearls, and all of good workmanship, which
we were told our old friend Nilos had had made for
himself in expectation of being created Patriarch of
Alexandria. How his monastery had managed to
retain possession of them I know not, nor the real
story of Nilos's dispute with the monks, but he was
clearly in very bad odour with his former brethren. His
name appeared on several of these vestments. Altogether we were much astonished at the display of
wealth on the part of this lately ruined convent. The

Archbishop told us afterwards that most of the monasteries had secret hoards of this kind, and that the treasuries of some of the larger monasteries far outdid the present one.

Esphigmenou possesses farms in Cassandra, Thasos, and near the Dardanelles. The following is a list of its churches :

Esocclesia.

1. The catholicon, dedicated to the Ascension (this was the ancient name of the monastery before it obtained that of Esphigmenou), containing the paracclesia of the Assumption and of the Archangels. ·

2. St. Constantine and St. Helen.
3. St. Gregory Palamas.[1]
4. St. Gennadius, Patriarch of Constantinople.
5. St. Nilos the Wise.[2]
6. St. Anthimus of Nicomedia.[3]

Exocclesia.

1. Assumption of the Blessed Virgin Mary.
2. All Saints.
3. The Holy Theodores, the General and the Tyro.[4]
4. St. Modestus.
5. The Holy Unmercenaries.
6. St. Anthony of Esphigmenou.

The monastery has depending on it one kelli, three calyvia, and one cathisma.

The Archbishop decided against going to Chilian-

---

[1] The champion of the Uncreated Light (see p. 194) and a former monk of Esphigmenou, afterwards Archbishop of Thessalonica.

[2] A magistrate of Constantinople and a disciple of St. Chrysostom ; afterwards he became a hermit at Mount Sinai. He died in 451. His festival is kept on November 12.

[3] Bishop of Nicomedia ; suffered martyrdom under Maximian.

[4] St. Theodore Stratelates suffered in the year 230. His festival is February 8. St. Theodore Tyron was martyred in 297. His feast day is on February 17. Both are soldier saints.

dari to-day; as we had arranged to catch a steamer for Salonica that was to touch at Daphne the next evening we were forced to go alone.

Our road lay through pretty country, which was partly covered with trees and wild shrubs, and partly consisted of cultivated fields and meadows. Here too we passed through the stubble of corn, and cornfields in Athos are rare, nearly all the grain being brought from distant farms on the mainland or on the islands. A ruin stands near the shore at the entrance of the glen at the far end of which Chiliandari is situated, away from the sea. This we afterwards learnt was the last remnant of the Monastery of St. Basil, which, as the monks of Chiliandari told us, had become a ruin before their monastery was built and was handed over to them.[1] They still use the catholicon of St. Basil as a church; the other buildings are almost entirely in ruins. We were sorry that we had no time to visit the remains of this ancient convent.

There is also belonging to Chiliandari another ruined monastery called Scorpion, situated about three hours' distance to the west, near the Canal of Xerxes and halfway between the two gulfs, in the centre of the promontory. Scorpion was absorbed into Chiliandari in 1330. Hardly anything is left of this house, so the monks said.

On our nearing Chiliandari the bells began to peal forth, and the chief monks met us outside the gateway and politely assisted us to alight; in fact, they treated us with much honour and ceremony, and fully merit the praise which Comnenus bestows upon them : Σέρβοι

---

[1] St. Basil was bought by Chiliandari in 1326. It is said to have been founded in the ninth century.

καὶ Βούλγαροι ἄνθρωποι ἀγαθοὶ καὶ φιλόξενοι. We were taken upstairs and treated to coffee and sweetmeats, during the consumption of which our friend with the hair, whom we had met in attendance on the metropolitan Michael, came in and greeted us warmly. We discussed topics connected with the monastery whilst breakfast was being prepared in an adjoining room.

Chiliandari, believed by Leake to occupy the site of the ancient town of Holophyxus, is of very early foundation, but all accounts of the original monastery have perished. In the first few years of the thirteenth century it was restored by St. Simeon and St. Sabbas under the following circumstances :[1] Stephen Nemanja (for he took the name of Simeon in religion) was the ruler of Servia in the reign of Alexius I. (1081–1118), and Sabbas was his second son. Sabbas, fired by religious zeal, left Servia secretly and came to Athos, intending to devote himself to the monastic life. Two years afterwards his father, hearing of his whereabouts, went to Athos to fetch him back to Servia, but Sabbas succeeded in persuading his father not only to leave him to follow religion in peace, but also to join him in the assumption of the monastic habit. So, leaving the kingdom of Servia to another son, Stephen took the vows with Sabbas at Vatopedi under the name of Simeon. Here they remained for a few years and then moved with some other Servian monks to the ruins of Chiliandari, which they restored (1198 ?). Simeon the king died a monk within its walls, but Sabbas returned to Servia and became archbishop there. In 1308 the Catalans invaded Chalcidice, and it

[1] Mouravieff; gathered from ancient charters.

was mainly due to the monks of Chiliandari, under their brave abbot Daniel, that the inhabitants of Mount Athos were able to offer such strenuous resistance to the invaders. Milotine, another Servian prince, built the catholicon. The monastery suffered heavily during the Greek war of independence ; at that time the Turks destroyed some of the buildings, carried off much of the plate, and reduced the monks to great poverty.

The name of the monastery presents difficulties : it has been variously derived from Χίλιοι ἄνδρες, 'a thousand men,' either because at one time it contained that number of monks or because it was once miraculously preserved from the attack of a thousand pirates ; Χίλια ἄντρα, 'a thousand caves,' from the numerous caverns in its neighbourhood ; Χίλιοι λέοντες, 'a thousand lions ; ' and lastly from a Bulgarian word meaning 'a hive of bees.'[1] Probably the first-named derivation is the right one.

There are at Chiliandari about seventy monks, of whom ten are Greeks, a few Roumanians, and the rest Bulgarians and Servians ; there are also thirty lay brethren, or servants. They follow the idiorrhythmic rule, although they have several times endeavoured to change it to the cœnobite, but have failed owing to their poverty. We were much surprised at hearing that the idiorrhythmic system was the more economical of the two. The monks explained that in this case each inmate cultivated his own little garden, and we were led to infer that when they worked for themselves

---

[1] Mr. W. R. Morfill, M.A., of Oriel College, Oxford, who has kindly endeavoured to verify for me several Slavonic references, informs me that he cannot discover such a word bearing any resemblance to Chiliandari.

individually they accomplished more than when they laboured for the common weal. They have two small farms in Cassandra and one large one at Cala-Maria, two kellia (the Holy Trinity and the Prodromos), besides twenty-three kellia which they own at Caryes.

MONASTERY OF CHILIANDARI.

Esocclesia.

1. The catholicon, dedicated to the Presentation in the Temple of the Mother of God.
2. St. Sabbas.
3. St. Demetrius.
4. The Holy Apostles.
5. The Nativity of the Mother of God.
6. The Protection of the Blessed Virgin.
7. St. George.
8. St. John of Ryllo.
9. The Archangels.

Exocclesia.

1. St. Tryphon.
2. St. Charalampes.
3. St. Stephen.
4. St. Basil.

The names of the epitropoi were Stephen and Nicephorus. After breakfast the monks took us to the catholicon.[1] It has two nartheces of equal size, with an ascent of four steps from the outer to the inner one. The frescoes are all of modern date. The part of this church most worthy of notice is the pavement, which is of mosaic and fine marbles. The throne in the quire is 250 years old, by the date on it; let into the front of its canopy are two ancient plaques, which were probably book covers in former days. In each plaque are twelve illuminations on vellum, representing scenes from the life of Our Lord, the subjects being delineated on a ground of gold and pearls, just as in the illuminated cross and book covers at St. Paul's. The pictures are covered with glass and set in silver-gilt filigree enriched with jewels. At the side of the throne is placed a staff, said to have belonged to the Emperor Andronicus Comnenus. It is of black ebony with a head formed of a piece of jasper, mounted in silver gilt and set with precious stones; it measures 4 feet 8½ inches in length. This staff is used by any bishop who comes to the church.

On the eastern side of the south-west dome pillar is placed a miraculous icon called the Παναγία Τρι-χεροῦσα, or the Three-handed Panaghia. The monks asked us if we observed anything curious about the icon, and after a few moments we noticed that the Holy Virgin (for it is a representation of the Mother and Child) had a third hand, of silver, affixed to the picture.

[1] Size of sanctuary: from north to south, including chapels, 34½ feet; across chord of east apse, 13 feet; from iconostasis to end of east apse, 18 feet. Nave: across transepts, 51 feet; from iconostasis to west wall of nave, 37 feet; to west wall of narthex, 64 feet. There are doors at the extremities of the transepts, which is a very unusual feature.

This is said to be the very icon before which St. John Damascene prayed after his hand had been cut off by the iconoclasts. On his rubbing the stump against the lips of St. Mary the hand was restored to him.[1]

Amongst the relics are a large piece of the Holy Rood,[2] set in a filigree reliquary, a curious cross of crystal said to contain three of Our Lord's Hairs, a leg of St. Simon Stylites, and a hand of St. Nicephorus. The monks denied all knowledge of the bloodstone chalice mentioned by Curzon.

The library contains, I should think, about 150 manuscripts, of which nearly fifty are on vellum. Many are in the Slavonic languages; I saw one of these, which was a copy of the Gospels with illuminations. Of those in Greek the earliest is a commentary of St. Chrysostom, in quarto, of the eleventh century; there is also a manuscript on paper of the fifteenth century, containing the liturgies of St. Chrysostom, St. Basil, and the Presanctified, with a few other offices; of the remaining Greek manuscripts on paper over seventy are ecclesiastical music books.

To our great disappointment we were unable to see the beautiful manuscript of Andronicus Comnenus, the monk who had the key of the press where it is kept in the catholicon being away in the vineyards (for the vintage had begun), too far off to be recalled before our departure; so my readers must be content with

---

[1] 'C'est une des plus vieilles et des plus remarquables peintures byzantines ou orientales. On l'apporta de Jérusalem en Servie, et de là au mont Athos, à Chiliandari, qui est peuplé de moines serbes. Cette Vierge est d'un beau caractère, mais un peu dure de figure, comme l'enfant Jésus qu'elle tient dans ses bras. Du reste, c'est une des plus précieuses et des plus honorées reliques de tout le mont Athos, où il y a tant des belles reliques.'—Didron, *Manuel d'Iconographie Chrétienne.*

[2] Given to St. Sabbas by the Emperor John Vataces.

Curzon's description of it and the knowledge that it is still to be seen, when fortune or the monks favour, in the Monastery of Chiliandari. He says :

This, to my admiration and surprise, was not only the finest manuscript on Mount Athos, but the finest that I had met with in any Greek monastery, with the single exception of the golden manuscript of the New Testament at Mount Sinai. It was a quarto evangelistarium, written in golden letters on fine *white* vellum. The characters were a kind of semi-uncial, rather round in their forms, of large size, and beautifully executed, but often joined together and having many contractions and abbreviations, in these respects resembling the Mount Sinai MS. This magnificent volume was given to the monastery by the Emperor Andronicus Comnenus about the year 1184 ; it is consequently not an early manuscript, but its imperial origin renders it interesting to the admirers of literary treasures, while the very rare occurrence of a *Greek* manuscript written in letters of gold or silver would make it a most desirable and important acquisition to any royal library.

In the library there are preserved several necklaces formed of prodigiously heavy chains and crosses, the property of former hermits and worn by them in penitence. The courtyard of Chiliandari is picturesque, the surrounding buildings being for the most part ancient, and growing in the midst of it are several fine cypresses. Soon after three o'clock we bade adieu to the good monks ; they seemed so pleased at our visit that we felt quite sorry that we could not stay the night with them, but it was absolutely necessary for us to sleep at Vatopedi.

The epitropoi escorted us out of the monastery, and the monks continued to ring the bells until we were out of sight. We put our mules into a trot and managed to get back to Esphigmenou in twenty minutes, when we hurried up to the guest chamber. Here we found the Archbishop in the midst of writing two letters of recommendation for Salonica and Athens that he had promised to give us, for although they might have been written a week before he had put off the labour until the very last moment.

When they were finished we descended to the gate. Our mules were ready, and it only remained to say our last farewells to the genial prelate, whose companionship had so greatly heightened the enjoyment of our journey on the Holy Mountain. On both sides, I think, there was real regret that the parting hour had come, and none of the three had the heart to make long speeches; so we thanked him for all his kindness, and tried to cheer ourselves by talking of what we would do in company another year. We both felt that unpleasant choking sensation inseparable from all sincere leave-takings as we kissed his hand for the last time, and when the Archbishop kissed our foreheads I noticed that tears were in his eyes.

In silence we walked away to the other end of the bridge which spans the little dry torrent bed in front of the monastery to where Peter and Pantele were standing at our mules' heads. The honest fellows seemed as sorry as their master to part with us; we increased their appreciation of us by a suitable largess.

'Good-bye, Pantele. Good-bye, Peter. When *next* we see you, Peter, you will be a holy deacon, singing in the church.'

'Ah, no,' said Peter. 'I am afraid the Archbishop is only joking; he does not *really* intend to make me one.'

'Oh, yes; he told us he would. Good-bye, Peter the Deacon!'

Away we went, down to the right, into the little

river-bed, whilst the Archbishop stood on the bridge gazing after us ; we could see him through the trees waving his handkerchief, but a turn of the road soon shut both him and Esphigmenou from our sight.

We made great haste, with the result that we reached Vatopedi a quarter of an hour before Angelos and the baggage. It was dusk when we entered the gate, and the monastery was closed for the night directly after our baggage arrived. We made a point of supping with the epitropoi in the little room where we had eaten our first meal on Athos, for this was the last we were to have with our old hosts.

CHAPTER XXIV.

Saturday, September $\frac{15}{3}$. We rose very early and packed up our baggage for our final departure. Whilst we were thus engaged the dicaios of St. Demetrius called and stayed some time in conversation with us. Then we went to wish good-bye to the epitropoi, who had on every occasion been so kind to us, and took glyko and coffee with them in the guest chamber. They and many of the chief monks came to the gate with us, and at a quarter to nine o'clock we started 'for England,' as we pleasantly persuaded ourselves. On the way to the Bay of Daphne we had to pass through Caryes and traverse the same ground as when we first mounted our mules at Athos. We reached the Seraï at half-past eleven, and asked the monks to prepare some breakfast for us whilst we went into the town. There we parted in different directions, O— going to the post office to get our letters, whilst I collected the engravings I had ordered in the bazaar when we were last in the capital. O— soon joined me and brought the unwelcome news that the officials at the post positively affirmed that no boat would leave Daphne that day for Salonica. However we determined to push on that evening to Xeropotamou, on the chance of the steamer calling at the port, for in the East it is impossible to arrive at the truth unless one sees and hears for oneself. O— also told me that the post-office clerk declared that he should not have known him ; he had grown so thin. And no wonder after a six weeks' experience of the Athos *régime !* And yet people do say that snails are fattening.

After breakfast at the Seraï we left Caryes and rode over the ridge to Xeropotamou, which we reached at five o'clock. Here our worst fears were confirmed. The old Russian merchant, whom we had met at Russico, having completed the devotions of his pilgrimage, was returning to his native land, and had bribed the steamer which was passing from Salonica to Constantinople to call, so that the steamer belonging to the same company, which was to have touched at Daphne on its way from Constantinople to Salonica, would not now diverge from its course. We determined to stay at Xeropotamou for the night, especially as we heard that two Greek travellers, M. Damalas and a brother professor from the University of Athens, were here, waiting, like ourselves, for an opportunity of leaving Athos. We soon fraternized with our companions in adversity, and began to discuss our prospects of escape from the Holy Mountain. Three courses alone were open to us : the first, to wait a fortnight for the next steamer. This we were very loth to do. The second, to go with the old Russian as far as the Dardanelles, land there, and wait for a western-bound vessel to take us back to Salonica. The third, to go overland to that town. This last plan was stoutly opposed by the monks, who said that if we attempted it we should certainly be captured by the brigands, folk (from their description) 'righte felonouse and foule and of cursed kynde.' The professors were not

particularly anxious to try the experiment, but we all
finally determined to sleep the night over it.

The next morning we held a fresh council and
decided to abandon the overland route ; for our acting
consul at Cavalla had told us that the country was
not safe, and had refused to allow us to go to Athos
by road. Only a week ago intelligence had come to
Athos that one of the principal pashas of Salonica had
been carried off to the mountains, after several of his
escort of thirty soldiers had been killed, and that an
enormous ransom was demanded for his release.   I
remembered also an ominous reply that I had received
from the consul-general at Salonica in answer to a
letter addressed to him on the subject before leaving
England, that all English travellers were warned that
they must take their own risk.   So it was arranged
that we should go to Russico and see what could be
done, whether there was any chance of another steamer
calling before very long or whether we could get the
use of the launch.   The professors would not go
with us, being in high dudgeon at the unceremonious
way in which they had been treated at Russico.   As
M. Damalas was a notorious anti-Russian and a frequent
correspondent of certain Athenian journals of Russo-
phobist complexion, this, perhaps, was not to be wondered at.   We walked to Russico that Sunday afternoon
and reached the monastery in time for vespers.

The monks prepared a good meal for us and were
most anxious that we should stay the night, but, as
we had no baggage with us, we declined, although
we agreed to sup with them.   Nothing could be done
about the launch ; it was wanted for other purposes ;
and besides the monks did not care to send it such a

c c 2

distance at this time of the year, when the gales were
expected. After supper at seven o'clock we left
Russico, promising to return the next day, and rode
back by the bright moonlight to Xeropotamou. Of
course the monastery was closed for the night, but by
dint of shouting we attracted the attention of our
friends in the room above, and were soon let in at the
gate. We had a long and interesting conversation
with M. Damalas, who spoke English perfectly. He
seemed to think that the future of Mount Athos de-
pended entirely upon what government succeeded that
of the Ottoman Empire. Russia he considered the
most probable, and of this Power he was the most
afraid, because he believed the Russians would carry
off everything of interest on the Holy Mountain and
gradually destroy the whole community. He hoped
that, on the contrary, some other Christian Power
would establish its rule over Athos, under the protection of which a college for the Orthodox clergy
might be established, and a school for music and
painting. He discussed the Athos relics in a sensible
and temperate manner, being anxious to preserve the
genuine in honour and esteem whilst rejecting those
which were clearly false. This, he said, had been
done to a great extent in free Greece, but at Athos
the monks believed so implicitly in *all* their relics that
this reformation would be a work of difficulty.

We had intended to start early the next morning
for Russico, but one thing and another prevented
our doing so. The first delay was caused by the
monks, who told us that, as they had already put
to death a fine cock for our especial delectation at
breakfast, they must insist upon our partaking of that

meal.   After breakfast the whole monastery went to
sleep, and when the siesta was over the monks discovered that there were no mules to be had, none
having as yet returned from the vineyards.   This
occasioned another delay of over an hour, and it was
three o'clock before we finally left the monastery.

On our arrival at Russico we dined by ourselves,
it being a fast day for the monks, but not for us, and
afterwards developed our last negatives.

Tuesday, September $\frac{18}{6}$. Throughout the whole of last
night a fierce gusty wind howled round the monastery.
The steamer was to call at Daphne this evening to
take the Russian pilgrim to Constantinople, and we
had half made up our minds to make the best of a bad
business and go in it to the Dardanelles.   Professor
Damalas and his friend had indeed decided to do
this; but last night's storm turned the scale.   The
autumnal gales were clearly at hand, if not already
upon us, and I for my part had no desire to be tossed
up and down for a couple of nights in a horrid little
Turkish steamer with no berths or decent food,
although perhaps I should not have needed much of
that!   O—, who always professes to like waves (though
I *have* seen him look rather pale on ship-board), declared himself to be moved by the opinion of the
monks, that, owing to the bad weather, the steamer
would probably pass Athos this evening without
stopping.   So, throwing all fears of brigands to the
winds, we resolved to imitate the example of the Great
King, who having been once caught in the stormy
Athos seas, took care the next time he passed that
way to go *overland*.   Prudence, however, counselled
us to keep our change of plan to ourselves, for in a

populous monastery like Russico, with hundreds of servants, artisans, and fishermen, it would be wonderful if there were not a knave or two, and knaves have friends.　When Europeans have been attacked by robbers or carried off by brigands in the East, the disasters have nearly always occurred through gossiping servants.

If times and routes are kept private, and plans continually altered at the last moment, my experience is that you may travel through the most disturbed districts in fair security.　In this case there was probably but little risk, for we afterwards found that the brigands were many miles off our route, but we took care to be on the safe side.

We had discovered from conversation with the guest-master, Heliodorus, that by taking a sailing-boat to the end of the gulf of the Holy Mountain we should gain a whole day by saving the land journey down the length of the promontory.　We arranged therefore to walk to Daphne and try to find a caïque that would take us.　Just as we were starting Angelos brought word that there was a little boat lying off the beach below Russico ; so leaving O— to pack up I went down to the shore with our dragoman.　Here I found a nice two-masted little craft of about two tons.

A bargain was soon struck with the owner, and I went back to finish the packing.　In ten minutes all the luggage was on board ; a keg of water and two loaves were hurriedly thrown into the boat, and we were preparing to follow, when two Turkish custom-house officers appeared and demanded that all our baggage should be landed to be examined.　Of course they had waited until everything was carefully stowed

away in the boat with a view of extorting backsheesh.
Appreciating this move, we were determined not to
yield one way or the other, and so at once flatly
refused, telling them that the thing was not to be
thought of for an instant. *We* have our luggage
examined ? Did they know to whom they were
talking ? Perhaps they were unaware of the friendship
that existed between us and the caimacan, their master ?
A pretty fuss he would make when he heard how his
friends had been treated !

The officers wavered for an instant at our lofty talk,
and a happy inspiration caused me to follow up the
attack with success. I pulled out my passport, and
handing it to Angelos bade him point out the royal
arms at the top and the Turkish *visé*; then turning
round as if the matter were quite settled, we both
stepped into the boat. Whereupon Angelos improved
the occasion by explaining in a few words the
tremendous import of the document—that it was
about ten times more valuable and conferred far
greater powers upon its fortunate possessors than a
firman itself, and that there was a special clause relating to the free passage of all baggage through the
custom-houses. The Turks took the paper into their
hands (they had evidently never seen a British passport
before), looked at it with as much reverence as if it
had borne the signature of the Prophet, returned it to
our dragoman with a salaam, and wished us a prosperous voyage. We set sail at half-past four.

A fresh breeze carried us into the middle of the
gulf; it dropped almost at the moment when we
turned and shaped our course so as to run down
between the promontories. The whole of the western

side of Athos was exposed to our view ; we could
see all the monasteries we knew so well, Xenophou,
Docheiariou, and behind us Xeropotamou high above
the sea, and, beyond, the little bays and creeks sheltering the convents that nestle under the shadow of the
mountain, whose great peak towers up in barren
grandeur above the trees clothing its base. Soon the
sun went down behind Longos, and the shadows fell
upon the convents on the shore, gradually creeping up
the side of the ridge until all was enveloped except the
peak itself. On we go past Docheiariou, the fitful
wind now bellying the sails and carrying us on a few
yards, now dropping until they idly flap against the
masts. The promontory soon appears but a great
black mass dividing sky from sea, relieved only by the
lights of woodmen's fires. We float dreamily along,
listening to the ripple of the waters on our keel and the
distant bells of Russico, for the hour of compline is at
hand. The stars shine brightly over our heads, and
the soft breeze blowing from the eastern shore wafts
the delicious scent of pine trees across the waters of
the gulf. Angelos is asleep at our feet, so is one of the
sailor monks ; the other, being the skipper, sits silently
at the helm, his arm pressed idly against the tiller, for
indeed there is but little work for him to do. The
spell of Athos seems still to be over us ; we are not yet
escaped from the enchantments of peace.

But in a few hours we shall be in a crowded
Eastern city, in a few days once more in the crater of
that restless, heaving volcano called modern Europe.
Farewell, quiet woods and silent rocks; farewell, old
courts and simple monks. Life is short ; perhaps we
may never see you more.

Our skipper was a monk of Xeropotamou ; he had served on board an English ship some twenty-five years ago and still spoke our language with ease. I asked him the name of his little vessel.

'The " Evangelisteria," '[1] said he.

'Ah,' said I, 'a good name.'

'Yes,' replied the monk, 'the best in all the world.'

It was now getting late. We had had nothing to eat since eleven A.M. and were therefore desperately hungry ; so we cut off large hunches from our loaves, washed them down with water from our keg, and laid ourselves on the hard planks to snatch a little rest. A few drops of rain fell, but the monks rigged up a canopy over our heads out of a spare sail, and so we kept quite dry. Just before closing my eyes I noticed some islands (Mulari) on our right : these lie off the narrowest part of the promontory, where Xerxes cut his canal.[2] The novelty of our situation did not

---

[1] The 'Evangelized,' i.e. St. Mary, referring to the Annunciation.

[2] We much regretted that we were unable to visit and investigate this interesting spot. We first tried to go by sea from Russico and then by land from Zographou, but having put off the journey until we began to be pressed for time we found it would take too long, and, most reluctantly, we had to abandon our project. Mr. Tozer, who visited the site in 1853, has for ever settled the question of the authenticity of the canal. He says, ' The isthmus through which it was cut is just a mile and a half in width, and the ground immediately about it is low, so that even in the middle, where there are some slight undulations, it hardly rises more than fifty feet above the sea. Thus the description of Herodotus is very accurate, as he speaks of it as "a neck of land about twelve furlongs across, the whole extent whereof, from the sea of the Acanthians to that over against Torone, is a level plain, broken only by a few low hills." Through this isthmus the Canal of Xerxes was cut, and the deep dyke which still remains, and forms the boundary of the Holy Mountain, is now called by the inhabitants *Provlaka*, which name is evidently the corruption of a word (προαύλαξ) signifying "the canal in front of the peninsula of Athos." Thus the doubts of Juvenal and other writers, both ancient and modern,

assist somnolence, and we neither of us slept much
until we reached the end of the gulf, and, running into
a little creek, anchored there for the remainder of the
night.

At daybreak we weighed anchor and sailed eastwards under a fresh breeze, and in an hour's time, just
as the sun rose, we beached the ' Evangelisteria ' in the
Bay of St. Nicholas. The land was quite bare, without
any sign of habitation, but in a few minutes we espied
a youth on the shore, and hailing him desired him to
go up to the village of St. Nicholas as fast as he could
and bring back mules for transport. We hauled all
our luggage on to the beach, and after bathing in the
sea sat down on our portmanteaux for breakfast. This
consisted of the remains of the loaves, a small tin of
tunny, and cold water instead of coffee.

By the time we had finished our meal and arranged
our baggage, the mules arrived ; we loaded them, and

as to the execution of Xerxes' project are proved to have been groundless.
In the middle, it is true, it is not traceable for some distance ; but it has
been suggested, with great probability, that this part was afterwards filled
up in order to allow a more ready passage into and out of the peninsula.
The canal is best traceable on the southern side, where it is deep and
continuous, varying in breadth from time to time from the soil having
accumulated in places, and marshy at intervals, even in summer ; in the
wet season a considerable stream of water is said to flow down through
it. Near the point where it reaches the sea on this side stood the ancient
town of Sane. The whole place was carefully surveyed for the Admiralty
by Captain Spratt. I may here mention also that when approaching
from this direction the neighbouring village of Erisso (Acanthus), which
lies on the other side of some low hills to the north-west, I passed a large
and high mound, which at first I took for the acropolis, until the real
acropolis came in view, with the remains of Hellenic walls on one of its
sides. I have little doubt that this was the tomb of Artachæes, who
superintended the cutting of the canal, for Herodotus speaks of his having
been buried at Acanthus and of a mound having been raised over his
grave by the whole Persian army.'—*The Highlands of Turkey*, vol. i.
ch. vi.

saying good-bye to the captain started for St. Nicholas.
It took us an hour to reach the village. On the way
we passed a gleaner in a cornfield ; we started and
looked at each other, for it was a woman ! And then
we smiled ; for we knew that the spell of the Holy
Mountain was broken. Of course every soul in
St. Nicholas came out to see us. We were taken
to the custom-house, where the officer insisted upon
opening the hamper. After some delay this matter
was settled, and fresh mules being obtained we left at
a quarter to nine, being anxious to out-travel all rumours
of our advance.

Our party consisted of six persons : ourselves,
mounted on three mules—the other two mules carrying the baggage—the owner of the caravan, who rode
the sorriest nag conceivable, and two sturdy young
muleteers who followed on foot. At first our road led
across the base of the central promontory of Longos,
and then, striking the eastern shore of the Gulf of
Cassandra, proceeded along the sea coast, which is
bordered by low cliffs of red sand. Shortly after noon
we dismounted and lunched under a mulberry tree in
a melon field, off dry bread and some melons which
our muleteers gathered for us. Again we proceeded
along the Gulf of Cassandra until we reached its limit,
when, continuing our straight course, we ascended a
tableland from which we had good views of the two
western promontories, the great peak of Athos behind
us and the Gulf of Salonica in front.

The country through which we had passed in
coming from St. Nicholas consisted partly of unculti-
vated land, covered with low thick bushes, and partly
of vineyards, corn-fields, and mulberry groves (for the

silkworms). It seemed to be very thinly populated ; we saw but few natives during our ride.

As it grew dark we descended to a small straggling village, but passed it, as our muleteers were anxious to reach a farm belonging to the Monastery of Zographou. It had been threatening to rain all day, and we had seen it pouring on the neighbouring hills. Now thunder and lightning commenced and caused us to urge forward the mules with all possible haste ; but it was a very black night and we could not proceed so fast as we wished for fear of missing the road. After an hour of this sort of riding we reached the farm, just in time to avoid the rain, and knocked furiously at the gate. In about five minutes we were admitted and were received by the monks with much hospitality.

We had an excellent supper, consisting of a strong brew of our preserved soup, fresh eggs, and sheep's milk, and then retired to bed, quite tired out, as it was half-past seven o'clock and we had been riding for twelve hours in the hot sun, after a broken night's rest and on very inadequate food.

Thursday, September $\frac{20}{8}$. Rose, very loath, at daybreak, and after breakfasting off eggs and preserved soup started from the farm at six o'clock. The storm had passed away during the night, leaving, however, clouds behind it. For this we were thankful, as the sun in these parts is, in the month of September, still too hot for comfort at midday. During the next four or five hours we rode over an undulating and little cultivated country, the tortoises crawling over the sandy soil being nearly the only sign of animal life. Last night we had questioned the monks as to their manner of farming, and they told us that, as they own very large tracts of land, they only cultivate a portion at a time, moving on from field to field until they have gone through the whole, which they do in about seven years. Owing to their thus allowing the land to lie fallow so long they use no manure, and yet raise large quantities of corn. They also cultivate grapes and silk; the latter they send to Salonica. We lunched under a wild pear tree off bread and hard-boiled eggs, and then starting afresh, in two hours' time gained the top of a hill, from whence we saw the great town of Salonica, lying between the hills and the sea, on the farther side of an immense plain which lay in front of us. I calculated the distance at four hours' journey, but it was nearer five before we reached the walls. We descended into the plain through a dry torrent bed, and after riding some little distance forded a stream and found ourselves on the remnants of a narrow, roughly paved road: this was the famous Via Egnatia.

Making all the haste we could to cover the road between us and the town before nightfall—for this was of course the part of the route we had most to fear, owing to the time that had elapsed since our departure from Athos had become known—we reached the suburbs of the town at about half-past six. The sight of our cavalcade astonished the natives, who at the time were full of the capture of their pasha. The authorities of the town had just published a declaration that they would not be responsible for the safety of those adventurous citizens who chose to prolong their drives beyond the outposts; hence no little excitement was created by two Englishmen riding in from the country with their portmanteaux stuffed with golden liras, for such is the annoying superstition respecting every British traveller. Soon we were safe within the white walls of Salonica, and at half-past seven drew rein at the doors of the Hôtel Colombo.

After a few days spent in exploring this interesting town—with the assistance of Mr. J. E. Blunt, C.B., our most hospitable consul-general, and of Mr. Crosbie, a Presbyterian missionary who has lived for many years in Salonica and is accurately acquainted with its antiquities—we left for England *viâ* Athens, Brindisi, and Rome (the latter in spite of the warnings we had received from Archbishop Philotheos, who feared we should be contaminated by papistry), and thence after a short stay we travelled direct to Paris.

On October 10, a familiar cry announced that our toils were over and the circle of our three months' journey was completed—' Restez, messieurs, dans les voitures pour le bateau. Calais!'

And now it is time for me to part from my readers, if indeed there be any that have borne so long with my old monks and have come with me to our journey's end.

My object throughout these pages has been two-fold. In the first place I have endeavoured to describe with some minuteness—often, I fear, rather wearisome to the ordinary reader—the present condition of the Athos monasteries and their contents, in order to furnish those few travellers who may visit the peninsula with a sort of handbook for their journey, and also that future historians of the Holy Mountain may have certain statistics and information for comparison with their own times. For that a complete history of

this strange community will be written some day I
have little doubt; it will need a long sojourn on the
promontory, hard work with camera and pencil, and
much patient investigation of charters and manuscripts
both at Athos and at St. Petersburg, whither a number
of documents relating to the monasteries seem to have
been carried.

Besides my description of Athos I have tried to give
a picture of the Greek Church as it is to-day, of the
Greek ecclesiastics and religious, and of the habits of
thought that obtain amongst them, and I have been
studiously careful that the picture should not err on the
side of flattery. The Catholic Church has been now
unhappily divided for over eight centuries, with the
result that the East has been operated upon by one
set of influences, the West by another. Peculiarities,
good and bad, have developed in each, and both in-
terpret the Holy Scriptures and the traditions of the
Church with a certain àmount of individuality. When
a river is divided into two streams each branch as it
runs along receives into its volume divers little brooks
and rivulets, different from those which go to swell the
volume of the other, so that you shall find at last that
the water in the one stream yields a different analysis
from that taken from the other. Thus it is with the
Churches possessed of several centuries of different
histories.

Whilst the Orientals can learn much from us we
can learn many things from them, and this study of
our fellow-Christians is the antidote to that excessive
insularity to which the Anglican Church is most particularly liable. Such a study too, by drawing us
closer to our brethren, helps us to prepare for the im-

pending struggle of Christendom against the gathering
forces of the Evil One. These are dark days; infidelity
is increasing, tolerant of everything but dogmatic truth,
and it seems as if before long the Church of Christ
would be purified from the evils of the great schism
in the eleventh century and the great rebellion in the
sixteenth by the fierce flames of martyrdom, and the
divided Communions be welded together upon the
anvil of persecution.

Suffer me to close these few remarks with two ex-
tracts from a work by Sir Paul Ricaut,[1] an old traveller
on the Holy Mountain, which are well worthy of our
consideration, especially as they were published with
the *imprimatur* of an Archbishop of Canterbury.

After telling us that he will not 'enter the Lists of
Disputation against any point maintained by the *Greek*
Church, but, however, shall boldly reprove it,' and
having spoken justly but temperately withal of its
coldness and formalism, he proceeds to recognize the
lessons which we can learn from our brethren in the
faith.

' Yet I cannot but almost retract what I have said,
when I consider how they are startled and affrighted
at the Sentence of Excommunication ; how strict and
frequent some are in their Confessions, how obedient
and submissive to the censure and injunction of the
Priest; which certainly do evidence some inward
tenderness of Conscience, and dispositions towards

---

[1] *The Present State of the Greek and Armenian Churches, Anno
Christi* 1678.   Written at the Command of his Majesty by Paul Ricaut,
Esquire, Late Consul at Smyrna, and Fellow of the Royal Society.
London, 1679.   Imprimatur hic Liber cui Titulus, *The Present State, etc.*
Car. Trumball Rev. in Christo Pat. ac Dom. Dom. Gul. Archiep. Cant. a
Sac. dom.   Ex Æd. Lamb. 8 Feb. $167\frac{8}{9}$.

being edifyed, and built up in a more perfect frame
and structure of Religion. But here I lose myself and
am amazed when I contemplate the light of the Gospel
which shines in our Islands, what daily Lectures we
hear from the Pulpits; the knowledge we have from
the Scriptures, expanded and laid open to us in our
own Tongue, the Divine Mysteries expounded by
learned Commentaries, and most Mechanicks amongst
us more learned and knowing than the Doctors and
Clergy of *Greece* : And yet, good God! That all this
should serve to render us more blind, or more perverse;
for who is it that values the Excommunication of a
Bishop, or other Ecclesiastical Censures? Who accounts of Vigils and Fasts according to the Institutions
of the Universal, and of their own Church? or weighs
the private Instructions of a Priest, who is the Monitor
of his Soul?[1] Nay, even those who profess Obedience
to the Church of *England*, and attribute an efficacy to
the power of the Keys, and would not for the world
be under an Excommunication, and hold themselves
obliged to celebrate the Feasts with devotion and
rejoycing, and account the non-observance thereof the
Characteristical point of a *Phanatic* : yet, when the
Anniversary Fasts take their turn, which impose the
same injunction on them of keeping holy, as do the
Feasts, they find excuses to evade the obligation, and
dispute against all Penance, Mortification, and Severi-
ties of life, as grounded on the Doctrine of Merits, and

---

[1] 'Another great help to support and maintain the Eastern Church, is
their Confession to a Priest—I know not how far the *Roman* Clergy may
have abused this Excellent evidence of repentance, this Ordinance of the
Gospel, this admirable means to inflame our devotion, and to guide and
instruct us in the rules of holy Living.'—*Present State of the Greek and
Armenian Churches, &c.*

D D

Works of Supererogation :   And in this manner elude
that admirable duty enjoyned by Christ himself, where
he saith, That *when the Bridegroom is taken away
from them then they should fast*, and would abolish
that signal mark of Christianity, which by its rigour
and frequency distinguishes it from all other Religions
in the World.   Some, I know, will be apt to attribute
this abridgment of the Clergies' power to their super-
eminent knowledge, and more clear light of Scripture,
that they are better instructed than to be guided by
their Priests, or to stand in awe of the condemnation
of a supercilious Prelate : but such Learning as this,
derived from the Principles of Pride and Licentious-
ness, is far worse than ignorance : and that Person who
is humble and submissive, apt and willing to be instructed, is a better Christian, and in a more secure
path and way to Godliness and Heaven, than he, that
having heard and read much, stands dangerously
towring on the presumptuous Pinnacle of his own
Reason.'

   ' For conclusion, In this manner this Mountain of
Athos is inhabited, and this is the Government amongst
these Religious men of the Greek Church, who are for
the most part good simple men of godly lives, given
greatly to devotion and acts of mortification ; for as
out of the abundance of the heart the mouth speaks, so
these men discoursing with a lively sense of God and
of his Service, we may without over-much credulity,
or easiness of belief, conclude them not only to be real
and moral good men, but such also as are something
touched with the Spirit of God; whose devotion and
affection to his Commands and Precepts, shall carry
them farther in their way to Heaven, than the wisdom

of the most profound Philosophers, or the wisest Clerks. *And that such people are found in the world, endowed with such Priviledges, in the Countries of the Grand Oppressour of Christendom, to God's Name be Glory and Honour, now and for ever. Amen.'*

APPENDIX.

———❦———

I.

THE DISPERSION OF THE WOOD OF THE CROSS.

THE Cross of Christ was discovered in A.D. 326 by the Empress Helena and Macarius, Patriarch of Jerusalem—an event which convulsed Christendom, and which is still commemorated by the Christian Church on May 3—the feast of the 'Invention of the Cross,' as it is called in the kalendar of our Book of Common Prayer.

The Holy Rood remained entire until A.D. 636, when, to provide against the possible calamity of its total destruction by the infidels, it was decided to divide it into nineteen portions. This was done, and the parts were distributed in the following proportion:

Constantinople . . . 3			Jerusalem 4	
Cyprus 2			Georgia 2	
Antioch 3			Alexandria 1	
Crete 1			Ascalon 1	
Edessa 1			Damascus . . . 1	

Rohault de Fleury calculates that the total volume of the Wood of the Cross was somewhere about 178,000,000 cubic millimetres. He has made a careful list of all the relics of the True Cross known to exist in Christendom at the present day, with their measurements, and finds the volume to be about 3,942,000 cubic millimetres, so that, as might have been expected, the greater part of the Holy Rood has disappeared. He also had the opportunity of making a microscopical

examination of different relics, and comes to the conclusion
that the Wood was either pine or something closely allied
to it.

Of places where relics of the Holy Cross have accumulated,
Mount Athos stands pre-eminent with a total volume of
878,360 cubic millimetres; then Rome with 537,587; Brussels,
516,090; Venice, 445,582; Ghent, 436,450, and Paris with
237,731. Hardly anything is left in England, and nearly all
of what exists amongst us is in the possession of members of
the Roman Church.

II.

GREEK ECCLESIASTICAL MUSIC.

The Byzantine musicians recognise eight modes, four
authentic and four *plagal.* I propose to give as specimens
melodies written in the Second Mode Plagal and the Fourth
Authentic.

The scale of the Second Mode Plagal is that used most
generally in the East, not only by the Greeks but also by
Mohammedans, nearly all the Turkish secular airs being
written within its compass. It is as follows :

Rather a trying sequence, you will say! But observe that
it is not founded upon the modern system of *octaves*, but is a
succession of similar *quints*, the final note of each being the
first of the ensuing one. Play the scale again, striking the
connecting notes twice so as to separate the quints, and you
will find the whole more tolerable to your ear.

Now for the example :

The foregoing can be played on a piano or other keyed instrument; but the next piece of music, written in the Fourth Authentic Mode, contains *quarter tones*, inadmissible in modern European music, and difficult of execution even when the sounds can be produced, as by the voice or by an instrument like the violin. This is the scale :

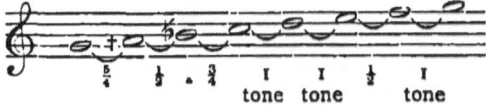

Here the signs † and ⅃ denote respectively the alteration of a quarter of a tone in ascending and a quarter of a tone in descending, or, so to speak, a *half-sharp* and a *half-flat*.

The melody I have chosen is that for one of the most solemn parts of the Oriental liturgy, the Cherubic Hymn, which is sung during the Great Entrance. This sublime composition, incapable of satisfactory translation, is said to have been added to the Constantinopolitan liturgy in the sixth century; the music, as given below, is probably coeval with the words. I originally intended to give the melody of Φῶς ἱλαρὸν, 'Hail Gladdening Light,' the evening hymn of the Eastern Church, as a specimen of a piece of music reputed to be ancient in the fourth century, but the composition was too long for this appendix. The music of the Cherubic Hymn, being very typical, very solemn, and of considerable antiquity, may be considered a fair substitute.

This is only the first portion of the hymn.   The following
is the translation of the whole, an asterisk being placed at the
end of our extract:

*Let us who mystically represent the Cherubim, and to the
quickening* Trinity sing the Trisagion, lay by at this time all
worldly cares, that we may receive the King of Glory, invisibly
attended by the Angelic Orders.   Alleluya, Alleluya, Alleluya.*

The Greek notation is quite different from the modern Western ; there is no stave, the musical sounds being represented by peculiar marks and accents placed over the words. I am indebted to the kindness of Monsieur L.-A. Bourgault-Ducoudray for the examples transposed into European notation, partly by the aid of the signs of which this French musician was, I believe, the inventor. Those who wish to pursue the study of Eastern music will do well to consult his *Etudes sur la Musique Ecclésiastique Grecque*, Hachette et Cie, Paris, 1877, a work which contains many other examples of the different Byzantine modes.

PRINTED BY
SPOTTISWOODE AND CO., NEW-STREET SQUARE
LONDON

E E

Map of
MOUNT ATHOS

BAY OF ERISSO

GULF OF THE HOLY MOUNTAIN

English Miles

Boundaries thus
Priories "
Author's Route "

Mulari Id

C. Pinay

Caterri

Kaphigmenou

From Cavalla

To St Nicholas

GULF OF SALONICA

Chalcidice
Salonica

London: Longmans & Co.

A Classified Catalogue

OF WORKS IN

GENERAL LITERATURE

PUBLISHED BY

LONGMANS, GREEN, & CO.

39 PATERNOSTER ROW, LONDON, E.C.

91 AND 93 FIFTH AVENUE, NEW YORK, AND 32 HORNBY ROAD, BOMBAY.

CONTENTS.

	PAGE
BADMINTON LIBRARY (THE)	12
BIOGRAPHY, PERSONAL MEMOIRS, &c.	9
CHILDREN'S BOOKS	32
CLASSICAL LITERATURE, TRANSLATIONS, ETC.	22
COOKERY, DOMESTIC MANAGEMENT, &c.	36
EVOLUTION, ANTHROPOLOGY, &c.	21
FICTION, HUMOUR, &c.	25
FUR, FEATHER AND FIN SERIES	15
FINE ARTS (THE) AND MUSIC	36
HISTORY, POLITICS, POLITY, POLITICAL MEMOIRS, &c.	3
LANGUAGE, HISTORY AND SCIENCE OF	20
LOGIC, RHETORIC, PSYCHOLOGY, &c.	17
MENTAL, MORAL, AND POLITICAL PHILOSOPHY	17
MISCELLANEOUS AND CRITICAL WORKS	38
POETRY AND THE DRAMA	23
POLITICAL ECONOMY AND ECONOMICS	20
POPULAR SCIENCE	30
RELIGION, THE SCIENCE OF	21
SILVER LIBRARY (THE)	33
SPORT AND PASTIME	12
STONYHURST PHILOSOPHICAL SERIES	19
TRAVEL AND ADVENTURE, THE COLONIES, &c.	11
WORKS OF REFERENCE	31

INDEX OF AUTHORS AND EDITORS.

	Page		Page		Page		Page
Abbott (Evelyn)	3, 22	Baring-Gould (Rev. S.)	21, 38	Butler (E. A.)	30	Dale (L.)	4
—— (J. H. M.)	3	Barnett (S. A. and H.)	20	Cameron of Lochiel	15	—— (T. F.)	14
—— (T. K.)	17, 18	Baynes (T. S.)	38	Campbell(Rev.Lewis)	21,22	Dallinger (F. W.)	5
—— (E. A.)	17	Beaconsfield (Earl of)	25	Chasseloup - Laubat (Marquis de)	13	Dauglish (M. G.)	9
Acland (A. H. D.)	3	Beaufort (Duke of)	13, 14	Chesney (Sir G.)	3	Davenport (A.)	25
Acton (Eliza)	39	Becker (W. A.)	22	Childe-Pemberton(W.S.)	9	Davidson (A. M. C.)	22
Adelborg (O.)	32	Beesly (A. H.)	9	Chisholm (G. C.)	31	—— (W. L.)	17, 20, 21
Æschylus	22	Bell (Mrs. Hugh)	14	Cholmondeley-Pennell (H.)	13	Davies (J. F.)	22
Ainger (A. C.)	14	Bent (J. Theodore)	11	Christie (R. C.)	38	Dent (C. T.)	14
Albemarle (Earl of)	13	Besant (Sir Walter)	3	Churchill(W. Spencer)	4, 25	De Salis (Mrs.)	36
Alcock (C. W.)	15	Bickerdyke (J.)	14, 15	Cicero	22	De Tocqueville (A.)	4
Allen (Grant)	30	Bird (G.)	23	Clarke (Rev. R. F.)	19	Devas (C. S.)	19, 20
Allgood (G.)	3	Blackburne (J. H.)	15	Climenson (E. J.)	10	Dickinson (G. L.)	4
Alverstone (Lord)	15	Bland(Mrs. Hubert)	24	Clodd (Edward)	21, 30	—— (W. H.)	38
Angwin (M. C.)	36	Blount (Sir E.)	9	Clutterbuck (W. J.)	12	Dougall (L.)	25
Anstey (F.)	25	Boase (Rev. C. W.)	6	Colenso (R. J.)	36	Dowden (E.)	40
Aristophanes	22	Boedder (Rev. B.)	19	Conington (John)	23	Doyle (Sir A. Conan)	25
Aristotle	17	Bonnell (H. H.)	38	Conway (Sir W. M)	14	Du Bois (W. E. B.)	5
Armstrong (W.)	13	Booth (A. J.)	38	Conybeare (Rev.W. J.) & Howson (Dean)		Dufferin (Marquis of)	14
Arnold (Sir Edwin)	11, 23	Bottome (P.)	25	Coolidge (W. A. B.)	11	Dunbar (Mary F.)	25
—— (Dr. T.)	3	Bowen (W. E.)	9	Corbett (Julian S.)	4	Dyson (E.)	26
Ashbourne (Lord)	3	Brassey (Lady)	11			Ebrington (Viscount)	15
Ashby (H.)	36	—— (Lord)	14			Ellis (J. H.)	15
Ashley (W. J.)	3, 20	Bright (Rev. J. F.)	3			—— (R. L.)	17
Avebury (Lord)	21						

Page

Frost (G.) - - - 38
Froude (James A.) 4,9,11,26
Fuller (F. W.) - - 5
Furneaux (W.) - - 30

Gardiner (Samuel R.) 5
Gathorne-Hardy (Hon. A. E.) - - 15, 16
Geikie (Rev. Cunningham) - - 38
Gibbons (J. S.) - 15
Gibson (C. H.) - 17
Gleig (Rev. G. R.) - 10
Gore-Booth (Sir H. W.) 14
Graham (A.) - - 5
—— (P. A.) - - 15, 16
—— (G. F.) - - 20
Granby (Marquess of) 15
Grant (Sir A.) - 17
Graves (R. P.) - - 9
Green (T. Hill) - 17, 18
Greene (E. B.) - - 5
Greville (C. C. F.) - 5
Grose (T. H.) - - 18
Gross (C.) - - 5
Grove (F. C.) - 13
—— (Lady) - 11
—— (Mrs. Lilly) - 13
Guiney (L. I.) - - 9
Gurdon (Lady Camilla) 26
Gurnhill (J.) - - 18
Gwilt (J.) - - 31

Haggard (H. Rider) 11, 26, 27, 38
Hake (O.) - - - 14
Halliwell-Phillipps (J.) 10
Hamilton (Col. H. B.) 5
Hamlin (A. D. F.) - 36
Harding (S. B.) - 5
Harmsworth (A. C.) 13, 14
Harte (Bret) - 27
Harting (J. E.) - 15
Hartwig (G.) - - 30
Hassall (A.) - - 8
Haweis (H. R.) - 9, 36
Head (Mrs.) - - 37
Heath (D. D.) - 17
Heathcote (J. M.) - 14
—— (C. G.) - 14
—— (N.) - - 11
Helmholtz (Hermann von) - - 30
Henderson (Lieut.-Col. G. F. R.) - 5
Henry (W.) - - 14
Henty (G. A.) - - 32
Herbert (Col. Kenney) 15
Higgins (Mrs. N.) - 9
Hill (Mabel) - - 5
Hillier (G. Lacy) - 13
Hime (H. W. L.) - 22
Hodgson (Shadworth) 18
Hoenig (F.) - - 38
Hogan (J. F.) - - 9
Holmes (R. R.) - - 4
Homer - - 22
Hope (Anthony) - 27
Horace - - 22
Houston (D. F.) - 5
Howard (Lady Mabel) 27
Howitt (W.) - - 11
Hudson (W. H.) - 30
Huish (M. B.) - 37
Hullah (J.) - - 37
Hume (David) - 18
—— (M. A. S.) - 4
Hunt (Rev. W.) - 6
Hunter (Sir W.) - 4
Hutchinson (Horace G.) 13, 16, 27, 38
Ingelow (Jean) - 23
Ingram (T. D.) - 6

James (W.) - 18, 21
Jameson (Mrs. Anna) 37
Jefferies (Richard) - 38
Jekyll (Gertrude) - 38
Jerome (Jerome K.) - 27
Johnson (J. & J. H.) 39
Jones (H. Bence) - 31
Joyce (P. W.) - 6, 27, 39
Justinian - - 18

Kant (I.) - - 18
Kaye (Sir J. W.) - 6

Page

Keary (C. F.) - - 23
Kelly (E.) - - 18
Kent (C. B. R.) - 6
Kerr (Rev. J.) - 14
Kielmansegge (F.) - 9
Killick (Rev. A. H.) - 18
Kitchin (Dr. G. W.) - 6
Knight (E. F.) - 11, 14
Köstlin (J.) - - 10
Kristeller (P.) - - 37

Ladd (G. T.) - - 18
Lang (Andrew) 6, 14, 16, 21, 22, 23, 27, 32, 39
Lapsley (G. T.) - 5
Lascelles (Hon. G.) 13, 15
Laurie (S. S.) - - 6
Lawley (Hon. F.) - 14
Lawrence (F. W.) - 20
Lear (H. L. Sidney) - 36
Lecky (W. E. H.) 6, 18, 23
Lees (J. A.) - - 12
Leighton (J. A.) - 21
Leslie (T. E. Cliffe) - 20
Lieven (Princess) - 16
Lillie (A.) - - 16
Lindley (J.) - - 31
Locock (C. D.) - 16
Lodge (H. C.) - - 6
Loftie (Rev. W. J.) - 6
Longman (C. J.) - 12, 16
—— (F. W.) - 16
—— (G. H.) - 12, 15
—— (Mrs. C. J.) - 37
Lowell (A. L.) - - 6
Lucian - - 22
Lutoslawski (W.) - 18
Lyall (Edna) - 27, 32
Lynch (G.) - - 6
—— (H. F. B.) - 12
Lyttelton (Hon. R. H.) 13
—— (Hon. A.) - 14
Lytton (Earl of) - 24

Macaulay (Lord) 6, 7, 10, 24
Macdonald (Dr. G.) - 24
Macfarren (Sir G. A.) 37
Mackail (J. W.) - 24
Mackenzie (C. G.) - 16
Mackinnon (J.) - 7
Macleod (H. D.) - 20
Macpherson (Rev. H. A.) 15
Madden (D. H.) - 16
Magnússon (E.) - 28
Maher (Rev. M.) - 19
Mallet (B.) - - 7
Malleson (Col. G. B.) 6
Marchment (A. W.) - 27
Marshman (J. C.) - 9
Maryon (M.) - - 39
Mason (A. E. W.) - 27
Maskelyne (J. N.) - 16
Matthews (B.) - 39
Maunder (S.) - - 31
Max Müller (F.) - 10, 18, 20, 21, 22, 27, 39
May (Sir T. Erskine) 7
McFerran (J.) - - 14
Meade (L. T.) - 32
Mecredy (R. J.) - 13
Melville (G. J. Whyte) 27
Merivale (Dean) - 7
Merriman (H. S.) - 27
Mill (John Stuart) - 18, 20
Millais (J. G.) - 16, 30
Milner (G.) - - 40
Mitchell (E. B.) - 13
Monck (W. H. S.) - 19
Montague (F. C.) - 7
Moore (T.) - - 31
—— (Rev. Edward) - 17
Morgan (C. Lloyd) - 30
Morris (Mowbray) - 13
—— (W.) - 22, 23, 24, 27, 28, 37, 40
Mulhall (M. G.) - 20
Murray (Hilda) - 33

Nansen (F.) - - 12
Nash (V.) - - 7
Nesbit (E.) - - 24
Nettleship (R. L.) - 17
Newman (Cardinal) - 28
Nichols (F. M.) - 9
Oakesmith (J.) - 22

Page

Ogilvie (R.) - - 22
Oldfield (Hon. Mrs.) 9
Onslow (Earl of) - 14
Osbourne (L.) - 28

Packard (A. S.) - 21
Paget (Sir J.) - 10
Park (W.) - - 16
Parker (B.) - - 40
Payne-Gallwey (Sir R.) - 14, 16
Pearse (H. H. S.) - 6
Pearson (C. H.) - 10
Peek (Hedley) - 14
Pemberton (W. S. Childe-) - 9
Pembroke (Earl of) - 14
Pennant (C. D.) - 15
Penrose (H. H.) - 33
Phillipps-Wolley (C.) 12, 28
Pierce (A. H.) - 19
Pitman (C. M.) - 14
Pleydell-Bouverie (E. O.) 14
Pole (W.) - - 17
Pollock (W. H.) - 13, 40
Poole (W. H. and Mrs.) 36
Poore (G. V.) - 40
Pope (W. H.) - 15
Powell (E.) - - 7
Powys (Mrs. P. L.) - 9
Praeger (S. Rosamond) 33
Prevost (C.) - - 13
Pritchett (R. T.) - 14
Proctor (R. A.) - 17, 30

Raine (Rev. James) - 6
Ramal (W.) - - 24
Ramsay (C. F.) - 7
Randolph (C. F.) - 7
Rankin (R.) - - 8, 25
Ransome (Cyril) - 3, 8
Reid (S. J.) - - 9
Rhoades (J.) - - 23
Rice (S. P.) - - 12
Rich (A.) - - 23
Richardson (C.) - 13, 15
Richmond (Ennis) - 19
Rickaby (Rev. John) 19
—— (Rev. Joseph) 19
Ridley (Lady Alice) 28
Riley (J. W.) - 24
Roberts (E. P.) - 33
Robertson (W. G.) - 37
Roget (Peter M.) - 20, 31
Rolls (Hon. C. S.) - 13
Romanes (G. J.) 10, 19, 21, 24
—— (Mrs. G. J.) 10
Ronalds (A.) - - 17
Roosevelt (T.) - 6
Ross (Martin) - 28
Rossetti (Maria Francesca) - 40
Rotheram (M. A.) - 36
Rowe (R. P. P.) - 14
Russell (Lady) - 9

Saintsbury (G.) - 15
Salomons (Sir D.) - 13
Sandars (T. C.) - 18
Sanders (E. K.) - 9
Savage-Armstrong (G. F.) 25
Scott (F. J.) - - 37
Scott-Montagu (Hon. J.) - 13
Seebohm (F.) - 8, 10
Selous (F. C.) - 12, 17
Senior (W.) - 14, 15
Seth-Smith (C. E.) - 14
Seton-Karr - - 8
Sewell (Elizabeth M.) 27
Shadwell (A.) - 40
Shakespeare - 27
Shand (A. I.) - 15
Shaw (W. A.) - 8
Shearman (M.) - 12, 13
Sheehan (P. A.) - 28
Sheppard (E.) - 8
Sinclair (A.) - 14
Skrine (C. F. H.) - 9
Smith (C. Fell) - 10
—— (R. Bosworth) - 8
—— (T. C.) - 5
Smith (W. P. Haskett) 12
Somerville (E.) - 28
Sophocles - - 23
Soulsby (Lucy H.) - 40

Page

Southey (R.) - - 40
Spedding (J.) - 9, 17
Spender (A. E.) - 12
Stanley (Bishop) - 31
Stebbing (W.) - 28
Steel (A. G.) - 13
Stephen (Leslie) - 12
Stephens (H. Morse) 8
Sternberg (Count Adalbert) - 8
Stevens (R. W.) - 40
Stevenson (R. L.) 25, 28, 39
Storr (F.) - - 17
Stuart-Wortley (A. J.) 15
Stubbs (J. W.) - 8
—— (W.) - 8
Suffolk & Berkshire (Earl of) - 14
Sullivan (Sir E.) - 14
Sully (James) - 19
Sutherland (A. and G.) 8
—— (Alex.) - 19, 40
—— (G.) - 40
Suttner (B. von) - 29
Swan (M.) - 29
Swinburne (A. J.) - 19
Symes (J. E.) - 20

Tait (J.) - - 7
Tallentyre (S. G.) - 10
Tappan (E. M.) - 33
Taylor (Col. Meadows) 8
Tebbutt (C. G.) - 14
Terry (C. S.) - 10
Thomas (J. W.) - 19
Thomson (H. C.)
Thornhill (W. J.) - 23
Thornton (T. H.) - 10
Thuillier (H. F.) - 40
Todd (A.) - - 8
Tout (T. F.) - - 7
Toynbee (A.) - 20
Trevelyan (Sir G. O.) 6, 7, 8, 9, 10
—— (G. M.) - 7, 8
Trollope (Anthony)- 29
Turner (H. G.) - 40
Tyndall (J.) - 9, 12
Tyrrell (R. Y.) - 22, 23

Unwin (R.) - - 40
Upton (F. K. and Bertha) 33

Van Dyke (J. C.) - 37
Vanderpoel (E. N.) - 37
'Veritas' - - 5
Virgil - - 23

Wagner (R.) - - 25
Wakeman (H. O.) - 8
Walford (L. B.) - 29
Wallas (Graham) - 10
—— (Mrs. Graham) - 32
Walpole (Sir Spencer) 8, 10
—— (Horace) - 10
Walrond (Col. H.) - 12
Walsingham (Lord) - 14
Ward (Mrs. W.) - 29
Warwick (Countess of) 40
Watson (A. E. T.) - 14
—— (G. L.) - 14
Weathers (J.) - 40
Webb (Mr. and Mrs. Sidney) - 20
—— (Judge T.) - 40
—— (T. E.) - 19
Weber (A.) - - 19
Weir (Capt. R.) - 14
Wellington (Duchess of) 37
Wemyss (M. C. E.) - 33
Weyman (Stanley) - 29
Whately (Archbishop) 17, 19
Whitelaw (R.) - 3
Whittall (Sir J. W.) - 40
Wilkins (G.) - 23
—— (W. H.) - 3
Willard (A. R.) - 12
Willich (C. M.) - 31
Witham (T. M.) - 14
Wood (Rev. J. G.) - 31
Wood-Martin (W. G.) 22
Wyatt (A. J.) - 24
Wylie (J. H.) - 8

Yeats (S. Levett) - 29
Yoxall (J. H.) - 29

Zeller (E.) - - 19

History, Politics, Polity, Political Memoirs, &c.

Abbott.—*A HISTORY OF GREECE.* By EVELYN ABBOTT, M.A., LL.D.

Part I.—From the Earliest Times to the Ionian Revolt. Crown 8vo., 10s. 6d.

Part II.—500-445 B.C. Crown 8vo., 10s. 6d.

Part III.—From the Peace of 445 B.C. to the Fall of the Thirty at Athens in 403 B.C. Crown 8vo., 10s. 6d.

Abbott.—*TOMMY CORNSTALK :* being Some Account of the Less Notable Features of the South African War from the Point of View of the Australian Ranks. By J. H. M. ABBOTT. Crown 8vo., 5s. net.

Acland and Ransome.—*A HANDBOOK IN OUTLINE OF THE POLITICAL HISTORY OF ENGLAND TO* 1896. Chronologically Arranged. By the Right Hon. A. H. DYKE ACLAND, and CYRIL RANSOME, M.A. Crown 8vo., 6s.

Allgood. — *CHINA WAR,* 1860 : *LETTERS AND JOURNALS.* By Major-General G. ALLGOOD, C.B., formerly Lieut. G. ALLGOOD, 1st Division China Field Force. With Maps, Plans, and Illustrations. Demy 4to. 12s. 6d. net.

Annual Register (The). A Review of Public Events at Home and Abroad, for the year 1901. 8vo., 18s.

Volumes of the *ANNUAL REGISTER* for the years 1863-1900 can still be had. 18s. each.

Arnold.—*INTRODUCTORY LECTURES ON MODERN HISTORY.* By THOMAS ARNOLD, D.D., formerly Head Master of Rugby School. 8vo., 7s. 6d.

Ashbourne.—*PITT : SOME CHAPTERS ON HIS LIFE AND TIMES.* By the Right Hon. EDWARD GIBSON, LORD ASHBOURNE, Lord Chancellor of Ireland. With 11 Portraits. 8vo., gilt top, 21s.

Ashley.—*SURVEYS, HISTORIC AND ECONOMIC :* a Volume of Essays. By W. J. ASHLEY, M.A. 8vo., 9s. net.

Bagwell.—*IRELAND UNDER THE TUDORS.* By RICHARD BAGWELL, LL.D. (3 vols.) Vols. I. and II. From the first invasion of the Northmen to the year 1578. 8vo., 32s. Vol. III. 1578-1603. 8vo., 18s.

Baillie.—*THE ORIENTAL CLUB, AND HANOVER SQUARE.* By ALEXANDER F. BAILLIE. With 6 Photogravure Portraits and 8 Full-page Illustrations. Crown 4to., 25s. net.

Besant.—*THE HISTORY OF LONDON.* By Sir WALTER BESANT. With 74 Illustrations. Crown 8vo., 1s. 9d. Or bound as a School Prize Book, gilt edges, 2s. 6d.

Bright.—*A HISTORY OF ENGLAND.* By the Rev. J. FRANCK BRIGHT, D.D.

Period I. *MEDIÆVAL MONARCHY:* A.D. 449-1485. Crown 8vo., 4s. 6d.

Period II. *PERSONAL MONARCHY.* 1485-1688. Crown 8vo., 5s.

Period III. *CONSTITUTIONAL MONARCHY*—1689-1837. Crown 8vo., 7s. 6d.

Period IV. *THE GROWTH OF DEMOCRACY.* 1837-1880. Crown 8vo., 6s.

Bruce.—*THE FORWARD POLICY AND ITS RESULTS ;* or, Thirty-five Years' Work amongst the Tribes on our North-Western Frontier of India. By RICHARD ISAAC BRUCE, C.I.E. With 28 Illustrations and a Map. 8vo., 15s. net.

Buckle.—*HISTORY OF CIVILISATION IN ENGLAND.* By HENRY THOMAS BUCKLE.

Cabinet Edition. 3 vols. Crown 8vo., 24s.
'*Silver Library* ' *Edition.* 3 vols. Crown 8vo., 10s. 6d.

Burke.—*A HISTORY OF SPAIN, FROM THE EARLIEST TIMES TO THE DEATH OF FERDINAND THE CATHOLIC.* By ULICK RALPH BURKE, M.A. Edited by MARTIN A. S. HUME. With 6 Maps. 2 vols. Crown 8vo., 16s. net.

Caroline, Queen.—*CAROLINE THE ILLUSTRIOUS, QUEEN-CONSORT OF GEORGE II. AND SOMETIME QUEEN REGENT :* a Study of Her Life and Time. By W. H. WILKINS, M.A., F.S.A., Author of ' The Love of an Uncrowned Queen '. 2 vols., 8vo., 36s.

Chesney.—*INDIAN POLITY :* a View of the System of Administration in India. B General Sir GEORGE CHESNEY, K.C.B. With Map showing all the Administrative Divisions of British India. 8vo., 21s.

History, Politics, Polity, Political Memoirs, &c.—*continued.*

Churchill (WINSTON SPENCER, M.P.).

THE RIVER WAR: an Historical Account of the Reconquest of the Soudan. Edited by Colonel F. RHODES, D.S.O. With 34 Maps and Plans, and 51 Illustrations from Drawings by ANGUS MCNEILL. Also with 7 Photogravure Portraits of Generals, etc. 2 vols. Medium 8vo., 36s.

NEW, REVISED AND CHEAPER EDITION. In One Volume. With Photogravure Portrait of Viscount Kitchener of Khartoum, and 22 Maps and Plans. 8vo., 10s. 6d. net.

THE STORY OF THE MALAKAND FIELD FORCE, 1897. With 6 Maps and Plans. Crown 8vo., 3s. 6d.

LONDON TO LADYSMITH VIÂ PRETORIA. Crown 8vo., 6s.

IAN HAMILTON'S MARCH. With Portrait of Major-General Sir Ian Hamilton, and 10 Maps and Plans. Crown 8vo., 6s.

Corbett (JULIAN S.).

DRAKE AND THE TUDOR NAVY, with a History of the Rise of England as a Maritime Power. With Portraits, Illustrations and Maps. 2 vols. Crown 8vo., 16s.

THE SUCCESSORS OF DRAKE. With 4 Portraits (2 Photogravures) and 12 Maps and Plans. 8vo., 21s.

Creighton (M., D.D., Late Lord Bishop of London).

A HISTORY OF THE PAPACY FROM THE GREAT SCHISM TO THE SACK OF ROME, 1378-1527. 6 vols. Cr. 8vo., 5s. net each.

QUEEN ELIZABETH. With Portrait. Crown 8vo., 5s. net.

HISTORICAL ESSAYS AND REVIEWS. Edited by LOUISE CREIGHTON. Crown 8vo., 5s. net.

Dale.—*THE PRINCIPLES OF ENGLISH CONSTITUTIONAL HISTORY.* By LUCY DALE, late Scholar of Somerville College, Oxford. Crown 8vo., 6s.

De Tocqueville.—*DEMOCRACY IN AMERICA.* By ALEXIS DE TOCQUEVILLE. Translated by HENRY REEVE, C.B., D.C.L. 2 vols. Crown 8vo., 16s.

Dickinson.—*THE DEVELOPMENT OF PARLIAMENT DURING THE NINETEENTH CENTURY.* By G. LOWES DICKINSON, M.A. 8vo., 7s. 6d.

Falkiner.—*STUDIES IN IRISH HISTORY AND BIOGRAPHY,* Mainly of the Eighteenth Century. By C. LITTON FALKINER. 8vo., 12s. 6d. net.

Fitzmaurice. — *CHARLES WILLIAM FERDINAND, DUKE OF BRUNSWICK:* an Historical Study. By Lord EDMUND FITZMAURICE. With Map and 2 Portraits. 8vo., 6s. net.

Froude (JAMES A.).

THE HISTORY OF ENGLAND, from the Fall of Wolsey to the Defeat of the Spanish Armada. 12 vols. Crown 8vo., 3s. 6d. each.

THE DIVORCE OF CATHERINE OF ARAGON. Crown 8vo., 3s. 6d.

THE SPANISH STORY OF THE ARMADA, and other Essays. Cr. 8vo., 3s. 6d.

THE ENGLISH IN IRELAND IN THE EIGHTEENTH CENTURY. 3 vols. Cr. 8vo., 10s. 6d.

ENGLISH SEAMEN IN THE SIXTEENTH CENTURY.
Cabinet Edition. Crown 8vo., 6s.
Illustrated Edition. With 5 Photogravure Plates and 16 other Illustrations. Large Cr. 8vo., gilt top, 6s. net.
' Silver Library ' Edition. Cr. 8vo., 3s. 6d.

THE COUNCIL OF TRENT. Crown 8vo., 3s. 6d.

SHORT STUDIES ON GREAT SUBJECTS.
Cabinet Edition. 4 vols. 24s.
' Silver Library ' Edition. 4 vols. Crown 8vo., 3s. 6d. each.

CÆSAR: a Sketch. Cr. 8vo., 3s. 6d.

SELECTIONS FROM THE WRITINGS OF JAMES ANTHONY FROUDE. Edited by P. S. ALLEN, M.A. Crown 8vo., 3s. 6d.

History, Politics, Polity, Political Memoirs, &c.—*continued.*

Fuller.—*Egypt and the Hinterland.* By Frederic W. Fuller. With Frontispiece and Map of Egypt and the Sudan. 8vo., 10s. 6d. net.

Gardiner (Samuel Rawson, D.C.L., LL.D.).

History of England, from the Accession of James I. to the Outbreak of the Civil War, 1603-1642. 10 vols. Crown 8vo., 5s. net each.

A History of the Great Civil War, 1642-1649. 4 vols. Cr. 8vo., 5s. net each.

A History of the Commonwealth and the Protectorate. 1649-1660. Vol. I. 1649-1651. With 14 Maps. 8vo., 21s. Vol. II. 1651-1654. With 7 Maps. 8vo., 21s. Vol. III. 1654-1656. With 6 Maps. 8vo., 21s.

The Student's History of England. With 378 Illustrations. Crown 8vo., gilt top, 12s.

Also in Three Volumes, price 4s. each.

What Gunpowder Plot Was. With 8 Illustrations. Crown 8vo., 5s.

Cromwell's Place in History. Founded on Six Lectures delivered in the University of Oxford. Cr. 8vo., 3s. 6d.

Oliver Cromwell. With Frontispiece. Crown 8vo., 5s. net.

German Empire (The) of To-day : Outlines of its Formation and Development. By 'Veritas'. Crown 8vo., 6s. net.

Graham.—*Roman Africa* : an Outline of the History of the Roman Occupation of North Africa, based chiefly upon Inscriptions and Monumental Remains in that Country. By Alexander Graham, F.S.A., F.R.I.B.A. With 30 reproductions of Original Drawings by the Author, and 2 Maps. 8vo., 16s. net.

Greville.—*A Journal of the Reigns of King George IV., King William IV., and Queen Victoria.* By Charles C. F. Greville, formerly Clerk of the Council. 8 vols. Crown 8vo., 3s. 6d. each.

Gross.—*The Sources and Literature of English History, from the Earliest Times to about* 1485. By Charles Gross, Ph.D. 8vo., 18s. net.

Hamilton.—*Historical Record of the 14th (King's) Hussars*, from A.D. 1715 to A.D. 1900. By Colonel Henry Blackburne Hamilton, M.A., Christ Church, Oxford ; late Commanding the Regiment. With 15 Coloured Plates, 35 Portraits, etc., in Photogravure, and 10 Maps and Plans. Crown 4to., gilt edges, 42s. net.

HARVARD HISTORICAL STUDIES.

The Suppression of the African Slave Trade to the United States of America, 1638-1870. By W. E. B. Du Bois, Ph.D. 8vo., 7s. 6d.

The Contest over the Ratificaton of the Federal Constitution in Massachusetts. By S. B. Harding, A.M. 8vo., 6s.

A Critical Study of Nullification in South Carolina. By D. F. Houston, A.M. 8vo., 6s.

Nominations for Elective Office in the United States. By Frederick W. Dallinger, A.M. 8vo., 7s. 6d.

A Bibliography of British Municipal History, including Gilds and Parliamentary Representation. By Charles Gross, Ph.D. 8vo., 12s.

The Liberty and Free Soil Parties in the North West. By Theodore C. Smith, Ph.D. 8vo., 7s. 6d.

The Provincial Governor in the English Colonies of North America. By Evarts Boutell Greene. 8vo., 7s. 6d.

The County Palatine of Durham : a Study in Constitutional History. By Gaillard Thomas Lapsley, Ph.D. 8vo., 10s. 6d.

The Anglican Episcopate and the American Colonies. By Arthur Lyon Cross, Ph.D., Instructor in History in the University of Michigan. 8vo., 10s. 6d,

Hill.—*Liberty Documents.* With Contemporary Exposition and Critical Comments drawn from various Writers. Selected and Prepared by Mabel Hill. Edited with an Introduction by Albert Bushnell Hart, Ph.D. Large Crown 8vo., 7s. 6d. net.

History, Politics, Polity, Political Memoirs, &c.—*continued*.

Historic Towns.—Edited by E. A. FREEMAN, D.C.L., and Rev. WILLIAM HUNT, M.A. With Maps and Plans. Crown 8vo., 3s. 6d. each.

Bristol. By Rev. W. Hunt.
Carlisle. By Mandell Creighton, D.D.
Cinque Ports. By Montagu Burrows.
Colchester. By Rev. E. L. Cutts.
Exeter. By E. A. Freeman.
London. By Rev. W. J. Loftie.
Oxford. By Rev. C. W. Boase.
Winchester. By G. W. Kitchin, D.D.
York. By Rev. James Raine.
New York. By Theodore Roosevelt.
Boston (U.S.) By Henry Cabot Lodge.

Hunter.—*A HISTORY OF BRITISH INDIA.* By Sir WILLIAM WILSON HUNTER, K.C.S.I., M.A., LL.D. Vol. I.—Introductory to the Overthrow of the English in the Spice Archipelago, 1623. With 4 Maps. 8vo., 18s. Vol. II.—To the Union of the Old and New Companies under the Earl of Godolphin's Award, 1708. 8vo., 16s.

Ingram. — *A CRITICAL EXAMINATION OF IRISH HISTORY.* From the Elizabethan Conquest to the Legislative Union of 1800. By T. DUNBAR INGRAM, LL.D. 2 vols. 8vo., 24s.

Joyce.—*A SHORT HISTORY OF IRELAND,* from the Earliest Times to 1603. By P. W. JOYCE, LL.D. Crown 8vo., 10s. 6d.

Kaye and Malleson.—*HISTORY OF THE INDIAN MUTINY,* 1857-1858. By Sir JOHN W. KAYE and Colonel G. B. MALLESON. With Analytical Index and Maps and Plans. 6 vols. Crown 8vo., 3s. 6d. each.

Kent.—*THE ENGLISH RADICALS:* an Historical Sketch. By C. B. ROYLANCE KENT. Crown 8vo., 7s. 6d.

Lang (ANDREW).

THE MYSTERY OF MARY STUART. With 6 Photogravure Plates (4 Portraits) and 15 other Illustrations. 8vo., 18s. net.

JAMES THE SIXTH AND THE GOWRIE MYSTERY. With Gowrie's Coat of Arms in colour, 2 Photogravure Portraits and other Illustrations. 8vo., 12s. 6d. net.

Laurie.—*HISTORICAL SURVEY OF PRE-CHRISTIAN EDUCATION.* By S. S. LAURIE, A.M., LL.D. Crown 8vo., 7s. 6d.

Lecky (The Rt. Hon. WILLIAM E. H.)

HISTORY OF ENGLAND IN THE EIGHTEENTH CENTURY.

Library Edition. 8 vols. 8vo. Vols. I. and II., 1700-1760, 36s.; Vols. III. and IV., 1760-1784, 36s.; Vols. V. and VI., 1784-1793, 36s.; Vols. VII. and VIII., 1793-1800, 36s.

Cabinet Edition. ENGLAND. 7 vols. Crown 8vo., 5s. net each. IRELAND. 5 vols. Crown 8vo., 5s. net each.

HISTORY OF EUROPEAN MORALS FROM AUGUSTUS TO CHARLEMAGNE. 2 vols. Crown 8vo., 10s. net.

HISTORY OF THE RISE AND INFLUENCE OF THE SPIRIT OF RATIONALISM IN EUROPE. 2 vols. Crown 8vo., 10s. net.

DEMOCRACY AND LIBERTY.
Library Edition. 2 vols. 8vo., 36s.
Cabinet Edition. 2 vols. Cr. 8vo., 10s. net.

Lowell.—*GOVERNMENTS AND PARTIES IN CONTINENTAL EUROPE.* By A. LAWRENCE LOWELL. 2 vols. 8vo., 21s.

Lumsden's Horse, Records of.—Edited by H. H. S. PEARSE. With a Map, and numerous Portraits and Illustrations in the Text. 4to.

Lynch.—*THE WAR OF THE CIVILISATIONS: BEING A RECORD OF 'A FOREIGN DEVIL'S' EXPERIENCES WITH THE ALLIES IN CHINA.* By GEORGE LYNCH, Special Correspondent of the 'Sphere,' etc. With Portrait and 21 Illustrations. Crown 8vo., 6s. net.

Macaulay (Lord).

THE LIFE AND WORKS OF LORD MACAULAY.
'Edinburgh' Edition. 10 vols. 8vo., 6s. each.
Vols. I.-IV. HISTORY OF ENGLAND.
Vols. V.-VII. ESSAYS, BIOGRAPHIES, INDIAN PENAL CODE, CONTRIBUTIONS TO KNIGHT'S 'QUARTERLY MAGAZINE'.
Vol. VIII. SPEECHES, LAYS OF ANCIENT ROME, MISCELLANEOUS POEMS.
Vols. IX. and X. THE LIFE AND LETTERS OF LORD MACAULAY. By Sir G. O. TREVELYAN, Bart.

History, Politics, Polity, Political Memoirs, &c.—*continued.*

Macaulay (Lord)—*continued.*

THE WORKS.

'*Albany' Edition.* With 12 Portraits. 12 vols. Large Crown 8vo., 3s. 6d. each.

Vols. I.-VI. *HISTORY OF ENGLAND, FROM THE ACCESSION OF JAMES THE SECOND.*

Vols. VII.-X. *ESSAYS AND BIOGRAPHIES.*

Vols. XI.-XII. *SPEECHES, LAYS OF ANCIENT ROME, ETC., AND INDEX.*

Cabinet Edition. 16 vols. Post 8vo., £4 16s.

Library Edition. 5 vols. 8vo., £4.

HISTORY OF ENGLAND FROM THE ACCESSION OF JAMES THE SECOND.

Popular Edition. 2 vols. Cr. 8vo., 5s.
Student's Edition. 2 vols. Cr. 8vo., 12s.
People's Edition. 4 vols. Cr. 8vo., 16s.
'*Albany' Edition.* With 6 Portraits. 6 vols. Large Crown 8vo., 3s. 6d. each.
Cabinet Edition. 8 vols. Post 8vo., 48s.
'*Edinburgh' Edition.* 4 vols. 8vo., 6s. each.

CRITICAL AND HISTORICAL ESSAYS, WITH LAYS OF ANCIENT ROME, etc., in 1 volume.

Popular Edition. Crown 8vo., 2s. 6d.
'*Silver Library' Edition.* With Portrait and 4 Illustrations to the 'Lays'. Cr. 8vo., 3s. 6d.

CRITICAL AND HISTORICAL ESSAYS.

Student's Edition. 1 vol. Cr. 8vo., 6s.
People's Edition. 2 vols. Cr. 8vo., 8s.
'*Trevelyan' Edition.* 2 vols. Cr. 8vo., 9s.
Cabinet Edition. 4 vols. Post 8vo., 24s.
'*Edinburgh' Edition.* 3 vols. 8vo., 6s. each.
Library Edition. 3 vols. 8vo., 36s.

ESSAYS, which may be had separately, sewed, 6d. each; cloth, 1s. each.

Addison and Walpole.	Frederick the Great.
Croker's Boswell's Johnson.	Ranke and Gladstone.
Hallam's Constitutional History.	Lord Bacon.
	Lord Clive.
Warren Hastings.	Lord Byron, and The
The Earl of Chatham (Two Essays).	Comic Dramatists of the Restoration.

MISCELLANEOUS WRITINGS, SPEECHES AND POEMS.

Popular Edition. Crown 8vo., 2s. 6d.
Cabinet Edition. 4 vols. Post 8vo., 24s.

SELECTIONS FROM THE WRITINGS OF LORD MACAULAY. Edited, with Occasional Notes, by the Right Hon. Sir G. O. TREVELYAN, Bart. Crown 8vo., 6s.

Mackinnon (JAMES, Ph.D.).

THE HISTORY OF EDWARD THE THIRD. 8vo., 18s.

THE GROWTH AND DECLINE OF THE FRENCH MONARCHY. 8vo., 21s. net.

Mallet.—*MALLET DU PAN AND THE FRENCH REVOLUTION.* By BERNARD MALLET. With Photogravure Portrait. 8vo., 12s. 6d.

May.—*THE CONSTITUTIONAL HISTORY OF ENGLAND* since the Accession of George III. 1760-1870. By Sir THOMAS ERSKINE MAY, K.C.B. (Lord Farnborough). 3 vols. Cr. 8vo., 18s.

Merivale (CHARLES, D.D.).

HISTORY OF THE ROMANS UNDER THE EMPIRE. 8 vols. Crown 8vo., 3s. 6d. each.

THE FALL OF THE ROMAN REPUBLIC: a Short History of the Last Century of the Commonwealth. 12mo., 7s. 6d.

GENERAL HISTORY OF ROME, from the Foundation of the City to the Fall of Augustulus, B.C. 753-A.D. 476. With 5 Maps. Crown 8vo., 7s. 6d.

Montague. — *THE ELEMENTS OF ENGLISH CONSTITUTIONAL HISTORY.* By F. C. MONTAGUE, M.A. Crown 8vo., 3s. 6d.

Nash.—*THE GREAT FAMINE AND ITS CAUSES.* By VAUGHAN NASH. With 8 Illustrations from Photographs by the Author, and a Map of India showing the Famine Area. Crown 8vo., 6s.

Owens College Essays.—Edited by T. F. TOUT, M.A., Professor of History in the Owens College, Victoria University, and JAMES TAIT, M.A., Assistant Lecturer in History. With 4 Maps. 8vo., 12s. 6d. net.

Powell and Trevelyan. — *THE PEASANTS' RISING AND THE LOLLARDS:* a Collection of Unpublished Documents. Edited by EDGAR POWELL and G. M. TREVELYAN. 8vo., 6s. net.

Randolph.—*THE LAW AND POLICY OF ANNEXATION,* with Special Reference to the Philippines; together with Observations on the Status of Cuba. By CARMAN F RANDOLPH. 8vo., 9s. net.

History, Politics, Polity, Political Memoirs, &c.—*continued.*

Rankin (REGINALD).

THE MARQUIS D'ARGENSON ; AND RICHARD THE SECOND. 8vo., 10s. 6d. net.

A SUBALTERN'S LETTERS TO HIS WIFE. (The Boer War.) Crown 8vo., 3s. 6d.

Ransome.—*THE RISE OF CONSTITUTIONAL GOVERNMENT IN ENGLAND.* By CYRIL RANSOME, M.A. Crown 8vo., 6s.

Seebohm (FREDERIC, LL.D., F.S.A.).

THE ENGLISH VILLAGE COMMUNITY. With 13 Maps and Plates. 8vo., 16s.

TRIBAL CUSTOM IN ANGLO-SAXON LAW: being an Essay supplemental to (1) 'The English Village Community,' (2) 'The Tribal System in Wales'. 8vo., 16s.

Seton-Karr.—*THE CALL TO ARMS,* 1900-1901 ; or a Review of the Imperial Yeomanry Movement, and some subjects connected therewith. By HENRY SETON-KARR, M.P. With a Frontispiece by R. CATON-WOODVILLE. Crown 8vo., 5s. net.

Shaw.—*A HISTORY OF THE ENGLISH CHURCH DURING THE CIVIL WARS AND UNDER THE COMMONWEALTH, 1640-1660.* By WILLIAM A. SHAW, Litt.D. 2 vols. 8vo., 36s.

Sheppard. — *THE OLD ROYAL PALACE OF WHITEHALL.* By EDGAR SHEPPARD, D.D., Sub-Dean of H.M. Chapels Royal, Sub-Almoner to the King. With 6 Photogravure Plates and 33 other Illustrations. Medium 8vo., 21s. net.

Smith.—*CARTHAGE AND THE CARTHAGINIANS.* By R. BOSWORTH SMITH, M.A. With Maps, Plans, etc. Cr. 8vo., 3s. 6d.

Stephens. — *A HISTORY OF THE FRENCH REVOLUTION.* By H. MORSE STEPHENS. 8vo. Vols. I. and II. 18s. each.

Sternberg. — *MY EXPERIENCES OF THE BOER WAR.* By ADALBERT COUNT STERNBERG. With Preface by Lieut.-Col. G. F. R. HENDERSON. Crown 8vo., 5s. net.

Stubbs.—*HISTORY OF THE UNIVERSITY OF DUBLIN.* By J. W. STUBBS. 8vo., 12s. 6d.

Stubbs. — *HISTORICAL INTRODUCTIONS TO THE 'ROLLS SERIES'.* By WILLIAM STUBBS, D.D., formerly Bishop of Oxford, Regius Professor of Modern History in the University. Collected and Edited by ARTHUR HASSALL, M.A. 8vo., 12s. 6d. net.

Sutherland.—*THE HISTORY OF AUSTRALIA AND NEW ZEALAND, from 1606-1900.* By ALEXANDER SUTHERLAND, M.A., and GEORGE SUTHERLAND, M.A. Crown 8vo., 2s. 6d.

Taylor.—*A STUDENT'S MANUAL OF THE HISTORY OF INDIA.* By Colonel MEADOWS TAYLOR, C.S.I., etc. Cr. 8vo., 7s. 6d.

Thomson.—*CHINA AND THE POWERS:* a Narrative of the Outbreak of 1900. By H. C. THOMSON. With 2 Maps and 29 Illustrations. 8vo., 10s. 6d. net.

Todd. — *PARLIAMENTARY GOVERNMENT IN THE BRITISH COLONIES.* By ALPHEUS TODD, LL.D. 8vo., 30s. net.

Trevelyan.—*THE AMERICAN REVOLUTION.* Part I. 1766-1776. By Sir G. O. TREVELYAN, Bart. 8vo., 16s.

Trevelyan.—*ENGLAND IN THE AGE OF WYCLIFFE.* By GEORGE MACAULAY TREVELYAN. 8vo., 15s.

Wakeman and Hassall.—*ESSAYS INTRODUCTORY TO THE STUDY OF ENGLISH CONSTITUTIONAL HISTORY.* Edited by HENRY OFFLEY WAKEMAN, M.A., and ARTHUR HASSALL, M.A. Crown 8vo., 6s.

Walpole.—*HISTORY OF ENGLAND FROM THE CONCLUSION OF THE GREAT WAR IN 1815 TO 1858.* By Sir SPENCER WALPOLE, K.C.B. 6 vols. Cr. 8vo., 6s. each.

Wylie (JAMES HAMILTON, M.A.).

HISTORY OF ENGLAND UNDER HENRY IV. 4 vols. Crown 8vo. Vol. I., 1399-1404, 10s. 6d. Vol. II., 1405-1406, 15s. (out of print). Vol. III., 1407-1411, 15s. Vol. IV., 1411-1413, 21s.

THE COUNCIL OF CONSTANCE TO THE DEATH OF JOHN HUS. Cr. 8vo., 6s. net.

Biography, Personal Memoirs, &c.

Bacon.—*The Letters and Life of Francis Bacon, including all his Occasional Works.* Edited by James Spedding. 7 vols. 8vo., £4 4s.

Bagehot.—*Biographical Studies.* By Walter Bagehot. Crown 8vo., 3s. 6d.

Bernards (The) of Abington and Nether Winchendon: A Family History. By Mrs. Napier Higgins. 2 Vols. 8vo.

Blount. — *The Memoirs of Sir Edward Blount, K.C.B., etc.* Edited by Stuart J. Reid, Author of 'The Life and Times of Sydney Smith,' etc. With 3 Photogravure Plates. 8vo., 10s. 6d. net.

Bowen.—*Edward Bowen: a Memoir.* By the Rev. the Hon. W. E. Bowen. With Appendices, 3 Photogravure Portraits and 2 other Illustrations. 8vo., 12s. 6d. net.

Carlyle.—*Thomas Carlyle:* A History of his Life. By James Anthony Froude.

1795-1835. 2 vols. Crown 8vo., 7s.
1834-1881. 2 vols. Crown 8vo., 7s.

Crozier.—*My Inner Life:* being a Chapter in Personal Evolution and Autobiography. By John Beattie Crozier, LL.D. 8vo., 14s.

Dante.—*The Life and Works of Dante Allighieri:* being an Introduction to the Study of the 'Divina Commedia'. By the Rev. J. F. Hogan, D.D. With Portrait. 8vo., 12s. 6d.

Danton.—*Life of Danton.* By A. H. Beesly. With Portraits. Cr. 8vo., 6s.

De Bode.—*The Baroness de Bode,* 1775-1803. By William S. Childe-Pemberton. With 4 Photogravure Portraits and other Illustrations. 8vo., gilt top, 12s. 6d. net.

Erasmus.

Life and Letters of Erasmus. By James Anthony Froude. Crown 8vo., 3s. 6d.

The Epistles of Erasmus, from his Earliest Letters to his Fifty-first Year, arranged in Order of Time. English Translations, with a Commentary. By Francis Morgan Nichols. 8vo., 18s. net.

Faraday.—*Faraday as a Discoverer.* By John Tyndall. Crown 8vo., 3s. 6d.

Fénelon : his Friends and his Enemies, 1651-1715. By E. K. Sanders. With Portrait. 8vo., 10s. 6d.

Fox.—*The Early History of Charles James Fox.* By the Right Hon. Sir G. O. Trevelyan, Bart. Crown 8vo., 3s. 6d.

Froude.—*Hurrell Froude:* Some Reprints and Reprinted Comments. With a Biographical Preface by the Editor, L. I. Guiney. With Illustrations. 8vo.

Granville.—*Some Records of the Later Life of Harriet, Countess Granville.* By her Granddaughter, the Hon. Mrs. Oldfield. With 17 Portraits. 8vo., gilt top, 16s. net.

Grey. — *Memoir of Sir George Grey, Bart., G.C.B.,* 1799-1882. By Mandell Creighton, D.D., late Lord Bishop of London. With 3 Portraits. Crown 8vo., 6s. net.

Hamilton.—*Life of Sir William Hamilton.* By R. P. Graves. 8vo. 3 vols. 15s. each. Addendum. 8vo., 6d. sewed.

Harrow School Register (The), 1801-1900. Second Edition, 1901. Edited by M. G. Dauglish, Barrister-at-Law. 8vo. 15s. net.

Havelock.—*Memoirs of Sir Henry Havelock, K.C.B.* By John Clark Marshman. Crown 8vo., 3s. 6d.

Haweis.—*My Musical Life.* By the Rev. H. R. Haweis. With Portrait of Richard Wagner and 3 Illustrations. Cr. 8vo., 6s. net.

Hunter.—*The Life of Sir William Wilson Hunter, K.C.S.I., M.A., LL.D.* Author of 'A History of British India,' etc. By Francis Henry Skrine, F.S.S. With 6 Portraits (2 Photogravures) and 4 other Illustrations. 8vo., 16s. net.

Jackson.—*Stonewall Jackson and the American Civil War.* By Lieut.-Col. G. F. R. Henderson. With 2 Portraits and 33 Maps and Plans. 2 vols. Cr. 8vo., 16s. net.

Kielmansegge.—*Diary of a Journey to England in the Years 1761-1762.* By Count Frederick Kielmansegge. With 4 Illustrations. Crown 8vo. 5s. net.

Biography, Personal Memoirs, &c.—*continued.*

Leslie.—*THE LIFE AND CAMPAIGNS OF ALEXANDER LESLIE, FIRST EARL OF LEVEN.* By CHARLES SANFORD TERRY, M.A. With Maps and Plans. 8vo., 16s.

Lieven. — *LETTERS OF DOROTHEA, PRINCESS LIEVEN, DURING HER RESIDENCE IN LONDON,* 1812-1834. Edited by LIONEL G. ROBINSON. With 2 Photogravure Portraits. 8vo., 14s. net.

Luther. — *LIFE OF LUTHER.* By JULIUS KÖSTLIN. With 62 Illustrations and 4 Facsimilies of MSS. Cr. 8vo., 3s. 6d.

Macaulay.—*THE LIFE AND LETTERS OF LORD MACAULAY.* By the Right Hon. Sir G. O. TREVELYAN, Bart.
Popular Edition. 1 vol. Cr. 8vo., 2s. 6d.
Student's Edition 1 vol. Cr. 8vo., 6s.
Cabinet Edition. 2 vols. Post 8vo., 12s.
'Edinburgh' Edition. 2 vols. 8vo., 6s. each.
Library Edition. 2 vols. 8vo., 36s.

Max Müller (F.)
THE LIFE AND LETTERS OF THE RIGHT HON. FRIEDRICH MAX MÜLLER. Edited by his Wife. With Photogravure Portraits and other Illustrations. 2 vols., 8vo.

MY AUTOBIOGRAPHY: a Fragment. With 6 Portraits. 8vo., 12s. 6d.

AULD LANG SYNE. Second Series. 8vo., 10s. 6d.

CHIPS FROM A GERMAN WORKSHOP. Vol. II. Biographical Essays. Cr. 8vo., 5s.

Meade.—*GENERAL SIR RICHARD MEADE AND THE FEUDATORY STATES OF CENTRAL AND SOUTHERN INDIA.* By THOMAS HENRY THORNTON. With Portrait, Map and Illustrations. 8vo., 10s. 6d. net.

Morris. — *THE LIFE OF WILLIAM MORRIS.* By J. W. MACKAIL. With 2 Portraits and 8 other Illustrations by E. H. NEW, etc. 2 vols. Large Crown 8vo., 10s. net.

On the Banks of the Seine. By A. M. F., Authoress of 'Foreign Courts and Foreign Homes'. Crown 8vo., 6s.

Paget.—*MEMOIRS AND LETTERS OF SIR JAMES PAGET.* Edited by STEPHEN PAGET, one of his sons. With 6 Portraits (3 Photogravures) and 4 other Illustrations. 8vo., 12s. 6d. net.

Place.—*THE LIFE OF FRANCIS PLACE,* 1771-1854. By GRAHAM WALLAS, M.A. With 2 Portraits. 8vo., 12s.

Powys.—*PASSAGES FROM THE DIARIES OF MRS. PHILIP LYBBE POWYS, OF HARDWICK HOUSE, OXON.* 1756-1808. Edited by EMILY J. CLIMENSON. 8vo., gilt top, 16s.

Râmakrishna : *HIS LIFE AND SAYINGS.* By the Right Hon. F. MAX MÜLLER. Crown 8vo., 5s.

Rich.—*MARY RICH, COUNTESS OF WARWICK* (1625-1678): Her Family and Friends. By C. FELL SMITH. With 7 Photogravure Portraits and 9 other Illustrations. 8vo., gilt top, 18s. net.

Rochester, and other Literary Rakes of the Court of Charles II., with some Account of their Surroundings. By the Author of 'The Life of Sir Kenelm Digby,' 'The Life of a Prig,' etc. With 15 Portraits. 8vo., 16s.

Romanes.—*THE LIFE AND LETTERS OF GEORGE JOHN ROMANES, M.A., LL.D F.R.S.* Written and Edited by his WIFE. With Portrait and 2 Illustrations. Cr. 8vo., 5s. net.

Russell. —*SWALLOWFIELD AND ITS OWNERS.* By CONSTANCE LADY RUSSELL, of Swallowfield Park. With 15 Photogravure Portraits and 36 other Illustrations. 4to., gilt edges, 42s. net.

Seebohm.—*THE OXFORD REFORMERS —JOHN COLET, ERASMUS, AND THOMAS MORE :* a History of their Fellow-Work. By FREDERIC SEEBOHM. 8vo., 14s.

Shakespeare. — *OUTLINES OF THE LIFE OF SHAKESPEARE.* By J. O. HALLIWELL-PHILLIPPS. With Illustrations and Facsimiles. 2 vols. Royal 8vo., 21s.

Tales of my Father.—By A. M. F., Author of 'Foreign Courts and Foreign Homes,' and 'On the Banks of the Seine'. Crown 8vo., 6s.

Tallentyre.—*THE WOMEN OF THE SALONS,* and other French Portraits. By S. G. TALLENTYRE. With 11 Photogravure Portraits. 8vo., 10s. 6d. net.

Victoria, Queen, 1819-1901. By RICHARD R. HOLMES, M.V.O., F.S.A., Librarian to the Queen. With Photogravure Portrait. Crown 8vo., gilt top, 5s. net.

Walpole.—*SOME UNPUBLISHED LETTERS OF HORACE WALPOLE.* Edited by Sir SPENCER WALPOLE, K.C.B. With 2 Portraits. Crown 8vo., 4s. 6d. net.

Wellington.—*LIFE OF THE DUKE OF WELLINGTON.* By the Rev. G. R. GLEIG, M.A. Crown 8vo., 3s. 6d.

Travel and Adventure, the Colonies, &c.

Arnold.—*SEAS AND LANDS.* By Sir EDWIN ARNOLD. With 71 Illustrations. Crown 8vo., 3s. 6d.

Baker (Sir S. W.).

EIGHT YEARS IN CEYLON. With 6 Illustrations. Crown 8vo., 3s. 6d.

THE RIFLE AND THE HOUND IN CEYLON. With 6 Illusts. Cr. 8vo., 3s. 6d.

Ball (JOHN).

THE ALPINE GUIDE. Reconstructed and Revised on behalf of the Alpine Club, by W. A. B. COOLIDGE.

Vol. I., *THE WESTERN ALPS:* the Alpine Region, South of the Rhone Valley, from the Col de Tenda to the Simplon Pass. With 9 New and Revised Maps. Crown 8vo., 12s. net.

HINTS AND NOTES, PRACTICAL AND SCIENTIFIC, FOR TRAVELLERS IN THE ALPS: being a Revision of the General Introduction to the 'Alpine Guide'. Crown 8vo., 3s. net.

Bent.—*THE RUINED CITIES OF MASHONALAND:* being a Record of Excavation and Exploration in 1891. By J. THEODORE BENT. With 117 Illustrations. Crown 8vo., 3s. 6d.

Brassey (The Late Lady).

A VOYAGE IN THE 'SUNBEAM'; OUR HOME ON THE OCEAN FOR ELEVEN MONTHS.

Cabinet Edition. With Map and 66 Illustrations. Cr. 8vo., gilt edges, 7s. 6d.
'Silver Library' Edition. With 66 Illustrations. Crown 8vo., 3s. 6d.
Popular Edition. With 60 Illustrations. 4to., 6d. sewed, 1s. cloth.
School Edition. With 37 Illustrations. Fcp., 2s. cloth, or 3s. white parchment.

SUNSHINE AND STORM IN THE EAST.

Popular Edition. With 103 Illustrations. 4to., 6d. sewed, 1s. cloth.

IN THE TRADES, THE TROPICS, AND THE 'ROARING FORTIES'.

Cabinet Edition. With Map and 220 Illustrations. Cr. 8vo., gilt edges, 7s. 6d.

Crawford. — *SOUTH AMERICAN SKETCHES.* By ROBERT CRAWFORD, M.A. Crown 8vo., 6s.

Fountain (PAUL).

THE GREAT DESERTS AND FORESTS OF NORTH AMERICA. With a Preface by W. H. HUDSON, Author of 'The Naturalist in La Plata,' etc. 8vo., 9s. 6d. net.

THE GREAT MOUNTAINS AND FORESTS OF SOUTH AMERICA. With Portrait and 7 Illustrations. 8vo., 10s. 6d. net.

Froude (JAMES A.).

OCEANA: or England and her Colonies. With 9 Illustrations. Cr. 8vo., 3s. 6d.

THE ENGLISH IN THE WEST INDIES: or, the Bow of Ulysses. With 9 Illustrations. Crown 8vo., 2s. boards, 2s. 6d. cloth.

Grove.—*SEVENTY-ONE DAYS' CAMPING IN MOROCCO.* By Lady GROVE. With Photogravure Portrait and 32 Illustrations from Photographs. 8vo., 7s. 6d. net.

Haggard.—*A WINTER PILGRIMAGE:* Being an Account of Travels through Palestine, Italy and the Island of Cyprus, undertaken in the year 1900. By H. RIDER HAGGARD. With 31 Illustrations from Photographs. Cr. 8vo., gilt top, 12s. 6d. net.

Heathcote.—*ST. KILDA.* By NORMAN HEATHCOTE. With 80 Illustrations from Sketches and Photographs of the People, Scenery and Birds by the Author. 8vo., 10s. 6d. net.

Howitt.—*VISITS TO REMARKABLE PLACES.* Old Halls, Battle-Fields, Scenes, illustrative of Striking Passages in English History and Poetry. By WILLIAM HOWITT. With 80 Illustrations. Crown 8vo., 3s. 6d.

Knight (E. F.).

WITH THE ROYAL TOUR : a Narrative of the Recent Tour of the Duke and Duchess of Cornwall and York through Greater Britain. With 16 Illustrations and a Map. Crown 8vo., 5s. net.

THE CRUISE OF THE 'ALERTE': the Narrative of a Search for Treasure on the Desert Island of Trinidad. With 2 Maps and 23 Illustrations. Crown 8vo., 3s. 6d.

WHERE THREE EMPIRES MEET: a Narrative of Recent Travel in Kashmir, Western Tibet, Baltistan, Ladak, Gilgit, and the adjoining Countries. With a Map and 54 Illustrations. Cr. 8vo., 3s. 6d.

THE 'FALCON' ON THE BALTIC: a Voyage from London to Copenhagen in a Three-Tonner. With 10 Full-page Illustrations. Crown 8vo., 3s. 6d.

Travel and Adventure, the Colonies, &c.—*continued.*

Lees.—*PEAKS AND PINES :* another Norway Book. By J. A. LEES. With 63 Illustrations and Photographs. Cr. 8vo., 6s.

Lees and Clutterbuck.—B.C. 1887 : *A RAMBLE IN BRITISH COLUMBIA.* By J. A. LEES and W. J. CLUTTERBUCK. With Map and 75 Illustrations. Crown 8vo., 3s. 6d.

Lynch. — *ARMENIA :* Travels and Studies. By H. F. B. LYNCH. With 197 Illustrations (some in tints) reproduced from Photographs and Sketches by the Author, 16 Maps and Plans, a Bibliography, and a Map of Armenia and adjacent countries. 2 vols. Medium 8vo., gilt top, 42s. net.

Nansen.—*THE FIRST CROSSING OF GREENLAND.* By FRIDTJOF NANSEN. With 143 Illustrations and a Map. Crown 8vo., 3s. 6d.

Rice.—*OCCASIONAL ESSAYS ON NATIVE SOUTH INDIAN LIFE.* By STANLEY P. RICE, Indian Civil Service. 8vo., 10s. 6d.

Smith.—*CLIMBING IN THE BRITISH ISLES.* By W. P. HASKETT SMITH. With Illustrations and Numerous Plans.

Part I. *ENGLAND.* 16mo., 3s. net.

Part II. *WALES AND IRELAND.* 16mo., 3s. net.

Spender.—*TWO WINTERS IN NORWAY :* being an Account of Two Holidays spent on Snow-shoes and in Sleigh Driving, and including an Expedition to the Lapps. By A. EDMUND SPENDER. With 40 Illustrations from Photographs. 8vo., 10s. 6d. net.

Stephen. — *THE PLAY-GROUND OF EUROPE* (The Alps). By Sir LESLIE STEPHEN, K.C.B. With 4 Illustrations. Crown 8vo., 3s. 6d.

Three in Norway. By Two of Them. With a Map and 59 Illustrations. Crown 8vo., 2s. boards, 2s. 6d. cloth.

Tyndall.—(JOHN).

THE GLACIERS OF THE ALPS. With 61 Illustrations. Crown 8vo., 6s. 6d. net.

HOURS OF EXERCISE IN THE ALPS. With 7 Illustrations. Cr. 8vo., 6s. 6d. net.

Willard.—*THE LAND OF THE LATINS.* By ASHTON R. WILLARD. With 11 Illustrations from Photographs. Crown 8vo., 5s. net.

Sport and Pastime.

THE BADMINTON LIBRARY.

Edited by HIS GRACE THE (EIGHTH) DUKE OF BEAUFORT, K.G., and A. E. T. WATSON.

ARCHERY. By C. J. LONGMAN and Col. H. WALROND. With Contributions by Miss LEGH, Viscount DILLON, etc. With 2 Maps, 23 Plates and 172 Illustrations in the Text. Crown 8vo., cloth, 6s. net; half-bound, with gilt top, 9s. net.

ATHLETICS. By MONTAGUE SHEARMAN. With Chapters on Athletics at School by W. BEACHER THOMAS ; Athletic Sports in America by C. H. SHERRILL ; a Contribution on Paper-chasing by W. RYE, and an Introduction by Sir RICHARD WEBSTER (Lord ALVERSTONE). With 12 Plates and 37 Illustrations in the Text. Cr. 8vo., cloth, 6s. net; half-bound, with gilt top, 9s. net.

BIG GAME SHOOTING. By CLIVE PHILLIPPS-WOLLEY.

Vol. I. AFRICA AND AMERICA. With Contributions by Sir SAMUEL W. BAKER, W. C. OSWELL, F. C. SELOUS, etc. With 20 Plates and 57 Illustrations in the Text. Crown 8vo., cloth, 6s. net; half-bound, with gilt top, 9s. net.

Vol. II. EUROPE, ASIA, AND THE ARCTIC REGIONS. With Contributions by Lieut.-Colonel R. HEBER PERCY, Major ALGERNON C. HEBER PERCY, etc. With 17 Plates and 56 Illustrations in the Text. Crown 8vo., cloth, 6s. net; half-bound, with gilt top, 9s. net.

Sport and Pastime—*continued.*

THE BADMINTON LIBRARY—*continued.*

Edited by HIS GRACE THE (EIGHTH) DUKE OF BEAUFORT, K.G., and A. E. T. WATSON.

BILLIARDS. By Major W. BROAD-FOOT, R.E. With Contributions by A. H. BOYD, SYDENHAM DIXON, W. J. FORD, etc. With 11 Plates, 19 Illustrations in the Text, and numerous Diagrams. Crown 8vo., cloth, 6s. net ; half-bound, with gilt top, 9s. net.

COURSING AND FALCONRY. By HARDING COX, CHARLES RICHARDSON, and the Hon. GERALD LASCELLES. With 20 Plates and 55 Illustrations in the Text. Crown 8vo., cloth, 6s. net ; half-bound, with gilt top, 9s. net.

CRICKET. By A. G. STEEL and the Hon. R. H. LYTTELTON. With Contributions by ANDREW LANG, W. G. GRACE, F. GALE, etc. With 13 Plates and 52 Illustrations in the Text. Crown 8vo., cloth, 6s. net ; half-bound, with gilt top, 9s. net.

CYCLING. By the EARL OF ALBEMARLE and G. LACY HILLIER. With 19 Plates and 44 Illustrations in the Text. Crown 8vo., cloth, 6s. net ; half-bound, with gilt top, 9s. net.

DANCING. By Mrs. LILLY GROVE. With Contributions by Miss MIDDLETON, The Hon. Mrs. ARMYTAGE, etc. With Musical Examples, and 38 Full-page Plates and 93 Illustrations in the Text. Crown 8vo., cloth, 6s. net ; half-bound, with gilt top, 9s. net.

DRIVING. By His Grace the (Eighth) DUKE of BEAUFORT, K.G. With Contributions by A. E. T. WATSON the EARL OF ONSLOW, etc. With 12 Plates and 54 Illustrations in the Text. Crown 8vo., cloth, 6s. net ; half-bound, with gilt top, 9s. net.

FENCING, BOXING, AND WRESTLING. By WALTER H. POLLOCK, F. C. GROVE, C. PREVOST, E. B. MITCHELL, and WALTER ARMSTRONG. With 18 Plates and 24 Illustrations in the Text. Crown 8vo., cloth, 6s. net ; half-bound, with gilt top, 9s. net.

FISHING. By H. CHOLMONDELEY-PENNELL.

Vol. I. SALMON AND TROUT. With Contributions by H. R. FRANCIS, Major JOHN P. TRAHERNE, etc. With 9 Plates and numerous Illustrations of Tackle, etc. Crown 8vo., cloth, 6s. net ; half-bound, with gilt top, 9s. net.

Vol. II. PIKE AND OTHER COARSE FISH. With Contributions by the MARQUIS OF EXETER, WILLIAM SENIOR, G. CHRISTOPHER DAVIS, etc. With 7 Plates and numerous Illustrations or Tackle, etc. Crown 8vo., cloth, 6s. net ; half-bound, with gilt top, 9s. net.

FOOTBALL. HISTORY, by MONTAGUE SHEARMAN ; THE ASSOCIATION GAME, by W. J. OAKLEY and G. O. SMITH ; THE RUGBY UNION GAME, by FRANK MITCHELL. With other Contributions by R. E. MACNAGHTEN, M. C. KEMP, J. E. VINCENT, WALTER CAMP and A. SUTHERLAND. With 19 Plates and 35 Illustrations in the Text. Crown 8vo., cloth, 6s. net ; half-bound, with gilt top, 9s. net.

GOLF. By HORACE G. HUTCHINSON. With Contributions by the Rt. Hon. A. J. BALFOUR, M.P., Sir WALTER SIMPSON, Bart., ANDREW LANG, etc. With 34 Plates and 56 Illustrations in the Text. Crown 8vo., cloth, 6s. net ; half-bound, with gilt top, 9s. net.

HUNTING. By His Grace the (Eighth) DUKE OF BEAUFORT, K.G., and MOWBRAY MORRIS. With Contributions by the EARL OF SUFFOLK AND BERKSHIRE, Rev. E. W. L. DAVIES, G. H. LONGMAN, etc. With 5 Plates and 54 Illustrations in the Text. Crown 8vo., cloth, 6s. net ; half-bound, with gilt top, 9s. net.

MOTORS AND MOTOR-DRIVING. By ALFRED C. HARMSWORTH, the MARQUIS DE CHASSELOUP-LAUBAT, the Hon. JOHN SCOTT-MONTAGU, R. J. MECREDY, the Hon. C. S. ROLLS, Sir DAVID SALOMONS, Bart., etc. With 13 Plates and 136 Illustrations in the Text. Crown 8vo., cloth, 9s. net ; half-bound, 12s. net.
A Cloth Box for use when Motoring, 2s. net

Sport and Pastime—*continued*.

THE BADMINTON LIBRARY—*continued*.

Edited by HIS GRACE THE (EIGHTH) DUKE OF BEAUFORT, K.G., and A. E. T. WATSON.

MOUNTAINEERING. By C. T. DENT. With Contributions by the Right Hon. J. BRYCE, M.P., Sir MARTIN CONWAY, D. W. FRESHFIELD, C. E. MATTHEWS, etc. With 13 Plates and 91 Illustrations in the Text. Crown 8vo., cloth, 6s. net ; half-bound, with gilt top, 9s. net.

POETRY OF SPORT (THE).— Selected by HEDLEY PEEK. With a Chapter on Classical Allusions to Sport by ANDREW LANG, and a Special Preface to the BADMINTON LIBRARY by A. E. T. WATSON. With 32 Plates and 74 Illustrations in the Text. Crown 8vo., cloth, 6s. net ; half-bound, with gilt top, 9s. net.

RACING AND STEEPLE-CHASING. By the EARL OF SUFFOLK AND BERKSHIRE, W. G. CRAVEN, the Hon. F. LAWLEY, ARTHUR COVENTRY, and A. E. T. WATSON. With Frontispiece and 56 Illustrations in the Text. Crown 8vo., cloth, 6s. net ; half-bound, with gilt top, 9s. net.

RIDING AND POLO. By Captain ROBERT WEIR, J. MORAY BROWN, T. F. DALE, THE LATE DUKE OF BEAUFORT, THE EARL OF SUFFOLK AND BERKSHIRE, etc. With 18 Plates and 41 Illusts. in the Text. Crown 8vo., cloth, 6s. net ; half-bound, with gilt top, 9s. net.

ROWING. By R. P. P. ROWE and C. M. PITMAN. With Chapters on Steering by C. P. SEROCOLD and F. C. BEGG ; Metropolitan Rowing by S. LE BLANC SMITH ; and on PUNTING by P. W. SQUIRE. With 75 Illustrations. Crown 8vo., cloth, 6s. net ; half-bound, with gilt top, 9s. net.

SHOOTING.

Vol. I. FIELD AND COVERT. By LORD WALSINGHAM and Sir RALPH PAYNE-GALLWEY, Bart. With Contributions by the Hon. GERALD LASCELLES and A. J. STUART-WORTLEY. With 11 Plates and 95 Illustrations in the Text. Crown 8vo., cloth, 6s. net ; half-bound, with gilt top, 9s. net.

Vol. II. MOOR AND MARSH. By LORD WALSINGHAM and Sir RALPH PAYNE-GALLWEY, Bart. With Contributions by LORD LOVAT and Lord CHARLES LENNOX KERR. With 8 Plates and 57 Illustrations in the Text. Crown 8vo., cloth, 6s. net ; half-bound, with gilt top, 9s. net.

SEA FISHING. By JOHN BICKERDYKE, Sir H. W. GORE-BOOTH, ALFRED C. HARMSWORTH, and W. SENIOR. With 22 Full-page Plates and 175 Illusts. in the Text. Crown 8vo., cloth, 6s. net ; half-bound, with gilt top, 9s. net.

SKATING, CURLING, TOBOGANING. By J. M. HEATHCOTE, C. G. TEBBUTT, T. MAXWELL WITHAM, Rev. JOHN KERR, ORMOND HAKE, HENRY A. BUCK, etc. With 12 Plates and 272 Illustrations in the Text. Crown 8vo., cloth, 6s. net ; half-bound, with gilt top, 9s. net.

SWIMMING. By ARCHIBALD SINCLAIR and WILLIAM HENRY, Hon. Secs. of the Life-Saving Society. With 13 Plates and 112 Illustrations in the Text. Crown 8vo., cloth, 6s. net ; half-bound, with gilt top, 9s. net.

TENNIS, LAWN TENNIS, RACKETS AND FIVES. By J. M. and C. G. HEATHCOTE, E. O. PLEYDELL-BOUVERIE, and A. C. AINGER. With Contributions by the Hon. A. LYTTELTON, W. C. MARSHALL, Miss L. DOD, etc. With 12 Plates and 67 Illustrations in the Text. Crown 8vo., cloth, 6s. net ; half-bound, with gilt top, 9s. net.

YACHTING.

Vol. I. CRUISING, CONSTRUCTION OF YACHTS, YACHT RACING RULES, FITTING-OUT, etc. By Sir EDWARD SULLIVAN, Bart., THE EARL OF PEMBROKE, LORD BRASSEY, K.C.B., C. E. SETH-SMITH, C.B., G. L. WATSON, R. T. PRITCHETT, E. F. KNIGHT, etc. With 21 Plates and 93 Illustrations in the Text. Crown 8vo., cloth, 6s. net ; half-bound, with gilt top, 9s. net.

Vol. II. YACHT CLUBS, YACHTING IN AMERICA AND THE COLONIES, YACHT RACING, etc. By R. T. PRITCHETT, THE MARQUIS OF DUFFERIN AND AVA, K.P., THE EARL OF ONSLOW, JAMES MCFERRAN, etc. With 35 Plates and 160 Illustrations in the Text. Crown 8vo., cloth, 9s. net ; half-bound, with gilt top, 9s. net.

Sport and Pastime—*continued.*

FUR, FEATHER, AND FIN SERIES.

Edited by A. E. T. Watson.

Crown 8vo., price 5s. each Volume, cloth.

. *The Volumes are also issued half-bound in Leather, with gilt top.   Price 7s. 6d. net each.*

THE PARTRIDGE. Natural History, by the Rev. H. A. Macpherson; Shooting, by A. J. Stuart-Wortley; Cookery, by George Saintsbury. With 11 Illustrations and various Diagrams. Crown 8vo., 5s.

THE GROUSE. Natural History, by the Rev. H. A. Macpherson; Shooting, by A. J. Stuart-Wortley; Cookery, by George Saintsbury. With 13 Illustrations and various Diagrams. Crown 8vo., 5s.

THE PHEASANT. Natural History, by the Rev. H. A. Macpherson; Shooting, by A. J. Stuart-Wortley; Cookery, by Alexander Innes Shand. With 10 Illustrations and various Diagrams. Crown 8vo., 5s.

THE HARE. Natural History, by the Rev. H. A. Macpherson; Shooting, by the Hon. Gerald Lascelles; Coursing, by Charles Richardson; Hunting, by J. S. Gibbons and G. H. Longman; Cookery, by Col. Kenney Herbert. With 9 Illustrations. Crown 8vo., 5s.

RED DEER.—Natural History, by the Rev. H. A. Macpherson; Deer Stalking, by Cameron of Lochiel; Stag Hunting, by Viscount Ebrington; Cookery, by Alexander Innes Shand. With 10 Illustrations. Crown 8vo., 5s.

THE SALMON. By the Hon. A. E. Gathorne-Hardy. With Chapters on the Law of Salmon Fishing by Claud Douglas Pennant; Cookery, by Alexander Innes Shand. With 8 Illustrations. Cr. 8vo., 5s.

THE TROUT. By the Marquess of Granby. With Chapters on the Breeding of Trout by Col. H. Custance; and Cookery, by Alexander Innes Shand. With 12 Illustrations. Crown 8vo., 5s.

THE RABBIT. By James Edmund Harting. Cookery, by Alexander Innes Shand. With 10 Illustrations. Cr. 8vo., 5s.

PIKE AND PERCH. By William Senior ('Redspinner,' Editor of the 'Field'). With Chapters by John Bickerdyke and W. H. Pope; Cookery, by Alexander Innes Shand. With 12 Illustrations. Crown 8vo., 5s.

Alverstone and Alcock.—*Surrey Cricket:* its History and Associations. Edited by the Right Hon. Lord Alverstone, L.C.J., President, and C.W. Alcock, Secretary, of the Surrey County Cricket Club. With 48 Illustrations. 8vo., 16s. net.

Bickerdyke.—*Days of My Life on Water, Fresh and Salt;* and other Papers. By John Bickerdyke. With Photo-etching Frontispiece and 8 Full-page Illustrations. Crown 8vo., 3s. 6d.

Blackburne. — *Mr. Blackburne's Games at Chess.* Selected, Annotated and Arranged by Himself. Edited, with a Biographical Sketch and a brief History of Blindfold Chess, by P. Anderson Graham. With Portrait of Mr. Blackburne. 8vo., 7s. 6d. net.

Dead Shot (The): or, Sportsman's Complete Guide. Being a Treatise on the Use of the Gun, with Rudimentary and Finishing Lessons in the Art of Shooting Game of all kinds. Also Game-driving, Wildfowl and Pigeon-shooting, Dog-breaking, etc. By Marksman. With numerous Illustrations. Crown 8vo., 10s. 6d.

Ellis.—*Chess Sparks;* or, Short and Bright Games of Chess. Collected and Arranged by J. H. Ellis, M.A. 8vo., 4s. 6d.

Folkard.—*The Wild-Fowler:* A Treatise on Fowling, Ancient and Modern, descriptive also of Decoys and Flight-ponds, Wild-fowl Shooting, Gunning-punts, Shooting-yachts, etc. Also Fowling in the Fens and in Foreign Countries, Rock-fowling, etc., etc., by H. C. Folkard. With 13 Engravings on Steel, and several Woodcuts. 8vo., 12s. 6d.

Sport and Pastime—*continued.*

Ford.—*THE THEORY AND PRACTICE OF ARCHERY.* By HORACE FORD. New Edition, thoroughly Revised and Re-written by W. BUTT, M.A. With a Preface by C. J. LONGMAN, M.A. 8vo., 14s.

Francis.—*A BOOK ON ANGLING:* or, Treatise on the Art of Fishing in every Branch; including full Illustrated List of Salmon Flies. By FRANCIS FRANCIS. With Portrait and Coloured Plates. Crown 8vo., 15s.

Fremantle. — *THE BOOK OF THE RIFLE.* By the Hon. T. F. FREMANTLE, V.D., Major, 1st Bucks V.R.C. With 54 Plates and 107 Diagrams in the Text. 8vo., 12s. 6d. net.

Gathorne - Hardy. — *AUTUMNS IN ARGYLESHIRE WITH ROD AND GUN.* By the Hon. A. E. GATHORNE-HARDY. With 8 Photogravure Illustrations by ARCHIBALD THORBURN. 8vo., 6s. net.

Graham.—*COUNTRY PASTIMES FOR BOYS.* By P. ANDERSON GRAHAM. With 252 Illustrations from Drawings and Photographs. Cr. 8vo., gilt edges, 3s. net.

Hutchinson.—*THE BOOK OF GOLF AND GOLFERS.* By HORACE G. HUTCHINSON. With Contributions by Miss AMY PASCOE, H. H. HILTON, J. H. TAYLOR, H J. WHIGHAM, and Messrs. SUTTON & SONS. With 71 Portraits from Photographs. Large crown 8vo., gilt top, 7s. 6d. net.

Lang.—*ANGLING SKETCHES.* By ANDREW LANG. With 20 Illustrations. Crown 8vo., 3s. 6d.

Lillie.—*CROQUET UP TO DATE.* Containing the Ideas and Teachings of the Leading Players and Champions. By ARTHUR LILLIE. With Contributions by Lieut.-Col. the Hon. H. NEEDHAM, C. D. LOCOCK, etc. With 19 Illustrations (15 Portraits), and numerous Diagrams. 8vo., 10s. 6d. net.

Locock.—*SIDE AND SCREW:* being Notes on the Theory and Practice of the Game of Billiards. By C. D. LOCOCK. With Diagrams. Crown 8vo., 5s. net.

Longman.—*CHESS OPENINGS.* By FREDERICK W. LONGMAN. Fcp. 8vo., 2s. 6d.

Mackenzie.—*NOTES FOR HUNTING MEN.* By Captain CORTLANDT GORDON MACKENZIE. Crown 8vo., 2s. 6d. net.

Madden.—*THE DIARY OF MASTER WILLIAM SILENCE:* a Study of Shakespeare and of Elizabethan Sport. By the Right Hon. D. H. MADDEN, Vice-Chancellor of the University of Dublin. 8vo., gilt top, 16s.

Maskelyne.—*SHARPS AND FLATS:* a Complete Revelation of the Secrets of Cheating at Games of Chance and Skill. By JOHN NEVIL MASKELYNE, of the Egyptian Hall. With 62 Illustrations. Crown 8vo., 6s.

Millais (JOHN GUILLE).

THE WILD-FOWLER IN SCOTLAND. With a Frontispiece in Photogravure by Sir J. E. MILLAIS, Bart., P.R.A., 8 Photogravure Plates, 2 Coloured Plates and 50 Illustrations from the Author's Drawings and from Photographs. Royal 4to., gilt top, 30s. net.

THE NATURAL HISTORY OF THE BRITISH SURFACE-FEEDING DUCKS. With 6 Photogravures and 66 Plates (41 in Colours) from Drawings by the Author, ARCHIBALD THORBURN, and from Photographs. Royal 4to., cloth, gilt top, £6 6s. net.

Modern Bridge.—By 'Slam'. With a Reprint of the Laws of Bridge, as adopted by the Portland and Turf Clubs. 18mo., gilt edges, 3s. 6d. net.

Park.—*THE GAME OF GOLF.* By WILLIAM PARK, Jun., Champion Golfer, 1887-89. With 17 Plates and 26 Illustrations in the Text. Crown 8vo., 7s. 6d.

Payne-Gallwey (Sir RALPH, Bart.).

THE CROSS-BOW: its History, Construction and Management. With numerous Illustrations. Medium 4to.

LETTERS TO YOUNG SHOOTERS (First Series). On the Choice and use of a Gun. With 41 Illustrations. Crown 8vo., 7s. 6d.

LETTERS TO YOUNG SHOOTERS (Second Series). On the Production, Preservation, and Killing of Game. With Directions in Shooting Wood-Pigeons and Breaking-in Retrievers. With Portrait and 103 Illustrations. Crown 8vo., 12s. 6d.

LETTERS TO YOUNG SHOOTERS. (Third Series.) Comprising a Short Natural History of the Wildfowl that are Rare or Common to the British Islands, with complete directions in Shooting Wildfowl on the Coast and Inland. With 200 Illustrations. Crown 8vo., 18s.

Sport and Pastime—*continued.*

Pole.—*THE THEORY OF THE MODERN SCIENTIFIC GAME OF WHIST.* By WILLIAM POLE, F.R.S. Fcp. 8vo., gilt edges, 2s. net.

Proctor.—*HOW TO PLAY WHIST: WITH THE LAWS AND ETIQUETTE OF WHIST.* By RICHARD A. PROCTOR. Crown 8vo., gilt edges, 3s. net.

Ronalds.—*THE FLY-FISHER'S ENTOMOLOGY.* By ALFRED RONALDS. With 20 coloured Plates. 8vo., 14s.

Selous.—*SPORT AND TRAVEL, EAST AND WEST.* By FREDERICK COURTENEY SELOUS. With 18 Plates and 35 Illustrations in the Text. Medium 8vo., 12s. 6d. net.

Mental, Moral, and Political Philosophy.

LOGIC, RHETORIC, PSYCHOLOGY, &C.

Abbott.—*THE ELEMENTS OF LOGIC.* By T. K. ABBOTT, B.D. 12mo., 3s.

Aristotle.

THE ETHICS: Greek Text, Illustrated with Essay and Notes. By Sir ALEXANDER GRANT, Bart. 2 vols. 8vo., 32s.

AN INTRODUCTION TO ARISTOTLE'S ETHICS. Books I.-IV. (Book X. c. vi.-ix. in an Appendix). With a continuous Analysis and Notes. By the Rev. E. MOORE, D.D. Crown 8vo., 10s. 6d.

Bacon (FRANCIS).

COMPLETE WORKS. Edited by R. L. ELLIS, JAMES SPEDDING and D. D. HEATH. 7 vols. 8vo., £3 13s. 6d.

LETTERS AND LIFE, including all his occasional Works. Edited by JAMES SPEDDING. 7 vols. 8vo., £4 4s.

THE ESSAYS: with Annotations. By RICHARD WHATELY, D.D. 8vo., 10s. 6d.

THE ESSAYS: with Notes. By F. STORR and C. H. GIBSON. Cr. 8vo., 3s. 6d.

THE ESSAYS: with Introduction, Notes, and Index. By E. A. ABBOTT, D.D. 2 Vols. Fcp. 8vo., 6s. The Text and Index only, without Introduction and Notes, in One Volume. Fcp. 8vo., 2s. 6d.

Bain (ALEXANDER).

MENTAL AND MORAL SCIENCE: a Compendium of Psychology and Ethics. Crown 8vo., 10s. 6d.
Or separately,
Part I. *PSYCHOLOGY AND HISTORY OF PHILOSOPHY.* Crown 8vo., 6s. 6d.
Part II. *THEORY OF ETHICS AND ETHICAL SYSTEMS.* Crown 8vo., 4s. 6d.

Bain (ALEXANDER)—*continued.*

LOGIC. Part I. *DEDUCTION.* Cr. 8vo., 4s. Part II. *INDUCTION.* Cr. 8vo., 6s. 6d.

THE SENSES AND THE INTELLECT. 8vo., 15s.

THE EMOTIONS AND THE WILL. 8vo., 15s.

PRACTICAL ESSAYS. Cr. 8vo., 2s.

Brooks.—*THE ELEMENTS OF MIND :* being an Examination into the Nature of the First Division of the Elementary Substances of Life. By H. JAMYN BROOKS. 8vo., 10s. 6d. net.

Crozier (JOHN BEATTIE).

CIVILISATION AND PROGRESS: being the Outlines of a New System of Political, Religious and Social Philosophy. 8vo., 14s.

HISTORY OF INTELLECTUAL DEVELOPMENT: on the Lines of Modern Evolution.

Vol. I. 8vo., 14s.
Vol. II. (*In preparation.*)
Vol. III. 8vo., 10s. 6d.

Davidson.—*THE LOGIC OF DEFINITION,* Explained and Applied. By WILLIAM L. DAVIDSON, M.A. Crown 8vo., 6s.

Green (THOMAS HILL).—THE WORKS OF. Edited by R. L. NETTLESHIP.

Vols. I. and II. Philosophical Works. 8vo. 16s. each.
Vol. III. Miscellanies. With Index to the three Volumes, and Memoir. 8vo., 21s.

LECTURES ON THE PRINCIPLES OF POLITICAL OBLIGATION. With Preface by BERNARD BOSANQUET. 8vo., 5s.

Mental, Moral and Political Philosophy—*continued*.

LOGIC, RHETORIC, PSYCHOLOGY, &C.

Gurnhill.—*THE MORALS OF SUICIDE.* By the Rev. J. GURNHILL, B.A. Vol. I., Crown 8vo., 6s. Vol. II., Crown 8vo.

Hodgson (SHADWORTH H.).

TIME AND SPACE: A Metaphysical Essay. 8vo., 16s.

THE THEORY OF PRACTICE: an Ethical Inquiry. 2 vols. 8vo., 24s.

THE PHILOSOPHY OF REFLECTION. 2 vols. 8vo., 21s.

THE METAPHYSIC OF EXPERIENCE. Book I. General Analysis of Experience ; Book II. Positive Science; Book III. Analysis of Conscious Action ; Book IV. The Real Universe. 4 vols. 8vo., 36s. net.

Hume.—*THE PHILOSOPHICAL WORKS OF DAVID HUME.* Edited by T. H. GREEN and T. H. GROSE. 4 vols. 8vo., 28s. Or separately, Essays. 2 vols. 14s. TREATISE OF HUMAN NATURE. 2 vols. 14s.

James (WILLIAM, M.D., LL.D.).

THE WILL TO BELIEVE, and Other Essays in Popular Philosophy. Crown 8vo., 7s. 6d.

THE VARIETIES OF RELIGIOUS EXPERIENCE: a Study in Human Nature. Being the Gifford Lectures on Natural Religion delivered at Edinburgh in 1901-1902. 8vo., 12s. net.

Justinian.—*THE INSTITUTES OF JUSTINIAN:* Latin Text, chiefly that of Huschke, with English Introduction, Translation, Notes, and Summary. By THOMAS C. SANDARS, M.A. 8vo., 18s.

Kant (IMMANUEL).

CRITIQUE OF PRACTICAL REASON, AND OTHER WORKS ON THE THEORY OF ETHICS. Translated by T. K. ABBOTT, B.D. With Memoir. 8vo., 12s. 6d.

FUNDAMENTAL PRINCIPLES OF THE METAPHYSIC OF ETHICS. Translated by T. K. ABBOTT, B.D. Crown 8vo, 3s.

INTRODUCTION TO LOGIC, AND HIS ESSAY ON THE MISTAKEN SUBTILTY OF THE FOUR FIGURES. Translated by T. K. ABBOTT. 8vo., 6s

Kelly.—*GOVERNMENT OR HUMAN EVOLUTION.* By EDMOND KELLY, M.A., F.G.S. Vol. I. Justice. Crown 8vo., 7s. 6d. net. Vol. II. Collectivism and Individualism. Crown 8vo., 10s. 6d. net.

Killick.—*HANDBOOK TO MILL'S SYSTEM OF LOGIC.* By Rev. A. H. KILLICK, M.A. Crown 8vo., 3s. 6d.

Ladd (GEORGE TRUMBULL).

PHILOSOPHY OF CONDUCT: a Treatise of the Facts, Principles and Ideals of Ethics. 8vo., 21s.

ELEMENTS OF PHYSIOLOGICAL PSYCHOLOGY. 8vo., 21s.

OUTLINES OF DESCRIPTIVE PSYCHOLOGY: a Text-Book of Mental Science for Colleges and Normal Schools. 8vo., 12s.

OUTLINES OF PHYSIOLOGICAL PSYCHOLOGY. 8vo., 12s.

PRIMER OF PSYCHOLOGY. Cr. 8vo., 5s. 6d.

Lecky.—*THE MAP OF LIFE:* Conduct and Character. By WILLIAM EDWARD HARTPOLE LECKY.

Library Edition, 8vo., 10s. 6d.

Cabinet Edition, Cr. 8vo., 5s. net.

Lutoslawski.—*THE ORIGIN AND GROWTH OF PLATO'S LOGIC.* With an Account of Plato's Style and of the Chronology of his Writings. By WINCENTY LUTOSLAWSKI. 8vo., 21s.

Max Müller (F.).

THE SCIENCE OF THOUGHT. 8vo., 21s.

THE SIX SYSTEMS OF INDIAN PHILOSOPHY. 8vo., 18s.

THREE LECTURES ON THE VEDANTA PHILOSOPHY. Crown 8vo., 5s.

Mill (JOHN STUART).

A SYSTEM OF LOGIC. Cr. 8vo., 3s. 6d.

ON LIBERTY. Crown 8vo., 1s. 4d.

CONSIDERATIONS ON REPRESENTATIVE GOVERNMENT. Crown 8vo., 2s.

UTILITARIANISM. 8vo., 2s. 6d.

EXAMINATION OF SIR WILLIAM HAMILTON'S PHILOSOPHY. 8vo., 16s.

NATURE, THE UTILITY OF RELIGION, AND THEISM. Three Essays. 8vo., 5s.

Mental, Moral, and Political Philosophy—*continued.*

LOGIC, RHETORIC, PSYCHOLOGY, &C.

Monck. — *An Introduction to Logic.* By William Henry S. Monck, M.A. Crown 8vo., 5s.

Pierce.—*Studies in Auditory and Visual Space Perception:* Essays on Experimental Psychology. By A. H. Pierce. Crown 8vo., 6s. 6d. net.

Richmond.—*The Mind of a Child.* By Ennis Richmond. Cr. 8vo., 3s. 6d. net.

Romanes.—*Mind and Motion and Monism.* By George John Romanes, Cr. 8vo., 4s. 6d.

Sully (James).

An Essay on Laughter: its Forms, its Cause, its Development and its Value. 8vo., 12s. 6d. net.

The Human Mind: a Text-book of Psychology. 2 vols. 8vo., 21s.

Outlines of Psychology. Crown 8vo., 9s.

The Teacher's Handbook of Psychology. Crown 8vo., 6s. 6d.

Studies of Childhood. 8vo., 10s. 6d.

Children's Ways: being Selections from the Author's 'Studies of Childhood'. With 25 Illustrations. Crown 8vo., 4s. 6d.

Sutherland. — *The Origin and Growth of the Moral Instinct.* By Alexander Sutherland, M.A. 2 vols. 8vo., 28s.

Swinburne. — *Picture Logic:* an Attempt to Popularise the Science of Reasoning. By Alfred James Swinburne, M.A. With 23 Woodcuts. Cr. 8vo., 2s. 6d.

Thomas.—*Intuitive Suggestion.* By J. W. Thomas, Author of 'Spiritual Law in the Natural World,' etc. Crown 8vo., 3s. 6d. net.

Webb.—*The Veil of Isis:* a Series of Essays on Idealism. By Thomas E. Webb, LL.D., Q.C. 8vo., 10s. 6d.

Weber.—*History of Philosophy.* By Alfred Weber, Professor in the University of Strasburg. Translated by Frank Thilly, Ph.D. 8vo., 16s.

Whately (Archbishop).

Bacon's Essays. With Annotations. 8vo., 10s. 6d.

Elements of Logic. Cr. 8vo., 4s. 6d.

Elements of Rhetoric. Cr. 8vo., 4s. 6d.

Zeller (Dr. Edward).

The Stoics, Epicureans, and Sceptics. Translated by the Rev. O. J. Reichel, M.A. Crown 8vo., 15s.

Outlines of the History of Greek Philosophy. Translated by Sarah F. Alleyne and Evelyn Abbott, M.A., LL.D. Crown 8vo., 10s. 6d.

Plato and the Older Academy. Translated by Sarah F. Alleyne and Alfred Goodwin, B.A. Crown 8vo., 18s.

Socrates and the Socratic Schools. Translated by the Rev. O. J. Reichel, M.A. Crown 8vo., 10s. 6d.

Aristotle and the Earlier Peripatetics. Translated by B. F. C. Costelloe, M.A., and J. H. Muirhead, M.A. 2 vols. Crown 8vo., 24s.

STONYHURST PHILOSOPHICAL SERIES.

A Manual of Political Economy. By C. S. Devas, M.A. Crown 8vo., 7s. 6d.

First Principles of Knowledge. By John Rickaby, S.J. Crown 8vo., 5s.

General Metaphysics. By John Rickaby, S.J. Crown 8vo., 5s.

Logic. By Richard F. Clarke, S.J. Crown 8vo., 5s.

Moral Philosophy (Ethics and Natural Law). By Joseph Rickaby, S.J. Crown 8vo., 5s.

Natural Theology. By Bernard Boedder, S.J. Crown 8vo., 6s. 6d.

Psychology. By Michael Maher, S.J., D.Litt., M.A. (Lond.). Cr. 8vo., 6s. 6d.

History and Science of Language, &c.

Davidson.—*LEADING AND IMPORT-ANT ENGLISH WORDS*: Explained and Exemplified. By WILLIAM L. DAVIDSON, M.A. Fcp. 8vo., 3s. 6d.

Farrar.—*LANGUAGE AND LANGUAGES*. By F. W. FARRAR, D.D., Dean of Canterbury. Crown 8vo., 6s.

Graham. — *ENGLISH SYNONYMS*, Classified and Explained: with Practical Exercises. By G. F. GRAHAM. Fcp. 8vo., 6s.

Max Müller (F.).

THE SCIENCE OF LANGUAGE. 2 vols. Crown 8vo., 10s.

Max Müller (F.)—*continued.*

BIOGRAPHIES OF WORDS, AND THE HOME OF THE ARYAS. Crown 8vo., 5s.

CHIPS FROM A GERMAN WORKSHOP. Vol. III. *ESSAYS ON LANGUAGE AND LITERATURE.* Crown 8vo., 5s.

LAST ESSAYS. First Series. Essays on Language, Folk-lore and other Subjects. Crown 8vo., 5s.

Roget.—*THESAURUS OF ENGLISH WORDS AND PHRASES.* Classified and Arranged so as to Facilitate the Expression of Ideas and assist in Literary Composition. By PETER MARK ROGET, M.D., F.R.S. With full Index. Crown 8vo., 9s. net.

Political Economy and Economics.

Ashley (W. J.).

ENGLISH ECONOMIC HISTORY AND THEORY. Crown 8vo., Part I., 5s. Part II., 10s. 6d.

SURVEYS, HISTORIC AND ECONOMIC. Crown 8vo., 9s. net.

Bagehot.—*ECONOMIC STUDIES.* By WALTER BAGEHOT. Crown 8vo., 3s. 6d.

Barnett.—*PRACTICABLE SOCIALISM*: Essays on Social Reform. By SAMUEL A. and HENRIETTA BARNETT. Crown 8vo., 6s.

Devas.—*A MANUAL OF POLITICAL ECONOMY.* By C. S. DEVAS, M.A. Cr. 8vo., 7s. 6d. (*Stonyhurst Philosophical Series.*)

Lawrence.—*LOCAL VARIATIONS IN WAGES.* By F. W. LAWRENCE, M.A. With Index and 18 Maps and Diagrams. 4to., 8s. 6d.

Leslie.—*ESSAYS ON POLITICAL ECONOMY.* By T. E. CLIFFE LESLIE, Hon. LL.D., Dubl. 8vo., 10s. 6d.

Macleod (HENRY DUNNING).

BIMETALLISM. 8vo., 5s. net.

THE ELEMENTS OF BANKING. Cr. 8vo., 3s. 6d.

THE THEORY AND PRACTICE OF BANKING. Vol. I. 8vo., 12s. Vol. II. 14s.

Macleod (HENRY DUNNING)—*contd.*

THE THEORY OF CREDIT. 8vo. In 1 Vol., 30s. net; or separately, Vol. I., 10s. net. Vol. II., Part I., 10s. net. Vol II., Part II. 10s. net.

INDIAN CURRENCY. 8vo., 2s. 6d. net.

Mill.—*POLITICAL ECONOMY.* By JOHN STUART MILL. *Popular Edition.* Cr. 8vo., 3s. 6d. *Library Edition.* 2 vols. 8vo., 30s.

Mulhall.—*INDUSTRIES AND WEALTH OF NATIONS.* By MICHAEL G. MULHALL, F.S.S. With 32 Diagrams. Cr. 8vo., 8s. 6d.

Symes. — *POLITICAL ECONOMY*: a Short Text-book of Political Economy. With Problems for Solution, Hints for Supplementary Reading, and a Supplementary Chapter on Socialism. By J. E. SYMES, M.A. Crown 8vo., 2s. 6d.

Toynbee.—*LECTURES ON THE INDUSTRIAL REVOLUTION OF THE 18TH CENTURY IN ENGLAND.* By ARNOLD TOYNBEE. 8vo., 10s. 6d.

Webb (SIDNEY and BEATRICE).

THE HISTORY OF TRADE UNIONISM. With Map and Bibliography. 8vo., 7s. 6d. net.

INDUSTRIAL DEMOCRACY: a Study in Trade Unionism. 2 vols. 8vo., 12s. net.

PROBLEMS OF MODERN INDUSTRY. 8vo., 5s. net.

Evolution, Anthropology, &c.

Avebury.—*THE ORIGIN OF CIVILISA-TION*, and the Primitive Condition of Man. By the Right Hon. LORD AVEBURY. With 6 Plates and 20 Illustrations. 8vo., 18s.

Clodd (EDWARD).

THE STORY OF CREATION: a Plain Account of Evolution. With 77 Illustrations. Crown 8vo., 3s. 6d.

A PRIMER OF EVOLUTION: being a Popular Abridged Edition of 'The Story of Creation'. With Illustrations. Fcp. 8vo., 1s. 6d.

Packard.—*LAMARCK, THE FOUNDER OF EVOLUTION*: his Life and Work, with Translations of his Writings on Organic Evolution. By ALPHEUS S. PACKARD, M.D., LL.D., Professor of Zoology and Geology in Brown University. With 10 Portrait and other Illustrations. Large Crown 8vo., 9s. net.

Romanes (GEORGE JOHN).

ESSAYS. Edited by C. LLOYD MORGAN. Crown 8vo., 5s. net.

AN EXAMINATION OF WEISMANN-ISM. Crown 8vo., 6s.

DARWIN, AND AFTER DARWIN: an Exposition of the Darwinian Theory, and a Discussion on Post-Darwinian Questions.

Part I. THE DARWINIAN THEORY. With Portrait of Darwin and 125 Illustrations. Crown 8vo., 10s. 6d.

Part II. POST-DARWINIAN QUESTIONS: Heredity and Utility. With Portrait of the Author and 5 Illustrations. Cr. 8vo., 10s. 6d.

Part III. Post-Darwinian Questions: Isolation and Physiological Selection. Crown 8vo., 5s.

The Science of Religion, &c.

Balfour. — *THE FOUNDATIONS OF BELIEF*: being Notes Introductory to the Study of Theology. By the Right Hon. ARTHUR JAMES BALFOUR. Cr. 8vo., 6s. net.

Baring-Gould.—*THE ORIGIN AND DEVELOPMENT OF RELIGIOUS BELIEF*. By the Rev. S. BARING-GOULD. 2 vols. Crown 8vo., 3s. 6d. each.

Campbell.—*RELIGION IN GREEK LITERATURE*. By the Rev. LEWIS CAMPBELL, M.A., LL.D. 8vo., 15s.

Davidson.—*THEISM*, as Grounded in Human Nature, Historically and Critically Handled. Being the Burnett Lectures for 1892 and 1893, delivered at Aberdeen. By W. L. DAVIDSON, M.A., LL.D. 8vo., 15s.

James.—*THE VARIETIES OF RELIGIOUS EXPERIENCE*: a Study in Human Nature. Being the Gifford Lectures on Natural Religion delivered at Edinburgh in 1901-1902. By WILLIAM JAMES, LL.D., etc. 8vo., 12s. net.

Lang (ANDREW).

MAGIC AND RELIGION. 8vo., 10s. 6d.

CUSTOM AND MYTH: Studies of Early Usage and Belief. With 15 Illustrations. Crown 8vo., 3s. 6d.

MYTH, RITUAL, AND RELIGION. 2 vols. Crown 8vo., 7s.

MODERN MYTHOLOGY: a Reply to Professor Max Müller. 8vo., 9s.

THE MAKING OF RELIGION. Cr. 8vo., 5s. net.

Leighton.—*TYPICAL MODERN CONCEPTIONS OF GOD*; or, The Absolute of German Romantic Idealism and of English Evolutionary Agnosticism. By JOSEPH ALEXANDER LEIGHTON, Professor of Philosophy in Hobart College, U.S. Crown 8vo., 3s. 6d. net.

Max Müller (The Right Hon. F.).

CHIPS FROM A GERMAN WORKSHOP. Vol. IV. Essays on Mythology and Folklore. Crown 8vo., 5s.

THE SIX SYSTEMS OF INDIAN PHILOSOPHY. 8vo., 18s.

CONTRIBUTIONS TO THE SCIENCE OF MYTHOLOGY. 2 vols. 8vo., 32s.

THE ORIGIN AND GROWTH OF RELIGION, as illustrated by the Religions of India. The Hibbert Lectures, delivered at the Chapter House, Westminster Abbey, in 1878. Crown 8vo., 5s.

INTRODUCTION TO THE SCIENCE OF RELIGION: Four Lectures delivered at the Royal Institution. Crown 8vo., 5s.

NATURAL RELIGION. The Gifford Lectures, delivered before the University of Glasgow in 1888. Crown 8vo., 5s.

PHYSICAL RELIGION. The Gifford Lectures, delivered before the University of Glasgow in 1890. Crown 8vo., 5s.

The Science of Religion, &c.—*continued.*

Max Müller (The Right Hon. F.)—*continued.*

ANTHROPOLOGICAL RELIGION. The Gifford Lectures, delivered before the University of Glasgow in 1891. Cr. 8vo., 5s.

THEOSOPHY, OR PSYCHOLOGICAL RELIGION. The Gifford Lectures, delivered before the University of Glasgow in 1892. Crown 8vo., 5s.

THREE LECTURES ON THE VEDÂNTA PHILOSOPHY, delivered at the Royal Institution in March, 1894. Cr. 8vo., 5s.

LAST ESSAYS. Second Series— Essays on the Science of Religion. Crown 8vo., 5s.

Oakesmith. — *THE RELIGION OF PLUTARCH:* a Pagan Creed of Apostolic Times. An Essay. By JOHN OAKESMITH, D.Litt., M.A. Crown 8vo., 5s. net.

Wood-Martin (W. G.).

TRACES OF THE ELDER FAITHS OF IRELAND: a Folk-lore Sketch. A Handbook of Irish Pre-Christian Traditions. With 192 Illustrations. 2 vols. 8vo., 30s. net.

PAGAN IRELAND: an Archæological Sketch. A Handbook of Irish Pre-Christian Antiquities. With 512 Illustrations. 8vo., 15s.

Classical Literature, Translations, &c.

Abbott.—*HELLENICA.* A Collection of Essays on Greek Poetry, Philosophy, History, and Religion. Edited by EVELYN ABBOTT, M.A., LL.D. Crown 8vo., 7s. 6d.

Æschylus.—*EUMENIDES OF ÆSCHYLUS.* With Metrical English Translation. By J. F. DAVIES. 8vo., 7s.

Aristophanes. — *THE ACHARNIANS OF ARISTOPHANES,* translated into English Verse. By R. Y. TYRRELL. Crown 8vo., 1s.

Becker (W. A.), Translated by the Rev. F. METCALFE, B.D.

GALLUS: or, Roman Scenes in the Time of Augustus. With Notes and Excursuses. With 26 Illustrations. Crown 8vo., 3s. 6d.

CHARICLES: or, Illustrations of the Private Life of the Ancient Greeks. With Notes and Excursuses. With 26 Illustrations. Crown 8vo., 3s. 6d.

Campbell.—*RELIGION IN GREEK LITERATURE.* By the Rev. LEWIS CAMPBELL, M.A., LL.D., Emeritus Professor of Greek, University of St. Andrews. 8vo., 15s.

Cicero.—*CICERO'S CORRESPONDENCE.* By R. Y. TYRRELL. Vols. I., II., III., 8vo., each 12s. Vol. IV., 15s. Vol. V., 14s. Vol. VI., 12s. Vol. VII. Index, 7s. 6d.

Harvard Studies in Classical Philology. Edited by a Committee of the Classical Instructors of Harvard University. Vols. XI., 1900; XII., 1901; XIII., 1902. 8vo., 6s. 6d. net each.

Hime.—*LUCIAN, THE SYRIAN SATIRIST.* By Lieut.-Col. HENRY W. L. HIME, (late) Royal Artillery. 8vo., 5s. net.

Homer.—*THE ODYSSEY OF HOMER.* Done into English Verse. By WILLIAM MORRIS. Crown 8vo., 6s.

Horace.—*THE WORKS OF HORACE, RENDERED INTO ENGLISH PROSE.* With Life, Introduction and Notes. By WILLIAM COUTTS, M.A. Crown 8vo., 5s. net.

Lang.—*HOMER AND THE EPIC.* By ANDREW LANG. Crown 8vo., 9s. net.

Lucian. — *TRANSLATIONS FROM LUCIAN.* By AUGUSTA M. CAMPBELL DAVIDSON, M.A. Edin. Crown 8vo., 5s. net.

Ogilvie.—*HORAE LATINAE:* Studies in Synonyms and Syntax. By the late ROBERT OGILVIE, M.A., LL.D., H.M. Chief Inspector of Schools for Scotland. Edited by ALEXANDER SOUTER, M.A. With a Memoir by JOSEPH OGILVIE, M.A., LL.D. 8vo., 12s. 6d. net.

Classical Literature, Translations, &c.—*continued.*

Rich.—*A Dictionary of Roman and Greek Antiquities.* By A. Rich, B.A. With 2000 Woodcuts. Crown 8vo., 6s. net.

Sophocles.—Translated into English Verse. By Robert Whitelaw, M.A., Assistant Master in Rugby School. Cr. 8vo., 8s. 6d.

Tyrrell. — *Dublin Translations into Greek and Latin Verse.* Edited by R. Y. Tyrrell. 8vo., 6s.

Virgil.

The Poems of Virgil. Translated into English Prose by John Conington. Crown 8vo., 6s.

The Æneid of Virgil. Translated into English Verse by John Conington. Crown 8vo., 6s.

Virgil—*continued.*

The Æneids of Virgil. Done into English Verse. By William Morris. Crown 8vo., 6s.

The Æneid of Virgil, freely translated into English Blank Verse. By W. J. Thornhill. Crown 8vo., 6s. net.

The Æneid of Virgil. Translated into English Verse by James Rhoades. Books I.-VI. Crown 8vo., 5s. Books VII.-XII. Crown 8vo., 5s.

The Eclogues and Georgics of Virgil. Translated into English Prose by J. W. Mackail, Fellow of Balliol College, Oxford. 16mo., 5s.

Wilkins.—*The Growth of the Homeric Poems.* By G. Wilkins. 8vo., 6s.

- - - -

Poetry and the Drama.

Arnold.—*The Light of the World:* or, The Great Consummation. By Sir Edwin Arnold. With 14 Illustrations after Holman Hunt. Crown 8vo., 5s. net.

Bell (Mrs. Hugh).

Chamber Comedies: a Collection of Plays and Monologues for the Drawing Room. Crown 8vo., 5s. net.

Fairy Tale Plays, and How to Act Them. With 91 Diagrams and 52 Illustrations. Crown 8vo., 3s. net.

Rumpelstiltzkin: a Fairy Play in Five Scenes (Characters, 7 Male; 1 Female). From 'Fairy Tale Plays and How to Act Them'. With Illustrations, Diagrams and Music. Cr. 8vo., sewed, 6d.

Bird. — *Ronald's Farewell,* and other Verses. By George Bird, M.A., Vicar of Bradwell, Derbyshire. Fcp. 8vo., 4s. 6d. net.

Dabney.—*The Musical Basis of Verse:* a Scientific Study of the Principles of Poetic Composition. By J. P. Dabney. Crown 8vo., 6s. 6d. net.

Ingelow (Jean).

Poetical Works. Complete in One Volume. Crown 8vo., gilt top, 6s. net.

Lyrical and other Poems. Selected from the Writings of Jean Ingelow. Fcp. 8vo., 2s. 6d. cloth plain, 3s. cloth gilt.

Keary.—*The Brothers:* a Fairy Masque. By C. F. Keary. Cr. 8vo., 4s. net.

Lang (Andrew).

Grass of Parnassus. Fcp. 8vo., 2s. 6d. net.

The Blue Poetry Book. Edited by Andrew Lang. With 100 Illustrations. Crown 8vo., gilt edges, 6s.

Lecky.—*Poems.* By the Right Hon. W. E. H. Lecky. Fcp. 8vo., 5s.

Poetry and the Drama—*continued*.

Lytton (The Earl of), (OWEN MEREDITH).

THE WANDERER. Cr. 8vo., 10s. 6d.

LUCILE. Crown 8vo., 10s. 6d.

SELECTED POEMS. Cr. 8vo., 10s. 6d.

Macaulay.—*LAYS OF ANCIENT ROME, WITH 'IVRY' AND 'THE ARMADA'.* By Lord MACAULAY.

Illustrated by G. SCHARF. Fcp. 4to., 10s. 6d.

———————————— Bijou Edition. 18mo., 2s. 6d. gilt top.

———————————— Popular Edition. Fcp. 4to., 6d. sewed, 1s. cloth.

Illustrated by J. R. WEGUELIN. Crown 8vo., 3s. net.

Annotated Edition. Fcp. 8vo., 1s. sewed, 1s. 6d. cloth.

MacDonald.—*A BOOK OF STRIFE, IN THE FORM OF THE DIARY OF AN OLD SOUL:* Poems. By GEORGE MACDONALD, LL.D. 18mo., 6s.

Morris (WILLIAM).

POETICAL WORKS—LIBRARY EDITION. Complete in 11 volumes. Crown 8vo., price 5s. net each.

THE EARTHLY PARADISE. 4 vols. Crown 8vo., 5s. net each.

THE LIFE AND DEATH OF JASON. Crown 8vo., 5s. net.

THE DEFENCE OF GUENEVERE, and other Poems. Crown 8vo., 5s. net.

THE STORY OF SIGURD THE VOLSUNG, AND THE FALL OF THE NIBLUNGS. Cr. 8vo., 5s. net.

POEMS BY THE WAY, AND LOVE IS ENOUGH. Crown 8vo., 5s. net.

Morris (WILLIAM)—*continued.*

THE ODYSSEY OF HOMER. Done into English Verse. Crown 8vo., 5s. net.

THE ÆNEIDS OF VIRGIL. Done into English Verse. Crown 8vo., 5s. net.

THE TALE OF BEOWULF, SOMETIME KING OF THE FOLK OF THE WEDERGEATS. Translated by WILLIAM MORRIS and A. J. WYATT. Crown 8vo., 5s. net.

Certain of the POETICAL WORKS may also be had in the following Editions :—

THE EARTHLY PARADISE.

Popular Edition. 5 vols. 12mo., 25s.; or 5s. each, sold separately.

The same in Ten Parts, 25s.; or 2s. 6d· each, sold separately.

Cheap Edition, in 1 vol. Crown 8vo., 6s. net.

POEMS BY THE WAY. Square crown 8vo., 6s.

⁎ For Mr. William Morris's other Works, see pp. 27, 28, 37 and 40.

Morte Arthur: an Alliterative Poem of the Fourteenth Century. Edited from the Thornton MS., with Introduction, Notes and Glossary. By MARY MACLEOD BANKS. Fcp. 8vo., 3s. 6d.

Nesbit.—*LAYS AND LEGENDS.* By E. NESBIT (Mrs. HUBERT BLAND). First Series. Crown 8vo., 3s. 6d. Second Series. With Portrait. Crown 8vo., 5s.

Ramal.—*SONGS OF CHILDHOOD.* By WALTER RAMAL. With a Frontispiece from a Drawing by RICHARD DOYLE. Fcp. 8vo., 3s. 6d. net.

Riley. — *OLD FASHIONED ROSES:* Poems. By JAMES WHITCOMB RILEY. 12mo., gilt top, 5s.

Romanes.—*A SELECTION FROM THE POEMS OF GEORGE JOHN ROMANES, M.A., LL.D., F.R.S.* With an Introduction by T. HERBERT WARREN, President of Magdalen College, Oxford. Crown 8vo., 4s. 6d.

Poetry and the Drama—*continued.*

Savage-Armstrong.—*BALLADS OF DOWN.* By G. F. SAVAGE-ARMSTRONG, M.A., D.Litt. Crown 8vo., 7s. 6d.

Shakespeare.

BOWDLER'S FAMILY SHAKESPEARE. With 36 Woodcuts. 1 vol. 8vo., 14s. Or in 6 vols. Fcp. 8vo., 21s.

THE SHAKESPEARE BIRTHDAY BOOK. By MARY F. DUNBAR. 32mo., 1s. 6d.

Stevenson.—*A CHILD'S GARDEN OF VERSES.* By ROBERT LOUIS STEVENSON. Fcp. 8vo., gilt top, 5s.

Wagner.—*THE NIBELUNGEN RING.* Done into English Verse by REGINALD RANKIN, B.A., of the Inner Temple, Barrister-at-Law.

Vol. I. Rhine Gold, The Valkyrie. Fcp. 8vo., gilt top, 4s. 6d.

Vol. II. Siegfried, The Twilight of th Gods. Fcp. 8vo., gilt top, 4s. 6d.

Fiction, Humour, &c.

Anstey (F.).

VOCES POPULI. (Reprinted from 'Punch'.)

First Series. With 20 Illustrations by J. BERNARD PARTRIDGE. Cr. 8vo., gilt top, 3s. net.

Second Series. With 25 Illustrations by J. BERNARD PARTRIDGE. Cr. 8vo., gilt top, 3s. net.

THE MAN FROM BLANKLEY'S, and other Sketches. (Reprinted from 'Punch'.) With 25 Illustrations by J. BERNARD PARTRIDGE. Cr. 8vo., gilt top, 3s. net.

Bailey.—*MY LADY OF ORANGE :* a Romance of the Netherlands in the Days of Alva. By H. C. BAILEY. With 8 Illustrations. Crown 8vo., 6s.

Beaconsfield (The Earl of).

NOVELS AND TALES. Complete in 11 vols. Crown 8vo., 1s. 6d. each, or in sets, 11 vols., gilt top, 15s. net.

Vivian Grey.	Sybil.
The Young Duke, etc.	Henrietta Temple.
Alroy, Ixion, etc.	Venetia.
Contarini Fleming, etc.	Coningsby.
	Lothair.
Tancred.	Endymion.

NOVELS AND TALES. THE HUGHENDEN EDITION. With 2 Portraits and 11 Vignettes. 11 vols. Crown 8vo., 42s.

Bottome.—*LIFE, THE INTERPRETER.* By PHYLLIS BOTTOME. Crown 8vo., 6s.

Churchill.—*SAVROLA :* a Tale of the Revolution in Laurania. By WINSTON SPENCER CHURCHILL, M.P. Cr. 8vo., 6s.

Crawford.—*THE AUTOBIOGRAPHY OF A TRAMP.* By J. H. CRAWFORD. With a Photogravure Frontispiece 'The Vagrants,' by FRED. WALKER, and 8 other Illustrations. Crown 8vo., 5s. net.

Creed.—*THE VICAR OF ST. LUKE'S.* By SIBYL CREED. Crown 8vo., 6s.

Davenport.—*BY THE RAMPARTS OF JEZREEL :* a Romance of Jehu, King of Israel. By ARNOLD DAVENPORT. With Frontispiece by LANCELOT SPEED. Crown 8vo., 6s.

Dougall.—*BEGGARS ALL.* By L. DOUGALL. Crown 8vo., 3s. 6d.

Doyle (Sir A. CONAN).

MICAH CLARKE : A Tale of Monmouth's Rebellion. With 10 Illustrations. Cr. 8vo., 3s. 6d.

THE REFUGEES : A Tale of the Huguenots. With 25 Illustrations. Cr. 8vo., 3s. 6d.

THE STARK MUNRO LETTERS. Cr. 8vo., 3s. 6d.

THE CAPTAIN OF THE POLESTAR, and other Tales. Cr. 8vo., 3s. 6d.

Fiction, Humour, &c.—*continued.*

Dyson.—*THE GOLD-STEALERS:* a Story of Waddy. By EDWARD DYSON, Author of 'Rhymes from the Mines,' etc. Crown 8vo., 6s.

Farrar (F. W., DEAN OF CANTERBURY).

DARKNESS AND DAWN: or, Scenes in the Days of Nero. An Historic Tale. Cr. 8vo., gilt top, 6s. net.

GATHERING CLOUDS: a Tale of the Days of St. Chrysostom. Cr. 8vo., gilt top, 6s. net.

Fowler (EDITH H.).

THE YOUNG PRETENDERS. A Story of Child Life. With 12 Illustrations by Sir PHILIP BURNE-JONES, Bart. Crown 8vo., 6s.

THE PROFESSOR'S CHILDREN. With 24 Illustrations by ETHEL KATE BURGESS. Crown 8vo., 6s.

Francis (M. E.).

FIANDER'S WIDOW. Cr. 8vo., 6s.

YEOMAN FLEETWOOD. With Frontispiece. Crown 8vo., 3s. net.

PASTORALS OF DORSET. With 8 Illustrations. Crown 8vo., 6s.

THE MANOR FARM. With Frontispiece by CLAUD C. DU PRÉ COOPER. Crown 8vo., 6s.

Froude.—*THE TWO CHIEFS OF DUNBOY:* an Irish Romance of the Last Century. By JAMES A. FROUDE. Cr. 8vo., 3s. 6d.

Gurdon.—*MEMORIES AND FANCIES:* Suffolk Tales and other Stories; Fairy Legends; Poems; Miscellaneous Articles. By the late LADY CAMILLA GURDON. Cr. 8vo., 5s.

Haggard (H. RIDER).

ALLAN QUATERMAIN. With 31 Illustrations. Crown 8vo., 3s. 6d.

ALLAN'S WIFE. With 34 Illustrations. Crown 8vo., 3s. 6d.

BEATRICE. With Frontispiece and Vignette. Crown 8vo., 3s. 6d.

BLACK HEART AND WHITE HEART, AND OTHER STORIES. With 33 Illustrations. Crown 8vo., 6s.

CLEOPATRA. With 29 Illustrations. Crown 8vo., 3s. 6d.

COLONEL QUARITCH, V.C. With Frontispiece and Vignette. Cr. 8vo., 3s. 6d.

DAWN. With 16 Illustrations. Cr. 8vo., 3s. 6d.

DR. THERNE. Crown 8vo., 3s. 6d.

ERIC BRIGHTEYES. With 51 Illustrations. Crown 8vo., 3s. 6d.

HEART OF THE WORLD. With 15 Illustrations. Crown 8vo., 3s. 6d.

JOAN HASTE. With 20 Illustrations. Crown 8vo., 3s. 6d.

LYSBETH. With 26 Illustrations. Crown 8vo., 6s.

MAIWA'S REVENGE. Cr. 8vo., 1s. 6d.

MONTEZUMA'S DAUGHTER. With 24 Illustrations. Crown 8vo., 3s. 6d.

MR. MEESON'S WILL. With 16 Illustrations. Crown 8vo., 3s. 6d.

NADA THE LILY. With 23 Illustrations. Crown 8vo., 3s. 6d.

SHE. With 32 Illustrations. Crown 8vo., 3s. 6d.

SWALLOW: a Tale of the Great Trek. With 8 Illustrations. Crown 8vo., 3s. 6d.

THE PEOPLE OF THE MIST. With 16 Illustrations. Crown 8vo., 3s. 6d.

THE WITCH'S HEAD. With 16 Illustrations. Crown 8vo., 3s. 6d.

Fiction, Humour, &c.—*continued.*

Haggard and Lang.—*The World's Desire.* By H. Rider Haggard and Andrew Lang. With 27 Illustrations. Crown 8vo., 3s. 6d.

Harte.—*In the Carquinez Woods.* By Bret Harte. Crown 8vo., 3s. 6d.

Hope.—*The Heart of Princess Osra.* By Anthony Hope. With 9 Illustrations. Crown 8vo., 3s. 6d.

Howard (Lady Mabel).

The Undoing of John Brewster. Crown 8vo., 6s.

The Failure of Success. Crown 8vo., 6s.

Hutchinson.—*A Friend of Nelson.* By Horace G. Hutchinson. Cr. 8vo., 6s.

Jerome.—*Sketches in Lavender: Blue and Green.* By Jerome K. Jerome, Author of 'Three Men in a Boat,' etc. Crown 8vo., 3s. 6d.

Joyce.—*Old Celtic Romances.* Twelve of the most beautiful of the Ancient Irish Romantic Tales. Translated from the Gaelic. By P. W. Joyce, LL.D. Crown 8vo., 3s. 6d.

Lang (Andrew).

A Monk of Fife; a Story of the Days of Joan of Arc. With 13 Illustrations by Selwyn Image. Crown 8vo., 3s. 6d.

The Disentanglers. With 7 Full-page Illustrations by H. J. Ford. Crown 8vo., 6s.

Lyall (Edna).

The Hinderers. Crown 8vo., 2s. 6d.

The Autobiography of a Slander. Fcp. 8vo., 1s. sewed.
Presentation Edition. With 20 Illustrations by Lancelot Speed. Crown 8vo., 2s. 6d. net.

Doreen. The Story of a Singer. Crown 8vo., 6s.

Wayfaring Men. Crown 8vo., 6s.

Hope the Hermit: a Romance of Borrowdale. Crown 8vo., 6s.

Marchmont.—*In the Name of a Woman:* a Romance. By Arthur W. Marchmont. With 8 Illustrations. Crown 8vo., 6s.

Mason and Lang.—*Parson Kelly.* By A. E. W. Mason and Andrew Lang. Crown 8vo., 3s. 6d.

Max Müller. — *Deutsche Liebe* (*German Love*): Fragments from the Papers of an Alien. Collected by F. Max Müller. Translated from the German by G. A. M. Crown 8vo., gilt top, 5s.

Melville (G. J. Whyte).

The Gladiators.	Holmby House.
The Interpreter.	Kate Coventry.
Good for Nothing.	Digby Grand.
The Queen's Maries.	General Bounce.

Crown 8vo., 1s. 6d. each.

Merriman.—*Flotsam:* A Story of the Indian Mutiny. By Henry Seton Merriman. With Frontispiece and Vignette by H. G. Massey. Cr. 8vo., 3s. 6d.

Morris (William).

The Sundering Flood. Cr. 8vo., 7s. 6d.

The Water of the Wondrous Isles. Crown 8vo., 7s. 6d.

The Well at the World's End. 2 vols. 8vo., 28s.

The Wood Beyond the World. Crown 8vo., 6s. net.

The Story of the Glittering Plain, which has been also called The Land of the Living Men, or The Acre of the Undying. Square post 8vo., 5s. net.

The Roots of the Mountains, wherein is told somewhat of the Lives of the Men of Burgdale, their Friends, their Neighbours, their Foemen, and their Fellows-in-Arms. Written in Prose and Verse. Square crown 8vo., 8s.

Fiction, Humour, &c.—*continued.*

Morris (WILLIAM)—*continued.*

A TALE OF THE HOUSE OF THE WOLFINGS, and all the Kindreds of the Mark. Written in Prose and Verse. Square crown 8vo., 6s.

A DREAM OF JOHN BALL, AND A KING'S LESSON. 12mo., 1s. 6d.

NEWS FROM NOWHERE; or, An Epoch of Rest. Being some Chapters from an Utopian Romance. Post 8vo., 1s. 6d.

THE STORY OF GRETTIR THE STRONG. Translated from the Icelandic by EIRÍKR MAGNÚSSON and WILLIAM MORRIS. Cr. 8vo., 5s. net.

THREE NORTHERN LOVE STORIES, AND OTHER TALES. Translated from the Icelandic by EIRÍKR MAGNÚSSON and WILLIAM MORRIS. Crown 8vo., 6s. net.

** For Mr. William Morris's other Works, see pp. 24, 37 and 40.

Newman (Cardinal).

LOSS AND GAIN : The Story of a Convert. Crown 8vo., 3s. 6d.

CALLISTA : A Tale of the Third Century. Crown 8vo., 3s. 6d.

Phillipps-Wolley.—*SNAP:* a Legend of the Lone Mountain. By C. PHILLIPPS-WOLLEY. With 13 Illustrations. Crown 8vo., 3s. 6d.

Ridley.—*ANNE MAINWARING.* By ALICE RIDLEY, Author of 'The Story of Aline'. Crown 8vo., 6s.

Sewell (ELIZABETH M.).

A Glimpse of the World.	Amy Herbert.
Laneton Parsonage.	Cleve Hall.
Margaret Percival.	Gertrude.
Katharine Ashton.	Home Life.
The Earl's Daughter.	After Life.
The Experience of Life.	Ursula. Ivors.

Cr. 8vo., cloth plain, 1s. 6d. each. Cloth extra, gilt edges, 2s. 6d. each.

Sheehan. — *LUKE DELMEGE.* By the Rev. P. A. SHEEHAN, P.P., Author of 'My New Curate'. Crown 8vo., 6s.

Somerville (E. Œ.) **and Ross** (MARTIN).

SOME EXPERIENCES OF AN IRISH R.M. With 31 Illustrations by E. Œ. SOMERVILLE. Crown 8vo., 6s.

THE REAL CHARLOTTE. Crown 8vo., 3s. 6d.

THE SILVER FOX. Cr. 8vo., 3s. 6d.

Stebbing.—*RACHEL WULFSTAN*, and other Stories. By W. STEBBING, author of 'Probable Tales'. Crown 8vo., 4s. 6d.

Stevenson (ROBERT LOUIS).

THE STRANGE CASE OF DR. JEKYLL AND MR. HYDE. Fcp. 8vo., 1s. sewed. 1s. 6d. cloth.

THE STRANGE CASE OF DR. JEKYLL AND MR. HYDE ; WITH OTHER FABLES. Crown 8vo., bound in buckram, with gilt top, 5s. net.

'Silver Library' Edition. Crown 8vo., 3s. 6d.

MORE NEW ARABIAN NIGHTS—THE DYNAMITER. By ROBERT LOUIS STEVENSON and FANNY VAN DE GRIFT STEVENSON. Crown 8vo., 3s. 6d.

THE WRONG BOX. By ROBERT LOUIS STEVENSON and LLOYD OSBOURNE. Crown 8vo., 3s. 6d.

Fiction, Humour, &c.—*continued.*

Suttner.—*LAY DOWN YOUR ARMS* (*Die Waffen Nieder*): The Autobiography of Martha von Tilling. By BERTHA VON SUTTNER. Translated by T. HOLMES. Cr. 8vo., 1s. 6d.

Swan.—*BALLAST.* By MYRA SWAN. Crown 8vo., 6s.

Trollope (ANTHONY).

THE WARDEN. Cr. 8vo., 1s. 6d.

BARCHESTER TOWERS. Cr.8vo.,1s.6d.

Walford (L. B.).

CHARLOTTE. Crown 8vo., 6s.

ONE OF OURSELVES. Cr. 8vo., 6s.

THE INTRUDERS. Crown 8vo., 2s. 6d.

LEDDY MARGET. Crown 8vo., 2s. 6d.

IVA KILDARE : a Matrimonial Problem. Crown 8vo., 2s. 6d.

MR. SMITH: a Part of his Life. Crown 8vo., 2s. 6d.

THE BABY'S GRANDMOTHER. Cr. 8vo., 2s. 6d.

COUSINS. Crown 8vo., 2s. 6d.

TROUBLESOME DAUGHTERS. Cr. 8vo., 2s. 6d.

PAULINE. Crown 8vo., 2s. 6d.

DICK NETHERBY. Cr. 8vo., 2s. 6d.

THE HISTORY OF A WEEK. Cr. 8vo. 2s. 6d.

A STIFF-NECKED GENERATION. Cr. 8vo. 2s. 6d.

NAN, and other Stories. Cr. 8vo., 2s. 6d.

Walford (L. B.)—*continued.*

THE MISCHIEF OF MONICA. Cr. 8vo., 2s. 6d.

THE ONE GOOD GUEST. Cr. 8vo. 2s. 6d.

' *PLOUGHED,*' and other Stories. Crown 8vo., 2s. 6d.

THE MATCHMAKER. Cr. 8vo., 2s. 6d.

Ward.—*ONE POOR SCRUPLE.* By Mrs. WILFRID WARD. Crown 8vo., 6s.

Weyman (STANLEY).

THE HOUSE OF THE WOLF. With Frontispiece and Vignette. Crown 8vo., 3s. 6d.

A GENTLEMAN OF FRANCE. With Frontispiece and Vignette. Cr. 8vo., 6s.

THE RED COCKADE. With Frontispiece and Vignette. Crown 8vo., 6s.

SHREWSBURY. With 24 Illustrations by CLAUDE A. SHEPPERSON. Cr. 8vo., 6s.

SOPHIA. With Frontispiece. Crown 8vo., 6s.

Yeats (S. LEVETT-).

THE CHEVALIER D'AURIAC. Crown 8vo., 3s. 6d.

THE TRAITOR'S WAY. Cr. 8vo., 6s.

Yoxall.—*THE ROMANY STONE.* By J. H. YOXALL, M.P. Crown 8vo., 6s.

Popular Science (Natural History, &c.).

Butler.—*OUR HOUSEHOLD INSECTS.* An Account of the Insect-Pests found in Dwelling-Houses. By EDWARD A. BUTLER, B.A., B.Sc. (Lond.). With 113 Illustrations. Crown 8vo., 3*s*. 6*d*.

Furneaux (W.).

THE OUTDOOR WORLD; or The Young Collector's Handbook. With 18 Plates (16 of which are coloured), and 549 Illustrations in the Text. Crown 8vo., gilt edges, 6*s*. net.

BUTTERFLIES AND MOTHS (British). With 12 coloured Plates and 241 Illustrations in the Text. Crown 8vo., gilt edges, 6*s*. net.

LIFE IN PONDS AND STREAMS. With 8 coloured Plates and 331 Illustrations in the Text. Crown 8vo., gilt edges, 6*s*. net.

Hartwig (GEORGE).

THE SEA AND ITS LIVING WONDERS. With 12 Plates and 303 Woodcuts. 8vo., gilt top, 7*s*. net.

THE TROPICAL WORLD. With 8 Plates and 172 Woodcuts. 8vo., gilt top, 7*s*. net.

THE POLAR WORLD. With 3 Maps, 8 Plates and 85 Woodcuts. 8vo., gilt top, 7*s*. net.

THE SUBTERRANEAN WORLD. With 3 Maps and 80 Woodcuts. 8vo., gilt top, 7*s*. net.

Helmholtz.—*POPULAR LECTURES ON SCIENTIFIC SUBJECTS.* By HERMANN VON HELMHOLTZ. With 68 Woodcuts. 2 vols. Cr. 8vo., 3*s*. 6*d*. each.

Hudson (W. H.).

BIRDS AND MAN. Large crown 8vo., 6*s*. net.

NATURE IN DOWNLAND. With 12 Plates and 14 Illustrations in the Text by A. D. McCORMICK. 8vo., 10*s*. 6*d*. net.

BRITISH BIRDS. With a Chapter on Structure and Classification by FRANK E. BEDDARD, F.R.S. With 16 Plates (8 of which are Coloured), and over 100 Illustrations in the Text. Crown 8vo., gilt edges, 6*s*. net.

Millais.—*THE NATURAL HISTORY OF THE BRITISH SURFACE FEEDING-DUCKS.* By JOHN GUILLE MILLAIS, F.Z.S., etc. With 6 Photogravures and 66 Plates (41 in Colours) from Drawings by the Author, ARCHIBALD THORBURN, and from Photographs. Royal 4to., £6 6*s*.

Proctor (RICHARD A.).

LIGHT SCIENCE FOR LEISURE HOURS. Familiar Essays on Scientific Subjects. Crown 8vo., 3*s*. 6*d*.

ROUGH WAYS MADE SMOOTH. Familiar Essays on Scientific Subjects. Crown 8vo., 3*s*. 6*d*.

PLEASANT WAYS IN SCIENCE. Crown 8vo., 3*s*. 6*d*.

NATURE STUDIES. By R. A. PROCTOR, GRANT ALLEN, A. WILSON, T. FOSTER and E. CLODD. Cr. 8vo., 3*s*. 6*d*.

LEISURE READINGS. By R. A. PROCTOR, E. CLODD, A. WILSON, T. FOSTER and A. C. RANYARD. Cr. 8vo., 3*s*. 6*d*.

** *For Mr. Proctor's other books see pp. 17 and 35, and Messrs. Longmans & Co.'s Catalogue of Scientific Works.*

Popular Science (Natural History, &c.)—*continued.*

Stanley.—*A Familiar History of Birds.* By E. Stanley, D.D., formerly Bishop of Norwich. With 160 Illustrations. Cr. 8vo., 3s. 6d.

Wood (Rev. J. G.).

Homes without Hands: A Description of the Habitations of Animals, classed according to their Principle of Construction. With 140 Illustrations. 8vo., gilt top, 7s. net.

Insects at Home : A Popular Account of British Insects, their Structure, Habits and Transformations. With 700 Illustrations. 8vo., gilt top, 7s. net.

Wood (Rev. J. G.)—*continued.*

Insects Abroad : A Popular Account of Foreign Insects, their Structure, Habits and Transformations. With 600 Illustrations. 8vo., 7s. net.

Out of Doors; a Selection of Original Articles on Practical Natural History. With 11 Illustrations. Cr. 8vo., 3s. 6d.

Petland Revisited. With 33 Illustrations. Cr. 8vo., 3s. 6d.

Strange Dwellings: a Description of the Habitations of Animals, abridged from 'Homes without Hands'. With 60 Illustrations. Cr. 8vo., 3s. 6d.

Works of Reference.

Gwilt.—*An Encyclopædia of Architecture.* By Joseph Gwilt, F.S.A. With 1700 Engravings. Revised (1888), with Alterations and Considerable Additions by Wyatt Papworth. 8vo., 21s. net.

Longmans' *Gazetteer of the World.* Edited by George G. Chisholm, M.A., B.Sc. Imperial 8vo., 18s. net; cloth, 21s. half-morocco.

Maunder (Samuel).

Biographical Treasury. With Supplement brought down to 1889. By Rev. James Wood. Fcp. 8vo., 6s.

The Treasury of Bible Knowledge. By the Rev. J. Ayre, M.A. With 5 Maps, 15 Plates, and 300 Woodcuts. Fcp. 8vo., 6s.

Treasury of Knowledge and Library of Reference. Fcp. 8vo., 6s.

Maunder (Samuel)—*continued.*

The Treasury of Botany. Edited by J. Lindley, F.R.S., and T. Moore, F.L.S. With 274 Woodcuts and 20 Steel Plates. 2 vols. Fcp. 8vo., 12s.

Roget. — *Thesaurus of English Words and Phrases.* Classified and Arranged so as to Facilitate the Expression of Ideas and assist in Literary Composition. By Peter Mark Roget, M.D., F.R.S. Recomposed throughout, enlarged and improved, partly from the Author's Notes, and with a full Index, by the Author's Son, John Lewis Roget. Crown 8vo., 9s. net.

Willich.--*Popular Tables* for giving information for ascertaining the value of Lifehold, Leasehold, and Church Property, the Public Funds, etc. By Charles M. Willich. Edited by H. Bence Jones. Crown 8vo., 10s. 6d.

Children's Books.

Adelborg.—*CLEAN PETER AND THE CHILDREN OF GRUBBYLEA.* By OTTILIA ADELBORG. Translated from the Swedish by Mrs. GRAHAM WALLAS. With 23 Coloured Plates. Oblong 4to., boards, 3s. 6d. net.

Alick's Adventures.—By G. R. With 8 Illustrations by JOHN HASSALL. Crown 8vo., 3s. 6d.

Brown.—*THE BOOK OF SAINTS AND FRIENDLY BEASTS.* By ABBIE FARWELL BROWN. With 8 Illustrations by FANNY Y. CORY. Crown 8vo., 4s. 6d. net.

Buckland.—*TWO LITTLE RUNAWAYS.* Adapted from the French of LOUIS DES-NOYERS. By JAMES BUCKLAND. With 110 Illustrations by CECIL ALDIN. Cr. 8vo., 6s.

Crake (Rev. A. D.).

EDWY THE FAIR; or, The First Chronicle of Æscendune. Cr. 8vo., silver top, 2s. net.

ALFGAR THE DANE; or, The Second Chronicle of Æscendune. Cr. 8vo., silver top, 2s. net.

THE RIVAL HEIRS: being the Third and Last Chronicle of Æscendune. Cr. 8vo., silver top, 2s. net.

THE HOUSE OF WALDERNE. A Tale of the Cloister and the Forest in the Days of the Barons' Wars. Crown 8vo., silver top, 2s. net.

BRIAN FITZ-COUNT. A Story of Wallingford Castle and Dorchester Abbey. Cr. 8vo., silver top, 2s. net.

Henty (G. A.).—EDITED BY.

YULE LOGS: A Story-Book for Boys. By VARIOUS AUTHORS. With 61 Illustrations. Crown 8vo., gilt edges, 3s. net.

YULE TIDE YARNS: a Story-Book for Boys. By VARIOUS AUTHORS. With 45 Illustrations. Cr. 8vo., gilt edges, 3s. net.

Lang (ANDREW).—EDITED BY.

THE VIOLET FAIRY BOOK. With 8 Coloured Plates and 54 other Illustrations. Crown 8vo., gilt edges, 6s.

THE BLUE FAIRY BOOK. With 138 Illustrations. Crown 8vo., gilt edges, 6s.

THE RED FAIRY BOOK. With 100 Illustrations. Crown 8vo., gilt edges, 6s.

THE GREEN FAIRY BOOK. With 99 Illustrations. Crown 8vo., gilt edges, 6s.

THE GREY FAIRY BOOK. With 65 Illustrations. Crown 8vo., gilt edges, 6s.

THE YELLOW FAIRY BOOK. With 104 Illustrations. Cr. 8vo., gilt edges, 6s.

THE PINK FAIRY BOOK. With 67 Illustrations. Crown 8vo., gilt edges, 6s.

THE BLUE POETRY BOOK. With 100 Illustrations. Crown 8vo., gilt edges, 6s.

THE TRUE STORY BOOK. With 66 Illustrations. Crown 8vo., gilt edges, 6s.

THE RED TRUE STORY BOOK. With 100 Illustrations. Cr. 8vo., gilt edges, 6s.

THE ANIMAL STORY BOOK. With 67 Illustrations. Cr. 8vo., gilt edges, 6s.

THE RED BOOK OF ANIMAL STORIES. With 65 Illustrations. Crown 8vo., gilt edges, 6s.

THE ARABIAN NIGHTS ENTERTAIN-MENTS. With 66 Illustrations. Cr. 8vo., gilt edges, 6s.

THE BOOK OF ROMANCE. With 8 Coloured Plates and 44 other Illustrations. Crown 8vo., gilt edges, 6s.

Lyall.—*THE BURGES LETTERS:* a Record of Child Life in the Sixties. By EDNA LYALL. With Coloured Frontispiece and 8 other Full-page Illustrations by WALTER S. STACEY. Crown 8vo., 2s. 6d.

Meade (L. T.).

DADDY'S BOY. With 8 Illustrations. Crown 8vo., gilt edges, 3s. net.

DEB AND THE DUCHESS. With 7 Illustrations. Cr. 8vo., gilt edges, 3s. net.

THE BERESFORD PRIZE. With 7 Illustrations. Cr. 8vo., gilt edges, 3s. net.

THE HOUSE OF SURPRISES. With 6 Illustrations. Cr. 8vo., gilt edges, 3s. net.

Children's Books—*continued.*

Murray. — *FLOWER LEGENDS FOR CHILDREN.* By HILDA MURRAY (the Hon. Mrs. MURRAY of Elibank). Pictured by J. S. ELAND. With numerous Coloured and other Illustrations. Oblong 4to., 6s.

Penrose. — *CHUBBY: A NUISANCE.* By Mrs. PENROSE. With 8 Illustrations by G. G. MANTON. Crown 8vo., 3s. 6d.

Praeger (ROSAMOND).

THE ADVENTURES OF THE THREE BOLD BABES: HECTOR, HONORIA AND ALISANDER. A Story in Pictures. With 24 Coloured Plates and 24 Outline Pictures. Oblong 4to., 3s. 6d.

THE FURTHER DOINGS OF THE THREE BOLD BABES. With 24 Coloured Pictures and 24 Outline Pictures. Oblong 4to., 3s. 6d.

Roberts. — *THE ADVENTURES OF CAPTAIN JOHN SMITH :* Captain of Two Hundred and Fifty Horse, and sometime President of Virginia. By E. P. ROBERTS. With 17 Illustrations and 3 Maps. Crown 8vo., 5s. net.

Stevenson.—*A CHILD'S GARDEN OF VERSES.* By ROBERT LOUIS STEVENSON. Fcp. 8vo., gilt top, 5s.

Tappan.—*OLD BALLADS IN PROSE.* By EVA MARCH TAPPAN. With 4 Illustrations by FANNY Y. CORY. Crown 8vo., gilt top, 4s. 6d. net.

Upton (FLORENCE K. AND BERTHA).

THE ADVENTURES OF TWO DUTCH DOLLS AND A 'GOLLIWOGG'. With 31 Coloured Plates and numerous Illustrations in the Text. Oblong 4to., 6s.

THE GOLLIWOGG'S BICYCLE CLUB. With 31 Coloured Plates and numerous Illustrations in the Text. Oblong 4to., 6s.

THE GOLLIWOGG AT THE SEASIDE. With 31 Coloured Plates and numerous Illustrations in the Text. Oblong 4to., 6s.

THE GOLLIWOGG IN WAR. With 31 Coloured Plates. Oblong 4to., 6s.

THE GOLLIWOGG'S POLAR ADVENTURES. With 31 Coloured Plates. Oblong 4to., 6s.

THE GOLLIWOGG'S AUTO-GO-CART. With 31 Coloured Plates and numerous Illustrations in the Text. Oblong 4to., 6s.

THE GOLLIWOGG'S AIR-SHIP. With 30 Coloured Pictures and numerous Illustrations in the Text. Oblong 4to., 6s.

THE VEGE-MEN'S REVENGE. With 31 Coloured Plates and numerous Illustrations in the Text. Oblong 4to., 6s.

Wemyss.—'*THINGS WE THOUGHT OF': Told from a Child's Point of View.* By MARY C. E. WEMYSS, Author of 'All About All of Us'. With 8 Illustrations in Colour by S. R. PRAEGER. Crown 8vo., 3s. 6d.

The Silver Library.

CROWN 8vo. 3s. 6d. EACH VOLUME.

Arnold's (Sir Edwin) Seas and Lands. With 71 Illustrations. 3s. 6d.

Bagehot's (W.) Biographical Studies. 3s. 6d.

Bagehot's (W.) Economic Studies. 3s. 6d.

Bagehot's (W.) Literary Studies. With Portrait. 3 vols., 3s. 6d. each.

Baker's (Sir S. W.) Eight Years in Ceylon. With 6 Illustrations. 3s. 6d.

Baker's (Sir S. W.) Rifle and Hound in Ceylon. With 6 Illustrations. 3s. 6d.

Baring-Gould's (Rev. S.) Curious Myths of the Middle Ages. 3s. 6d.

Baring-Gould's (Rev. S.) Origin and Development of Religious Belief. 2 vols. 3s. 6d. each.

Becker's (W. A.) Gallus : or, Roman Scenes in the Time of Augustus. With 26 Illus. 3s. 6d.

Becker's (W. A.) Charicles : or, Illustrations of the Private Life of the Ancient Greeks. With 26 Illustrations. 3s. 6d.

Bent's (J. T.) The Ruined Cities of Mashonaland. With 117 Illustrations. 3s. 6d.

Brassey's (Lady) A Voyage in the 'Sunbeam'. With 66 Illustrations. 3s. 6d.

Buckle's (H. T.) History of Civilisation in England. 3 vols. 10s. 6d.

Churchill's (W. Spencer) The Story of the Malakand Field Force, 1897. With 6 Maps and Plans. 3s. 6d.

Clodd's (E.) Story of Creation: a Plain Account of Evolution. With 77 Illustrations. 3s. 6d.

Conybeare (Rev. W. J.) and Howson's (Very Rev. J. S.) Life and Epistles of St. Paul. With 46 Illustrations. 3s. 6d.

Dougall's (L.) Beggars All: a Novel. 3s. 6d.

Doyle's (Sir A. Conan) Micah Clarke. A Tale of Monmouth's Rebellion. With 10 Illusts. 3s. 6d.

The Silver Library—*continued.*

Doyle's (Sir A. Conan) The Captain of the Polestar, and other Tales. 3s. 6d.

Doyle's (Sir A. Conan) The Refugees: A Tale of the Huguenots. With 25 Illustrations. 3s 6d.

Doyle's (Sir A. Conan) The Stark Munro Letters. 3s. 6d.

Froude's (J. A.) The History of England, from the Fall of Wolsey to the Defeat of the Spanish Armada. 12 vols. 3s. 6d. each.

Froude's (J. A.) The English in Ireland. 3 vols. 10s. 6d.

Froude's (J. A.) The Divorce of Catherine of Aragon. 3s. 6d.

Froude's (J. A.) The Spanish Story of the Armada, and other Essays. 3s. 6d.

Froude's (J. A.) English Seamen in the Sixteenth Century. 3s. 6d.

Froude's (J. A.) Short Studies on Great Subjects. 4 vols. 3s. 6d. each.

Froude's (J. A.) Oceana, or England and Her Colonies. With 9 Illustrations. 3s. 6d.

Froude's (J. A.) The Council of Trent. 3s. 6d.

Froude's (J. A.) The Life and Letters of Erasmus. 3s. 6d.

Froude's (J. A.) Thomas Carlyle: a History of his Life.
1795-1835. 2 vols. 7s. 1834-1881. 2 vols. 7s.

Froude's (J. A.) Cæsar: a Sketch. 3s. 6d.

Froude's (J. A.) The Two Chiefs of Dunboy: an Irish Romance of the Last Century. 3s. 6d.

Froude's (J. A.) Writings, Selections from. 3s. 6d.

Gleig's (Rev. G. R.) Life of the Duke of Wellington. With Portrait. 3s. 6d.

Greville's (C. C. F.) Journal of the Reigns of King George IV., King William IV., and Queen Victoria. 8 vols., 3s. 6d. each.

Haggard's (H. R.) She: A History of Adventure. With 32 Illustrations. 3s. 6d.

Haggard's (H. R.) Allan Quatermain. With 20 Illustrations. 3s. 6d.

Haggard's (H. R.) Colonel Quaritch, V.C.: a Tale of Country Life. With Frontispiece and Vignette. 3s. 6d.

Haggard's (H. R.) Cleopatra. With 29 Illustrations. 3s. 6d.

Haggard's (H. R.) Eric Brighteyes. With 51 Illustrations. 3s. 6d.

Haggard's (H. R.) Beatrice. With Frontispiece and Vignette. 3s. 6d.

Haggard's (H. R.) Allan's Wife. With 34 Illustrations. 3s. 6d.

Haggard (H. R.) Heart of the World. With 15 Illustrations. 3s. 6d.

Haggard's (H. R.) Montezuma's Daughter. With 25 Illustrations. 3s. 6d.

Haggard's (H. R.) Swallow: a Tale of the Great Trek. With 8 Illustrations. 3s. 6d.

Haggard's (H. R.) The Witch's Head. With 16 Illustrations. 3s. 6d.

Haggard's (H. R.) Mr. Meeson's Will. With 16 Illustrations. 3s. 6d.

Haggard's (H. R.) Nada the Lily. With 23 Illustrations. 3s. 6d.

Haggard's (H. R.) Dawn. With 16 Illusts. 3s. 6d.

Haggard's (H. R.) The People of the Mist. With 16 Illustrations. 3s. 6d.

Haggard's (H. R.) Joan Haste. With 20 Illustrations. 3s. 6d.

Haggard (H. R.) and Lang's (A.) The World's Desire. With 27 Illustrations. 3s. 6d.

Harte's (Bret) In the Carquinez Woods and other Stories. 3s. 6d.

Helmholtz's (Hermann von) Popular Lectures on Scientific Subjects. With 68 Illustrations. 2 vols. 3s. 6d. each.

Hope's (Anthony) The Heart of Princess Osra. With 9 Illustrations. 3s. 6d.

Howitt's (W.) Visits to Remarkable Places. With 80 Illustrations. 3s. 6d.

Jefferies' (R.) The Story of My Heart: My Autobiography. With Portrait. 3s. 6d.

Jefferies' (R.) Field and Hedgerow. With Portrait. 3s. 6d.

Jefferies' (R.) Red Deer. With 17 Illusts. 3s. 6d.

Jefferies' (R.) Wood Magic: a Fable. With Frontispiece and Vignette by E. V. B. 3s. 6d.

Jefferies (R.) The Toilers of the Field. With Portrait from the Bust in Salisbury Cathedral. 3s. 6d.

Kaye (Sir J.) and Malleson's (Colonel) History of the Indian Mutiny of 1857-8. 6 vols. 3s. 6d. each.

Knight's (E. F.) The Cruise of the 'Alerte': the Narrative of a Search for Treasure on the Desert Island of Trinidad. With 2 Maps and 23 Illustrations. 3s. 6d.

The Silver Library—*continued.*

Knight's (E. F.) Where Three Empires Meet: a Narrative of Recent Travel in Kashmir, Western Tibet, Baltistan, Gilgit. With a Map and 54 Illustrations. 3*s.* 6*d.*

Knight's (E. F.) The 'Falcon' on the Baltic: a Coasting Voyage from Hammersmith to Copenhagen in a Three-Ton Yacht. With Map and 11 Illustrations. 3*s.* 6*d.*

Köstlin's (J.) Life of Luther. With 62 Illustrations and 4 Facsimiles of MSS. 3*s.* 6*d.*

Lang's (A.) Angling Sketches. With 20 Illustrations. 3*s.* 6*d.*

Lang's (A.) Custom and Myth: Studies of Early Usage and Belief. 3*s.* 6*d.*

Lang's (A.) Cock Lane and Common-Sense. 3*s.* 6*d.*

Lang's (A.) The Book of Dreams and Ghosts. 3*s.* 6*d.*

Lang's (A.) A Monk of Fife: a Story of the Days of Joan of Arc. With 13 Illustrations. 3*s.* 6*d.*

Lang's (A.) Myth, Ritual, and Religion. 2 vols. 7*s.*

Lees (J. A.) and Clutterbuck's (W. J.) B.C. 1887, A Ramble in British Columbia. With Maps and 75 Illustrations. 3*s.* 6*d*

Levett-Yeats' (S.) The Chevalier D'Auriac. 3*s.* 6*d.*

Macaulay's (Lord) Complete Works. 'Albany' Edition. With 12 Portraits. 12 vols. 3*s.* 6*d.* each.

Macaulay's (Lord) Essays and Lays of Ancient Rome, etc. With Portrait and 4 Illustrations to the 'Lays'. 3*s.* 6*d.*

Macleod's (H. D.) Elements of Banking. 3*s.* 6*d.*

Marshman's (J. C.) Memoirs of Sir Henry Havelock. 3*s.* 6*d.*

Mason (A. E. W.) and Lang's (A.) Parson Kelly. 3*s.* 6*d.*

Merivale's (Dean) History of the Romans under the Empire. 8 vols. 3*s.* 6*d.* each.

Merriman's (H. S.) Flotsam: A Tale of the Indian Mutiny. 3*s.* 6*d.*

Mill's (J. S.) Political Economy. 3*s.* 6*d.*

Mill's (J. S.) System of Logic. 3*s.* 6*d.*

Milner's (Geo.) Country Pleasures: the Chronicle of a Year chiefly in a Garden. 3*s.* 6*d.*

Nansen's (F.) The First Crossing of Greenland. With 142 Illustrations and a Map. 3*s.* 6*d.*

Phillipps-Wolley's (C.) Snap: a Legend of the Lone Mountain With 13 Illustrations. 3*s.* 6*d.*

Proctor's (R. A.) The Orbs Around Us. 3*s.* 6*d.*

Proctor's (R. A.) The Expanse of Heaven. 3*s.* 6*d.*

Proctor's (R. A.) Light Science for Leisure Hours. 3*s.* 6*d.*

Proctor's (R. A.) The Moon. 3*s.* 6*d.*

Proctor's (R. A.) Other Worlds than Ours. 3*s.* 6*d.*

Proctor's (R. A.) Our Place among Infinities: a Series of Essays contrasting our Little Abode in Space and Time with the Infinities around us. 3*s.* 6*d.*

Proctor's (R. A.) Other Suns than Ours. 3*s.* 6*d.*

Proctor's (R. A.) Rough Ways made Smooth. 3*s.* 6*d.*

Proctor's (R. A.) Pleasant Ways in Science. 3*s.* 6*d.*

Proctor's (R. A.) Myths and Marvels of Astronomy. 3*s.* 6*d.*

Proctor's (R. A.) Nature Studies. 3*s.* 6*d.*

Proctor's (R. A.) Leisure Readings. By R. A. PROCTOR, EDWARD CLODD, ANDREW WILSON, THOMAS FOSTER, and A. C. RANYARD. With Illustrations. 3*s.* 6*d.*

Rossetti's (Maria F.) A Shadow of Dante. 3*s.* 6*d.*

Smith's (R. Bosworth) Carthage and the Carthaginians. With Maps, Plans, etc. 3*s.* 6*d.*

Stanley's (Bishop) Familiar History of Birds. With 160 Illustrations. 3*s.* 6*d.*

Stephen's (Sir Leslie) The Playground of Europe (The Alps). With 4 Illustrations. 3*s.* 6*d.*

Stevenson's (R. L.) The Strange Case of Dr. Jekyll and Mr. Hyde; with other Fables. 3*s.* 6*d.*

Stevenson (R. L.) and Osbourne's (Ll.) The Wrong Box. 3*s.* 6*d.*

Stevenson (Robert Louis) and Stevenson's (Fanny van de Grift) More New Arabian Nights.—The Dynamiter. 3*s.* 6*d.*

Trevelyan's (Sir G. O.) The Early History of Charles James Fox. 3*s.* 6*d.*

Weyman's (Stanley J.) The House of the Wolf: a Romance. 3*s.* 6*d.*

Wood's (Rev. J. G.) Petland Revisited. With 33 Illustrations. 3*s.* 6*d.*

Wood's (Rev. J. G.) Strange Dwellings. With 60 Illustrations. 3*s.* 6*d.*

Wood's (Rev. J. G.) Out of Doors. With 11 Illustrations. 3*s.* 6*d.*

Cookery, Domestic Management, &c.

Acton. — *MODERN COOKERY.* By ELIZA ACTON. With 150 Woodcuts. Fcp. 8vo., 4s. 6d.

Angwin. — *SIMPLE HINTS ON CHOICE OF FOOD,* with Tested and Economical Recipes. For Schools, Homes, and Classes for Technical Instruction. By M. C. ANGWIN, Diplomate (First Class) of the National Union for the Technical Training of Women, etc. Crown 8vo., 1s.

Ashby. — *HEALTH IN THE NURSERY.* By HENRY ASHBY, M.D., F.R.C.P., Physician to the Manchester Children's Hospital. With 25 Illustrations. Crown 8vo., 3s. net.

Bull (THOMAS, M.D.).

HINTS TO MOTHERS ON THE MANAGEMENT OF THEIR HEALTH DURING THE PERIOD OF PREGNANCY. Fcp. 8vo., sewed, 1s. 6d.; cloth, gilt edges, 2s. net.

THE MATERNAL MANAGEMENT OF CHILDREN IN HEALTH AND DISEASE. Fcp. 8vo., sewed, 1s. 6d.; cloth, gilt edges, 2s. net.

De Salis (Mrs.).

À LA MODE COOKERY: Up-to-date Recipes. With 24 Plates (16 in Colour). Crown 8vo., 5s. net.

CAKES AND CONFECTIONS À LA MODE. Fcp. 8vo., 1s. 6d.

DOGS: A Manual for Amateurs. Fcp. 8vo., 1s. 6d.

DRESSED GAME AND POULTRY À LA MODE. Fcp. 8vo., 1s. 6d.

DRESSED VEGETABLES À LA MODE. Fcp. 8vo., 1s 6d.

DRINKS À LA MODE. Fcp. 8vo., 1s. 6d.

De Salis (Mrs.)—*continued.*

ENTRÉES À LA MODE. Fcp. 8vo., 1s. 6d.

FLORAL DECORATIONS. Fcp. 8vo., 1s. 6d.

GARDENING À LA MODE. Fcp. 8vo. Part I., Vegetables, 1s. 6d. Part II., Fruits, 1s. 6d.

NATIONAL VIANDS À LA MODE. Fcp. 8vo., 1s. 6d.

NEW-LAID EGGS. Fcp. 8vo., 1s. 6d.

OYSTERS À LA MODE. Fcp. 8vo., 1s. 6d.

PUDDINGS AND PASTRY À LA MODE. Fcp. 8vo., 1s. 6d.

SAVOURIES À LA MODE. Fcp. 8vo., 1s. 6d.

SOUPS AND DRESSED FISH À LA MODE. Fcp. 8vo., 1s. 6d.

SWEETS AND SUPPER DISHES À LA MODE. Fcp. 8vo., 1s. 6d.

TEMPTING DISHES FOR SMALL INCOMES. Fcp. 8vo., 1s. 6d.

WRINKLES AND NOTIONS FOR EVERY HOUSEHOLD. Crown 8vo., 1s. 6d.

Lear. — *MAIGRE COOKERY.* By H. L. SIDNEY LEAR. 16mo., 2s.

Poole. — *COOKERY FOR THE DIABETIC.* By W. H. and Mrs. POOLE. With Preface by Dr. PAVY. Fcp. 8vo., 2s. 6d.

Rotheram. — *HOUSEHOLD COOKERY RECIPES.* By M. A. ROTHERAM, First Class Diplomée, National Training School of Cookery, London; Instructress to the Bedfordshire County Council. Crown 8vo., 2s.

The Fine Arts and Music.

Burne-Jones. — *THE BEGINNING OF THE WORLD:* Twenty-five Pictures by EDWARD BURNE-JONES. Medium 4to., Boards, 7s. 6d. net.

Burns and Colenso. — *LIVING ANATOMY.* By CECIL L. BURNS, R.B.A., and ROBERT J. COLENSO, M.A., M.D. 40 Plates, 11¼ by 8¾ ins., each Plate containing Two Figures—(a) A Natural Male or Female Figure; (b) The same Figure Anatomatised. In a Portfolio, 7s. 6d. net.

Hamlin. — *A TEXT-BOOK OF THE HISTORY OF ARCHITECTURE.* By A. D. F. HAMLIN, A.M. With 229 Illustrations. Crown 8vo., 7s. 6d.

Haweis (Rev. H. R.).

MUSIC AND MORALS. With Portrait of the Author, and numerous Illustrations, Facsimiles, and Diagrams. Cr. 8vo., 6s. net.

MY MUSICAL LIFE. With Portrait of Richard Wagner and 3 Illustrations. Crown 8vo., 6s. net.

The Fine Arts and Music—*continued.*

Huish, Head, and Longman.— *SAMPLERS AND TAPESTRY EMBROIDERIES.* By MARCUS B. HUISH, LL.B.; also 'The Stitchery of the Same,' by Mrs. HEAD; and 'Foreign Samplers,' by Mrs. C. J. LONGMAN. With 30 Reproductions in Colour, and 40 Illustrations in Monochrome. 4to., £2 2s. net.

Hullah.— *THE HISTORY OF MODERN MUSIC.* By JOHN HULLAH. 8vo., 8s. 6d.

Jameson (Mrs. ANNA).

SACRED AND LEGENDARY ART, containing Legends of the Angels and Archangels, the Evangelists, the Apostles, the Doctors of the Church, St. Mary Magdalene, the Patron Saints, the Martyrs, the Early Bishops, the Hermits, and the Warrior-Saints of Christendom, as represented in the Fine Arts. With 19 Etchings and 187 Woodcuts. 2 vols. 8vo., 20s. net.

LEGENDS OF THE MONASTIC ORDERS, as represented in the Fine Arts, comprising the Benedictines and Augustines, and Orders derived from their Rules, the Mendicant Orders, the Jesuits, and the Order of the Visitation of St. Mary. With 11 Etchings and 88 Woodcuts. 1 vol. 8vo., 10s. net.

LEGENDS OF THE MADONNA, OR BLESSED VIRGIN MARY. Devotional with and without the Infant Jesus, Historical from the Annunciation to the Assumption, as represented in Sacred and Legendary Christian Art. With 27 Etchings and 165 Woodcuts. 1 vol. 8vo., 10s. net.

THE HISTORY OF OUR LORD, as exemplified in Works of Art, with that of His Types, St. John the Baptist, and other persons of the Old and New Testament. Commenced by the late Mrs. JAMESON; continued and completed by LADY EASTLAKE. With 31 Etchings and 281 Woodcuts. 2 vols. 8vo., 20s. net.

Kristeller. — *ANDREA MANTEGNA.* By PAUL KRISTELLER. English Edition by S. ARTHUR STRONG, M.A., Librarian to the House of Lords, and at Chatsworth. With 26 Photogravure Plates and 162 Illustrations in the Text. 4to., gilt top, £3 10s. net.

Macfarren. — *LECTURES ON HARMONY.* By Sir GEORGE A. MACFARREN. 8vo., 12s.

Morris (WILLIAM).

ARCHITECTURE, INDUSTRY AND WEALTH. Collected Papers. Crown 8vo., 6s. net.

HOPES AND FEARS FOR ART. Five Lectures delivered in Birmingham, London, etc., in 1878-1881. Cr 8vo., 4s. 6d.

AN ADDRESS DELIVERED AT THE DISTRIBUTION OF PRIZES TO STUDENTS OF THE BIRMINGHAM MUNICIPAL SCHOOL OF ART ON 21ST FEBRUARY, 1894. 8vo., 2s. 6d. net. (*Printed in 'Golden' Type.*)

SOME HINTS ON PATTERN-DESIGNING: a Lecture delivered at the Working Men's College, London, on 10th December, 1881. 8vo., 2s. 6d. net. (*Printed in 'Golden' Type.*)

ARTS AND ITS PRODUCERS (1888) *AND THE ARTS AND CRAFTS OF TO-DAY* (1889). 8vo., 2s. 6d. net. (*Printed in 'Golden' Type.*)

ARCHITECTURE AND HISTORY, AND WESTMINSTER ABBEY. Two Papers read before the Society for the Protection of Ancient Buildings. 8vo., 2s. 6d. net. (*Printed in 'Golden' Type.*)

ARTS AND CRAFTS ESSAYS. By Members of the Arts and Crafts Exhibition Society. With a Preface by WILLIAM MORRIS. Crown 8vo., 2s. 6d. net.
. For Mr. William Morris's other Works, see pp. 24, 27, 28 and 40.

Robertson.— *OLD ENGLISH SONGS AND DANCES.* Decorated in Colour by W. GRAHAM ROBERTSON. Royal 4to., 42s. net.

Scott. — *THE PORTRAITURES · OF JULIUS CÆSAR:* a Monograph. By FRANK J. SCOTT. With many Full-page Plates and Illustrations in the Text. Small 4to.

Vanderpoel. — *COLOUR PROBLEMS:* a Practical Manual for the Lay Student of Colour. By EMILY NOYES VANDERPOEL. With 117 Plates in Colour. Square 8vo., 21s. net.

Van Dyke.— *A TEXT-BOOK ON THE HISTORY OF PAINTING.* By JOHN C. VAN DYKE. With 110 Illustrations. Cr. 8vo., 6s.

Wellington.— *A DESCRIPTIVE AND HISTORICAL CATALOGUE OF THE COLLECTIONS OF PICTURES AND SCULPTURE AT APSLEY HOUSE, LONDON.* By EVELYN, Duchess of Wellington. Illustrated by 52 Photo-Engravings, specially executed by BRAUN, CLÉMENT, & Co., of Paris. 2 vols., royal 4to., £6 6s. net.

Miscellaneous and Critical Works.

Annals of Mathematics (under the Auspices of Harvard University). Issued Quarterly. 4to., 2s. net each number.

Auto da Fé and other Essays: some being Essays in Fiction. By the Author of 'Essays in Paradox' and 'Exploded Ideas'. Crown 8vo., 5s.

Bagehot.—*LITERARY STUDIES.* By WALTER BAGEHOT. With Portrait. 3 vols. Crown 8vo., 3s. 6d. each.

Baker. — *EDUCATION AND LIFE:* Papers and Addresses. By JAMES H. BAKER, M.A., LL.D. Crown 8vo., 4s. 6d.

Baring-Gould.—*CURIOUS MYTHS OF THE MIDDLE AGES.* By Rev. S. BARING-GOULD. Crown 8vo., 3s. 6d.

Baynes. — *SHAKESPEARE STUDIES,* and other Essays. By the late THOMAS SPENCER BAYNES, LL.B., LL.D. With a Biographical Preface by Professor LEWIS CAMPBELL. Crown 8vo., 7s. 6d.

Bonnell. — *CHARLOTTE BRONTË, GEORGE ELIOT, JANE AUSTEN:* Studies in their Works. By HENRY H. BONNELL. Crown 8vo.

Booth.—*THE DISCOVERY AND DE-CIPHERMENT OF THE TRILINGUAL CUNEI-FORM INSCRIPTIONS.* By ARTHUR JOHN BOOTH, M.A. With a Plan of Persepolis. 8vo. 14s. net.

Charities Register, The Annual, *AND DIGEST:* being a Classified Register of Charities in or available in the Metropolis. 8vo., 4s.

Christie.—*SELECTED ESSAYS.* By RICHARD COPLEY CHRISTIE, M.A., Oxon. Hon. LL.D., Vict. With 2 Portraits and 3 other Illustrations. 8vo., 12s. net.

Dickinson.—*KING ARTHUR IN CORN-WALL.* By W. HOWSHIP DICKINSON, M.D. With 5 Illustrations. Crown 8vo., 4s. 6d.

Essays in Paradox. By the Author of 'Exploded Ideas' and 'Times and Days'. Crown 8vo., 5s.

Evans.—*THE ANCIENT STONE IM-PLEMENTS, WEAPONS AND ORNAMENTS OF GREAT BRITAIN.* By Sir JOHN EVANS, K.C.B. With 537 Illustrations. 8vo., 28s.

Exploded Ideas, *AND OTHER ESSAYS.* By the Author of 'Times and Days'. Cr. 8vo., 5s.

Frost. — *A MEDLEY BOOK.* By GEORGE FROST. Crown 8vo., 3s. 6d. net.

Geikie.—*THE VICAR AND HIS FRIENDS.* Reported by CUNNINGHAM GEIKIE, D.D., LL.D. Crown 8vo., 5s. net.

Haggard (H. RIDER).

A FARMER'S YEAR: being his Commonplace Book for 1898. With 36 Illustrations. Crown 8vo., 7s. 6d. net.

RURAL ENGLAND. With 23 Agricultural Maps and 56 Illustrations from Photographs. 2 vols., 8vo.

Hoenig. — *INQUIRIES CONCERNING THE TACTICS OF THE FUTURE.* By FRITZ HOENIG. With 1 Sketch in the Text and 5 Maps. Translated by Captain H. M. BOWER. 8vo., 15s. net.

Hutchinson.—*DREAMS AND THEIR MEANINGS.* By HORACE G. HUTCHINSON. 8vo., gilt top, 9s. 6d. net.

Jefferies (RICHARD).

FIELD AND HEDGEROW: With Portrait. Crown 8vo., 3s. 6d.

THE STORY OF MY HEART: my Autobiography. Crown 8vo., 3s. 6d.

RED DEER. With 17 Illustrations. Crown 8vo., 3s. 6d.

THE TOILERS OF THE FIELD. Crown 8vo., 3s. 6d.

WOOD MAGIC: a Fable. Crown 8vo., 3s. 6d.

Jekyll (GERTRUDE).

HOME AND GARDEN: Notes and Thoughts, Practical and Critical, of a Worker in both. With 53 Illustrations from Photographs. 8vo., 10s. 6d. net.

WOOD AND GARDEN: Notes and Thoughts, Practical and Critical, of a Working Amateur. With 71 Photographs. 8vo., 10s. 6d. net.

Miscellaneous and Critical Works—*continued.*

Johnson (J. & J. H.).

THE PATENTEE'S MANUAL : a Treatise on the Law and Practice of Letters Patent. 8vo., 10s. 6d.

AN EPITOME OF THE LAW AND PRACTICE CONNECTED WITH PATENTS FOR INVENTIONS, with a reprint of the Patents Acts of 1883, 1885, 1886 and 1888. Crown 8vo., 2s. 6d.

Joyce.—*THE ORIGIN AND HISTORY OF IRISH NAMES OF PLACES.* By P. W. JOYCE, LL.D. 2 vols. Crown 8vo., 5s. each.

Lang (ANDREW).

LETTERS TO DEAD AUTHORS. Fcp. 8vo., 2s. 6d. net.

BOOKS AND BOOKMEN. With 2 Coloured Plates and 17 Illustrations. Fcp. 8vo., 2s. 6d. net.

OLD FRIENDS. Fcp. 8vo., 2s. 6d. net.

LETTERS ON LITERATURE. Fcp. 8vo., 2s. 6d. net.

ESSAYS IN LITTLE. With Portrait of the Author. Crown 8vo., 2s. 6d.

COCK LANE AND COMMON-SENSE. Crown 8vo., 3s. 6d.

THE BOOK OF DREAMS AND GHOSTS. Crown 8vo., 3s. 6d.

Maryon.—*HOW THE GARDEN GREW.* By MAUD MARYON. With 4 Illustrations. Crown 8vo., 5s. net.

Matthews.—*NOTES ON SPEECH-MAKING.* By BRANDER MATTHEWS. Fcp. 8vo., 1s. 6d. net.

Max Müller (The Right Hon. F.).

COLLECTED WORKS. 18 vols. Crown 8vo., 5s. each.

Vol. I. *NATURAL RELIGION:* the Gifford Lectures, 1888.

Vol. II. *PHYSICAL RELIGION:* the Gifford Lectures, 1890.

Vol. III. *ANTHROPOLOGICAL RELIGION:* the Gifford Lectures, 1891.

Vol. IV. *THEOSOPHY;* or, Psychological Religion : the Gifford Lectures, 1892.

CHIPS FROM A GERMAN WORKSHOP.

Vol. V. Recent Essays and Addresses.

Vol. VI. Biographical Essays.

Vol. VII. Essays on Language and Literature.

Vol. VIII. Essays on Mythology and Folk-lore.

Vol. IX. *THE ORIGIN AND GROWTH OF RELIGION*, as Illustrated by the Religions of India: the Hibbert Lectures, 1878.

Vol. X. *BIOGRAPHIES OF WORDS, AND THE HOME OF THE ARYAS.*

Vols. XI., XII. *THE SCIENCE OF LANGUAGE :* Founded on Lectures delivered at the Royal Institution in 1861 and 1863. 2 vols. 10s.

Vol. XIII. *INDIA :* What can it Teach Us ?

Vol. XIV. *INTRODUCTION TO THE SCIENCE OF RELIGION.* Four Lectures, 1870.

Vol. XV. *RÂMAKRISHNA :* his Life and Sayings.

Vol. XVI. *THREE LECTURES ON THE VEDÂNTA PHILOSOPHY,* 1894.

Vol. XVII. *LAST ESSAYS.* First Series. Essays on Language, Folk-lore, etc.

Vol. XVIII. *LAST ESSAYS.* Second Series. Essays on the Science of Religion.

Miscellaneous and Critical Works—*continued.*

Milner.—*COUNTRY PLEASURES:* the Chronicle of a Year chiefly in a Garden. By GEORGE MILNER. Crown 8vo., 3s. 6d.

Morris.—*SIGNS OF CHANGE.* Seven Lectures delivered on various Occasions. By WILLIAM MORRIS. Post 8vo., 4s. 6d.

Parker and Unwin.—*THE ART OF BUILDING A HOME :* a Collection of Lectures and Illustrations. By BARRY PARKER and RAYMOND UNWIN. With 68 Full-page Plates. 8vo., 10s. 6d. net.

Pollock.—*JANE AUSTEN :* her Contemporaries and Herself. By WALTER HERRIES POLLOCK. Cr. 8vo., 3s. 6d. net.

Poore (GEORGE VIVIAN, M.D.).

ESSAYS ON RURAL HYGIENE. With 13 Illustrations. Crown 8vo., 6s. 6d.

THE DWELLING HOUSE. With 36 Illustrations. Crown 8vo., 3s. 6d.

THE EARTH IN RELATION TO THE PRESERVATION AND DESTRUCTION OF CONTAGIA : being the Milroy Lectures delivered at the Royal College of Physicians in 1899, together with other Papers on Sanitation. With 13 Illustrations. Crown 8vo., 5s.

Rossetti. - *A SHADOW OF DANTE :* being an Essay towards studying Himself, his World and his Pilgrimage. By MARIA FRANCESCA ROSSETTI. Crown 8vo., 3s. 6d.

Shadwell. — *DRINK : TEMPERANCE AND LEGISLATION.* By ARTHUR SHADWELL, M.A., M.D. Crown 8vo., 5s. net.

Soulsby (LUCY H. M.).

STRAY THOUGHTS ON READING. Fcp. 8vo., 2s. 6d. net.

STRAY THOUGHTS FOR GIRLS. 16mo., 1s. 6d net.

STRAY THOUGHTS FOR MOTHERS AND TEACHERS. Fcp. 8vo., 2s. 6d. net.

Soulsby (LUCY H. M.)—*continued.*

STRAY THOUGHTS FOR INVALIDS. 16mo., 2s. net.

STRAY THOUGHTS ON CHARACTER. Fcp. 8vo., 2s. 6d. net.

Southey.—*THE CORRESPONDENCE OF ROBERT SOUTHEY WITH CAROLINE BOWLES.* Edited by EDWARD DOWDEN. 8vo., 14s.

Stevens.—*ON THE STOWAGE OF SHIPS AND THEIR CARGOES.* With Information regarding Freights, Charter-Parties, etc. By ROBERT WHITE STEVENS. 8vo., 21s.

Sutherland.—*TWENTIETH CENTURY INVENTIONS :* a Forecast. By GEORGE SUTHERLAND, M.A. Crown 8vo., 4s. 6d. net.

Thuillier.—*THE PRINCIPLES OF LAND DEFENCE, AND THEIR APPLICATION TO THE CONDITIONS OF TO-DAY.* By Captain H. F. THUILLIER, R.E. With Maps and Plans. 8vo., 12s. 6d. net.

Turner and Sutherland.—*THE DEVELOPMENT OF AUSTRALIAN LITERATURE.* By HENRY GYLES TURNER and ALEXANDER SUTHERLAND. With Portraits and Illustrations. Crown 8vo., 5s.

Warwick.—*PROGRESS IN WOMEN'S EDUCATION IN THE BRITISH EMPIRE :* being the Report of Conferences and a Congress held in connection with the Educational Section, Victorian Era Exhibition. Edited by the COUNTESS OF WARWICK. Cr. 8vo. 6s.

Weathers.—*A PRACTICAL GUIDE TO GARDEN PLANTS.* By JOHN WEATHERS, F.R.H.S. With 159 Diagrams. 8vo., 21s. net.

Webb.—*THE MYSTERY OF WILLIAM SHAKESPEARE :* a Summary of Evidence. By his Honour Judge T. WEBB, sometime Regius Professor of Laws and Public Orator in the University of Dublin. 8vo., 10s. 6d. net.

Whittall.—*FREDERICK THE GREAT ON KINGCRAFT,* from the Original Manuscript ; with Reminiscences and Turkish Stories. By Sir J. WILLIAM WHITTALL, President of the British Chamber of Commerce of Turkey. 8vo., 7s. 6d. net.

www.ingramcontent.com/pod-product-compliance
Lightning Source LLC
Chambersburg PA
CBHW052343110726
47901CB00005B/1333